POLITICS IS SHOWBUSINESS FOR UGLY PEOPLE

HORRIBLE PEOPLE

A PERILOUS STRUGGLE AGAINST THE DARK ARTS OF POLITICS

RICHARD EVANS

852 PRESS

852

PRESS

First published in 2024 by 852 Press,
Suite 12, 12 Eshelby Drive, Airlie Beach, Queensland 4802 Australia
www.852Press.com.au
10 9 8 7 6 5 4 3 2 1

 A catalogue record for this book is available from the National Library of Australia

National Library of Australia Cataloguing-in-Publication entry:
Author: Evans, Richard
Title: Horrible People / by Richard Evans
ISBN: 978-0-6455544-5-8 (paperback)
ISBN: 978-0-6455544-6-5 (eBook)
Australian fiction.
Cover Design: 852 Press

For my colleagues who shared my political journey.

Dean, Caroline, Anthony, Denise, and Jill.
Jennifer, Bronwyn, Pam, Sandra, and Millie.
&
The fantastic volunteers who served the Cowan community.

In a world where power often leads to corruption, it is vital for principled individuals to stand for election, no matter their party affiliation. They fight for liberty and freedom, countering those who seek power for selfish ideological ends. Their courage and commitment ensure that democracy thrives, and the people's voice can prevail.

Let us then stand and support those who wish to serve and rid ourselves of the Horrible People.

RICHARD EVANS, AUTHOR

Politics have no relation to morals.

NICCOLO MACHIAVELLI

A politician thinks of the next election, a statesman of the next generation.

JAMES FREEMAN CLARKE

THE MAJOR PLAYERS

POLITICIANS:

Jack Hudson	Member for Gellibrand
Senator Stephanie Morgan	Factional Leader (Opposition)
Alexander Windsor	Member for Adelaide
Ramsey MacDonald	Member for Cowan (Government)
Irene Mosely	Prime Minister
Ramon Chopra	Opposition Leader
Peter Raffles	Leader aspirant (Opposition)

HUDSON'S FRIENDS:

Chrissie Woodward	Chief of Staff
Dale Bower	IT Guru
Charlie O'Brien	Military Colleague
Billy Tyrrell	Military Colleague
Madelaine Booker	Journalist

HORRIBLE PEOPLE:

Eddie Collins	Local party leader (Gellibrand)
Oleg Rusnek	Union Leader
Toby Martin	Gellibrand candidate
Manaaki Henari	Maru Hunters Motorcycle gang leader

CHAPTER

1

No matter how many people gather at Aussies' Cafe in parliament house for coffee, the wooden floors echo with the heels of apparatchiks busy with national affairs. The cafe remains the central hub for politicians wishing to share news or expose a colleague, adding another notch to their Machiavellian belt. Journalists gossiped with politicians, lobbyists chatted with advisers, and unimportant staff strained to overhear covert conversations.

Paddy Campbell, the Minister for Industrial Relations, valued a daily coffee before question time to check notes, preparing himself for unexpected questions. It was all part of the role, and he relished it.

During the previous election, the government promised to enact legislation amending laws that force unions and employer groups to pay income tax. The minister remained under pressure from the prime minister to get it through the parliament.

Campbell's former union connections cautioned him to defer and obfuscate warning that trouble would come his way if he didn't. They wanted to keep their financial models private and employer groups shared the same view. Neither party was pleased. The quiet winks and nods for sealing agreements were about to be laid bare.

Unions and employer groups used various forms of persuasion to stymie the minister but fell short. Rogue unions adopted a campaign of personal abuse and intimidation directed toward the minister, while employer groups embraced their preferred weapon of advertising to vilify the government and the minister. No organisation wanted their lucrative secret business models reformed, and Campbell found himself isolated within the government.

The prime minister demanded the legislation be enacted. She set out a specific strategy for workplace reform and insisted the minister deliver on her promises. Campbell had little option other than to bring legislation forward for debate, but reassured unions their financial reporting would not change. They remained sceptical of his promise and demanded his sacking.

'Can I join you for a moment?'

Campbell glanced up and grinned when he saw a nodding Madeline Booker leaning over him with a beaming smile and coffee in hand.

'Sure, take a seat. What can I do for you?'

Booker stepped over the wooden chair and squeezed down, arranging her latte and resting on her forearms. 'I've heard a whisper you'll be tabling legislation next week. Is that true?'

'I can neither confirm nor deny such a proposition,' Campbell said, straightening his papers, shifting them away from the journalist's roving eye. 'Who told you that?'

Booker tapped her nose and grinned. 'I have my sources.' She took a sip, glancing over her shoulder to check if anyone might be listening. 'I'm informed you are not regulating as rigorously as proposed, and you have moderated many of the reporting requirements.'

Campbell said nothing, his face unmoved, not even a hint of acknowledgement. Booker studied it, searching for any twitch, flick, or wink to corroborate her suggestion. She got nothing.

'I'm also reliably informed the Cabinet rejected your softening of the regulations. They requested you to go harder on the commercial disclosures to reduce the increasing frequency of unions engaging in unrelated commercial business,' Booker said, locking his eyes. 'Are you feeling under pressure, Paddy?'

Campbell didn't respond. His tongue worked the back of his teeth, holding her gaze, his lips pouting. 'When are we having dinner?'

Booker slumped back. 'When you're single.'

'Come on Maddie, surely a minister can have dinner with a journalist without her thinking it's a date?'

'You have a reputation.'

'Nothing for which I'm ashamed.'

'Yes, well, you should be,' Booker leaned close, 'are you under pressure to amend your legislation?'

Campbell smirked, trailing a finger across his cheek. 'I

suppose what I can tell you is that I have listened to all interested parties, noting their concerns. I will table legislation that will deliver the promises we made during the election.'

'Are you going to end union commercial enterprises receiving unfair tax shelters?'

He gnawed at the inside of his bottom lip, an expressionless stare directed at her. 'Come have dinner with me. I promise I will provide you with a briefing on what happened and how the legislation is framed.'

Booker dropped her head. 'When?'

Campbell smiled; eyebrows arched. 'Next week?'

'So, you'll be introducing your legislation next week?'

Campbell frowned, sat straighter, and glanced around. 'I didn't say that.'

'Yeah, you did.' Booker rose. 'That's all I needed to know, thanks.'

'Dinner?'

'Not happening.'

'Still the bitch, I see,' Campbell called as she walked off, a hint of a smile playing on his lips. He suspected she'd be back, just like the others. Politics was a game, and he loved playing.

After finishing his coffee, he gathered his papers and made his way back to his office, his mind racing with strategies to deal with the opposition in Question Time. He glanced over his shoulder, uneasy. He couldn't shake the impression he was being followed. He swerved and turned.

There was no one there.

CHAPTER
2

Campbell moved his family to the safe electorate of Gellibrand when pre-selected sixteen years ago and enjoyed walking the peninsula of Williamstown. The magnificent view back across the bay to the city of Melbourne never failed to lift his spirits. He often walked to his office when scheduled for constituent work, keeping to the paths along the shoreline past the football ground and Time-Ball Tower.

He preferred dinners and lunches in the historic village with those seeking influence, and tonight was no different. When a message came urging dinner with the boss of the Building Workers Union, he insisted on Pelicans Landing at Gem Pier. He enjoyed their marinara with extra chilli, with the view of the city adding spectacular ambience.

He arrived on time for the seven o'clock dinner, clasping hands and acknowledging locals at the bar as he squeezed through. Oleg Rusnek was halfway through a beer when

Campbell joined him at a corner table in the adjoining restaurant. They nodded and smiled as Campbell settled, hands conspicuously still. A waiter was quick to attend. Campbell ordered a sherry. Rusnek smirked.

'Thanks for coming out, Oleg. It's always nice to show folks what the village offers.'

Rusnek squinted out at the view of the city and nodded. 'It's impressive. You are fortunate.'

Campbell paused for a moment, gnawing at his bottom lip. 'I suppose you are here to talk about the legislation.'

'I'm here to enjoy dinner. If we can resolve issues we share, that is a bonus.'

Campbell nodded, then waved to the waiter. For the next ninety minutes, they talked about weather, football, and the current state of politics in the United States while enjoying a meal. A casual chat over dinner with the feared union boss was not what he had in mind when he agreed to the meeting.

'I'm tabling the legislation next week,' Campbell said, as an espresso arrived.

'The union is keen to expand our business model. We cannot serve members on subscriptions alone. We need flexibility to create alternate revenue channels to pay for high demand services,' Rusnek said as he drank the last of his wine.

'The legislation won't touch anything which serves your members, but...' the Minister paused for a moment, 'it will require your other, non-member, commercial enterprises to step out from the shadow of protection from the Fair Work Commission and undergo corporations' law scrutiny.'

'I'm sorry to hear that.' Rusnek clenched his hands, rubbing his thumbs against his pointers.

'We have evidence of employer and union executives exploiting Fair Work tax arrangements for personal gain. This must stop.'

'Why?'

'The prime minister promised she would accept the recommendations of the Royal Commission.'

'You assured me this wouldn't happen. You have broken your word.'

Campbell hesitated, wiping his chin. 'I'm a government minister. I take direction from my prime minister.'

'You cannot bring this legislation forward,' Rusnek almost growled the words. 'We will not allow it.'

Campbell gulped, stretching up his chin to clear his throat. 'Why?'

'Our business is our business.' Rusnek said, staring at the minister. 'We will deal with those who threaten our business model.'

Campbell swallowed, his throat dry. He coughed. 'Are you threatening me?'

Rusnek paused, cupped his stubbled chin, running his fingers along his jaw, then smiled. 'Of course, I'm not threatening you. I am a humble servant to my members. I only ask that you reconsider your position by allowing us to establish and operate legitimate enterprises free from this regulation.'

'What legitimate enterprises are we talking about?'

'We have a superannuation fund.'

'No issue.'

'We have an education arm training union officials and members.'

'Again, no issue.'

'We have a finance company.'

'That is a potential problem.'

'Why?'

'The Securities Commission should be monitoring it.'

'Unacceptable.'

Campbell shrugged, raising his eyebrows. 'What else do you have?'

'We're in the early stages of establishing a bank, a communications company, a distribution hub, a building company, and...'

'Wait up,' Campbell raised his hand. 'You are registering a building company?'

'Amongst other things, yes.'

'You are a building union. How can you expect to establish a building company?' Campbell almost laughed.

'I see no problem,' Rusnek sucked his teeth, 'it would mean a project would progress cooperation across the entire site.'

'You don't consider it as a conflict of interest?'

'There is no reason we cannot tender for the construction of major buildings,' Rusnek shifted in his chair, leaning forward, 'it would mean we can guarantee projects get completed on time and on budget,' he grinned, 'unlike now.'

'That is a ridiculous idea,' Campbell said, shaking his head. 'You expect to win tenders as a union?'

'There is not one reason we cannot establish our own CBD building company.'

Campbell rested back in his chair. 'Yeah, there is,' he said. 'It's called monopolistic behaviour and borders on breaching the Consumer and Competition Act.'

'We can establish it under the current law. We cannot under your new law.'

'That might be a good thing, quite frankly.'

Rusnek fisted the table, rattling glasses, and remaining condiments, his faced skewed into a wince. Staff milled closer as other diners glanced over. Lowering his voice, he stated, 'We will defend any threat to our business model. You owe us. We expect you to meet your obligations. Get me?'

'I owe you nothing,' Campbell said. 'We don't have any arrangements. I have been grateful for your generous donations, but you cannot expect me to protect you from legislation that is focused on cleaning up corruption.'

Rusnek scowled, tightening his lips, unable to speak.

'I suspect you should take advice on the legislation to iden-tify what it means to your union,' Campbell stood, peering down at him. 'This legislation is to force criminals out. If that means you need to reflect on your future, then so be it. Thanks for dinner.' He left, leaving Rusnek tapping fingers on the edge of the table. As Campbell walked from the dining room, he heard a smashing glass.

THE MINISTER BOUNCED down the front steps, wanting to clear the area in case Rusnek followed or a confederate waited. The boss was not a man to be trusted, and unquestionably one to be feared. He strode to the corner and considered what to do. Take the shortcut home through the darkened streets or take his preferred route along the foreshore. He moved over to an unlit area by a large tree and surveyed the area. He detected nothing suspicious and headed home along the shoreline. He needed to clear his head, and a stroll would settle his anxiety before arriving home to deal with his young family preparing for the weekend.

He called the prime minister to let her know the meeting outcome. 'He's not happy.'

'This legislation is to clean up the union movement and rid them of thugs like him. We all know what they're doing. It's time to clean the house.'

'Easy for you to say. You don't have to face them.'

'This is why you get paid the big bucks, Paddy,' the prime minister said. 'I'm grateful for the work you are doing.'

'How much?'

'How much, what?' the prime minister sounded confused.

'How grateful are you?'

'You're putting your hand out?'

'It's politics, Irene,' Campbell smiled as he stepped his pace out a little quicker. 'I scratch your back, you scratch mine.'

'What do you want?'

'Treasury.' He checked over his shoulder as a car passed.

'Not available.'

'It soon will be.'

'How so?'

Campbell smirked as he said, 'Your little mate, Stevie, got caught with his pants down, literally. Some blokes never learn.'

'It seems you never do.'

'Oh Irene, please,' Campbell said. 'His troubles will hit the media next week. When I table the legislation, the subsequent sex scandal gets pushed from the front page. You should thank me.'

'Okay, let's talk next week, but just remember, Paddy.'

'Yeah?' Campbell smiled as he checked around again. 'What's that?'

'Karma could be closer than you think.'

'Irene, I suspect it is you who should be worried about that hocus pocus,' Campbell said now passing the Prince of Wales Hotel. 'You and I will be a successful partnership, you'll see.'

'Yeah, right. Just get the legislation into the House, then we can talk. You don't need to reveal Stephen.' The prime minister ended the call.

Campbell texted his wife he would be home soon. She pinged back, texting she looked forward to seeing him. He quickened his pace as he reached the illuminated bluestone Time-ball tower and gazed out over the bay toward the coastal suburbs in the east. He passed three rugged-up fishermen. A lycra-clad runner startled him as he bolted past at an impressive pace.

There was no traffic, and the runner was now well in front, so Campbell slowed his pace to enjoy a peaceful stroll. He switched his thinking to sharing a wine and the news of his promotion with his wife. He never heard the running footsteps.

'Hey. What are you doing?' he yelled.

The aggressive force of the grapple almost knocked him off his feet as two of the fishermen wrapped their arms around him. He struggled to free himself from their gang tackle. Then, like an illegal rugby move, they picked him up and walked him to the metal railing fence. He grabbed hold of the gripping arms as he looked at what faced him below.

'Hey, don't do this; don't you know who I am?'

'We know ya're.'

The men speared him with lethal force into ragged rocks six feet below. He didn't feel a thing.

CHAPTER

3

The sun was out, and cafe owners slogged to meet Saturday breakfast orders. Eddie Collins worked his rounds talking to retailers, shaking hands with locals who appreciated his quips and sociable banter. He was a personality in the village, and everyone either knew him or knew of him. Like salt and pepper, he seemed to be into everything. He served as president of the Chamber of Commerce, chair of the Historical Society, secretary of the Library Advisory Council and long-time member of various community groups including schools and churches. If someone wanted something done, Eddie was the man to talk to.

Politics was never too far away from his chats with locals. He was the patron of three city councillors, and National Party president for the federal electorate of Gellibrand. He served as treasurer in the state division for the past ten years, holding the deciding vote in most party forums. Many questioned why he never stood for city council. His clichéd response was "too busy", which hid his aspiration of becoming a senator in the national parliament.

Collins started his glad-handing early every Saturday, always ending up at the Parade Deli for coffee. His sunlit reserved table allowed him to nod and shake hands as locals squeezed past during the peak late morning rush. Enjoying a coffee in the sun was one of his favourite pastimes.

'Hi Jo, is Dion on the jump this morning?'

'He's making coffee every morning, you know that Mr Eddie,' she smiled as she delivered water and wiped his table. 'The usual, for you?'

'Should I deny myself the best coffee in Williamstown?'

'You're laying it on thick this morning.'

'Jo, you know I love ya.'

'Hey, what about Campbell?'

'What about him?' Collins said with a sniff. 'Has he deigned to visit us? We never see him and he's useless for the community.'

'Oh my gosh, haven't you heard?' Jo lifted her hand to shield her eyes from the sun. 'They found him dead this morning, floating out by Gellibrand Pier.'

'I did hear sirens early.' Collins shook his head.

'They're not sure how long he'd been in the water or how he got there,' Jo said. 'I had a copper in this morning getting an early feed.'

'Must have been drunk and fell in,' Collins scoffed.

'That's a mean thing to say, Eddie Collins, you should be ashamed.'

'He deserves no sympathy from me for the things he's done. He signed off on the bluestone church in Stevedore Street being demolished.'

'Yeah, maybe, but let's not speak ill of the dead,' Jo said, leaving for his coffee.

Collins reached for his phone and pushed a well-used number. 'Hi honey, how's business this morning?' Collins said. 'It's busy here. Hey, good news, they found Paddy Campbell dead this morning.'

'That's terrible. Why is that good news?' Alice Collins said.

'There's opportunity in every crisis.' Collins cupped his hand around his phone. 'It means a by-election. If you run, we increase your profile for your mayoral campaign.'

'It's a little early to be talking about this, Ed, surely.'

'If we want you elected, then we have to start planning,' Collins said, scanning around to see if anyone was listening. 'This will be a great opportunity for us.'

'Let's talk about it later. I'm not comfortable discussing it now.'

'Righto love, talk soon,' Collins said, ending the call as he received his coffee. He spooned in half a teaspoon of sugar and stirred as he scrolled through his contacts, settling on the senator's number.

'Senator? Eddie Collins,' he said to the recorded message bank. 'Not sure if you have heard. Police discovered Paddy Campbell dead this morning, which means there will be a by-election. I have the perfect candidate. Can you call me to discuss it? Thanks.'

'Wheeling and dealing, as usual, Eddie?' a customer asked from the next table.

'Oh hi, John,' Collins smiled. 'Terrible news about Paddy Campbell, isn't it?'

'Ah, no wonder you're excited. Are you you going to run?'

'No way,' Collins shook his head. 'Safe seat, no chance.'

'Times change. I reckon it might be time.'

'Yeah, nah, not this seat. The same party has held it since it was proclaimed,' Collins stated. 'Anyway, how's the bench, busy?'

'Crime is a never-ending pastime for many fools. So yes, I'm always busy.'

Someone saying hello and asking about the chamber of commerce interrupted Collins, so he left John to enjoy his eggs. He continued listening to those who sought a chat to discuss local issues. He was on his second latte when the senator returned his call.

'Sad news about Campbell,' the senator said. 'What's the reaction in your part of town?'

'No significant loss,' Collins said. 'He's a party hack with a poor reputation.'

'I suppose a by-election will be called once the dust settles. The speaker will probably declare it next week.'

'You reckon an election in seven weeks?'

'Not sure we should bother. It'd be a waste of money and resources for a campaign we can't win.'

Collins glanced over at the judge. 'It might be time for a change. You never know.'

'Got a candidate in mind?'

'As it happens, I do. I will need to speak to her.'

'You run the show out there, so run whoever you like.'

'Thanks Stephanie, that's what I hoped you'd say.'

'This could be a good time for you to recruit more members to bolster your hold on state council delegates. You know what I mean?'

'You'll have all the delegates you need at the AGM, I promise you,' Collins smiled.

'I know I can trust you, Edward. Your turn will come soon enough.'

'When?'

'Either next vacancy or the one after that.'

'You said that before Patterson retired.'

'Yes, I did.'

Collins waited for further explanation, but it didn't come. 'I trust you, Senator, and you know you can trust me.'

'Please let me know when they announce the date of the by-election.'

Before Collins could respond, the phone went dead. He slipped it back into his jacket, reflecting on the exchange wondering if he was being played.

CHAPTER
4

Madeleine Booker was enjoying the morning sun and papers while lying in bed propped by abundant pillows when the call from her editor came. The early Saturday morning call surprised her, and she rolled back among the pillows pushing the answer button.

'You are kidding me,' she said sitting up, when told the Campbell news.

'I want you to follow this, Maddie. It may mean a few trips to Melbourne, at least until the by-election result.'

'It should be an easy win for the government, so what do you want me to look for?'

'There's been plenty of intrigue around the legislation he was due to table in the House. Maybe his death has something to do with it.'

'Do they know the cause?'

'Fully dressed and found in the water? Well, let's just state the obvious: he wasn't taking a midnight swim.'

'Accident or murder?' Booker asked.

'Too early to say. He's a union man double crossing his union mates, so I'm guessing foul play. Maybe the thugs finally got to him.'

'They're not all thugs, boss.'

'I'd start with the Building Workers Union.'

'Do you think the legislation might have had something to do with it?'

'This is what I pay you for, Maddie,' he said. 'I want you to answer that question. I suspect there are union heavies breathing a sigh of relief this morning. Potential suspects, the lot of them. Can you get on to it today?'

'Sure boss.' Booker tossed the phone aside when it went dead.

'You gotta go?'

'I need to get to Melbourne for a few days.'

'That'll be sad. I will miss you.'

'You say that, but you jump at every opportunity to travel with your boss.'

'He needs me on the road. The guy is hopeless.'

'If he is so bad, why is he still leader and why don't you change offices?'

'He is leader because no one else wants the job. At least not right now. I stay with him because there is no one else I want to work for.'

'But surely there are others who can help you get what you want.'

'No one that I can see. I'll just wait for my opportunity.'

'Anything I can do for you?'

'What would you suggest, girlfriend?'

Booker curled her hair as she gazed at her lover. 'Do you think we will ever become a public item?'

'Why would you ask that? I'm enjoying what we do, aren't you?'

'I'm just confused about how I feel about you. I wonder if we should take the next step?'

'By next step, you mean marriage?'

'Noohoohooho,' Booker cringed. 'But maybe we could share a bed more often. Perhaps we could be seen together more often. Hold your hand maybe.' She took a hand and placed it across her chest.

'Let's talk about it after the election.'

'Why then?'

'I'm pushing for a role in Foreign Affairs. If we win, and we have a chance, then I will ask the leader to appoint me Chief of Staff to the minister.'

'Will we have a conflict of interest?'

'Of course not, because I won't tell you anything. It will mean I'll be travelling more and that will be unfair to you and your needs.'

Booker smiled. 'I have a strong need right now.' She brushed away her hair, leaning over.

'You get me going when you kiss like that.'

'Woody, I want a little more than just being a girlfriend.' She snuggled closer. 'If I must wait, I will.'

'You're so cute.'

Booker ran her fingers across her.

CHAPTER
5

The exterior of the impressive house in Victoria Street displayed its stately World War One grandeur, but the inside renovations modernised it. Collins invested heavily in the house soon after marrying Alice, thinking it would increase its capital value and build a sizeable nest egg for their later years. Their stubborn adult children remained ensconced, although lost in the enormous house, providing plentiful privacy in the parents' wing.

'Hey, Ali, you about?' Collins called, passing through the stained-glass front door.

'Out back. Bring a wine.'

Collins fetched two glasses and a chilled bottle of Riesling to the back deck, slumping into the cushioned couch with his wife. After pouring the glasses and setting the bottle on the glass-topped table, he proposed a toast. 'Here's to the next mayor.'

Alice grinned, then, clinking his extended glass, took a sip, relaxing deeper into the cushions. 'I'm not so sure it's a good idea.'

'What are you worried about?'

'The cafe needs me. The staff need me, otherwise nothing gets done. I don't think I can afford time away.'

Collins gazed out onto his lush green garden, sipping wine, then asked, 'What's really worrying you?'

'Money. It's making a loss. We had another bad day today. We can't afford to keep going. What would it say about the president of the chamber of commerce to have a failed business?'

Collins didn't respond.

'Darling, I understand you want me to run for mayor. I simply don't believe I can do it.'

'I'm confident you'll be successful. However, we need to raise your profile. That's why you should nominate for the party in the by-election.'

'I dropped in to have a chat with Tracey on the way home. She's devastated.'

'No doubt.' Collins took another sip. 'Does she know what happened?'

'Not a clue,' Alice said. 'Police have told her nothing. They are doing an autopsy tomorrow. She doesn't have a clue what she's going to do.'

'She doesn't?' Collins shifted among the cushions. 'Wasn't she planning to leave him?'

'Paddy made it too hard for her. She did not have the

support she needed around her. He was always away, and when he was home, he wasn't. Poor thing. I don't understand why you want to do the same thing.'

'What? Do you think all politicians are selfish toads like Campbell?'

'I'm not saying you'd do the same things as Paddy, darling. I just don't get why anyone would want to go into that cesspit with all the other vipers.'

Collins chuckled. 'Yeah, nice one.' He paused for a moment, sipping his wine. 'It's been a dream of mine since before we met. That's the reason I do all this for us.'

'For us, or you?'

'It's for us, hon, only ever for us,' Collins said. 'It's taken me years to get to this position. We can't waste it now.'

Alice drained her glass and held it out. 'I need an injection of funds if you want me to run for mayor.'

'Okay, I'll speak to the bank.' Collins stretched for the bottle and refilled her waggling glass. 'In the meantime, will you at least think about nominating for the by-election?'

'No other candidate?'

'No one will want it.'

'Will you run the campaign?'

'Of course I will. Plus, we'll have the funds to do it.'

Alice took a sip and gnawed her upper lip. 'If Tracey doesn't mind, then I'll give it a go.'

'Why should she mind?'

'She may think we're disrespecting Paddy.'

'Disrespecting him?' Collins scoffed. 'What was she

thinking when she received information about him and the journalist in Canberra?'

'Never proven.'

'You know full well it's true,' Collins scoffed.

'Let me talk to Trace first. That's all I'm saying.'

'Then let's toast,' Collins leaned toward his wife. 'Here's to the next mayor of the city.'

CHAPTER

6

The laneway cafe, off Collins Street, is always busy for lunch, noisy inside, crowded at the small iron tables outside. Jack Hudson preferred the bustle of the lane to the grinding coffee, voices barking orders and the echoing chatter of patrons. Although chairs were not as comfortable outside, the buzz of the lane was a little more agreeable.

Wednesdays are Charlie's lunch day. Hudson appreciates the break with his friend away from the repetitive, boring work assigned to him as an analyst for a stockbroking firm. Why he agreed to join and stay at the firm troubled him for months, but loyalty was in his DNA. Relishing a substantive sandwich with Charlie every week broke up the monotony. When his mate's beaming face sidled up to the table, Hudson smiled.

'Have you ordered?'

'As it happens, I have,' Hudson said. 'The usual I would have thought.'

'You champion,' said O'Brien, as he turned his chair so he could watch the strollers. 'Don't you just love these warm days?' he said, ogling two pretty girls, 'How has your week been?'

'The analytical rubbish I'm doing is a waste of time—such a boring, fruitless task.'

'What do you want to do?'

'Contribute,' Hudson said. 'I want to serve the community.'

'You've already done your time, mate. Now it's your time to make money.'

'There's more to life than money, Charlie.'

'Mate, are you crazy? Money provides everything.'

'Not everything,' Hudson said, leaning back, allowing a waiter to place the sandwiches before them. 'Thank you.' He smiled. 'It can't get my job back.'

'What do you want to do?'

'Will the police take me? Or am I too old?'

'It's not your age; it's your back.'

'It's feeling better. Maybe I could get a gig with the coppers.'

'Have you thought about the church?'

'Don't be stupid.'

'You just said you want to serve the community and money isn't important.'

'I'm serious. There must be something I could do,' Hudson mumbled, chewing a mouthful.

O'Brien took a large bite, eyeing Hudson, chomping his sandwich before taking another generous bite. Wiping his lips and chin with a paper serviette, he began nodding, waiting for his mouth to clear. 'Thought about politics?'

Hudson raised his eyebrows, bouncing his head about. 'Not really.'

'Service and money. The perfect combination.'

'Charlie, I don't want money. I don't need it.'

'Mate, everyone needs it. Your service pension will not support you,' he took another generous bite, then mumbled, 'why not think about politics? You'd be perfect.'

'Which party?'

'Doesn't matter,' O'Brien said. 'Although, given your background, I reckon the Nationals would be a better match.'

'I've never voted for them. Why would I join them?'

'A few reasons.' O'Brien finished his sandwich and wiped his face. 'You are military. You are a hero. You are university educated. You come from the other side of the tracks, and... and you're not corruptible.'

'Why the Nationals? I don't understand.'

O'Brien shook his head, smiling. 'You're such a naïve bugger, aren't you?' He turned to watch a short skirt stroll by. 'Corruption is everywhere in politics. More so with the government than the opposition.'

'Logic like that says the Nationals are just as bad.'

'They probably are,' he laughed. 'I'm just saying you may have a better chance of getting a gig with them than the other mob, that's all.'

'Trash my ideals for the sake of getting ahead? Yeah—no thanks.'

'They are both the same on policy.' O'Brien leaned on the table and counted off on his fingers. 'They are for less government. Which you agree, right?' Hudson nodded. 'They are for less tax; high defence spending; and they are tougher with China than the other mob. These are issues you always bang on about. It makes sense they could be a good match for you.'

'I've never considered politics,' said Hudson, scratching his cheek for a moment, then wincing. 'You could be right. It would allow me to serve.'

'Jackson, my ole friend, I reckon politics is the type of job you would excel. You should give it careful consideration.'

'Yeah, maybe.'

'If you want to serve the community, then there isn't much on offer. You can't be a first responder because of your back. Charities and community groups would drive you nuts because you would want to be out there taking risks, charging over that literal top. To me, it makes sense. Politics may be your answer.'

'Let me think about it.'

'Righto, you think about it. Next week you can bleat to me again about how bad your life is.'

'What do you want me to do?'

'I have a local branch meeting tomorrow night. Come along and judge for yourself.'

'That surprises me.'

'Mate, you know nothing about me, and that's the way I like it.'

CHAPTER

7

Hudson parked his car opposite the office of the state member for Blackburn fifteen minutes before the nominated time and observed people entering. Some struggled with the door, others pushed it with confidence. Most seemed to know each other. He decided it was a good idea to walk over at five minutes before the scheduled time, but as he stepped from his car, Charlie O'Brien startled him by flicking his ear.

'What the heck?'

'Mate, you have lost a bit of your vigilance if you let folks like me get the better of you.'

'Charlie, you're a goose.' Hudson locked his car and trotted after him. 'You were always the best at getting in with no one noticing.'

'Such a long time ago.'

They pushed through the office front door to join party members assembled in a meeting room, taking the empty seats down front. The mingling members surprised Hudson, as they seemed older and most with thick grey hair. There were a couple of younger attendees who appeared to assess him, then chat about their conclusions behind cupped hands.

Five minutes after the nominated time an untidy, over-weight speaker approached the lectern. Hudson shook his head as he scrutinised the man, curious why he had not bothered tucking his shirt that dangled to one side, his collar unfastened and loosened tie askew. He flicked on the microphone.

'Thanks for coming. For those who don't know me, I'm Jeremy Briggs, the Member for Blackburn. I welcome you to my humble abode. Tonight, the agenda seems packed with discussion points. I'm looking forward to hearing from you. I note we have fresh faces with us, so welcome. I hope you will consider completing a membership form before you leave. We love getting our numbers up.'

Hudson scanned a sheet of paper passed to him over his shoulder as Briggs spoke. The agenda listed several populist topics such as immigration, aborigines, welfare, and China. He took a deep breath, making a silent, disappointed snort breathing out.

'I remind members we observe Chatham House rules, and we insist on respect for speakers who may have a differing view. Australia is a fantastic country, and we respect each other and those who have contributed to its greatness. Having said that, I call upon Max to provide a small prayer and bless our deliberations this evening.'

An old bloke with a small, tattered book, tassels marking

pages shuffled to the front. Hudson tapped O'Brien on the thigh, raising his eyebrows when his friend turned to him.

'Heavenly Father, we come to you this evening asking for your guidance, wisdom, and support as we begin this meeting. Help us engage in meaningful discussion; allow us to grow closer as a group and nurture the bonds of community. Fill us with your grace, Lord God, and continue to remind us that all that we do here this evening, all that we accomplish, is for the pursuit of truth and the service of the community. We ask these things in your name. Amen.'

'Very nice, Max,' Briggs said. 'Who would like to start, with the first agenda item, a motion to close detention centres?'

'I will,' said Max, standing in his place. 'This motion is ludicrous. It should not even be considered. These people want to come here to screw our generous welfare system. In my opinion, anyone who jumps the queue should not be considered for the government's ill-advised refugee status. They are not refugees, and that's bloody obvious. They come to exploit our legal system and can go home any time, but they don't. We should never allow them into the community. I stand against closing any centres as they act as a deterrent.'

'Good on ya, Maxie.' A voice said, from the back.

'Furthermore, as patriots we must fight to maintain our sovereignty and send them back.'

Applause rippled through the meeting as the old bloke sat down.

'Thanks, Max,' said Briggs. 'Anyone wanting to speak for the motion?'

'Not likely.' The voice down back said.

'Anyone?' Briggs scanned the room, settling on a woman close to the window. 'Annabelle?'

The woman stood and perused the members. Some dropped their heads while others crossed arms, tilting their heads back.

'I put this motion on the agenda because I think it is important for us to speak about these social issues.'

'You're at a meeting for the wrong party.' An unidentified voice said, tinged with anger. 'Go join the Greens.'

'Let her speak,' interrupted Briggs.

Hudson turned to watch Annabelle make her argument.

'I'm a patriot, like Max says. I am also a Christian, and we should do the Christian thing by welcoming desperate folk who seek sanctuary.'

'Father, forgive her for she knows what she says,' the voice said.

Hudson glimpsed over his shoulder to gaze at the burly man.

'Let her speak, Greg,' Briggs insisted.

Burly man crossed his arms and turned away.

'In saying Australia should accept refugees and not imprison them, I am not suggesting we should ignore complex political and social consequences. I'm saying that we must base our discussion on an accurate understanding of the facts. We must use that discussion to strengthen a principled, rules-based system. Instead, Greg and Max bully and often mislead us based on ill-informed assumptions, inflated rhetoric, and exaggerated numbers. This manufactured approach is a familiar tactic to generate fear. It creates arguments amongst us that are wrong and dangerous.'

Hudson raised an eyebrow and faced the front as Annabelle sat.

'Is there a speaker against the motion?' Briggs asked, then pointed to the burly Greg who stood, crossing his arms, resting them on his ballooned gut.

'I wasn't going to speak, but I feel I must after Annabelle's predictable violin playing. By giving up our right to select who comes here and under what circumstances they are allowed to arrive, we create a free-for-all which ignores the most vulnerable who need our help. Once you are in Australia, your chances of being deported are minimal. We may feel sorry for Somali doctors and engineers, but in a world in which a child dies every minute from malaria they should not have first call on our generosity. These boat people's lives are not endangered, and they do not face persecution in refugee camps or in their own country. They are the young and strong and come for economic reasons. They should stay home and help their own people rebuild.'

'Let us hope our weak federal politicians resist the hypocritical and legalistic assault of the refugee lobby and stick to the policy that returns most of them. We should not allow our legal system to be used against us. We will then send a powerful signal down the line. To the people smugglers in Pakistan, Afghanistan, or Somalia that it is not worth risking the expensive journey. Australians want security and the rule of law on our border.'

As he sat, the applause seemed more animated.

'I suspect I know the mood of the meeting,' Briggs smiled. 'All those in favour of the motion say aye,' no response, 'to the contrary, no,' a loud no was shouted in response, 'I think the nays have it and I declare the motion lost.' A loud applause followed the announcement.

For the rest of the meeting, Hudson and O'Brien listened quietly to motions and questions about government social welfare policies, street gangs, Chinese spying, and parents' decisions to institutionalise their children in childcare. The robust debate's underlying theme focused on protecting the community from those who seek to give it away. Patriots and patriotism continued to be mentioned and its use riled Hudson, especially whenever directed at new immigrants.

After two hours, Briggs wound the meeting up, accepting the nod from a staffer that supper waited in another room. 'Members, before we adjourn to supper and the magnificent cakes our ladies have brought for our enjoyment. I would like to acknowledge those attending for the first time. If they wouldn't mind, perhaps they can share their thoughts about the experience.'

Hudson shook his head when O'Brien turned with encouraging eyes and bouncing eyebrows.

'Would you like to say a few words, sir?' Briggs directed his comment to Hudson who shook his head.

'Yes, he would,' O'Brien cajoled.

Hudson ruffled his fingers through his hair, then straightened as he stood, moving to the lectern as Briggs stepped aside. 'Good evening, my name is Jack Hudson. I too am a patriot,' many in the audience smiled. 'I served my country in the military along with Charlie O'Brien here.' He pointed to his friend. 'We saw service in various conflicts around the globe. Indeed, it may surprise you to learn that Charlie here received the Star of Gallantry, second to the VC, for his actions during perilous action in Sudan including an operation that resulted in my release from rebels. So, when you owe your life to someone, and they ask you to attend a political meeting you are obliged to do so.'

A ripple of applause crept through the members.

'Like you I'm a patriot who is prepared to fight for my country and the principles that we hold dear. I fight for those who cannot. I fight for those seeking liberation, justice, and freedom.' Hudson paused, then eyed O'Brien who nodded encouragement. After taking in a breath, he continued. 'Unlike you, I stand for the things that bind this country. I do not support the manner and attitudes of division within our community. From what I heard tonight, there is no way I would ever contemplate joining a party which displays such contempt toward our community and those who work hard to make Australia great.'

No one spoke, coughed, or shifted in their chair. Every eye now directed toward Hudson.

'We are a country of immigrants who built this nation with their hands and the sweat on their brow as their only assets. We built a society which can provide the best health service and education systems in the world. Yet all I hear from you tonight are complaints. All I hear is whining and absolute disrespect for those patriots who provided you with the liberty to say whatever you like. I hear no strategy for the future, just complaints about the government needing to do more.'

'I share your thoughts about the current state government and wonder why your party doesn't win elections. I then look at your local member. Then I understand.'

Briggs snapped a look at him.

'Nice man that he is. I reckon he is caring, with a sharing soul, but he is an example of why your party remains in opposition. If he is the best, you offer the community, then I would hate to meet your worst. To slovenly appear before you with tie askew, no jacket, shirt hanging out, and scuffed shoes tells me a lot about the man, the politician and indeed his party.'

Briggs straightened his tie.

'How in heaven's name can a leading politician like Mr Briggs appear as a community leader dressed like a vagrant? If he does not exact standards upon himself, how can he expect his party and his community to raise beyond such standards? Fact is, he can't. The quality of your debate this evening also reflects these poor standards. You started with a prayer seeking to bring wisdom and guidance. You then ignore this appeal and delve deep into the lowest common denominator.'

'I will reflect on this meeting and the comments made by many of you. I will then determine if I should get involved with a party devoid of common sense. I'm disappointed with this meeting's outcomes. It is two hours of my life I will never get back and perhaps squares the ledger with my friend.'

'Don't get me wrong, I honour your commitment and your passion. I would fight to protect your views, but I also encourage you to consider the bigger picture rather than the tiny jigsaw piece you are trying to force in.' He was not expecting a response, but when Annabelle stood to clap, he smiled and nodded.

O'Brien forced a cup of tea and a curried sandwich into Hudson's hand so he could get the inevitable feedback from the members. Most seemed positive and supportive. He didn't talk to Max or Greg, and Jeremy Briggs didn't say goodbye.

'Thanks for that Charlie, I reckon I'll apply for the police force tomorrow.'

'Let's have lunch and have a chat about it.'

Hudson respected his friend but wasn't sure he would alter his thinking. He shook his head most of the way back to Surrey Hills.

CHAPTER

8

The mysterious Oleg Rusnek proved elusive for Madeleine Booker, seeking a comment about the death of Minister Campbell. Telephone calls went unreturned, emails not responded, and fronting up to his office was a waste of time, as she was told to wait for his return, which never came. She needed a comment about the impact the minister's death may have on the IR legislation tabled by the prime minister. She waited on the footpath outside a Melbourne construction site, trying to confirm if the union boss was there.

Safety officers requested three times, she move on. She ignored their direction, insisting on seeing Rusnek, so loitered behind the metal barrier. Workers moved about the site and trucks delivered materials. Loads lifted by cranes to the loaded needed to be. Workers were transported to their level using rickety elevators. Construction progressed beyond the fifty floors above with lower levels at various stages of completion.

Windows were installed up to level thirty, and it appeared they were in the final stages of completing internal fittings on lower floors. As she waited for any sign of Rusnek, she commiserated with the women passing the site demeaned by taunts and cat calls. Community attitudes to such behaviour may have changed, but sexism remained fair game on this building site.

'Are you the journalist?' A voice behind the gate asked.

'Yeah,' Booker turned to him. 'I'm waiting to see Rusnek.'

'Come through.' The unlocked gate swung open for her to enter. 'Stay close.'

Booker skipped closer, following the hulk with a tiny hard-hat plastered with stickers and a tight fluoro vest, his big boots pounding on the metal stairs leading to offices erected over the footpath.

'Take a seat, he won't be long. Stick this on ya scone.' The man tossed her an orange hard-hat. She put it on before adjusting and tightening the plastic suspension inside. While scanning the room, she assumed it to be a central site information hub. Blueprints were pinned to walls and spread across drafting tables. In another room, several men were loafing, chatting, and laughing.

Rusnek emerged from an office almost ten minutes later, and the banter stopped.

'Is Gerry about?'

'Thirty-seven, boss.'

Rusnek grabbed a fluro vest from the wall hanger, tossing it at Booker. 'Put this on and stay close.'

He bounced down the stairs, crossing the forecourt to a

wire caged elevator, pushing up a slide and stepping in, waving at Booker to enter. He pushed a button, and the wobbly lift rose against the tower at an uncomfortable speed. The air was frosty as they rushed past floors. Booker looked out over the park opposite, watching the tree line getting smaller with pedestrians indistinguishable. The wobbly cage increasing her anxiety as it shook higher. She tightened her grip on the cold metal rail, turning her body away from the openness.

When the lift crunched to a bouncing stop, Rusnek pushed open the slide and stepped out onto an open floor. Wind whipping through the open space chilling her further, and she held her vest a little tighter as she stepped out. She looked around, but saw no one.

'What do you want with me?'

The lift cranked into action and dropped away. Booker moved to the safety of the centre of the concrete floor, nearer to the central lift core. 'I wanted to speak to you about Minister Campbell.'

'He's dead, so what's the point?'

'I'm told you had dinner with him the night he died.'

Rusnek zipped his jacket. 'Yeah? So what?'

'Did you talk about the legislation?'

Rusnek considered her for a moment. She shivered. 'Of course we did.'

'Angry words and raised voices?'

'Not really.'

'Broken glass?'

'I'm passionate about my members.'

'I'm told you threatened him.'

'Police don't think so.'

'Waiters do.'

'You meddling?'

'I'm trying to understand what happened to him.'

'As I understand it, he may have had a few drinks, perhaps one too many, and stumbled off the edge of the wall.'

'Climbed over the guardrail, did he?'

'Listen, lady,' Rusnek said. Perhaps he had issues at home. Conceivably, he was fooling around and got caught. He may have been stressed about money. Maybe he took pills. I don't know, and I don't care.'

'Or maybe he wasn't doing what he was told.'

'What does that mean?'

'Your union doesn't want this legislation. Campbell was pushing it through. I'm sure none of you and your union mates wanted it done.'

'Nothing to do with me.'

'I researched your annual reports.' Rusnek's face tightened with visible anger. 'It seems you are increasing consolidated revenue but not reporting net profit.'

'We are a registered member organisation, and a not-for-profit entity.'

'I noticed key personnel expenditure increased.'

'I gave my blokes a pay rise, so what?'

'Give yourself one?'

'None of your business, lady.' Rusnek moved to the edge of the concrete floor. 'What I pay my blokes is my business.'

'Not your members?'

'They approved the financials.'

'How come the increase in contracted management fees increased fourfold?'

'Again, lady, this is none of your damn business. Only members should care. They don't.' Rusnek stood gazing out into the breeze, across Hobson's Bay to Williamstown.

'You give yourself and key personnel significant wage increases. You raise management fees, and you think no one should be interested?' Booker said, keeping her distance. 'I suspect the new legislation will clean up these ambiguities. That's why I think Campbell, how shall I say, slipped and fell after dinner with you?'

Rusnek faced her, chuckling. 'You reckon he was murdered?'

'Plenty of people were standing in the queue.'

'Murdered?'

'Easy to do when no one is looking.'

'Like now?' Rusnek rushed her, grabbing the vest at her chest, slapping the helmet off, twirling her to the edge of the concrete slab. He shoved her back until her feet had nowhere to go. He pushed her out further, leaning her back over the edge.

She gripped his wrist as he held tight and shook her.

'You think it's this easy to murder someone?'

Booker screamed. 'Take me back.' Her head dropped back. She stared up at the outside of the building. 'Take me in.' Her gasping becoming erratic.

'If I wanted to kill someone,' he bellowed. 'I wouldn't drop them onto a rock. I would drop them off a building. Or throw them in a concrete hopper, never to be seen again.'

'Take me back in. Please take me back,' Booker screamed, her body in lockdown. 'I'm scared.'

'You think you can blame me as if I'm some sort of criminal?' Rusnek shook her rigid body. 'You think you can stupidly come on my site and disrespect me? You think you can accuse me?'

'I'm sorry. I'm sorry,' Booker pleaded. 'I'm just doing my job. I'm sorry. Bring me in. Please bring me in.'

Rusnek surrendered, pulling her in, flinging her away from the edge. She crumpled into a sobbing ball. 'Never offend me again. Do you understand?'

Booker didn't respond.

'Do you understand?'

She snivelled a yes.

Rusnek stepped away, engaging his radio. 'Can you send a safety officer up to the thirty-seventh level? I have a site visitor who has had an episode and feels overwhelmed by the height and feels unsafe. She'll need help, so maybe bring a nurse.'

'On their way, boss.'

'I'll leave you now, lady. I don't expect to see you again.'

WHEN RUSNEK RETURNED to the site office, several union officials from another CBD site were waiting to inform him of the Maru boys paying a visit. 'About ten of the bastards.

They unsettled the cement drivers, delaying the concrete pour.'

'Anyone injured?'

'Only pride. They got the better of us, boss.'

'That's too bad,' Rusnek slumped into his chair, 'shut the site down. Shut it down for two days. Let's talk with the builders and demand health and safety reparations. They ought to protect us a little better, don't you think?'

'Representatives or managers?'

'I think we go see the big boys.' Rusnek smiled. 'They can donate a cheque to the holiday bonus fund and a bag of wellness cash for the boys involved.'

'On to it.' The union official left, but as he got to the door, he paused, then stepped back into the office. 'Boss, you have a visitor.'

'The journalist?'

'No, Henari. You want me to get some boys?'

Rusnek stroked his lip as if it had hair, the corners of his mouth sagging. He nodded. 'It'll be fine. Show him in.' Rusnek tossed his feet onto the corner of the desk as he pushed back in his chair. He checked his nails as he waited.

Henari filled the doorway as he moseyed in, an even bigger man behind. He pulled back a chair from the desk and sat, the plastic at its limit of stability. His associate remained standing by the door.

'Take a seat,' Rusnek said, as he smiled at the brazenness of his visitor. 'You come to apologise?'

'What are you talking about, man?'

'Your brief visit to the Cathedral this morning.'

'Just reminding a few drivers who they should be loyal to.'

Rusnek eyed the man. 'You are so provocative.'

'Making a living is not provocative.'

'Living off me is,' Rusnek said, glaring at Henari.

'I'm not here for trouble, Oleg. I'm here to negotiate.'

'Negotiate what?' Rusnek scoffed.

'The boys decided the other day that we should talk to you about branching out our services.'

'Your services?'

Henari laughed. 'Yeah.'

'What services?'

'We reckon we can grow your membership.'

'Recruitment?'

'Yeah. We reckon we can help you get what you want.'

'And what do I want?'

'You want political influence? Unlike other unions in the party, you lack the same status. You need more influence, but you don't have the numbers,' Henari said. 'I reckon you want to dominate the union movement. You can only do that with members. If you have influence in the union movement, you have influence in the government.'

'I already have that.'

'No, you don't. If you did, the IR legislation would never have seen the light of day. Campbell was never on your side.'

'I still reckon I can stop it.'

'What are you smokin', man?' Henari scoffed. 'You have no

chance. Unless you control the prime minister, and you don't control the prime minister.'

'Who does?'

Henari tapped his nose as he grinned. 'The one with the numbers. And you don't have them,' he said. 'I reckon I can recruit them for you.'

'Oh yeah? How do you propose to do that?'

'You have most of the CBD sites locked in. The only way to increase numbers is to merge with other unions. I reckon we can make that happen.' Rusnek pursed his lips, considering the idea. 'A bigger union means you have more votes in the party. More votes mean more influence.'

'Maybe.'

'But here's the real kicker,' Henari smiled. 'I reckon you can also dominate the parliamentary side of the party. More numbers for you means controlling preselections. You could even influence the prime minister's preselection.'

'How can you do that?'

'We bring significant numbers into the party in various federal electorates. They then vote for the key branch adminis-trative positions. Once you control those positions, you hand-pick your preferred people to do your bidding in the federal and state parliaments. You will never have to bother with out-of-control ministers again.'

Rusnek dropped his feet, leaning into his desk, picking up a paper clip, straightening it, before twirling it. 'How many?'

'Of the twenty-five seats the party holds federally in this

state, I reckon we could get seventeen plus all the senate seats. Although that might be a little harder, but not impossible.'

'Interesting,' Rusnek glanced up. 'What do you want?'

'Three things,' Henari shifted in his seat, the legs buckled almost collapsing. 'We want a clear run at the supply channel.'

'The transport union runs that.'

'Not for long. They are thinking about merging their construction division with you.'

'News to me.'

'And them,' Henari mocked. 'Second, we want to run several business interests through your corporate business model.'

'Like what?'

'Pornography and gaming.'

Rusnek nodded, squeezing out his bottom lip. 'It's possible.'

'Third, we want thirty percent of the parliamentary seats reserved for my mob.'

Rusnek nodded. 'Where do you get the new member numbers from?'

'Our client base is broad and relies on our product supply, if you know what I mean.' Henari flicked the tip of his nose. 'A signature and an address will be no problem.'

'How many do you reckon?'

'Immediately?' Henari smiled. 'Over four thousand. We can take that to twenty within a few months.'

Rusnek raised his eyebrows, whistling through his teeth. 'Let me think about it.'

'What's there to think about?'

Rusnek smirked at the challenge. 'Since establishing my union, I've only made decisions considering all the aspects of a deal. It has allowed me to be the only player in CBD construction in most capital cities. We don't rush. We don't wilt under intimidation.'

'I meant no offence.'

'None taken,' Rusnek smirked. 'Believe me when I say a deal is possible. I will need to think about it.'

Henari stood, pulling away the chair jammed on his hips. 'If you agree, I will ask the prime minister to defer the legislation.' He leaned across the desk, offering his hand.

'You influence the prime minister?'

'Let's just say she has a desire, and I meet it.'

Rusnek glanced at the offered hand, then engaged Henari's eyes. 'I'll let you know in a few days. I need to sort out the Cathedral first.'

Henari accepted the rebuke indicating to his man they should leave.

Rusnek watched them go. He gnawed his upper lip as he listened to them thump down the metal stairs. As they left the site, a sudden rush of retributive adrenalin surged through him. He sprang out of his chair, picking up his aluminium baseball bat, and headed out the office.

———

BOOKER SAT on a low stone wall at the park opposite the building site, trying to clear her head and overcome the anxiety still gushing through her. She struggled to control her shaking body and hoped the sun would comfort her. She considered whether to call her editor and pull the plug on her assignment when she observed two enormous men in bikie colours outside the building site straddle black Harley Davidsons. They secured their matte black helmets when, surprisingly, Rusnek rushed from the gate wielding a baseball bat. His first swing took off the mirror of one bike. The riders tried to reposition their stands so they could get off.

The next swing hit a rider in the helmet; the back swing taking out the glass of the headlamp of the other bike. Both riders were between a rock and a hard place as they could not get off and needed to absorb the blows to ride off. Both revved their throttles while shielding themselves from the vicious swipes. One sped off. The other took a blow to the face. The helmet took most of the heat, but the nose shattered.

Rusnek stopped his attack, pointed his bat at the bikie, and shouted. 'You ever come to my sites again, you ask permission, get me?'

The bikie struggled to turn his bike.

Rusnek panted, watching. 'Come see me in two days, and we will talk again.'

The bike roared off as Booker finished taking snaps of the ruckus with her phone. Rusnek spotted her and began striding across the street. She collected her bag and ran off. 'I told you,' Rusnek shouted. 'I never want to see you again, you bitch.'

Booker didn't look back. She sprinted, hoping Rusnek's demand would come true.

CHAPTER

9

Senator Morgan enjoyed her life. From an early age, she abandoned the suburbs and the miserable existence her parents and friends expected. By mastering the art of manipulation, she employed any means necessary, to attain her aspirations. She developed an understanding of the fragilities of humans, particularly the limitations of men. They were wonderfully supportive of her career, but hopelessly complicit in acts of disloyalty. She understood their triggers.

She was lucky to be appointed as a clerical assistant to an ambitious business owner who took a shine to her. One Christmas, she complied with his drunken innuendo. Her employment was secure after taking compromising selfies of her boss during his ill-judged dalliance. Once was enough to secure a relationship of trust. When he won the election for a seat in the state parliament, she moved to his electorate office. As soon as he became minister, she took over the position of his senior adviser. Manipulating the numbers, he secured her endorsement when a vacancy for the senate came. She kept the photos on file just in case she needed them.

Now she rarely returns to Frankston, preferring Melbourne city living and indulging in a two-week holiday to Chile each year. Parliamentary Services located her office to a tower down the New York end of Bourke Street. She lived a stylish existence in a loft apartment off a laneway at the eastern end of the city, close to her gym and anonymous salsa dance clubs. She boxed three times a week, swam 1500 metres twice, and tossed weights around in four sessions a week. Fit and hard had been her motto for years and others admired her.

Eddie Collins vaguely knew her background, but remained sceptical about her claimed influence within the party. He complied with her requests to deliver votes at party preselections and supported her in party meetings, acknowledging she promised the golden ticket for his political ambition. She insisted he widen his network and deliver more votes for her on the state executive. This proved an ongoing challenge. Outside of Gellibrand, few party officials identified him as an influencer.

After waiting twenty minutes for his scheduled appointment, Collins grew a little bored with examining the streetscape below. He counted the cranes on the skyline and assumed if there was so much construction activity the economy must be improving, contrary to the media narrative. BWU signs and flags dominated the cranes.

'The senator will see you now, Mr Collins,' the receptionist announced. Collins pushed off the windowsill to follow her.

'Edward, take a seat. Would you like a drink?'

'Got a beer?'

'Sure, take a seat on the lounge. I'll get one for you.' The staffer went to a cupboard opening a refrigerator. She pulled a beer, flicking off the top.

'The bottle is fine, thanks.'

'Senator?'

'No thanks, I have a workout in an hour. A water would be good.'

Collins took a quick sip of beer as Morgan joined him in a soft leather chair opposite.

'What's the news, Edward?' Morgan smiled, catching him glimpsing at her legs as she crossed them. 'You are the party's key finance man. So, tell me, what's happening?'

Collins cleared his throat. 'Donations are coming in since we commenced making calls to the usual suspects. Indeed, I would suggest we are ten percent ahead of this time last election.'

'That's terrific. You must be very pleased,' she said. 'Previous treasurers never scored your results, let me tell you.'

'I'm putting in place a better ledger system for party campaign accounts, so reporting becomes faster and more accurate. This will allow the campaign team to make real-time decisions.'

'Yeah, good,' Morgan said. 'What's happening with Gellibrand?'

'The speaker issued writs today for an election in five weeks. Nominations close in two weeks, which means preselection next week.'

'Is it winnable?'

'Not likely,' Collins said. 'Although there has been a shift in demographics. Boundaries have changed since the last election. A stronghold region for the government has been consigned to the neighbouring seat. We think the margin is now seven percent.'

'What do you want?'

'We conduct the preselection as usual,' said Collins. 'A member will put up his hand as he always does. I suspect there may be a novice nominating. The candidate we select though will be Alice Collins.' He took a quick slug of beer.

'Any relation?'

'My wife. I recall you met last year.'

'Oh, that's right. She owns a restaurant.'

'Cafe.'

'She keen?'

'We're using it to raise her profile for a run for mayor early next year.'

'I wouldn't broadcast that news to anyone. It may damage her profile. Especially during the campaign.' Morgan unhooked her legs and stretched for her water, catching Collins gawking. She enjoyed it and gave him another quick glimpse of lace as she straightened.

Collins coughed and sipped a little more. 'She'll be fine. We have a good team, and we have plenty of money. We don't have to seek money from the State Division.'

'You do a great job, don't you?'

'I like it. Someone needs to step up.' Collins paused for a moment. 'When do you think I will be rewarded?'

'Rewarded? What do you mean?'

'Senate preselection,' Collins gulped, his throat tightened. 'When do you reckon I'll be elected to that seat you promised?'

'I've told you many times, Edward, all in good time.' Morgan shifted in her chair. 'The next vacancy is yours, or maybe the one after.'

'You've said that before. I just need to know when it is my turn.'

'Edward, you are being a little too assertive right now. I feel somewhat threatened by you.'

Collins raised his palm. 'Sorry Senator, I mean no disrespect. I need to make arrangements for my business commitments. I'm a forward planner, that's all.'

'Just be careful with your tone. It's not appropriate.'

Collins grimaced. 'I meant no offence. I apologise.'

'Apology accepted. Now get going with your plans and let's secure Alison's preselection.'

Collins nodded as he stood, offering his hand. 'Her name is Alice.'

'Yes, that's what I said.'

Collins withdrew his hand before she could grasp it and moved to the door. 'Thank you for seeing me, Senator. I'll keep you advised.'

'Keep up the good work, Edward,' she said as he left. 'Hell will freeze over before you sit next to me in the senate my perving little friend.'

'JUST RELAX,' O'Brien said, straightening Hudson's tie. 'The Senator runs the show in Victoria. She is better to have on your side than trying to secure a preselection without her.'

'I told you the other night I'm not interested.'

'Mate, the way you handled that diverse group was incredible. You have the potential to be a first-rate politician.' O'Brien brushed Hudson's shoulders. 'I still get a chuckle out of it. Morgan heard about the meeting and wanted to meet you.'

'It's not what I want. I want to serve not be of service to the racists and bigots.'

'You think all of Australia is like that?'

'It's reflective,' Hudson stepped away from the preening. 'I imagine they exist everywhere and even on the other side.'

'Look, Jack,' O'Brien smiled. 'Let's just play the game. Get pre-selected for a comfortable state seat, then let's do the things we want to do?'

'I'm not sure I want to work with the folks I met the other night,' Hudson said. 'What an idiot Briggs is. How is he getting a career out of this?'

'They reckon he might be our leader one day.'

'That news really startles me.'

'You frightened?' O'Brien mocked. 'Yeah, right.'

Hudson checked his watch. 'She's late. Let's go.' He moved to the exit.

'Mate, not everything runs by the clock. Not in politics at least.'

'This is the problem. I see no discipline,' Hudson said, dragging open the door. 'Let's go.'

As they waited in the lift lobby for a car, Hudson again checked his watch as the ping of an elevator arriving gained his focus. The doors slid open, and Morgan stepped out.

She judged her situation. 'Sorry to keep you, gentlemen. I wish to apologise. There's no excuse, but I got held up.'

'By whom?' Hudson asked.

Morgan hesitated, then smiled at him. 'A constituent wanting to talk about her mother in aged care,' she lied. 'If you follow me, we can have our chat.'

'After you.' Hudson waved his hand. O'Brien slapped him on the shoulder.

'I suspect you are pressed for time, so please, take a seat.' Morgan extended her hand. 'I'm Stephanie Morgan.'

'Jack Hudson.'

'We've met, Senator,' O'Brien took her hand. 'Last year's state conference.'

'Oh right, yes I remember.' Morgan waited until they sat in the lounge, then sat, crossing her legs. Neither one of them noticed.

'Senator, thanks for agreeing to see us,' O'Brien said. 'We appreciate it.'

'Why are you here?'

'You invited us,' O'Brien grinned. 'The lady said it had to do with the Blackburn branch meeting.'

'Oh, that's right,' Morgan relaxed. 'You two caused a kerfuffle.'

'More Jack than me.'

Morgan laughed. 'You called Briggs a slob?'

'Not really,' Hudson smirked. 'His presentation was inappropriate. I called him out on it.'

Morgan smiled, considering the men for a moment. Hudson seemed different. 'Do you have political ambitions?'

'Not really.'

'Yes, he does,' O'Brien cut in. 'He just doesn't know it yet. Jack is the kind of bloke we need in parliament.'

'State or federal?'

'I would prefer state, if there are opportunities,' Hudson said. 'They're closer to the community. That's where I want to be.'

'Interesting,' Morgan said, scrutinising Hudson. 'I would have thought federal parliament is more your style.'

'I've done enough travelling. I would rather stick close to home.'

'You married?'

'Not even close.'

'Parents alive?'

'We lost dad in Afghanistan. Mum lives with one of my sisters in Malvern.'

'Which seat do you think would be a good for you?' Morgan

asked, steepling her hands under her nose and cupping her chin with her thumbs.

'Burwood,' Hudson said, without hesitation. 'I'll win it back and shift it into safe seat territory.'

Morgan raised her eyebrows, hiding a smile behind her hands. 'And how do you propose to do that?'

'By doing something different,' Hudson said.

'What might that be?'

'Telling the truth. If I do, I will gain the confidence of voters.'

Morgan felt a sharp twinge in her diaphragm as it tightened as if under threat. She considered Hudson and then glanced over at O'Brien. 'What's your plan?'

'Yeah, nah, no plans.' He shifted in his seat. 'I'm not ready, unlike Jack here. The way he spoke the other night was incredible. I think the party needs him.'

Morgan agreed. Hudson was what they needed, but she wouldn't recommend him. Too much charisma, too many smarts, and an aggressive arrogance that threatened her. He needed to be stopped dead in his ambitious tracks. 'I reckon we should prepare you for the next state election,' Morgan said. 'I think you should get campaign experience before then. I have an idea for you.'

She unwrapped her legs and moved to her desk, disappointed the men didn't drop their gaze. Morgan picked up the phone handpiece, prodding a button, then scrutinised the men as she waited. 'Hello, Cheryl? Stephanie here. When are you planning to close preselection nominations for Gellibrand?' She fisted her hip and gazed out across the bay to Williamstown, listening to the response. 'I have a quality candidate for you. I shall get his nomination in before the close of business tomorrow. When is the cut off time?' She took a note, replacing the handpiece without saying goodbye.

Morgan sat scribbling notes, listing out action items to be followed. She buzzed her assistant to join them, beckoning the men to move to the chairs at the desk. 'Jack, this is the plan,' she looked up and smiled, 'to prepare you for Burwood, there is an opportunity to learn preselection techniques and campaign experience in the federal seat of Gellibrand.'

'Where's Gellibrand?'

'See that peninsular over there,' she pointed to Williamstown, 'that's a lovely part of Melbourne. It is a strong seat for the government. Minister Campbell was involved in a tragic incident the other week and now a by-election is due. It's a seven percent margin and we can't win it. But here's the point: it will provide you with valuable experience addressing a preselection conference. And if you win preselection, a campaign.'

'Are you sure, Senator?' O'Brien asked.

'Where else do you get experience?' Morgan squinted. 'We must move fast. You need to be a member. We need to complete the nomination form and get it into Exhibition Street before five tomorrow. Sandra here will help you complete the forms. I will sign them off and deliver them in time. Any questions?'

Hudson seemed bewildered but shrugged.

'Very good,' Morgan smiled. 'You're a fast learner. Go with Sandra and complete the forms. Let's reconvene in thirty minutes.'

Hudson eyed O'Brien, already standing and offering his hand to help him out of the chair. Hudson took it and slapped his friend on the back as they followed the adviser. Morgan watched them leave, her fingers steepled in front of her face a frown creasing her forehead.

When they were alone, O'Brien asked, 'You reckon she just flashed us?'

'Like Sharon Stone, you mean?'

'Was it deliberate?'

'I don't know.' Hudson smiled. 'I must say, it was all a little weird. How can you make things happen like that when she doesn't even know me? Is this what politics is like?'

'Mind you, she's built like a brick shithouse,' O'Brien laughed. 'I wouldn't want to tackle her. Did you notice her biceps?'

'Her hair was a little damp,' Hudson said. 'I reckon she was talking crap about the constituent. I wouldn't mind betting she just had a workout.'

'Except for her hair, I wouldn't mind adding her to the dance card.'

'What's wrong with her hair?'

'Women should wear a wig when it's short and thinned out like that.'

'You don't.'

'Yeah, but I'm not trying to be glamorous.'

Hudson scoffed. 'That is for sure my friend.'

'I still wouldn't mind a dance or two with her.'

'Can't you ever think of anything else?' Hudson frowned.

'Mate, when you get a glimpse of lace, what else is there?'

'You are a crazy man,' said a chuckling Hudson.

———

'SENATOR, are you sure you want to do this?' Sandra asked after the men finished their tasks and left. 'This will put the wind-up, Collins.'

'What did you think about them?'

'Charming, well dressed, with a rare air of confidence and charisma.'

'Exactly,' Morgan nodded. 'A clear and present danger for the party.'

'That's good for us, surely?'

'Not good for us,' Morgan frowned. 'No doubt they will be successful politicians. Which means they will undermine my network of numbers. We can't have that.'

The staffer shook her head. 'So why have Hudson run in Gellibrand?'

'He will lose,' Morgan smirked. 'He is then labelled as a loser with no potential. Nothing worse than having a losing campaign on your CV.'

'Collins has the numbers.'

'I've told Hudson to get out and meet the delegates. He could turn it around.'

'If he doesn't?'

'Even better,' Morgan said. 'If you can't win preselection in a seat, we can't win. What does that say about you?'

Sandra nodded, pursing her lips. 'You think he is that bad?'

'No gorgeous. I think he is that good. I don't want the hassle of his rivalry.'

CHAPTER

10

The first preselection delegates to meet on Hudson's list of thirty were Jess Titter and her friend Mavis Gruber. Long-time members of the National Party and the complete opposite to stereotype. These women survived on social welfare, living in state housing with hordes of children and husbands struggling to maintain a job.

Soon after nominations closed, Hudson received an invitation to drop-in for tea and cake. He parked his car outside the Steam Packet Hotel and wandered past the unkempt houses along Aitken Street looking for the number, finding the townhouse in a small private cul-de-sac. Screaming kids played on plastic scooters and battered trikes in the driveway, avoiding the inevitable call in.

The well-worn wire screen door rattled when Hudson knocked. As he waited, he perused the neighbourhood, noting maintenance was not a priority. The door opened and a waft of warm sweet air washed over him. The smell of fresh bakery brightened his smile as a very plump woman asked him to step in.

'Thanks for coming Mr Hudson, I'm Jess. We spoke this morning.'

There was no hallway, so he couldn't squeeze past. He waited for her to step back along the dark passage, allowing him to move into the lounge room. A much thinner woman with grey hair tied back waited. Hudson smiled as he spotted her untamed, Einstein-like wisps of shorter grey hair.

'Hello, you must be Mavis.' Hudson offered his hand. Unlike her friend, she applied makeup as best she could. It seemed she was going out of her way to impress him.

He sat as directed on the soft vinyl sofa. As Jess hurried her clanking preparations in the small kitchen, Mavis asked a question. 'Were you in the military?' He detected a northern England accent.

'I was. Ten years.'

'My Dougie was in the navy for three years. He seemed to enjoy it.'

'Oh, that's interesting,' Hudson smiled. 'I thought the navy required a minimum six-year enlistment. But I could be wrong.'

'No, you're right,' Mavis said. 'They discharged him medically unfit. He's now on a TPI pension.'

'Badly wounded?'

'No, he never served on a ship,' Mavis said. 'He lost the tip of his finger playing touch rugby in the mess.'

Hudson raised his eyebrows. 'And now he's on a totally and permanently incapacitated pension?'

'Yeah. Nice little earner, that one.' Mavis smiled as the tea arrived, served on a ply-wood tray. 'How come you left the military?'

'Injury, I'm afraid.'

'You're on the TPI as well? And you want to become a politician?' Mavis asked. 'That's a little cheeky, don't you think?'

'Not on the TPI, I'm afraid.' Hudson leaned forward. 'Hey, this looks terrific, Jess. Did you bake this black forest?'

'Would you like a piece?'

'Is the Pope a Catholic?'

'I think he is,' Jess said, giggling. She sliced generous portions, passing a plate to him.

Hudson forked in a generous mouthful. He shook his head, recognising the unique baking skill of his host. 'That's beautiful,' he said. 'That probably ranks as the best I've ever tasted.'

'You see, Mavis? He's only been here a few minutes and already sounding like a politician.'

Mavis had cream clinging to her mouth as she nodded. Too much cake stuffed in her mouth to comment.

'Mr Hudson, we don't know you. We wondered why a smart man like you, dressed the way you are would be talking to us. Convincing us to vote for you in a political race that you can't win. Why do you want to represent us?'

'Call me Jack, please.' He knew his prepared answer would not cut it, so decided the truth might work for him. 'Senator

Morgan recommended it to me. She believed if I'm to learn grassroots politics, then I should learn why folks like yourselves continue to work for the party in electorates that don't respond to our messages. I'm here to learn, to listen, and to lean on your experience so I can better represent the party, no matter what they ask me to do.'

Jess nodded. She cast a glance at Mavis who also nodded, stretching for more cake. 'That sounds good, but are you in it to win it?'

'What's the point of not committing yourself one hundred percent?' Hudson said. 'I know it will be difficult. But, if we deliver the right message and give the community enough reasons to change their vote, then nothing is impossible. Improbable it may be, but not impossible.'

'What's your view on abortion?' Mavis asked.

'I believe a woman has a choice. That choice is at conception.'

'That's a provocative thing to say,' Jess said.

'It's what I believe. Would you prefer I speak the words you want to hear?'

'No, but it's provocative.'

'I believe in the sanctity of life. This means I do not agree with late-term abortions. I recognise there are times when the health of the mother should be the priority, but when conception happens, then there are two other voices who should be part of the decision.'

Mavis seemed confused. 'Two other voices?'

'The father and the baby,' Hudson said.

Jess poured another cup for him. 'It's not really a baby though, is it?'

'What is it then?' Hudson asked. 'A clump of cells with a unique DNA? A living thing heading for life outside the woman's body?'

'It's a woman's choice,' Mavis said.

'Indeed, it is,' Hudson agreed. 'At conception.'

'What's your view on immigration?' Jess asked.

'What do you want me to say?' Hudson paused. 'That I think we take too many? Or, that immigration is vital to the economic well-being of our community?'

'We think there are too many who come here taking advantage of our pensions,' Mavis said.

Hudson smirked at the irony as he thumbed his bottom lip. 'Fact is, most folks who migrate come to work and build businesses. Like yourself, Mavis,' Hudson said. 'I reckon you migrated. I'm also guessing you have contributed as a taxpayer. I'm also guessing your children will work and raise a family growing the economy. It's hard-working folks like you who have made this country great. I welcome folks just like you.'

Jess slumped back in her chair, checking her watch. 'I have to get the kids' tea ready. Can I just finish on a couple of quick questions?'

'Sure, fire away.' Hudson finished his tea placing the cup and saucer back on the cluttered coffee table.

'Are you married?'

'No.'

'Will you move to the electorate if you win?'

'Yes, of course.'

'Pets?'

Hudson laughed. 'No. I have no pets.'

'Last one,' said Jess. 'What do you value most?'

Hudson paused for a moment. He gazed at Jess, and said, 'HEL.'

Her mouth dropped open.

'It's an acronym. Honesty, Ethics, and Loyalty.'

'Interesting. Do you have any questions, Mavis?'

'I think you've done well, and I like you,' Mavis said, using the back of her hand to wipe her mouth. 'I know I'm not supposed to say this, but you have my vote.'

Jess tapped Mavis' knee. 'Hush now. No doubt, Jack will learn how we vote on the day.'

Hudson took her cue and stood. 'That cake was beautiful. I hope we can do it again.'

'You don't have to say that, Jack.'

'Yeah, I know. But it's the truth, and honesty is one of my values.' He offered his hand. They were all smiles as they ushered him out.

He shook his head as he strolled away, smirking as he recalled the questions and the surroundings. He pondered why he had agreed to this new life, dealing with people he thought were quirky.

As he passed the Steam Packet, he checked his watch, deciding he had time for a beer to wash away the cake before moving on to his next appointment. He found a place at the bar and scanned the throng.

'A pot of draught, thanks,' he said to the barman.

'Geezus Christ,' a voice yelled. 'Now I've seen everything.'

Hudson searched about for the voice, wondering if it referred to him. He saw a familiar beaming face at the other end of the bar.

Hudson collected his beer, pushing through to his former comrade. 'Captain Hudson, I thought you would be dead by now.'

'Billy Tyrrell, what the hell are you doing here?' They hugged, slapping each other before settling in for a chat. 'If I recall, you live in Perth. What are you doing here?'

'No work for an old digger over there. I relocated to get a job. I work down at the dockyard, restoring wooden boats. What are you up to?'

'I live over in Surrey Hills. I work as an analyst for a stockbroker.'

'Of course you do,' Tyrrell scoffed. 'Sounds boring to me. What brings you here?'

'Strange as it may sound, I'm standing for election.'

'You takin' that prick Campbell's place?'

'Nah, Hudson laughed. 'I'm running for the other mob.'

'You are kidding me. You have no chance.'

'I'm sticking my toe in the political waters to see how it feels.'

'Be careful of the sharks, Skip. There's a heap of them about, including the late Mr Campbell.'

'I don't expect to win.' Hudson took a sip of beer, checking his watch. 'I'm just learning the craft before standing for a seat over the other side of the city.'

'Well, you would know hostile territory when you see it. Hey, it's nice to see you, Skip.'

'Yeah, good to see you, Billy,' Hudson squeezed his colleague's shoulder.

'The last time I heard from you, they repatriated you after Sudan.'

'I spent six months in the hospital after the explosion. If Charlie O'Brien didn't come to my rescue, I'd still be there in some dingy cell.'

'Charlie got a gong, apparently.'

'Yeah, he did. Just like you. You were brilliant.'

'Need any help with this political thing?'

'I'm meeting with delegates over the next few days. I'm catching up with a Geoff Dougan. Maybe I can come back for a chat once I'm done with him.'

'You can rely on Dooges, unlike others who resemble peacocks or, more likely, liar birds. If you get up, I may have to change my vote.'

'Only if you believe, Billy,' Hudson drained his beer. 'You going to be here for a while.'

'I owe you, Skip, so sure, I'll be here.'

'You're a good man, Billy.'

CHAPTER
11

The comrades lounged in Hudson's living room, working on a speech thirty kilometres from the Williamstown Town Hall where he would deliver it. The organisers allocated him twenty minutes to say whatever he wanted and then move to questions from the almost fifty delegates. They overused coffee mugs during the afternoon and now enjoyed a chilled beer.

'I reckon it's done,' Charlie O'Brien said as he scanned the speech. 'This'll get you the nomination, for sure.'

Hudson stretched for the papers when offered them. 'You don't think it's a little pompous?'

'Nah, you nail most of the issues.'

Billy Tyrrell glugged his beer, studying his colleagues. 'I suppose we have the words, but I reckon it isn't authentic.'

'You think I should add more?'

'No, I reckon you don't read it.' Billy took another slug. 'If you read it, it won't sound like you. You know what I mean? From the heart. There's not enough of you in the words.'

Hudson brushed his thumb across his chin. 'So just learn it and recite it?'

'Geez no. You could stuff the whole thing up.' Billy sat forward, placing his beer on the table. 'I reckon you rehearse it as much as you can tonight. Only use a single sheet of paper which you take from your jacket after you're behind the lectern.' Billy glanced at O'Brien. 'Do they have a lectern?'

O'Brien nodded. 'Probably.'

'You look calm and composed. If you fumble with a folder, you may get heavy sighs. You eyeball them as you slip out your sheet of paper. Without breaking your gaze, you smile and straighten it. Then, you're off.'

'How can I get two thousand words onto a sheet of paper?'

'Dot points, mate.' Billy grinned. 'You have your key points listed. You refer to them when you need to move to the next point.'

Hudson nodded. 'I get you.'

'If you don't have a lectern, you would be in trouble finding a place to put your folder,' Tyrrell said, drinking the last of his beer.

'Good point,' Hudson said, struggling from his chair. 'Want another frothy?'

Tyrrell laughed. 'Do bears shit in woods?'

Hudson moved to the kitchen, fetching three bottles and a bag of potato chips.

'What questions do you think they'll ask, Charlie?'

'You better have an opinion on the tax system. I expect they will bring up immigration and will certainly discuss health policy.'

'What about my background?'

'Just promise to move if you win,' Billy said.

'No, I mean my military service.'

'You said it all in the nomination form, so why worry?' O'Brien said.

Hudson paused for a good gulp of beer, then burped as he wiped his mouth with the back of his hand. 'I'm a little worried they may raise it.'

O'Brien considered him for a moment. 'If someone raises it, then deflect by saying general things like, it was tough, we were in daily fire fights, and several friends were killed.'

'Too bloody many,' Tyrrell said.

Hudson pouted out his bottom lip, gazing at him. 'You're right, mate, way too many.'

'Can't do much about that now. Just deflect if you get a question.'

Hudson took another gulp, finishing his bottle, standing, and moving to the refrigerator. 'Anyone want another?'

Tyrrell raised his eyebrows, glancing at O'Brien. 'Yeah, why not?'

'Here's a question for you,' O'Brien raised his voice. 'What are your plans for detention centres, Mr Hudson?'

'I'M glad you asked that question, Jess,' Hudson smirked. 'I believe we have a compassionate migration program, which I support. I especially support the policy of bringing folks to this country who can help grow it, rather than coming for our pension benefits and a holiday.' Delegates nodded. 'I especially believe we are a compassionate country, and we should do our best to assist in the global refugee problem. There are many who deserve a better life and it is our good fortune we offer one that can provide security from the ravages of war. But...' Hudson scanned the room, 'what I cannot support is the scourge of people smuggling. I support the use of detention centres to send a strong, coherent message to these criminals.'

Questioned by delegates for almost an hour, he was the last candidate. He would have preferred to be number three, right in the middle of the candidate presentations. Eddie Collins drew names from a woollen cap with no one seeing the names he announced. Collins slotted him into last place.

The candidates assembled in a small anteroom downstairs, while the delegates met upstairs in the former council chamber of the gracious Town Hall, restored to its 1920s grandeur. An old bloke Hudson came to learn was a former navy man, came prepared with sandwiches, and a thermos of coffee, which he didn't share. He told Hudson he nominated for the ten previous elections, convinced he could win the seat. 'Gellibrand is primed to change. We just need the right candidate.'

The young kid was first and returned, smiling and confident within twenty minutes. He had no questions asked of him, so assumed his short address gave the delegates everything they needed to know about him. The next candidate was a well-presented woman from Newport. Hudson learned she lectured in politics at Victoria University. She was back within an hour, a little drained, but pleased with her experience. She wanted to go through a political process to add practical learnings to her undergraduate curriculum.

Third was Alice Collins. Hudson considered the possibility she may be related to the president. As they waited, the old bloke enjoyed a sandwich and relaxed, sipping his coffee. He must have assumed Collins would be awhile, and she was almost two hours. When she entered the waiting room, she seemed chirpy.

The old bloke was back in thirty minutes, surprising Hudson.

'Good afternoon,' Hudson smiled and reached for his slip of paper. It wasn't there. 'I appreciate the opportunity meeting with you today,' he checked his other pocket, without luck. 'I hope we can enjoy these moments we have together.'

Trained to remain calm in a crisis, Hudson stepped from behind the lectern, moving closer to the delegates. 'That's better. I don't want to have any barriers between us, now or in the future. I plan to serve you, the community, and the party with respect and responsibility. Nothing should come between us in reaching that goal.' Nervous he may have been, but he started powerfully, remembering the dot points Billy Tyrrell insisted on, and finished almost twenty minutes later, as planned.

Eddie Collins led the questions with standard policy

queries, which could trip up those unprepared. Several allies, including Geoff Dougan, asked easy questions that he answered confidently. Eddie Collins asked the last question.

'Is there anything in your service record we should know, Mr Hudson?'

Hudson was ready for the question but paused for a moment to breathe. 'My injury sustained in combat led to my repatriation from the service. Standing to attention on parade for hours limits me, and sitting in a foxhole can be a problem. Other than that, I have full mobility, but not good enough for the military.'

'Is that it?' Collins asked.

Hudson considered him for a moment, curious if he may have known. 'Yes, that's it. I am proud to have served. I look forward to doing so again, but in a different theatre of combat.'

Several delegates laughed, as others smiled, except Collins, who was frowning.

———

'RIGHTIO, DELEGATES,' Collins was standing at the lectern. 'Let's have an indicative show of hands. Those who support Denis McInerny?' Three members from the Young Nationals raised their hands.

'Professor Moncrieff?' Ten hands went up.

'Alice Collins?' Thirty hands shot into the air.

'Ron Hall?' No hands were raised.

'Jackson Hudson?' Two hands rose, hesitated, then dropped.

'Based upon that show of hands I can declare a winner, but I'm in your hands,' Collins knew to treat his numbers with sensitivity and respect. 'Would you like to discuss the nomination and proceed to a formal vote?'

'What's the point?' Dougan asked.

'I want to make sure everyone has an opportunity to have their say,' Collins said.

'We can't win, so what's the point in treating this vote like it meant something?' Dougan stood. 'I wouldn't mind calling it a day and having a beer.'

'Just wait, Geoff, please,' Collins raised a calming hand. 'If everyone agrees, then I'll call up the candidates and announce the result. Is it the will of the delegates that we select Alice Collins to represent the party at the forth coming by-election for the seat of Gellibrand?'

There were plenty of nods, and some restless delegates began shifting in their seats.

'All those of that opinion say aye,' some delegates murmured a yes, 'to the contrary no,' no one responded. 'I think the ayes have it. Mavis, can you ask the delegates to come up?'

As they waited, Collins explained campaign news and assigned various roles for those volunteers keen to get involved. After a few moments, the anxious candidates filed into the room in speaking order.

'Thank you for nominating for preselection. We thank you for your time and the effort you have all made,' Collins said.

'After a long day and a tight vote, we are pleased to announce that Alice Collins has been elected as the candidate for the seat of Gellibrand. Congratulations.'

The applause was loud, and Hudson joined in. As delegates mingled about congratulating Alice, Dougan pulled Hudson aside.

'You got two.'

'Two?' Hudson's jaw dropped. 'I could have sworn I had fifteen certainties. Folks said to my face they were going to vote for me.'

'Jack, learn a lesson.' Dougan grasped his hand and shook it firmly. 'It's the one with the numbers who counts them. Nothing is ever certain unless you have them.'

'Thanks Geoff, I appreciate your support.'

'Billy Tyrrell is a mate of mine and I owe him, so I was happy to help you,' Dougan said as he began to leave. 'You're wasting your time doing this. You should be in a safe seat and on the front bench.'

'This was supposed to give me experience.'

'It has that. I'm not sure the loser tag is what you want. Be careful Jack.'

———

'Congratulations, darling.' Collins hugged his wife once they returned home. 'You were marvellous.'

'Not sure I presented that well. I lost my place a few times. The words were hard to read.'

'You were the best,' Collins smiled. 'Fancy a cuppa?'

'Something stronger I think, darling,' Alice flopped onto the couch. 'How did the soldier perform? He seemed like a nice man.'

'A tad pompous for my liking. Typical eastern suburbs rich boy,' Collins said. 'We don't need his kind over in the west, that's for sure.'

Collins opened a bottle of wine, grabbed two glasses, and strolled over to the lounge. Jobs have been allocated to the team. Now you can relax until we generate media.'

'I hope this all works out as planned. Cheers.'

CHAPTER
12

Hudson didn't hang around after the conference, arriving home with a barbeque chicken, chips, and a tub of coleslaw from the Red Rooster drive-through. He noticed the folded slip of paper – which should have been in his jacket – sitting on the bench as he placed his paper bag of food. He let out a chuckle and went off to change into Sloppy Joes. As he was passing the front door, a thump startled him.

Charlie O'Brien was at the door, a bottle of champagne in one hand and a long neck beer in the other. 'Which one do we open?' he said, with raised brows and twinkling wide eyes.

'Come in. I have water open,' Hudson smirked.

'You're kidding? You got done over?'

'Want some chicken, Charlie?'

'I thought this was a shoo-in?' O'Brien followed Hudson into the kitchen. 'I thought the flasher said we were done and dusted.'

'Obviously, she doesn't hold the numbers in Gellibrand.'

'What a waste of time.'

'Hey, wait up,' Hudson broke open the chicken bag. 'We reunited with Billy. We wouldn't have done that if I didn't stop for a beer.'

'Yeah, you're right.'

Hudson spooned coleslaw onto the plates, tore off the legs and shook out chips before sliding dinner to O'Brien, now perched on a stool at the bench. 'Mind you, I only did that to wash away the ghastly black forest cake,' Hudson laughed. 'Those two-faced women told me to my face they were voting for me.'

'Politics,' O'Brien chortled. 'Don't you love it?'

'Not as much as you,' Hudson said, shoving chips into his mouth and sliding a fork to him.

'I suspect we should go talk to the senator,' O'Brien said, forking coleslaw into his mouth before tearing a bite of chicken. 'This was only ever about getting experience.'

'Some experience,' Hudson sighed. 'People lying to your face.'

'Harden up, young man. Politics is about numbers, so let's go find some. We then pick a safe seat, and Bob's your uncle. You are a future minister.'

'Yeah, simple.' Hudson picked up his drumstick, sucking the meat from it. His mouth full when he asked, 'Is there a chance the senator set us up?'

'Maybe,' O'Brien said, wiping his mouth. 'Why would she do that?'

'Who the hell knows? This is all new to me.'

'There is always a sense of deceit and duplicity when it comes to politics,' O'Brien mumbled as he chewed. 'From what I can gather, if you don't have the numbers, you bare your bum to the one who has.'

Hudson opened a wipe and cleansed his fingers and mouth. 'What do we do now?'

CHAPTER
13

Breaking and smashing bottles being emptied into a city dumpster, disturbs Stephanie Morgan most weekend nights. The noise of the city often disrupts life in a CBD loft apartment. She doesn't hear the drunks, but she sometimes hears the bottled glass from the nearby bars and the incessant reverse beeping of early morning trucks. Tonight, she remained fidgety and the city noise bothered her.

The senator continued thinking about Hudson failing the previous weekend. The fact that he continued to disturb her despite losing the preselection unsettled her. She hadn't changed her mind. He remained a threat to her power if he were ever successful in reaching the federal or even the state parliament. He held the charisma of leadership all politicians wanted, and she needed to stop him before he usurped her privileged position.

Despite attempting to read dull briefing papers, she found

them stimulating. Although she found it too believable, she attempted to read the latest political thriller. She enjoyed a cup of hot chocolate, followed by an Irish coffee that had no effect. At midnight, she completed a fifteen-minute workout, hoping this would help her sleep. Two hours later, she thought about the State Council meeting later that morning. The thought of discussing finance and planning issues for the next federal election was not appealing. She needed to be switched on and alert for any discussion. Looking for relief, she pounded her pillow.

'This is ridiculous.'

She tossed off her sheet, headed to the shower, and turned up the heat, hoping it would relax her and clear her mind. Patting and rubbing herself dry, she felt a twinge of need and chose to go out. She combed product into her hair until it was slicked back, slipped into a plum-coloured, tight lace frock: a very short tube, with a plunging neckline with half sleeves. She grabbed her black Jimmy Choo sandals from the top of her shoe rack and strapped them on. Then, reconsidering, she slipped into underwear. With eye makeup applied, she slipped on a black wrist sweatband, pushing her door key into a small hidden pocket. She left her phone and any ID behind as she usually did when she went dancing. Her face was made up enough that she would not be recognised if some miscreant took a photo.

Along the darkened lane just metres from her apartment building, she could hear the music of Latino reggaeton. The doorman waved her through, and she gingerly descended the steep staircase. Various neon colours illuminated the tiny room with most of the small crowd dancing. She moved to the bar, and the bartender slid her a glass of double shot bourbon on the rocks. The barman smiled and nodded. Morgan acknowledged the service and took a sip. She turned to watch the dancers move to the intoxicating music.

Ricardo's was a hidden bar she frequented when she craved to dance or to have a little fun. It closed when enthusiasm dropped off in time for breakfast. She always came to dance and did not feel the need to be a senator. She paid her monthly account through bank transfer on time from a bank account she didn't declare. Going by the name Valentina, she took precautions to remain unknown to others.

The music had her hips moving to the raw beat. She finished her bourbon, then moved to the centre of the dance space, stepping, twerking, and writhing to the beat. An arm slipped around her and snatched at her. Turning abruptly, she slapped him with such force that it staggered him away. As she watched him go, her hips found the rhythm again.

She closed her eyes and moved to the beat. When she opened them, she noticed a young man in a white singlet watching her. She pointed and beckoned him. He danced toward her. She stroked his face before whipping her hips. They moved into a merengue bachata. First apart, and when she pulled him close, they moved together. She moved against his black jeans, almost resting on his thigh. They twirled through each other's arms, swayed their hips, and danced close for thirty minutes until they both agreed enough. Morgan stepped to the bar, filmed in sweat. A bourbon slid to her. She gulped it down, crushing the shard of ice. Stretching to search past dancers, she couldn't see her dance partner. She glimpsed him disappearing down a dark passageway. She pushed away from the bar and followed.

Morgan found him bent over a washroom basin sluicing. He was wet, his silver chain dangling from his hip. He turned to recognise her entering, and he straightened. She thrust herself at him, kissing and gnawing. He didn't struggle and moved into her rhythm.

'I need you now,' Morgan demanded, turning to a familiar stall hoisting her lace.

CHAPTER

14

The senator was always on time for the 1 PM start and sat opposite the president at the large wooden board table in a windowless room on the sixth floor. The National Party owned its own building in Exhibition Street, within walking distance of Senator Morgan's apartment. Her patron's advice was that being five minutes early to a meeting was equivalent to being five minutes late, and she subscribed to it. With a coffee from her preferred cafe, she sat as usual, scanning the national newspaper as delegates wandered in.

On the Victorian Administrative Committee, she acted as the representative for the federal leader. It was the most powerful party committee and to be elected required support from branch delegates. She always managed the numbers for her favourites seeking to be appointed. The Committee set agendas for other party committees such as policy and membership and reviewed operational decisions regarding campaign finance.

Eddie Collins took his usual position at the end of the table so he could spread out files to answer finance questions. 'Good afternoon, Senator,' Collins said, pouring himself a glass of water at the refreshment station.

'Hello, Edward,' Morgan didn't look up, 'I note a small piece in the paper today about your wife, Alison. I wonder how that is possible?'

'Her name is Alice. What is it?'

According to the newspaper, she is the confirmed candidate for Gellibrand. She states she is looking forward to the challenge,' Morgan said, still not looking up. 'I would suggest nothing is certain until this committee agrees.'

'Just procedural, I'd reckon.' Unsettled by the senator's comment, Collins hesitated, perhaps now regretting briefing the Hancock Media journalist.

'You think?' Morgan eyed him. 'Are you moving ahead of the party? That's presumptuous, don't you think?'

'Precedence suggests confirmation will be today,' Collins said, clearing his throat, resuming his seat.

'We shall see,' Morgan said, as she closed, then folded her newspaper.

The president took his place, all smiles and enthusiasm, placing files before him, preparing for the meeting. 'Nice to see you, Stephanie. You are looking well.'

'Yes, I had a good hard workout this morning,' Morgan said, a smile brushing her lips for a moment.

'Not sure how you keep it up,' the president said. 'I admit, though, you look terrific.'

'So do you, Bryan,' Morgan said, a touch caustic.

The president scanned the table, seeking attention, and then opened the meeting. Discussion remained overly formal for much of the first agenda items. The president then requested Eddie Collins to present the accounts. He delved into detail, glazing over the eyes of his colleagues. They only required a brief update, not the accounting detail Collins delivered every meeting. As he listed expenditure, Morgan picked up a substantial expenditure item within the campaign expenses and queried it.

'We purchased corflutes for election day for those seats needing support.'

'The election is months away. Why do we need to purchase these items now?'

'We made an offer to the printer to prepay for the posters. They accepted. It will reduce our costs during the campaign.'

'Fair enough,' the president said.

'Who is the printer?' Morgan asked.

Collins shifted in his seat. 'Williamstown Chronicle.'

'You?'

'Umm, yes. I disclosed this in the ledger,' Collins said.

'You are prepared to accept prepayment on a job that may cost you more later?' Morgan asked. 'Seems extraordinary.'

Collins wriggled again. 'My donation to the party.'

Morgan swung in her seat as she studied the nervous man, avoiding her gaze at the end of the table. She wrote a note in her journal. Collins glanced at her, averting her gaze. His eyes flicked back to the president, seeking to wind up his presentation.

'If it's logged it should be fine,' the president said. 'Can we move on?'

The meeting progressed through a campaign overview, a policy discussion, and a briefing on the proposed preselection process for the next state and federal elections. Ratifying the candidate for the Gellibrand by-election was the last item on the agenda.

'We have a terrific candidate, Alice Collins,' the president advised. 'She has already established a campaign team and is all systems go for the election. Nominations close next Tuesday, so we need to ratify our decision today. Can I seek a formal motion?'

Collins leaned forward. 'I move the recommended candidate for the seat of Gellibrand, Alice Collins, to be approved.'

'Is there a seconder?' Someone raised their hand, 'Thank you, Rosemary. Is there any discussion?'

Morgan straightened, crawling her wheeled chair forward. 'Can I suggest Edward withdraws from the meeting while we discuss this motion?'

'I'm the president of this division.'

'And your wife is the nominated candidate. You have a conflict of interest.'

'Ed, can you step out for a few minutes while we discuss this nomination, please,' the president nodded.

Collins thumped his file closed, and strode from the room,

glancing at a smirking Morgan. Once the door stopped rattling, the president asked, 'Do you have any issues with the nomination, Steph?'

She licked her bottom lip and took a deep breath. 'Imagine for a moment we were to win the seat,' she clasped her hands staring at the president, 'what do you think the leader would say when Alice Collins turns up in Canberra for her first party room meeting?'

'I reckon he would appreciate her win.'

'He would then hope she says nothing in parliament and has zero interaction with the media.'

'What are you saying? She's not good enough?'

'I'm suggesting, if there is a chance for a win, then we should ask if she is the right candidate.'

'What are you seeing that we aren't, Senator?' Rosemary, the president of the Women's Division asked.

'With the right candidate, polling shows we could win.'

'Why do you think Alice is the wrong candidate?'

Morgan turned to her. 'I think as a federal candidate she is a very talented local councillor.'

'That's a bit rough, Stephanie,' the president said.

Morgan didn't respond, scrutinising the others. She wondered if they were agreeing or simply didn't care. 'It is obvious to me that Alice is Edward's candidate,' Morgan continued. 'He runs the division. He runs the numbers, and I am told he runs the local council. I'm also advised on good authority that Alice will be running for mayor in a few months. He is using this preselection to raise her profile.'

'What's wrong with that?' Rosemary asked.

Morgan scoffed. 'Nothing.' She smiled, glancing down at her hands, 'if we're running a nepotism organisation that rewards those who hold the numbers. Nothing at all.'

'What are you suggesting?' the president asked.

Morgan steepled her fingers, pausing for the effect needed before suggesting such an outrageous political move. 'I think we should override the recommendation and appoint a candidate that better reflects the high standards we hold.'

'No way,' Rosemary scoffed.

'We have a chance of winning.' Morgan lied. 'I'm suggesting we ought to consider a candidate we are proud to represent us in federal parliament.'

'Do you have one in mind?'

'As it happens, I do.' She opened a file, distributing thirty single sheets of a smiling headshot with an impressive CV.

'Wasn't this guy a candidate?' the president asked.

'He was. He is the type of candidate we need to nurture for the state parliament, if he is unsuccessful in Gellibrand.' Morgan set a narrative to limit Hudson's prospects.

'Candidates with previous losses often struggle in future races.'

'Not this gentleman,' Morgan said, studying her colleagues. 'He is highly credentialed, educated, and comes with a well-regarded military service which may attract voters in Gellibrand.'

'Gellibrand is a safe government seat. Why would you give him mission impossible?'

'Because, Mr President, if we ratify him, then we may win.' Morgan pressed her lips together to hide her lie.

'I must admit he looks good, literally and figuratively,' Rosemary said, checking out the photo.

'He may swing women to us,' Morgan said, smiling at her.

'You think this will be better for us?' the president asked.

'I have spoken to the leader,' the senator lied again. 'He likes the idea, encouraging me to recommend this change.'

'Could I just get a show of hands to support the senator's idea?' All but two hands went up. 'How do we tell Eddie?' the president asked.

'Let me convey the news,' Morgan said, standing and moving to the door. 'I need to use the bathroom, anyway.'

Morgan stepped from the room finding Collins reading a newspaper in a corner office. 'Edward,' Collins squinted when she entered. 'I have good and bad news for you.'

A rush of anxiety rushed through him. 'Oh yes, what have I done now?'

'You have done very well, frankly,' Morgan said, sitting opposite and watching his eyes dip to her crossing legs. 'The mood of the meeting is for endorsing Alice.'

'This is great news and a relief. I assumed it might be a problem.'

'No, that's bad news,' Morgan said. 'It means you may never get the gig in the senate.'

Collins dropped the newspaper on the coffee table between them. He wiped his jaw, ruffling his lips with a knuckle. 'What's the connection? I don't understand?'

'It seems there is a view within the party, not in the committee room, that you use your numbers a little too much for the benefit of others. This may reflect on your character during any future nomination you have in mind,' Morgan nodded encouragement. 'This means it may impact your support when it becomes your turn for the senate.'

Collins turned away, staring out the window.

'Edward, if I were you, I would think about giving up Gellibrand. You know we can't win.'

Collins still gazing outside, gulped and nodded. 'Yeah, we can't win.'

'We think we should sacrifice the soldier. He revealed to me he wants the next senate vacancy and appears to be getting support.'

'Say what?' Collins turned to her.

'Yes, it seems he is working hard to raise his profile in the party. He thinks a senate seat may be an option.' Morgan paused, licking her bottom lip as she stared at Collins. 'That's why I think we should throw him on the losers' pile where his ambition balloon will deflate without a pop.'

'You think a loss will end his ambition for the senate?'

'Imagine Edward, if you ran for the seat at the by-election,' Morgan said. 'You have the numbers, the reputation, and a history of working for the party. But then imagine if you lost. People would label you as a loser. Do you reckon you would get the senate seat?'

Collins' tense body gradually relaxed as he found a position that brought him comfort. 'You're right. Once a loser, always a loser.'

'It's your decision, and I'm sure the Committee will support you. My recommendation is you allow a vote against your motion then install Hudson into the loser's folder.'

Collins shifted again. 'What about Alice?'

'Encourage her to run for mayor. If she does, I'll campaign for her.'

Collins breathed, tightening his lips, then nodding. 'Okay, let's do it.'

'Wise decision, Edward.' Morgan uncrossed her legs, flashing him his reward. 'This is a brave decision you have made, and you will be compensated. Let me talk to the Committee and advise them of your decision. They'll be sensitive toward you, so let's not talk about it, okay?'

Collins lifted his eyes and nodded.

When Morgan resumed her chair, she perused the concerned members. 'Edward is a good party man and took the news be very well,' Morgan glanced at the president. 'He will accept the change and does not want to discuss it. Feeling both embarrassment and concern, he worries for his wife. He doesn't want to discuss the matter any further.

'That's fine with us,' the president said as he checked the others for confirmation. 'Bring him in, Mike.'

When Collins resumed his seat, the president moved through the motion. The party took little time to ratify Jackson Hudson as their candidate for the by-election of Gellibrand.

Morgan rested a finger to her lips, hiding a smirk as the meeting closed.

CHAPTER
15

Hudson and O'Brien persuaded security that they had an appointment with Senator Morgan, and after a confirming call, security directed them to the lift lobby. Another security guard unlocked the buttons, pushing the senator's level before securing it again. It didn't take long for the two men to be relaxing in the senator's office enjoying a glass of Chardonnay.

'I have news for you,' Morgan said, once past the friendly chit-chat. 'The endorsement for Gellibrand came to the Administrative Committee today. The Committee rejected the Alice Collins nomination. I have to say there was much debate. The meeting decided we should nominate someone else. That person is you, Jackson.'

The men said nothing. Hudson held his breath for a moment then blew out, his cheeks ballooning. The senator watched them smiling, playing the tip of her tongue along her lips. 'Anyone?' she asked. 'Anyone?'

O'Brien cast an eye toward Hudson, then said, 'What does it mean?'

'It means Jackson will be our candidate at the by-election. Let's hope he does well.'

'Cheers to that.' O'Brien raised his glass. He glanced at Hudson who seemed stunned. 'I think Jack is grateful. He's a little shocked by the news.'

'What happens now?' Hudson asked.

'You get a campaign up and running. If you're lucky, you win.'

'Simple,' O'Brien smiled.

Hudson winced. 'Yeah, if you say so.'

Morgan enjoyed the moment. The two soldiers seemed out of their depth in dangerous waters. 'I spoke to the leader before you arrived. We agreed we need to support you.'

'Will Collins run the campaign?' Hudson asked.

'Unlikely, considering his wife has been sacked.'

'He's a party man,' said O'Brien. 'Surely, he'll help out.'

'Who knows what the sleazy perv will do?'

'Not a friend?' Hudson queried.

'He has his advantages, but he has never had a chardonnay in my office.'

'Then we must be privileged,' O'Brien said with a smile.

'I think we will need the party structure to help us,' Hudson said.

Morgan's phone vibrated on her desk. 'Come straight up. Use the door near the washrooms, it's open.'

The men exchanged glances; their brows etched in puzzlement.

'That was your new campaign manager. She's a senior policy adviser for the leader and lives in Canberra. We asked her to manage your campaign, and she came down this evening.'

'Nice one,' O'Brien said, glancing at Hudson who bounced his head still confused.

'For me?' Hudson said. 'In an unwinnable seat?'

'We think you can win. That's the reason we got rid of Collins. We didn't think we would win with her.' Morgan emptied her glass, pouring the rest of the bottle into O'Brien's glass before moving to her refrigerator.

'Why me?' Hudson said. 'The professor was the better candidate.'

Morgan returned with a bottle of chardonnay and an extra glass for her guest.

'We think your background will attract the male and female voters. The swinging voters will also like you.'

'Hello?'

'Ah, Christine, there you are. Come in.' Morgan strode to her with arms open.

'Hi, sorry I'm late. I had trouble getting a taxi.' She wheeled a small travel bag with a garment pack attached. 'Good to see you, Senator.' They hugged.

Breaking away, Morgan said. 'Christine, let me introduce

you to Charles O'Brien,' they shook hands, 'and this strapping young man is Jackson Hudson, our candidate for Gellibrand.'

'Jack, please,' he offered his hand, 'the senator explained you are my new campaign guru.'

'Chrissie Woodward, pleased to meet you,' she said, taking Hudson's hand, 'we have much to discuss.'

'I apologise for dragging you down here, Christine,' Morgan handed her a wine, 'but you are the best.'

'There's no need to gild the lily, Senator,' she took a quick sip, 'I'm sure these boys will find out,' she released a broad smile, 'I was at mum's enjoying a lamb roast when the leader called. Now I'm here. What's the plan?'

Hudson grinned at her. 'I'm a recruit. I haven't done basic training, so I'm keen to learn.'

'How much money do you have?'

'The party doesn't pay?' O'Brien questioned.

Woodward shook her head, drawing in her bottom lip.

'We pay some bills, but not all,' Morgan said.

'Collins?' O'Brien asked.

'Not likely. He could surprise us with printing support,' Morgan glanced around the other subdued three. 'He owns a print shop and also publishes the local rag.'

'Well, that's something at least,' Woodward said. 'He may offer editorial.'

'You'll need to meet with Collins and get his people on the committee,' Morgan said. 'Elections are won with money and people. You haven't got money, so you'll need people.'

'I'll call him tomorrow,' Woodward said. 'Where do you live?'

'Surrey Hills,' Hudson said.

'I'm guessing that is in the eastern suburbs. Sounds too posh for the west.'

'You'd be guessing right.'

'I want you moved into the electorate by tomorrow. So, when you submit your nomination, you ensure you have an address within the electorate to provide. 'Sleep wherever you like. Just make sure you have an address in the electorate.'

'Shouldn't be a problem,' said O'Brien, grinning at Hudson.

'Look, I'm not going to mayonnaise it for you,' Woodward said, finishing her wine. 'Winning seats is a tough ask. Particularly when they are safe government seats. If we run a grassroots campaign and get your face in front of people, you may get over the line.

'That's a little cynical,' Hudson said.

'Not cynical, Jack,' smiled Woodward. 'There's a reason good-looking people are in politics. You look good, so you have a chance, but it'll be hard work. You'll be required to knock on doors and meet as many people as you can,' she waved her glass at the senator, 'if you don't, I can guarantee you won't win.'

Hudson turned to the senator and asked. 'Should I be doing this, if I can't win?'

'A lot of folks have placed their faith in you, Jackson. Don't let them down.'

'OLEG, with this by-election going on, will the legislation be deferred? Toby Martin asked, sitting at a table working through his nomination form.

'Not likely,' Rusnek said as he watched the kid. 'Once you are in parliament, you can work to amend it or get it stopped. It passed the lower house the other day.'

'What do you mean?'

'Toby, have you done any research on parliament and its procedures?'

'Yeah, of course.'

'What have you learned?'

'They have a generous superannuation scheme.'

'Anything on parliamentary standing orders and procedures?'

'I looked at it,' Toby glanced at Rusnek. 'It all seemed too wordy for me.'

Rusnek pressed his bottom teeth along his upper lip until it hurt. 'Look, Toby,' he straightened. 'You need to get across your requirements if you are going to be of any value to me.'

'Don't worry boss, it'll be fine.'

Rusnek scoffed, stepping away, staring out the window at the building site. 'We need to discharge this legislation. You need to guarantee that will be the case and do what you have to do.'

'Boss, it'll be fine.' Martin sidled over, placing an arm around Rusnek's shoulders. 'Who's the dude standing against me?'

'Some soldier.'

'We whack him hard, don't worry,' Martin dropped his arm. 'Once that's done then I'll blow up the parliament to get that legislation stopped.'

Rusnek turned and grinned, cupping Martin's face. 'You are a good boy. Now get that form done so we can get it to the electoral office before it closes, otherwise we're stuffed.'

Martin moved back to the desk. 'What does this mean - holding an office of profit under the Crown?' He frowned.

'Just tick the no box.'

CHAPTER
16

Hudson arrived every morning between six and eight at the traffic lights in Melbourne Road at the entrance to the West Gate Bridge. Woodward warned him, electors needed to see him seven times before they remembered him. He waved and shook his Vote for Hudson corflute sign so the crazy candidate seeking attention could amuse drivers. At eight he headed for a primary school, passing out brochures outlining his service record and values. He rejected Woodward's suggestion of a military portrait displaying his gallantry and service medals. He instead settled for a casual, smiling head shot. Several parents ignored him but many hovered for a chat.

Once the morning school run was done, he headed for a shopping centre until eleven to meet voters. Then he door-knocked registered swinging voters until it was time for the afternoon school run. Once schools emptied, he headed to sporting fields to chat with parents watching their children. He stuck to the netball courts where mothers were most likely chatting as their daughters had fun. Woodward recognised they needed to lift the female vote and insisted he meet as many as possible. At five o'clock, he headed for the major roads, where peak hour drivers were heading home. At around six thirty, he headed to a pub for a meal. He always selected a night when meal specials maximised the potential to meet locals.

Once the day was done, he headed for the campaign office which ended up being the house he rented as his electorate address. They brought in basic furniture and connected the internet, allowing them to manage contacts even more than the daily handshakes. Hudson remained convinced they should do more on social media, yet Woodward insisted voters also needed to see him in the trenches. He understood the analogy.

Woodward persuaded him the battle zone was the streets surrounding the safe government voting booths. She declared the government candidate would never bother to doorknock or visit those areas, convinced that the voters' loyalty was unshakable. She clarified the strategy in terms of guerrilla fighting and the need to outflank the government's candidate at his weakest point.

'Apathy loses battles,' Hudson agreed.

Woodward drove him hard like any drill sergeant. He had worn through two pairs of campaign shoes by the time he reached a neat house. As he walked past a car in the driveway, he noticed a backyard pool. With his foot braced against the wired door, he knocked. Pets would often attack, crashing out the door to get at him, so he learned to expect an attack. One time a cat flew at his head, pinning its claws into the wire, distressing its owner. He helped release the Burmese and made the owner a cup of tea to calm him. He hoped he received his vote.

His doorknocking system was straightforward and uncomplicated. Tap once. Knock a little harder the second time, then, if again no answer, thump it.

The thump didn't get a reaction at this house, but he heard a distant dog. Nothing worse than dogs. They were his worst enemy. He mustered up the courage to knock on doors, but his heart raced, and palms sweated at the thought of encountering a snarling dog. Rottweilers were the scariest and abundant in the safer government suburbs. Little terriers were the most rabid and noisiest and didn't fear a stranger.

He stepped away from the door, listing a 'not at home' in his log and marched off to the next house. As he moved off the porch, he checked through the carport to the pool. At that precise moment, a woman walked out from behind the house sweeping leaves, stark naked. He fretted for a moment about what to do, so froze. A flimsy fence between him and her. Then he spotted a Doberman chewing on a tennis ball beside her.

The woman turned to sweep more leaves and noticed Hudson. She emitted an anxious squeal, dropping the broom, bending over, and covering her chest. The dog responded, dropping the ball, snarling, strutting toward him, determining if the stranger was a threat.

'It's all right,' Hudson backed away, a hand in the air. 'I'm not wearing my glasses.' The baying Doberman rushed at the fence, hitting it hard, bouncing off. 'I'll come back later.'

Hudson skedaddled out of the driveway to his car parked further along the street. Jumping in before searching for any frothing canine keen to rip him apart. The Taliban were frightening, but nothing like a vicious black dog in Williamstown.

He called it a day.

CHAPTER
17

Woodward agreed to a *Meet the Candidates* debate at the community centre ten days prior to election day. She organised various party helpers to attend with signs to support Jack, instructing them to loudly display their support. The Williamstown Chronicle insisted all candidates attend so constituents could learn more about them. Eddie Collins hosted the event, ensuring all candidates kept speeches to time, and selected someone with hands raised from the crowd to ask a question of each candidate.

All candidates dressed appropriately, except for the government's candidate who showed up in work boots, overalls, and a fluoro vest. Rusnek suggested wearing the garb so Martin would appeal to workers. He wanted him to declare it was time workers stayed united and elected a representative for them. Martin spoke about the government's plan to hurt unions with legislation and suggested he would stop the assault. Woodward moved to the front of the audience, snapping photographs of him pointing at the audience, fist clenched, and contorted taut face with an aggressive fist salute.

Collins asked for questions, promising only one per candidate, and pointed to a confederate. 'My question is to Toby Martin,' the woman projected. 'What are you going to do for the workers of Gellibrand?'

Martin took off his hard hat, ambling toward the lectern, placing the helmet where he could read Rusnek's notes inside. The union boss received a text from an unknown source, advising his candidate should prepare for this specific question. Martin listed off his demands for infrastructure works to relieve traffic congestion. He floated the idea of helping workers increase their economic welfare by establishing a union bank and finance company, receiving loud applause. He even suggested developing vacant government industrial land in the electorate into a centralised distribution hub with road and rail connections.

'While this land remains idle, we cannot build a strong labour force in the electorate.' Another round of loud applause had him smiling and waving. 'I promise you all,' Martin said, putting his helmet back on, 'I will work every day ensuring working families are helped up the ladder of opportunity.' Spontaneous applause erupted again. 'The workers united, will never be defeated.' He chanted the slogan several times with his fist in the air. 'The workers united, will never be defeated.'

He may have expected a stronger response because only

one or two joined in. When he realised he earned little support, he stopped and resumed his seat.

Collins was quick to the microphone, pointing to another confederate. 'My question is to Mr Hudson.' The questioner was reading a slip of paper. 'We have heard much about Muslim immigration and refugees, but I would like you to explain why Australia provides funding to Israel and comment on constant community disruption.'

Woodward looked at Collins, noticing a weasel-faced smirk behind his hand as he sat at a chair away from the candidates.

Hudson raised his eyebrows and twisted his face as he took in a large breath, readying himself for a response as he strode to the lectern. Woodward was now convinced Collins was setting him up for a public humiliation to be reported in Collins' newspaper the next day.

'Thank you for the question,' Hudson began, smiling at the questioner. 'These are important questions, and all politicians should be able to respond.'

Woodward smirked a strained pout, wondering how her novice candidate would deal with a foreign policy issue that no one in the audience understood.

'There are two parts to your question, so allow me to deal with them,' Hudson gripped the side of the lectern a little harder as he scanned the audience. 'There are implications in your question that suggest Muslim immigration is too high and perhaps is a bad thing.' Hudson paused for a moment to locate the questioner and catch his gaze. 'Three percent of the Australian population is Muslim. The fastest growing religion in Australia is Hinduism, and fifty-three percent of Australians are Christians, with a staggering thirty percent of Australians identifying as having no religion. Although I wouldn't mind betting these folks come with some morals-based faith. So, this implied notion that Australia is being overrun by a certain religion, based on the figures, is wrong.' Hudson caught Woodward's eye; she nodded.

'To your point about Israel,' Hudson searched for the questioner but couldn't see him. 'Australia does not send foreign aid to Israel. Indeed, Australia and Israel have a healthy, but modest, commercial relationship. Last year two-way goods and services trade amounted to roughly $1.3 billion. Israel is the only democracy in the Middle East and whilst we don't send foreign aid; we support their existence contrary to popular belief,' Hudson said. 'I hope that reassures you.' Hudson studied the audience. 'Folks, Australia is a dynamic, diverse and variable community. We welcome people from all over the world and all we ask is that they have a go. If they do, then this country will provide them with a rewarding future. I recognise its many benefits and look forward to representing our community in the federal parliament.'

There was no response as Hudson stepped away from the lectern, resuming his seat. Someone clapped, then someone else. Then a ripple of applause evolved into a heavy ovation. Hudson found Woodward's eye and smiled. Woodward tapped her forehead in an admiring salute. It was the first time a politician impressed her.

CHAPTER
18

W oodward complained almost daily to Eddie Collins about providing resources or people for the election campaign. Volunteers were the most important. The campaign wanted to deploy them to attend polling booths on election day to distribute how-to-vote cards. Additionally, the campaign assigned volunteers to attend the pre-poll voting at the local electoral office. Collins did not return calls or respond to emails. Campaign material he forwarded was out of date. He provided a list of party volunteers but did not include contact details. She remained under no illusion, Collins did not support the campaign.

She encouraged Charlie O'Brien to call Hudson's military connections. Although both he and Hudson were reluctant, the willingness of the military volunteers they enlisted surprised them. Just like any military exercise, they appointed booth captains for all fifty-five booths. These former soldiers called upon their connections. Within a week, all booths were manned and prepared for election day. Each site underwent reconnoitring. The network agreed upon lists of equipment and shared ideas. It turned into a military campaign.

On the rare occasions Hudson visited the campaign office for a break, he complained about the lack of local support, suggesting the party should organise itself better, like how the government party organises its union membership. He continued to be annoyed by volunteers from the other side of politics, in their red shirts, harassing citizens at train and bus stations. There seemed to be more than a hundred enthusiastic campaigners seeking to convince voters Toby Martin was their man.

Hudson's calls to the senator and Collins went unanswered. The flimsiness of the party's commitment becoming clear. Chrissie Woodward's resourcefulness and Charlie O'Brien's enthusiasm convinced him that he would have been thrown into the basket of political also-rans if he didn't receive their help.

When he swung his feet onto a table covered with brochures, he blew out a heavy sigh, then took a slug of beer from his stubbie. His feet were sore. His shoes exposing his weariness, with both soles almost worn through. He glanced about the open space. Everything they could do was done. Tomorrow, the troops must persuade enough voters at the polling booths to switch their votes to Hudson.

He was looking forward to a shower and a good night's

sleep. In his mind, visiting the booths two or three times, shaking hands, and smiling was all he needed to do tomorrow. Then it would be over. 'Is this how marginal seat members' work on every campaign?' Hudson asked as Woodward ended a phone call.

'It's a little more hectic,' she smiled, examining her candidate.

'You are kidding,' Hudson took another generous slug. 'No wonder everyone wants a safe seat.'

'Including me,' Woodward laughed. 'But not yet.'

'Do you reckon we can improve the margin?' Hudson asked, combing his fingers through his hair. 'I know it'll be difficult to win. I'm hoping to reduce the margin, so it doesn't dent my prospects for a state seat.'

'You have done well. You surprised me.'

'I did what you told me.' Hudson raised his eyebrows. 'Without you, I would know nothing.'

'You're a born politician, Jack,' Woodward said, moving to a seat at the table. 'If you want to deal in the political cesspit with all these horrible people, you just have to keep reminding yourself you are.'

'I'm learning, I must say.'

'Collins has been useless. I suspect this is deliberate,' Woodward said. 'What he did at the community debate was appalling.'

'I had to laugh at the government's candidate. What were they thinking?'

'They expect to win the seat. They want to show Gellibrand is very different to when Campbell had it,' Woodward said. 'I reckon he died for a reason.'

'They can't be that arrogant.'

'Welcome to politics. A certain amount of arrogance is a primary requirement.'

Hudson nodded, gnawing at his lower lip. 'I have much to learn.'

'You may not get another chance unless we lift your vote tomorrow.'

'Is the party that shallow?'

'Ever wonder why they pushed you into this seat after you finished almost last at preselection?'

'I didn't really think about it too much. I didn't have the time.'

'I reckon the dark arts are at play here, my friend.' Woodward winked and nodded. 'Someone doesn't want you anywhere near the parliament.'

'So, why did they send you?'

'Good question,' Woodward smiled. 'I suspect they are testing me, rather than you.'

'Crumbs. Does that mean someone has set me up?'

'Maybe.'

'By whom?'

'Well, not Collins. Maybe one of his friends.'

'The senator?'

'You may well say that.' Woodward said, tapping her nose. 'I couldn't possibly comment.'

'Here's to a good day tomorrow,' Hudson saluted his bottle toward her.

Woodward smiled, nodding. 'You don't think you've finished for the day, do you?'

Hudson checked his watch. 'Ten o'clock? I would have thought knocking doors would be a tad late.'

'There's a dinner dance at the Royal Yacht Club. Perhaps you could pay a visit and say good night.'

'You are kidding me. Seriously?'

'I'm not asking Jack. There could be votes there, so move your arse.'

———

THIRTY MINUTES later Hudson was standing in the carpark handing out brochures as members left the building. He wished them a good evening and asked for their vote the next day.

'Bit late for you to be doing this, isn't it?' A voice came out of the dark.

'Sir, I'm working hard for your vote. If it means standing in the dark in a carpark wishing you a good evening, then I'm prepared to do it to convince you I'm your man.'

'Son, this is a working man's town. We vote for the government.'

'What have you got to lose voting for someone else?'

'I've lived here since I was a kid,' the man stopped, his wife holding his arm. 'My dad voted for the workers. His dad voted for the workers, and I was expected to follow his example. So, I did.' He offered his hand. 'In all that time, you are the first candidate I have met. I'm very pleased to meet you.'

'Sir, I want to change the system,' Hudson said. 'I've learnt over the last few weeks that it's the values of the politician that are important, not the party. I've tried to be authentic and meet as many constituents as I could to show them who I am.'

'Douglas Smythe is my name, and this is my lovely wife, Wendy.'

'Ma'am.'

'Why aren't you standing for a safe seat, like everyone else?' Smythe kept a firm grip.

'In my opinion, a few battle scars are required to secure any victory. I remain confident. I hope to improve the vote.'

'Not win?'

'Sir, I'm not arrogant enough to believe I can change the hearts and minds of the people of Gellibrand. I have to give them a reason, so maybe they'll decide it's time for a change.'

'You seem to be very impressive, and I wish you well,' Smythe released his hand and smiled, touching him on the shoulder. 'You're right, maybe it is time for a change.'

'Hey Dougie, who are you talking to?' Another couple came from the clubhouse.

'This impressive young man is Jack Hudson.'

'Blimey, the candidate?'

'Yes,' Smythe said. 'I'm hoping with our vote he will be our next member of the federal parliament.'

'If you reckon, we should vote for him, then we will.'

'There you go, Jack, that's four votes. I hope that helps.'

'Sir, I appreciate your support.'

After receiving hearty goodbyes and well wishes, Hudson watched them go. He smirked, hoping changing lifelong voting patterns, if only briefly, proved that easy.

CHAPTER
19

Hancock Media interrupted the evening movie with Breaking News from the election tally room.

'Good evening,' Naomi McKinnon announced. 'There is breaking news this evening that will rock the government. The safe seat of Gellibrand, never held by the Nationals, is in peril of being lost in an unprecedented result. Our reporter at the tally room, Madeleine Booker, is here with an update. Maddie, what is the status of the count?'

'Yes, good evening, Naomi,' Booker said. 'In an unprecedented outcome for the Gellibrand by-election, no winner has been confirmed. Latest two-party preferred results have the parties neck and neck. The government held the by-election because of the mysterious death of Industrial Relations Minister Paddy Campbell, who was found floating near the dockyard a little over six weeks ago. Police are yet to provide specific information about the circumstances surrounding his death. The police investigation is still ongoing.'

Stephanie Morgan stopped stretching to listen to the broadcast. She turned up the volume.

'The current result has the Nationals' candidate, Jack Hudson, leading by thirty votes. Although, we have had three lead changes within the last hour. We are yet to hear from either party leaders. I have with me the government's candidate, Toby Martin.'

Martin stepped closer as Booker signalled. 'Mr Martin, what is your response to the election result?'

Martin dropped his head, smiled, and then raised it, gazing at the high ceiling. 'I'm shocked. This is unexpected. I will claim victory when we have all votes counted. It's been close; however, I remain confident I have the numbers.'

'You delivered the party an unprecedented result. Has the prime minister been in touch?'

'I haven't spoken to anyone.'

'That surprises me.'

'Why would it surprise you?'

'It seems your party has dropped you like a hot potato,' Booker said.

'I'm gonna win the seat. Then, we make changes in Canberra, trust me.'

'It looks like it's going to be a stressful night for you. Thanks for talking to us.'

'Yeah, thanks, luv.'

Booker raised her eyebrows, wincing as he walked away.

'Naomi, it seems one candidate is confident about the result,' Booker said, grinning. 'It's way too early to tell at this stage.'

'How long before we have a result, Maddie?'

'I've spoken to the returning officer. She advises me that the result may take a week.'

Morgan stretched for her phone, swiping it to connect with Eddie Collins. 'Not the result we wanted, Edward.'

'It still appears likely the government will win,' Collins said.

'We need to have capable scrutineers in place to ensure Hudson doesn't win,' said Morgan, sitting cross-legged on her mat. 'We can't afford to win this seat.'

'I know.' Collins paused for a moment. 'We did all we could to hold him back.'

'Yes, I'm aware,' Morgan said. 'They are likely to go ahead with a recount tomorrow, so ensure we have our scrutineers there and not his.'

'I'm onto it.'

'MATE, HOW TALENTED ARE YOU?' O'Brien said, clinking the neck of his bottle against Hudson's.

'Too early to say,' Hudson took a sip. 'We gave them a good run though, didn't we?'

'More than that, my friend. I reckon you'll get a nod for a seat now.'

'Any feedback from the trenches?'

'Heaps. Let's have a debrief next week,' O'Brien said. 'Bottom line, there were some hostilities at several booths. We were able to contain any firefights. It seems there were a few union members wearing bikie colours who didn't take too kindly to our strategy.'

'Casualties?'

'Plenty of body bags. Them, not us.'

Hudson smiled as he held out his bottle. 'They will get over it someday.'

'Roger that,' O'Brien said, chuckling.

Hudson spotted Woodward on the phone, gesturing to him to come over. He squeezed through well wishes to the desk in the corner with Woodward gripping the handset to muffle the noise.

'The leader would like a word.'

'*Who?*'

'Ramon Chopra.'

'Oh right,' smiled Hudson, taking the hand piece. 'Mr Chopra, good evening?'

'Jack, you have been a mighty success young man. We are very proud of you.'

'Thank you, sir,' Hudson glimpsed at Woodward. 'But this is Chrissie's victory. We could not have done it without her.'

'She is the best, that's for sure. I'm glad I have her on my team,' Chopra said. 'When we know the result, we will speak again. If you are successful be ready to come to Canberra to meet the team.'

'There's a long way to go, and I wouldn't be overconfident just yet.'

'The vote is close, that's for sure,' Chopra said. 'You have been mighty, and we can all learn from your effort, win or lose. That's why I want to meet with you.'

'I'll be happy to fly up, sir.'

'Very good, young man. You should be very proud. See you soon.'

The call ended before Hudson could add anything. He shrugged and passed the handset back to a grinning Woodward.

'What happens now?'

CHAPTER
20

S crutineers examined each individual ballot paper in a small room at the Melbourne head office of the Electoral Commission during the recount. They disputed a vote when they saw a mark that didn't appear to show clear voter intention. The government scrutineers won every challenge. Opposition scrutineers seldom disputed a vote for Martin. On one occasion, the electoral officer raised an obvious false vote in favour of Martin. The government disputed this suggestion, and the opposition conceded, adding to Martin's total.

Hudson's team asked for two recounts, surprising the returning officer, only to concede further votes to Martin. They left satisfied after the fifth recount provided a clear winner. The government then called for another recount, just to make sure, and votes shifted again.

Both candidates attended the declaration of the poll a few

days later, with Martin in his hardhat garb and Hudson elegantly dressed, as always.

'After six recounts and distributing preferences, we are now prepared to declare a winner for the Electoral Division of Gellibrand,' announced the returning officer, as uninterested as any bureaucrat, 'There were 112,313 votes cast, which is a ninety-two-point-three percent turnout. Of this total, there were 4,267 votes marked informal, leaving 108,046 formal votes allocated after preferences.'

Chrissie Woodward slipped her hand into Hudson's and gripped. Morgan watched from her Canberra office, a bottle of champagne already popped and sitting on ice, with a Waterford flute in hand. Rusnek, watching via a streaming service on his phone, was enjoying a latte confident of the result.

'After allocating preferences, Candidate Toby Martin, 54,021 votes.'

Woodward tightened her grip.

'Candidate Jackson Hudson, 54,025,' the officer announced. 'I declare the winner, Jackson Hudson.'

Hudson didn't move even as Woodward flung into his arms for a hug, pulling at his neck to kiss him. Martin had already left, slamming the glass door bouncing its Venetian privacy blinds.

'I will kill the bastard,' Rusnek bellowed, slapping the table, overturning his coffee.

'Fuck me,' Morgan said, staring at the television, sculling her champagne.

CHAPTER
21

C hrissie Woodward took it upon herself to escort Hudson to Canberra before she returned to the Opposition Leader's office. Knowing which parliamentary accounts to charge, she booked his flight and accommodation. To ensure his safety and proper identification, she committed to escorting him through parliamentary security and completing forms for his identification tags. When she introduced him to the Speaker and the Opposition Whip's clerk, they directed him to his allotted office. Following that, she introduced him to the Clerk of the House who provided guidance on the schedule for the induction program.

The location of his office on the second floor didn't bother him, even though the Whip hadn't done him any favours. Woodward led him through to the plush suite, where he marvelled at the furniture and fittings. Even the ensuite excited him, but he found the refrigerator in the kitchenette too small, until he discovered another one in the cocktail cabinet that housed his television.

'The walls look a little bare at the moment. You will eventually fill them, as you're entitled to three works of art from the parliament collection,' Woodward said.

'I appreciate this, Chrissie,' Hudson said, as he sat on a hard chair beside her, scanning the room. 'This is incredible.'

'Just remember one thing, Jack,' Woodward waited for him to look at her, 'the parliament has many folks keen to assist you. They will do as you say. Chauffeurs will drive you to the airport and your home, here and in Melbourne. They will ferry you around Canberra when you need it. There are many, many people who will now think you are a member of the A-team, which you are, but, remember one thing,' Woodward locked eyes with him, 'you are now a VIP, know it, but never ever show it.'

Hudson didn't respond. He eyed her, appreciating the wisdom and the work she did to get him there. 'How many staff am I entitled to?'

'Four,' Woodward said. 'As a backbencher, especially in a marginal seat, it's all about constituent enquiries.'

'No procedural manual?'

Woodward squawked a laugh. 'You're kidding, right? Politicians think they know everything. They aspire to be individuals, and they claim their electorates are different, so they each do things differently. You will make it up and learn as you go. Choose your staff shrewdly.'

'What about you?'

Woodward dropped her enthusiasm, turning away, filling her lungs. 'I'm a senior policy adviser to Chopra, specialising in foreign affairs,' she said, facing him. 'I also want to be a politician. I'm thinking I'm in the best position staying with him to reach that goal.'

'Fair enough,' Hudson said. 'Given the work you did in getting us over the line, I just thought I'd ask.'

'Four votes,' she smiled. 'I suspect you are the one who got those.'

'I reckon I know when, too.'

'When – at the debate?'

'Nope.' Hudson crossed his legs and smiled. 'It was you actually,' he watched her doubtful face and grinned. 'You pushed me out to the yacht club, remember? I came across Mr and Mrs. Smythe, who staunchly support the red party. I got chatting with them and his mate. They promised they would vote for me. Four of them.'

'You're kidding me?'

'Not at all,' Hudson smirked, nodding. 'If it wasn't for you kicking me out of the campaign office on Friday night, I would not have met them, and they would not have voted for me.'

'I don't believe it.'

'It's true, so when I say I owe you, then I do.'

Woodward paused for a moment, taking off her glasses. 'You know, Jack,' she said, her eyes soft, 'originally this was just a project for me. To be frank with you, I didn't care whether you won or lost,' she tugged at the end of her nose, 'but you impressed me so much with your response to that set up question at the debate. I changed my mind about you.'

'What did I say?' Hudson said, squinting.

'It's not what you said, more the tone that you said it.'

'I pooed my pants when the question was asked.'

'I reckon that was Collins, such a bastard.' Woodward brushed her finger under her nose a few times. 'It was more the way you said we all have a duty to offer ourselves and the community to those who migrate here. Then you knocked the questioner's head right off with facts which just rolled out. How did you know that?'

'Always speak with authority when asked those types of questions. They'll correct you if you're wrong. Most wouldn't know.'

'I checked what you said.'

'Was I close?'

'Almost exact. How would you know that?'

'I study Middle Eastern economies as a hobby.'

'You see, Jack.' Woodward laughed. 'That's why I like you.'

'So come work with me,' Hudson grinned. 'On assignment from the leader's office until the next election. Then if we win, let's rethink it.'

'Why would I want to come live in Melbourne?'

'The coffee is excellent.'

'I need more than that.'

'The latest census shows males outnumber females in the forty to fifty age group.'

Woodward frowned, cocking her head. 'Your point?'

'Your social life may pick up?' Hudson smirked, eyebrows bouncing and eyes wide.

'Is that statistic, right?

'Well, did it sound right?'

'Say it with confidence and authority, I see what you mean.' She laughed.

'Come on, Chrissie, it'll be fun.'

Woodward didn't respond as she placed the arm of her glasses at the corner of her mouth to consider Hudson. 'Okay,' she replaced her glasses, 'I want my role to be chief of staff on the highest pay scale and I want to travel with you to Canberra.'

Hudson shrugged. 'Done.'

'And, on condition I go back to the leader's office any time I ask.'

Hudson waggled his head. 'Agreed.'

'And, when it comes to advice from me, you take it.'

Hudson offered his hand. 'Yes, ma'am.'

Woodward brushed his hand aside, standing dragging him up, then hugging him.

'Thank you, Jack. You are a good man, and you are going to be an influential politician.'

Hudson felt her warmth and tightened his arms.

'With you by my side, we may make that happen.'

They separated, a little uncomfortable with the familiarity. Hudson stepped away toward the desk. 'Is this yours?' He pointed to it.

'I'm next door, she pointed to a door. Remember, VIP.'

'Never show it, gotcha.'

'And by the way, Jack,' Woodward said, smirking. 'My social preference is the female demographic.'

CHAPTER
22

'Ah, Mr Hudson, I believe?' a well-dressed dandy approached Jack with his hand out. 'Now, is it Jackson or Jacob?'

'It's Jack,' he said, as he was being led by an attendant to the party room when the fellow sidled up.

'My name is Alexander Windsor. I'm the member for Adelaide,' he said. 'Most folks call me Alexander, but never Sandy or Al.'

'Nice to meet you, Alexander.'

'I was elected at the last election – a novice just like you.'

'A few more days on the clock than me, I'd reckon.'

'It's a little intimidating at first, but once you are used to it, then it all seems like boarding school. Coming to the meeting?'

'Yes, I'm yet to meet anyone.'

'Well, sit with us. It'll be a hoot.' Windsor heaved open the glass door, and they strolled into a room half full of colleagues standing and sitting amongst the beech-wood chairs with green inserts. Everything, it seems, is green in the House of Representatives.

Hudson shook hands with colleagues he vaguely knew from news reports. He scanned the room, spotting celebrity politicians and former ministers who ignored him. A huge woman squeezed into his row and sat next to Windsor.

'This is the wonderful Jack Hudson, Joyce, the new Member for Gellibrand.'

'You're Senator Morgan's boy, is that right?'

Hudson didn't let go of the offered sweaty hand, caught her eye, searched for humour, and got none. 'As it happens, I have little to do with the good senator.'

'Well, that's a positive start. Welcome to the team.'

As they settled, Windsor leaned over to whisper. 'The senators have little respect for each other. They're both after a job.'

'It's a steep learning curve, but I reckon I'm getting it.' Hudson nodded as he surveyed the settling politicians.

'Let's have lunch together. Any plans?'

'None.'

'Then let's meet in the dining room. It'll be a hoot.'

The room became silent when Ramon Chopra, positioned at the front of the meeting, stood. 'Colleagues, we have a very special guest here with us today. It is my great pleasure to welcome our newest member, Jack Hudson, the first Nationals member to win Gellibrand.'

The room erupted in applause. Hudson stood, smiled, and waved.

'It is always terrific to welcome new members to the parliament. In particular, those who win a seat off the government.'

'Enjoy it while you can,' a voice said, from the back.

'Would you like to say a few words, Jack?'

He wasn't expecting the leader's call and experienced hands were interested in the testing response. Hudson paused for a moment, dropped his head, and tugged at his lip. He then straightened, standing almost to attention. 'Thank you, Leader. I especially want to thank you for assigning Christine Woodward to my campaign for if it wasn't for her, I would not be here,' Hudson caught Morgan's eye, sitting on a lounge chair amongst the senior members. 'I also want to single out Senator Morgan for her efforts during the campaign. She was diligent and ruthless in getting what she wanted. I hope the win provides her a terrific reaction.' Morgan understood his message. 'I will work hard to keep the seat. I will work with you to win the government benches. I promise not to let you down.'

As he sat a rousing chorus of 'Hear, hear' thundered through the room.

'Not to be underestimated, I suspect,' Joyce Tregenza whispered. Windsor nodded as he cupped and stroked his nose.

———

'EDWARD, it's so nice of you to take my call. How are you?'

'Still reeling after the result, I can't believe it.'

'Nor can I,' Morgan said as she walked from the party meeting. 'I suppose the bright side is that once he loses in a general election his career is over,' she changed her tone, 'you will ensure he doesn't win, won't you?'

'The election or should we take him out at preselection?'

'He walks on water at the moment, so to block him at preselection we would need juicy gossip. Can you deliver?'

'I assure you, he won't be in the parliament after the next election.'

'Good lad.'

'When will my turn come?'

'Edward, there is one thing you must realise.' Morgan's tone sharpened. 'Your turn will come when I say so. Stop asking. Keep working for the cause would be my advice. Otherwise, I will seek more willing partners.'

Collins didn't have the chance to respond. He checked his phone, contemplating throwing it before his deep breaths calmed him.

CHAPTER
23

The Australian parliament sits for eighteen weeks a year and is a hive of activity when it's sitting. The building's population increases to over five thousand politicians, staffers, and others who manage the building. It's like a ghost town when politicians are back in their electorates. Aussies' cafe, the internal sidewalk deli, was the meeting centre for casual connections. The time of day determined the length of the queue and Chrissie Woodward was five minutes before handing Madeline Booker her cappuccino and a sugar sleeve.

'How do you think your bloke will go?' Booker asked as she stirred her coffee.

'I reckon he is of exceptional value. I don't see him winning the next election, though,' Woodward said, sipping her latte. 'It was a miracle he won this time. He won't do it again.'

'Why are you working for him?'

'Chopra has given me a leave of absence,' Woodward

checked the nearby tables, looking for any listeners. 'I feel a little sorry for him.'

Booker smirked. 'How come?'

'If he wasn't here, he would make a very capable State MP. I feel a somewhat responsible for getting him here.'

'Campbell's murder might have helped.'

'You still reckon it was murder? I understand the police report to the prime minister advised misadventure.'

'Yeah, righto.' Booker licked her spoon of froth. 'It's a much bigger story than that.'

'Why would someone want to murder him?' Woodward seemed unconvinced.

'Power and money are the usual suspects.'

'I still don't get it. Why would Campbell be upsetting folks?' Woodward asked. 'Industrial relations may be brutal on the docks, but that is no reason to knock him off.'

'Not sure it's the docks,' Booker wiped her lip of coffee froth. 'He had carriage of the new laws providing greater scrutiny on unions. I reckon this could be the reason.'

'Any leads?'

'None. Although he did have dinner with the moron from the BWU earlier that night.'

'Rusnek?'

'The thug almost killed me.'

'What? Did you call the police? What did he do?'

'I spoke to a contact with the federal police. She advised me his union is dangerous, and I should steer clear. I didn't formalise a report.'

'Why not take it further?'

Booker checked over her shoulder. 'I'm working on a theory. This is the reason I wanted to talk to you.'

Woodward pouted. 'So not because we are friends?' She made air quotes.

'Woody, sorry.' She reached for Woodward's hand, 'you know what I mean. I have a proposition for you that may help me expose the moron and his union.'

Woodward shook her head. 'Not sure what I can do.'

'There's two things,' Booker said. 'I'm told the union runs Gellibrand for the government.'

'They put up a dud candidate and knew nothing about campaigning.'

'That's the reason I need your ears and eyes. They'll run a candidate against your man. I just need intel from the coal face.'

'No problem,' Woodward finished her coffee. 'What else?'

Booker winced as she studied Woodward. 'I need a huge favour concerning your man.'

'Oh, yes? Pray tell me what you need?'

'I would like him to join a parliamentary committee,' Booker said, wincing.

'Which one?'

'They moved the inquiry into the IR legislation to a Joint House committee.'

'Which one?'

'Corporations and Financial Services,' Booker said. 'Chaired by the government. Deputy Chair is Stephanie Morgan.'

'Interesting,' Woodward said.

'Why do you say that?'

'Morgan doesn't strike me as a bright senator. She seems more focused on numbers than policy.' Woodward peeked over her shoulder as she leaned forward. 'She delivers numbers for Chopra, and the two of them remain close. That's why they assigned me to Gellibrand.'

'Are you sure someone didn't set you up?'

'How do you mean?'

'I heard the senator is not happy with the result,' Booker said.

Woodward contemplated the information, nodding, flicking her eyes about the tables. 'What do you want Jack to do?'

'I want him on the committee, so you get access to the papers.'

'Wait up.' Woodward held her hand up. 'That sounds like a breach of parliamentary practice if you expect me to pass you information.'

'No. It's a friend helping another friend expose inappropriate and corrupt behaviour.'

'There are no friends here. You know that.' Woodward shifted, preparing to leave.

Booker watched, waiting until she looked at her. 'All I'm asking is that you show me any information that could be linked to the BWU and Campbell before anyone else sees it.'

'Maddie, you're asking me to breach, and I don't like it, friend or not.' She began to move.

'Can we have dinner this week before you return to Melbourne?'

Woodward stopped, studying the journalist. 'Yes, I would like that. It's been a while, and I miss you.' She smiled and began leaving. 'I'll talk to Jack and see what he thinks. I expect he'll prioritise his seat until the election.'

'Thanks, I'll call you with a time and place.'

'Sleepover?'

'Of course.'

CHAPTER
24

Hudson considered Windsor a touch pompous with his manner, but enjoyed his wit, hilarity, and outrageous observations of colleagues whenever he joined him for a social drink.

'How do think we're travelling, Jack?'

'I'm a novice in this political business.' Hudson sipped his beer, enjoying the time with colleagues. 'My learning curve is almost straight up. There is much to learn.'

'The thing is, Jack, and this is an important point to learn,' Windsor said, balancing back on the two wooden legs of his chair, feet on the marble coffee table, glass of chardonnay in hand. 'You have as much right as anyone else in this place. We are all equals, and the Leader just happens to be the first amongst equals. So, how do you think we are travelling?'

'I think we have a chance of winning the next election if we offer the electorate solid policies.'

'In what portfolios?'

'Foreign Affairs, we still don't have a viable policy in the Middle East. Our attitude to southern Asia is questionable given our free trade policies. And we rely too much on China.'

'What would you recommend?'

'I think we should look at the Indian Ocean. We could provide leadership and bring together a multilateral trading and security agreement.'

'How long have you been a politician?' another colleague, Bob Patterson asked.

Hudson laughed, saying. 'I have an interest in foreign affairs.'

'Don't we all?' Patterson laughed. 'Nudge-nudge, wink-wink.'

Windsor dropped his chair to the four legs. 'It seems to me, Bobby, that we may have increased the intelligence of the party.'

'I would play those cards close to your chest,' opined Stewart McPherson, the longest serving member of the group, still yet to be promoted after sixteen years.

'Is that your sage advice, Stewie?' Windsor squealed. 'That strategy has done your career well hasn't it? Sooner or later, you need to play a card in this game.'

'You gotta know when to show 'em,' Patterson sang. 'Know when to fold them. Know when to walk away, know when to run.'

'It seems old Stewie is playing a game of patience,'

screeched Windsor, bringing others to a rousing laugh. 'By himself.'

'I reckon I'll get the full deck when we bone Chopra,' McPherson voiced over the laughter.

'Chop, chop, you reckon, Stewie?' Windsor giggled, chopping his hand.

'We can't change the leader this close to the election, can we?' Hudson asked. The men fell silent, responding only when bells calling a division in the House encouraged them to move.

Hudson tracked in behind the group as they strode to the chamber. He had little idea what they were voting on. The whip stated in no uncertain terms that he should never miss a vote. As he walked into the chamber, he sat on the front bench, reserved for ministers during question time. He felt privileged and humbled by its history.

The media often portrays politicians as constantly yelling abuse, but Hudson came to learn the other side of the aisle was just as full of bluster and wit as his side. He was interested in why raucous members treated the process of the parliament with frivolity, much like the boarding school attitudes he had seen in movies. He preferred a low profile.

After the division and counting of the votes, on legislation he wasn't aware, he rejected Windsor's invitation to return for a drink. He strolled back to his own office in a corner of the second floor. Woodward was busy working when he entered.

'Is that you, Jack?'

Hudson didn't respond until he was at his desk. The door to the staff office was open and Woodward sat at her desk.

'How has your day been?'

'Exhausting,' Hudson slumped into his green leather chair. 'There's a leadership challenge coming.'

She came to the door. 'You are kidding. Who's counting the numbers?'

'Will you talk with Ramon's people?'

'Jack, I'm yours, and only yours, until I'm with someone else,' she fisted a hip. 'Otherwise, we'll never trust each other.'

'Fair enough,' Hudson nodded. 'I had a drink with a bunch of backbenchers before the division. It was Stewart McPherson who raised it.'

'How?'

'What do you mean?'

'Machiavellian or Ricky Gervais?' Woodward leaned on the door jamb, as Hudson shrugged. 'Serious or satire?'

'Hmm, I don't know. No one responded. Then the bells rang.'

'Whose office were you in?'

'Alex Windsor.'

'Ah, then I suspect Machiavellian.'

'Is he The Prince?'

'More like court jester. No one knows where he stands on anything.'

'He's wonderful fun.'

'Also, extremely dangerous.'

'He's just a bony-arsed kid,' Hudson said.

'Young he may be, but he shafted a shadow minister to win preselection. The media are becoming more fascinated with him as he talks on various policy issues,' Woodward said. 'Trust him at your peril.'

'Should I trust anyone?'

'Maybe folks on the other side. No one on our side of the parliament.'

'That's a touch cynical,' Hudson said.

'You'll see. They will step over you to get in front of you,' Woodward moved back to her desk. 'Stewart McPherson is an appropriate example. Nothing will ever happen to him. He may as well retire.'

Hudson considered the comment for a moment. He then swung his foot onto the desk.

Woodward raised her eyebrows. 'You've made yourself at home.'

Embarrassed by the reproach, he dropped his foot, then grinned. 'I was just thinking about McPherson,' he said. 'I think I would rather put my hand up and speak on policy while I can, rather than take the compliant path.'

'What are you saying?'

'We may not win the next election,' Hudson glanced at Woodward, 'doesn't mean we won't, though.'

Woodward scoffed. 'Nice save.'

Hudson shrugged. 'If we are only here for a few months, wouldn't it be worthwhile to stake a claim on an issue?'

'Anything in mind?'

'I'm thinking about foreign affairs,' Hudson said. 'Maybe my experience could be useful.'

'How many voters in Gellibrand care about the Middle

East peace negotiations?' Hudson grimaced. 'How many, do you reckon, think the next trade deal with Indonesia will benefit them?'

'You're saying to forget it and concentrate on campaigning for the next few months?'

'No,' Woodward smiled, taking off her glasses. 'I think you should step up and make a mark, but only on issues impacting your voters.'

'Such as?'

'The rate of the pension.'

'I think it should be raised,' said Hudson.

'Then say so,' Woodward said, tapping her nose. 'I suspect the party may go to the next election with that as policy. So why not lead on it?'

'Isn't that a little cheeky?'

'You either want a profile, or you don't?' Hudson grimaced and nodded. 'I also think jobs are important,' Woodward said.

'Yes, but everyone talks jobs.'

'Then focus your discussion,' she said. 'Rather than talk jobs, talk about unions.'

'Gellibrand is a workers' electorate.'

'So, refine it again.

'I don't understand.'

'There is legislation going through the parliament calling for Registered Organisations, like unions and employer groups to have their financial reporting move from the Fair Work Commission to the tax department, opening them up to the regulator.'

Hudson frowned. 'What does that mean?'

'It means they will be subject to different rules. It means the tax department could see their total revenue for the first time.'

'They don't report now?'

'They don't pay tax. By taking advantage, they have launched various commercial operations that compete unfairly.'

'Like what?'

'Retail employers started a communications company, providing services at below market rates. A union started a finance company, lending money to members at lower than competitive rates. They can do this because they don't pay tax.'

'Sounds like a scam.'

'Hence the legislation, which caused a huge stink,' Woodward said. 'Campbell had carriage of it. It's still in the parliament in a joint House Inquiry.'

'Interesting.'

'Do you want to join the Inquiry?'

'How does that work?'

'You can join various committees. I happen to know there is a vacancy for the Corporations and Security Committee. If you want it, then I'll talk to the Leader's office and get you appointed.'

'You think it would be good for the campaign?'

'Let's put it this way,' Woodward said. 'It exposes you to controversial legislation giving you authority to speak on it within the electorate.'

Hudson prodded a pen into his mouth. 'Maybe.'

'Plus, it'll open up media contacts,' Woodward said. 'Madeleine Booker is running background on it hoping to get a story. She thinks Campbell's death may have something to do with the legislation.'

'Hasn't the police reported?'

'I think the next step is the coroner. They have no clear evidence on what might've happened.'

'If they don't think it's murder, what could it have been?'

'Misadventure, suicide, who knows?'

'Lucky for me though,' Hudson said.

Woodward moved from her desk with a file. 'This is the CV of Dale Bower,' she flicked it open, examining it over his shoulder. 'He comes to us from the party's head office. A media and tech head who will help us get our act together.'

'I thought we were okay,' Hudson glanced up, 'we won, didn't we?'

'It might be advantageous to have a pro.'

'I'm in your hands, Chrissie. You make the decisions about staff.'

Woodward smiled, flipping the file closed and stepping off. 'Correct response. I'll let him know.'

CHAPTER
25

Hudson remained a little anxious, stepping into the formal members' dining room, for the first time. He regularly stuck close to Chrissie Woodward, enjoying the clatter of the staff cafeteria, reminding him of communal meals in the military. The formal dining room was a little different. More like the formality of the senior officer's mess. A staff member led him to a table by the expansive windows offering a view across the small valley to the Shrine of Remembrance, where he waited for his luncheon companion.

'Would you like a glass of wine, Mr Hudson?' the maître d' asked.

Hudson raised an eyebrow in response. He wondered how he knew his name. 'A Chardonnay would be perfect, thank you.'

'We have a superb Margaret River on the list today. It won't be long.'

As Hudson studied the place setting, he spotted the Coat of Arms on almost everything. He felt humble yet privileged to be allowed into this special place. He glimpsed about the various tables, noticing ministers, members, and senators, in discussion with guests. Wait staff attentively scurried among the tables.

He felt a gentle hand touch his shoulder, pulling his attention to the senator who stood above him with her practiced smile of political seduction. 'Jackson, so pleased you could join me.'

Hudson stood, offering his hand, clutching his napkin with the other.

'Please, stay seated. We are all equal here.'

Hudson had already shaken her warm smooth hand and waited for her to sit before resuming his seat. As he settled a server delivered his glass of wine and a flute of champagne.

'Here's cheers to you, Jackson, and again, congratulations on a great win.'

Hudson smiled, and clinked glasses. 'Without your support, Senator, I'm not sure we would have won.'

'I did nothing.' Morgan smiled over her glass as she took a sip. 'My gosh, that is spectacular.' She took another sip before placing the glass. 'Penfolds does a fine Cuvée.'

'Never got into the champagnes, I'm afraid.'

'You are missing something with this nice little number.' Morgan cupped her chin with her thumb, a finger resting on her lips, contemplating Hudson. 'Tell me Jackson, what do you expect to achieve whilst you are here?'

'Re-election, Senator.'

'Fine answer. But really, what are you after?'

Hudson pondered a response. 'I suppose it's all connected,' he said. 'I want to win the seat again and therefore I'll be working on issues important to my electorate.'

Morgan gazed at him, stroking her lips. 'Interesting.' She paused, switching her gaze to Ramon Chopra walking past, greeting a table of suits. 'What do you think of the leader?'

'I don't know him. I suspect he is leader for a reason. He seems decent enough.'

'It's not talent I can assure you,' Morgan scoffed. 'Numbers keep him there. Mine mostly.'

Hudson grimaced. He raised his eyebrows. 'Should we be discussing this here?'

'The acoustics in this place are terrible, deliberately so. They didn't want conversations overheard. Did you notice?'

Hudson listened, and couldn't detect a conversation.

'We can talk about these things because I hear you've already been talking about them.'

His throat tightened, rushing a sip of wine to loosen it.

'Don't be nervous, Jackson,' she dropped her hand to his resting arm, 'we all talk in this place.'

Hudson cleared his throat. 'There was some chatter. I suspected it was only a joke.'

'No one jokes about leadership, Jackson, no one.'

'I support the leader.'

'Don't we all.' Morgan sat back, crossing her legs.

'I wanted to talk to you about something.'

'How can I help?'

Hudson coughed into his napkin. 'I'm thinking about joining your committee.'

'Which one?'

'The Inquiry into the Registered Organisations legislation.'

'Why?' Morgan's stomach fluttered.

'I think the issues are important in Gellibrand. I want to leverage off it.'

'Interesting,' Morgan stretched for her flute.

'You're the lead chair of the inquiry, so I thought I should ask you first to get your view before I make an application.'

Morgan drained her glass, indicating to a server for a refill. They also took the opportunity to order lunch. As they waited, Hudson was careful not to say too much about his office arrangements and the campaign. Morgan probed him for information, subtly, but enough for Hudson to recall Chrissie's advice before he left his office. *Tell her everything, but say nothing.*

'Are you married, Jackson?' Morgan asked, pushing her plate away after three mouthfuls.

Hudson snorted, 'No.'

'Gay?'

'Why do you ask?'

'Oh, I don't know,' Morgan studied him, running her tongue around her teeth, searching for food. 'Handsome man, beefy boy, not married and pushing forty. Perhaps that's a sign,' Morgan squeezed a smirk, enjoying Hudson squirm. 'This place is full of boys being boys. You know what I mean?'

'Actually, I don't.'

'It's okay, Jackson. I don't care,' Morgan smiled. 'Just be careful. This is a dangerous place. That's all I'm saying.'

Hudson considered the clear and present danger may be sitting in front of him. He finished his meal and set the cutlery for the server. He dabbed his lips, resting the napkin on the side of the table.

'My reason for wanting lunch with you today was to assess your loyalties,' Morgan said. 'To get the things we want, Victorians in this place need to work together. I provide the numbers for the leader. One in, all in. Do you understand?'

Hudson nodded, 'I think so. You promise the numbers to the leader. We support you when we need to.'

'Exactly.'

'When do you support us?'

Morgan tightened her lips, then raised an eyebrow. 'You support me, I support you. That's the way it works in this game of political survivor.'

'No need to outwit and outlast?' Hudson smiled. Morgan didn't understand and shook her head. 'We are a team is what I think you are saying. A team within a team.'

'Exactly.' Morgan nodded.

Hudson clasped his hands, dropping them to his lap, and nodded.

'This is why I don't want to hear any more gossip about McPherson,' Morgan said. 'Can I have your assurance about that?'

Hudson paused for a moment. 'I won't stop talking to folks. Perhaps I can report back like some undercover agent,' Hudson said, struggling to sound serious. 'When I learn something, you'll be the first to know.'

Morgan remained unsure about his tone. She turned and waved the air to the maître de wishing to sign her account. When she completed the protocol, she stood, adjusting her skirt along her thighs.

'If you want anything, Jackson, then call me, okay?'

Hudson remained seated, scrutinising her as she straightened. 'Thanks for lunch, Senator. I appreciate it,' he said. 'Feel assured, I will let you know if I learn anything about the leadership.'

Morgan smiled, running her fingers through her hair, and stepping off, leaving Hudson to finish his coffee.

———

As THE SENATOR stepped through the doors of the dining room, she rang her office.

'Sandra?' She pushed through the heavy glass doors of the walkway to the Senate wing. 'Hudson thinks he is a chance to join the Inquiry committee. Call the secretariat and change their minds for me please,' she smiled. 'I'm just going to have a walk through the media gallery. See you soon.'

CHAPTER
26

The weeks since the election loss had not gone well for Oleg Rusnek. He brooded at his empty home, downing half a bottle of bourbon most nights. His problematic headache and dehydration the following day on worksites morphed into belligerent responses for the slightest transgression. Union officials knew to steer clear and kept visitors away until well into the afternoon. Toby Martin hadn't surfaced.

Four weeks after the election, Trades Hall summoned Rusnek for an urgent meeting of the union heads to discuss the government's legislation and determine a course of action to oppose it. They remained concerned about the attack on their business models convinced the government was working to reduce their influence within the party. The collection of big thick men made themselves comfortable around a boardroom table famous for the bloodstain in its centre.

Rusnek's tongue was working overtime to minimise its dryness. No amount of water could reduce the thick cover of dehydration. He was yet to switch on. The ten o'clock meeting a tad too early for him. Right then, he decided se should perhaps give up his nightly lament.

'Any suggestions, Ollie?' The State Secretary asked.

'About what?'

'About killing this legislation?'

Rusnek sniffed, waiting for a moment, stroking his bristled face, cupping his chin, his scarred fist under his nose. 'Maybe I was mistaken.'

'Mistaken? What do you mean?'

'I thought it would be easy to get one of ours in there to sort it out. Just like we do on site.'

'Welcome to politics ole son,' another comrade said. 'It's more subtle than your brash bullying.'

Rusnek turned and glared at the official through drooped eyelids. 'Campbell was not a friend, and avoided us,' he said. 'He got what was due.' No one spoke; however, there were rumours, but this was the closest they had come to any admission. He scanned the table, then said, 'Someone did us a favour.' He laughed, no one else did.

'The question is, how do we kill the legislation without harming anyone else in the process?' the secretary asked.

A bushy bearded fellow, too big for a single chair said, 'It's the government's bill, why don't we change the government?'

The meeting remained silent for a few moments. Officials

with eyes down fiddled with their hands, to avoid engaging. 'The government is our party, so, we can't do that,' someone suggested.

Rusnek cleared his throat. 'If they are us, why are they bringing in this legislation?' The officials fidgeted, avoiding his glare. 'They aren't our friends,' he continued. 'Why don't we end the careers of those who don't support us?'

'More drownings?'

Rusnek glared at the bushy beard. 'No,' he sneered. 'We change the balance of numbers. We bring in our members at preselection to vote against the morons who are against us. If we aren't successful in doing that, we bring votes against them at the ballot box on election day.'

'How do we do that?' the secretary asked.

'I have over ten thousand votes ready to be used against our enemies.'

'Geezus! Where from?' bushy beard asked.

Rusnek nodded with a smug look. 'I have the troops. I just need to know if you want to go to war.'

'How would you do it?'

'We move into an electorate prior to the AGMs,' Rusnek said. 'We then vote our people into the preselection delegate roles.'

'What about election day?'

'Simple.' Rusnek wiped the back of his neck. 'We sign them onto the electoral roll, and they then vote as a bloc against the sitting member.'

'You can do this?'

Rusnek nodded.

The officials glimpsed at each other. Some rolled eyes, or raised an eyebrow of doubt, others nodded.

'What's the greatest threat a bully has?' Rusnek asked.

'They don't call you iron bar for nothing,' a comrade joked.

'It's the threat that's important, not the act,' Rusnek said. 'We must show we are serious with the leadership and then they will comply,' he said, grinning. 'It's always the threat that creates the doubt and fear.'

'What are you suggesting?'

'Before we mobilise our troops, we negotiate with the prime minister, the minister and perhaps the chair of the Committee inquiring into the legislation. We talk about what we want. If they don't support us, we then threaten their numbers.'

'I'm loath to say it, but I think Ollie has a good point.'

Rusnek responded in a taunt tone. 'You are loath, why are you loath?'

'Your history doesn't show a strong preference for conciliation and arbitration.'

'We are construction workers,' Rusnek joked. 'What do you expect?'

The secretary breathed, reducing his anxiety. 'Can I recommend Ollie heads a negotiation team to begin discussions with party officials, including the prime minister and the new minister?'

Rusnek leaned back in his chair, glancing over to his rival

bushy beard, who nodded support. 'I will develop a strategy. If anyone has any ideas, then let me know.'

'Are you running Toby Martin again?'

Rusnek shrugged. 'It may have been a mistake to run, Toby.'

'I hear he's in Queensland,' the secretary chuckled.

Rusnek tightened his face and looked about the faces. 'He is on assignment for me.'

CHAPTER
27

The leader and the shadow treasurer, Peter Raffles, asked Senator Morgan to join them in discussing the Registered Organisation legislation prior to the regular party meeting. She strolled into the office, following the direction of a young woman at the front desk, her name she could never remember. The men relaxed on a couch and a chair. She had visited the office many times and still considered it underwhelming.

'Steph, thanks for coming in,' Chopra said, pointing out a seat to her. 'Just out of the shower?'

'Finished a workout fifteen minutes ago,' she said, smiling as she sat, crossing her legs, checking the men's eyes, never disappointed with the reaction.

'You look fantastic.'

'So, do you Peter. Are they new shoes?'

Raffles shifted in his chair. 'No, these are my Canberra ones. Very comfortable for all the walking required.'

Morgan leaned forward, resting her chin on her knuckles, smiling. 'Yes, they look it.'

Chopra scoffed at the by-play. 'We want to talk to you about the legislation your committee is reviewing.'

'The union bashing one, or the banks?'

'The Registered Organisations bill,' Chopra said. 'Are you getting submissions?'

'We have well over a hundred,' Morgan said. 'Surprisingly, most of them are from employer groups.'

'What's their position?' Raffles asked, trying not to allow his eyes to wander over her.

'They are resolutely against it. They state it curtails their ability to raise funds independent of their members.'

'The unions think the same?' Raffles asked.

'Exactly the same argument. It's as if they have taken the same advice.'

'What will you be recommending?'

'Too early to say, as we are yet to call witnesses.'

'Gut feel?' Chopra asked.

'Leader, I never have a gut feeling.' Morgan slunk back in her chair. 'What I try to do is have an open mind.'

Raffles grimaced at the retort. 'We are trying to grasp whether or not to support it in the Senate.'

Morgan smirked a little, raising an eyebrow. 'If I was leader, I would support the legislation because it will bring the unions to heel.'

'The employer groups?'

'They have enough money, and don't embezzle funds,' Morgan said, raising her eyebrows. 'Although, there was that moron at the accountants who tried.'

'I don't want to come out in favour of the legislation if you find it is no good,' Chopra said.

'I will talk to you before tabling the report, but it is likely the parliament will support it.'

Chopra glanced at Raffles, who nodded.

'This is what we needed to know. Thanks, Steph,' Chopra said, smugly smiling showing the meeting was over.

'I have a question before I leave.'

'Shoot.'

'Why is Hudson being added to the committee?' She glanced at Chopra, then at Raffles. 'He is a novice, so why start him in a Joint House committee?'

Chopra glimpsed at Raffles, who leaned forward and said, 'It was my decision. I made it because I felt he needed to be active before the election. This Inquiry has relevance in his seat, given he knocked off the union official.'

'You never thought to speak to?'

'I okayed it,' Chopra said. 'I reckon it is important he cuts his teeth on economic issues rather than foreign affairs, which was his first choice.'

'So, no reference to me?'

'Sorry Steph. I didn't think it would worry you,' Raffles said.

'Nothing worries me, Peter.' Morgan looked at him. 'Whilst

I'm the Victorian senior member, nothing ever worries me. And whilst I remain the senior member, nothing should worry you.'

'We didn't decide to undermine you and threaten your support, Steph,' Chopra said, shifting forward. 'We just thought it was a marvellous idea for Hudson to get his teeth stuck into something of substance.'

'Well, given it was an unexpected election result, I suspect spending any time in developing Hudson would be a waste of resources. He has oncer obviously stamped on his career.'

'No prospect of winning again?' Raffles asked.

'Not a gossamer thread of a chance,' Morgan stood and squeezed past. 'We need to win the election, so we must win seats. We should not invest in seats we can't win just because someone looks good.'

'Thanks for your advice, Steph,' Chopra said, flopping back, wincing as he glanced at Raffles. When the door closed. 'She's got balls, that one,' Chopra said

Raffles laughed. 'Did you check out her guns?' He asked. 'She must be pumping iron every day.'

'Pumping something,' said Chopra. 'I don't trust her. Do you think she's solid?'

'How many votes does she bring to the table?'

'Victoria, and Tasmania, maybe she has cred in South Australia.'

'Not sure she is that influential, but I'll keep an eye on her,' Raffles said.

'From what I saw, you didn't take your eyes off her once she sat down,' Chopra chuckled. 'It was embarrassing.'

Raffles chuckled. 'Her guns – did you see those guns?'

'Let's hope she doesn't get to use them.'

CHAPTER
28

Rather than track back to her office, Morgan visited her favourite dandy for a tea and a chat before the party meeting. She strolled past the chamber, yet to open for the day. She poked her head into the Whip's office for a quick hello and then into Windsor's office, near the security entrance to the parliament.

'Alexander, darling, are you here?' Morgan called as she entered the foyer. She sauntered through the open door, smiling at the young man working the phone.

Windsor ended his call and skipped to her, kissing her on both cheeks in an exaggerated manner.

'Are you never off the phone. counting numbers, darling?'

'Senator, you know what the game is about. So, I keep score.' Windsor cackled. 'Would you like a tea before our meeting?'

'That's why I'm here,' said Morgan as she sprawled on the

leather couch, sitting neatly in the centre, stretching her arms along the back. 'I've just been to see the leader and rather than walk back, I thought I would come visit.'

'The pleasure is all mine, girlfriend,' Windsor said before sticking his head through the staff door, asking for tea. 'I have French Earl Grey for you.'

'You are a pet, always spoiling me.'

'Too early for champagne,' Windsor cackled.

'Never too early for a little fizz.' Morgan winked.

Windsor stopped. 'What fizz are you talking about?'

'The drinking kind, of course, Alexander.' They cackled again.

'Now tell me. Why were you with the leader? Something interesting I hope?'

Before she could answer, the outer door opened and Peter Raffles tracked in, closing the inner door for privacy.

'Oh Peter, thanks for dropping in. Stephie was just telling me she was in the leader's office.' Windsor ushered him to a chair. 'Would you like a tea?'

'No tea for me.' Raffles smiled. 'I was just with Steph at the meeting with Ramon.'

'Oh, how exciting. What were you scheming?'

Raffles leaned back in his chair, blowing out his cheeks, raising his eyebrows, glancing at Morgan. 'The game is afoot,' he said.

Windsor glanced at Morgan, then back to Raffles. 'What happened?'

Morgan laughed and straightened to the edge of the couch

when the tea arrived. 'The leader is about to commit himself to the Registered Organisations legislation,' she said, nodding a thanks to Windsor's staffer passing her the tea.

'He is now committed. I think we can now pivot him and tag its failure to him,' Raffles said.

'If you want the leadership prize, then we must move now. We can't wait until closer to the election,' Morgan said before sipping her tea.

'Hawke, Gillard, and Rudd moved late,' Windsor said.

'With respect Alexander, Peter is no Hawkie. The other two were in government,' Morgan said.

'Fair enough,' Raffles said. 'If we move on him, will you bring your numbers?'

Morgan shrugged. 'I had to work hard to get them to support Chopra, so I'm unsure about switching them again to vote against him.'

'Put it this way lovely, unless we have your numbers we can't move,' Windsor said.

'What do you want?' Raffles asked.

Morgan now had him where she wanted. She placed her cup and saucer on the marble coffee table and leaned back, brushing her fingers through her short hair, pushing and prodding it into place. 'Front bench.'

Raffles scoffed. 'Everyone wants to sit on the front bench.'

'You want the numbers then that's the price,' she said, trailing a finger along her jaw.

'Embassy somewhere?'

Morgan shrugged. 'I'm too young to be leaving the senate.'

'I can't give everyone a job,' Raffles shook his head.

'As I said, if you want my numbers the price for prime minister comes at a high rate of commission.'

'Crumbs darling,' Windsor said. 'You play the game hard.'

Morgan glanced at Windsor and then at Raffles, running her tongue across the back of her teeth, and smiled as if waiting to eat.

'President of the Senate,' Morgan said. 'If I can't have a front bench position, then I demand to be president.'

Raffles leaned back, checked Windsor, who was nodding a little as he tugged the tip of his nose. 'Done.'

CHAPTER
29

Eddie Collins wasn't much of a drinker. He enjoyed a wine with his wife, after a long day at the newspaper, or perhaps a brandy when he felt stressed by politics. He wasn't a drinker, but knew the power of alcohol to loosen tongues, which was the reason he stepped into the Steam Packet Hotel just across from the Chronicle's editorial office. The man he pursued, Billy Tyrrell, leaned against the bar talking to other locals. Billy was a well-known figure in the area, known for his generosity, but scarred by his army service. Collins recognised him working alongside Hudson during the campaign and suspected they were comrades, perhaps sharing a deeper connection than a fleeting salute.

'Hey, Billy, how's it going?' Collins called from the other end of the bar after being served a pint of draught.

'Eddie, how's it going with you?'

Collins made his way down the bar, dragging a stool to sit

beside his target. Billy seemed open to the company. 'Did I see you helping our new local member during the election?'

'Aye, ya did.' Tyrrell smiled as he drew a sip. 'Good man, Jack.'

'That he is,' Collins agreed. 'He did well to win a safe seat off the government.'

'Like a military campaign. We had the troopers out for him.'

'Did you serve with him?'

'He was my captain.' Tyrrell chuckled. 'Captain, my captain.'

'Yeah.' Collins laughed as he took a generous mouthful of beer. 'I bet you saw plenty. He seems to have done heaps, given his record.' Tyrrell eyed Collins, then took a sip, glancing about the bar. 'I mean he's a hero, isn't he?'

'That's what they say,' Tyrrell said.

Collins nodded, sensing wariness about the questions. 'I should do a profile on you for the paper, linking it to Hudson,' Collins suggested. 'It would be a fascinating read.'

'Not sure I would want to do that.'

'Oh, don't be so humble.' Collins regarded him as he swigged another mouthful. 'Were you with him in Malakal?'

Tyrrell ignored him, finishing his glass, placing it on its side at the bar. 'That's me. Thanks for the chat, Eddie,' Tyrrell said, sliding off his stool.

'Did I say something wrong?' Collins said. 'I was about to buy you a round.'

'Nah, I'm fine,' Tyrrell said, brushing past him. 'I don't

want to talk about any of that. If you want a profile linked to the captain, I suggest you speak with the RSL.'

'Why the brush-off?'

'What happens in battle stays in battle. I don't want to raise ghosts of the past.'

'How come?'

'Too much money spent on therapy.'

'See you, Billy.' Collins watched him leave. 'Take care.' He glanced at the attendant wiping a glass with a white towel, watching Tyrrell leave, then shake her head as he left. 'Something wrong with Billy?' Collins asked.

She placed the glass on a shelf above and came over to clear Tyrrell's glass. 'He has his moments.'

'He seems okay,' Collins drained his glass, passing it to her. 'Do you know what he's worried about? Anything I can help with?'

'He doesn't talk about it. I suspect he went through something in Sudan. That's what he says when he's had a few.'

'Yeah, it was tough for them,' Collins prompted.

'Something about a black op in a village.'

'Dark and stormy, maybe,' Collins suggested, and she laughed.

'Can I get you anything else?'

'No, I'm good. I just remembered I left something in the office.'

'See you, Ed. Are you coming in for lunch later this week?'

'Maybe. See you, Sandy.'

He marched back to his historic building across from the

hotel, rather than strolling home, tapping in the SAS Australia into his search engine. When he started scrolling, but he didn't know what he was hoping to find. An hour later, he had compiled a list of operations various SAS units had undertaken in Sudan. He focused on Sabre Squadrons one and four, well known for clandestine operations during the civil war. They listed casualties and decorations that were awarded. Neither Jackson Hudson nor Charles O'Brien appeared in the records.

CHAPTER

30

Madeleine Booker checked her reflection in the washroom mirror, fussing with her hair. One stubborn strand refused to settle, and she regretted not applying more product. Uncharacteristically, she wore lipstick for her meeting with Jack Hudson. After straightening her vest and adjusting her jeans, she used her phone to check the back of her hair. It looked weird, so she prodded some more.

Slinging a heavy leather satchel carrying all her needs, over her shoulder, she stepped off for her appointment, breathing to settle a brewing anxiety. When she arrived, Chrissie Woodward skipped from her office to greet her.

'You look different.'

'Just a little rouge.'

'Interesting,' Woodward grinned. 'He won't be long. He's just on the phone to the Leader.'

'No issue.' Booker followed her into the office. 'I received a weird email this afternoon.'

'About what?'

'Not sure who it was from. The Gmail address is basic and anonymous,' Booker said. 'It suggested I should check Jack's military record.'

Woodward grimaced as if an unpleasant odour passed through. 'Why would they do that? There's nothing to see there.'

'He was in Special Services, wasn't he?'

'Covert operations, I believe.'

'Is his record open?'

'Not sure. Why don't you ask him?'

Booker nodded. 'Are we still up for dinner tonight?'

'Sure, I expect to be finished here by seven.'

'Suits me,' Booker smiled. 'I'm looking forward to it.'

'Work-related, right?' Woodward checked.

Booker smirked. 'I thought we're not talking business when you stay over.'

Woodward grinned. 'Well, I'd better behave to get an invitation.'

'I hope you won't mind a good laugh.'

'So long there as there's no tickling involved.' Woodward brushed the tingle from her forearms.

'Deal,' Booker said.

The door seal broke, and Hudson stepped out to speak to Woodward. 'Chrissie, the leader wants me to represent him at the Shrine later this month. Could you liaise with his office for details? I said I would if there are no conflicts in the electorate.'

'I'll follow it up.'

'You're Maddie Booker, aren't you,' Hudson said. 'I saw you on election night. How come you didn't interview me? You two catching up?'

Booker couldn't speak. She tried to get words out, but she stumbled over them.

'Maddie is here for her appointment, which is listed in your daily program,' Woodward said.

'Okay,' Hudson cast a glimpse at Booker. 'Well, you had better come in.'

Booker sidled past Woodward's desk. 'Wish me luck.'

'You'll be fine. Do you want a tea?'

'If his nibs is having one, then yes.'

'Go in,' Woodward said, slipping her glasses off and moving toward the kitchenette on the other side of the foyer. Booker tapped on the door as she entered.

'Come in Madeleine, please,' Hudson said, smiling and gesturing her toward the couch. 'I'm sorry I wasn't ready for you.'

Booker felt flushed. She dropped her satchel to the floor, taking a hard chair by the couch. 'I appreciate you giving me time.'

'What would you like to talk about?' Hudson asked.

'Umm.'

'Cat got your tongue?'

Booker dropped her hand into the satchel, searching for a

pad as she maintained eye contact. 'I want to talk to you about the Registered Organisations legislation.'

Hudson grinned. 'Not my successful win in Gellibrand, then?'

'Ahhh.'

'Are you okay? You look a little flushed,' Hudson asked. 'Would you like some water?'

She cleared her throat, wiping her forehead. 'I'm not writing about the glamour of politics, Mr Hudson. I'm more of an investigative reporter.'

'Call me Jack, please.'

Booker shifted in her chair, filling her lungs then exhaling through her nose. 'I need your help, if that is possible?'

Hudson grinned. 'Anything is possible, Madeleine. You just need to ask.'

Booker gnawed the end of her pen as she flipped through her notes. 'Umm. Call me Maddie, please.' She coughed.

'Okay, Maddie.' Hudson leaned forward, resting his arms on his knees. 'What are you wanting?'

Booker gulped, stuttering a little before clearing her throat again. 'Umm,' she brushed back the strand of hair. 'I'm investigating the Campbell death and I'm trying to determine if there are any links to the legislation.'

'Do you think someone murdered him?'

'I don't know what to think at this stage. I have an open mind.'

Woodward delivered the tea, then closed the doors, leaving them in a sealed office.

'It's a long bow to link the two, I would have thought,' Hudson said, sipping his tea.

'We have confirmed he had dinner with Oleg Rusnek earlier in the evening.'

'And he is?'

'The boss of the Building Workers Union,' Booker dropped her head, grimacing as she glanced back. 'A ruthless bastard.'

'You sound as if you personally know.'

'You could say that.' She shook her head. 'I have an acute distaste for men like him, and the violence they execute. Execute being the operative word associated with him.'

Hudson sipped his tea, studying her. 'Has he been violent to you?'

'You could say that?'

'Police involved?'

'No evidence, and then it becomes "he said, she said," which means women lose again.'

'That's a touch cynical, wouldn't you say?'

'The figures back me up.' Booker sipped her tea, then sipped again.

'I haven't come across him.'

'That's interesting because his man was your opponent during the by-election.'

'Is that right?' Hudson nodded. 'Best I keep an eye out, then.'

'Might be a good idea,' Booker placed her cup down. She sat still for a moment, then said, 'Jack, the reason I wanted to talk to you is about the Inquiry and perhaps sharing information.'

'From what I know of the parliament that would be a breach of procedures.'

Booker breathed in, grinning. 'I'm not asking you to leak information.'

'What information are you after?'

'Rusnek,' Booker winced. 'I need to know if he is influencing the committee.'

'Political thuggery?' Hudson smiled.

'You could say that.' Booker nodded. 'I reckon he is answerable for Campbell's death. I reckon he is active in other criminal activities.'

'Big claim. Any evidence?'

'I have footage of him smashing the leader of the Maru Hunters on a city street.'

'Who are they?'

'A drug syndicate operating as a motorcycle gang.'

'Are you sure you should be here? You'd be better off at the crime desk.'

'I was but asked to come here for a change of scenery. Less stress, apparently.'

'Not what you expected?'

'There are more rogues in this place than in the drug scene.'

Hudson raised his eyebrows. 'What do you need from me?'

'Evidence of any influence. A read of any submissions from his union and any other submission you may think his union has influenced.' Booker raised her eyebrows, pursing her lips through a skewed smile. 'I believe Campbell's death and this legislation are connected, and I want to know why.'

Hudson leaned back. 'I can't promise anything, but if I hear anything, I'll let you know.'

Booker prepared herself to leave, tucking her pad and pen away. 'Just one last question, out of left field.'

'Shoot.'

Booker cocked her head at his response. 'Where do I get a copy of your military record? Would DVA help?'

Hudson shook his head with eyebrows raised as he eyed her. 'Classified I think,' he said. 'Why would you need to know?'

'Why is it restricted?'

'They assigned me to various covert duties. That remains classified for another ten years, if I recall.' Hudson stood and moved to the door. Booker had no choice but to scurry out.

'Would the DVA help?'

'Not sure, maybe.' Hudson was about to close the door. 'Why?'

'It's nice to know who I'm dealing with.'

'That's funny.' Hudson grinned. 'So do I,' he said, as he closed the door.

Woodward appeared from her office as she heard the door close. 'How was he?'

'Strange, if I'm honest,' Booker said.

'In what way?' Woodward said, moving closer.

'He reacted when I asked him about his military service.'

'Anything I should be worried about?'

'No, but his demeanour changed when I raised it. Very defensive.'

'Really?'

'It's not important, but he just seemed sensitive to enquiry.'

'I'll have a word and maybe report tonight.'

Thanks, gorgeous.' Booker stroked Woodward's arm. 'No issue with me.'

Once Booker was in the corridor, she stopped, dropped her satchel to the floor, crouched and searched for her pad. Confused, she remained unsure of her reaction to him. She knew him. His background was largely familiar to her. She had read his profile and followed his campaign. Chrissie had shared with her information about the type of man he was. Despite reviewing his photographs, his presence flummoxed her. *Totally unbelievable.*

'That was really weird.'

CHAPTER
31

'Who are you?' Hudson was back in his electorate office after parliamentary sittings, standing in the doorway of a small, glassed office, examining the back of a massive mop of plum-coloured curls falling over an enormous shirt.

A chubby smiling face, covered by enormous spectacles turned to recognise the voice. 'Hi, Mr Hudson,' he said, standing and offering a hand. 'I'm Dale Bower. I started yesterday. Thanks for the opportunity.'

'Welcome to the team, Dale.' Hudson squeezed his sweaty hand. 'What is your speciality in politics?'

'That would be branding and social media.'

'A troll then?'

Bower released his handshake, dropping into a frown. 'More than that. I plan to increase your vote.'

Hudson grinned, liking the response. 'How old are you?'

'Age has nothing to do with my capability,' Bower said, flopping his arms across his belly. 'I have been associated with three winning campaigns thought unwinnable. I have a master's in electrical engineering, a Grad Cert in computer science, a master's in communication, with a Grad Cert in digital online comms.'

'Why are you here, then?' Hudson asked. 'With that sort of background, I would have thought there were other opportunities.'

'Two reasons,' Bower said, frowning. 'Pretty people get those jobs. As you can see, I don't fit that mould. Second, I'm impressed by your numbers. I reckon you are a chance of having an amazing political career. I want to attach my baggage to you.'

'You don't have any baggage do you, Dale?'

'What I meant was I think you are going places. I want to be on that journey with you.'

'Impressive,' Hudson grinned. 'Welcome aboard.'

'I'll have numbers for you and Chrissie later this morning, which may either get you enthusiastic or drop you in the dumps.'

'Well, rather than wait, why don't we do that now?' Hudson said. 'Let me get settled and come see me in five minutes.'

'Are you a visual person or do you prefer a data dump?'

'You are an interesting lad. I would prefer visual briefings.'

Bower spun back to his desk. 'See you in five.' Hudson backed out of the office and moseyed along to his own.

As he passed Woodward's desk, he said, 'Interesting selection with the big boy.'

'You've met?'

'We just had a quick chat, and we are meeting with you in five minutes for a briefing.'

'I told you he was good.'

'Let's hope he does the job you want, because I have no idea what he'll be doing.'

———

WOODWARD CARRIED MUGS OF TEA, a pen in her mouth and a pad under her arm when she entered the lounge outside Hudson's office. Bower followed with a thick leather satchel and a pile of papers.

'What have you got to tell us, young man?' Hudson said as he sat in a club chair.

'I collect data, and I translate that into strategy.'

'What data?'

'Voter behaviour, demography, social influences, and other quantitative data pulled from various research, including the census. The qualitative data comes from various university studies.'

'How long will it take to get a handle on Gellibrand?'

'How do you mean?' Bower seemed confused, glancing at Woodward.

'What I mean is,' Hudson paused. 'We have eight months

to an election. How long before you review Gellibrand so we can prepare for the campaign?'

Bower shifted in his seat. 'I thought I was going to give you a briefing.'

'Yes, you are,' Hudson said.

'I've completed the review,' Bower said. 'I already have a reasonable understanding of what is required to get you over the line.'

Hudson glanced at a beaming Woodward, then back at Bower.

'I told you he was good.'

'I'm beginning to realise that.'

'Bottom line, Mr Hudson if we fail to take swift action, you will not be re-elected.'

Hudson chortled, then said, 'We won just a few weeks ago. We can do the same again.'

Bower raised his eyebrows, shook his head, and turned to Woodward, who nodded encouragement. 'It wouldn't matter how many doors you knocked, or babies you kissed, you won't win.'

Hudson dropped back into his chair, steepling his fingers in front of his face, his thumbs under his nose, elbows resting on the arms of the chair. He squinted, then nodded, taking a noisy deep breath.

'I'm guessing this is a dumps moment for you,' Bower smiled.

'Hah!' His comment took Hudson by surprise. 'I reckon you

and I are going to have some fun, Dale. You remind me of an interesting sergeant I used to have.'

'Hold that thought,' Bower said, passing out papers. 'These are the figures in diagrammatic form and if you allow me to explain, they may convince you we have a chance.'

Hudson flicked through the stapled papers, glancing at Woodward who seemed concerned with the diagrams. 'Basically, you are down with women. Older men like you, working men don't like you. Small business operators don't even know you.'

'So, no one?'

'You did well in several strong government booths, but the prevailing attitude of those who voted for you was that they wanted to send a message to the government.'

'Which is what?'

'Don't take us for granted. Which they did by running Toby Martin. His campaign was a shocker. They didn't spend too much money countering your work.'

'So, what you are telling me is if they run a reasonable candidate against me, we lose.'

'Easily.'

Hudson pushed out his bottom lip and shook his head, frowning.

'If they run a woman, you'll be smashed.'

Hudson glanced over at Bower who seemed concerned about the impact of the information he was providing. 'What's the good news?'

'I reckon you can win.'

Hudson beamed. 'What's he smokin', Chrissie?'

'If he says you can win, then I reckon we should listen.' Woodward encouraged Bower with a smile and nod.

He cleared his throat. 'We drop this idea of doorknocking and go to the biggest demographic we can influence.'

'How do we do that? Advertising?' Hudson asked.

'We establish a strong presence on social media.' Bower slid to the edge of his chair, showing a chart. 'The demography of the electorate with the most influence is working families. Mums and dads under fifty with children of voting age still living at home.'

'How do I get to them without knocking on doors?'

'Social media,' Bower smiled. 'We get you on Instagram with quirky campaign photos. On X commenting on policy. Facebook with activities in the electorate, and Snapchat.'

Hudson grimaced, rubbing fingers across his forehead, then sighed.

'Boss, you don't have to do a thing. That's why I'm here.'

Hudson peeked at Woodward. 'He's good, Jack, that's why he's here.'

'As you can tell from my lack of enthusiasm, I'm no geek when it comes to social media.'

'Geeks are so naughties,' Bower frowned. 'We're called influencers now.'

Hudson sniffed a smile. 'If you can get me re-elected, then I'll call you brilliant.'

'It won't be easy. We'll need to schedule several things to get active.'

'Like what?'

'Working families are not huge fans of unions,' Bower said. 'This will mean your work on your new committee becomes campaign relevant. Any media leverage from your committee work will be beneficial to your numbers.'

'Why don't they like unions?'

'Women don't like their bullying macho nature. Men don't like them wasting money on social and political campaigns.'

'Anything else?' Hudson bounced his hands on the arm of his chair, dancing his fingers.

Bower chewed at his bottom lip. 'Can I ask you to get rid of the beard?'

Hudson shuddered, stifling a laugh. 'Numbers don't like it?'

Bower lifted his eyebrows. 'You could say that. Either grow a full one or shave. The bristles are not working with women.'

Hudson wiped his stubbled chin. 'Anything else?'

Bower glanced at Woodward. 'What's wrong Dale?' she asked.

'At the moment, there's chatter around on social media which could bite us.'

'Like what?' she asked.

Bower shifted in his chair. 'There is a story going around casting aspersions about Mr Hudson's military career.'

Hudson frowned. 'What in particular?'

'Nothing specific. Plenty of political trolling encouraging examination of your injury and the manner the army discharged you.'

Hudson dropped his head back, gazing at the ceiling.

'Is there anything we should be concerned about?' Bower asked.

Hudson hadn't stirred, only moving his jaw as if chewing gum.

'Jack?' Woodward interrupted.

He straightened and glanced at them, rocking his head. 'Nothing to see here. Let's move on with our day.'

Bower closed his files, collecting his papers and moved off. Woodward waited for him to leave. 'Are you okay?'

'I'm fine,' Hudson responded.

'Anything I should be concerned about?'

'Nothing to concern you,' Hudson glanced over and smiled. 'There is nothing in my file that would cause any concern.'

As Woodward left the lounge, she turned back. 'If we are to trust one another, then there can be no secrets.'

Hudson nodded, his face taut. 'That's my understanding.'

CHAPTER
32

'I love this view, Stephie,' Windsor said, accepting a glass of chilled Sauvignon Blanc. 'A wonderful wine can always take a little ice, I say,' he said with a chuckle. 'Thank you, darling.'

'I wouldn't know. I don't drink that much.'

'Not what I heard.' Windsor snorted.

Morgan smirked behind her glass as she assessed Windsor. 'Cheers.'

'This is the problem with you senators.' Windsor waved at the window. 'No constituents to worry about means a gorgeous view like that.'

'Secure two hundred and fifty-one votes at state council and you can have a similar view.'

'The senate is not for me.'

'So then, endure the complaining constituents, elections

every three years and the party morons who hate you. And for what?'

'I can't be prime minister in the senate.'

'John Gorton was?'

'Yes, but not really. He moved to the House of Representatives.' Windsor checked his nails. 'The House is where the action is and that's what I love about politics. My career progress is taking a safe seat, tick.' Windsor flicked a finger. 'Sit on the backbench for three years, then I secure a junior ministry when next in government. Move back to opposition after ten years as a senior leader on the front bench. Then I become prime minister when the party wins again.' He took a sip of wine. 'Should take twenty-six years, I reckon.'

Morgan smirked. 'Nice to be ambitious.'

'Will you still be around?'

'A grumpy old senator in her seventies, not likely.'

'Maybe I can appoint you to something. What would you like?'

'Embassy in Santiago would do me fine.'

'Chile?' he yelped. 'You have got to be joking – why not Paris?'

'Better dancers in Chile.' She winked.

Windsor laughed out loud. 'You dirty old tart.'

Morgan sipped her wine, waiting for him to settle. 'What are we going to do about Chopra?'

'I was thinking about it on the plane,' Windsor said. 'Our polling is not good and with just eight months to the election, I reckon we're in trouble.'

'I share that view.' Morgan crossed her legs dismayed Windsor didn't sneak a peek. 'Although I'm not sure Peter is the right man.'

'Any man is a better man than Chopra, surely.'

'Not a woman?' Morgan asked.

'No one is credible enough to go up against Prime Minister Mosely. She would chew her up and spit her out.' Windsor waggled his empty glass. 'No, we need the contrast of a man against a woman.'

Morgan moved to the sideboard, opened the refrigerator, snatching the bottle from the door before it closed. She smiled at Windsor as she refilled his glass and topped up hers.

Windsor studied her as she moved about and sighed as she sat. 'You are a lean, mean machine, aren't you?'

'I work out two, maybe three times a day.'

'Crumbs. No wonder you have magnificent legs.'

'Alexander, get your mind off my body and onto the leadership,' she said, crossing her legs slow enough to find his gaze. Windsor accepted the invitation. She smiled as she took a sip of wine. 'If we are to move on the leader, then we need a reason and we need to find it soon. We only have eight months to state a case for a change of government.'

Windsor engaged her eyes a little embarrassed by her smile. 'If we don't win government, then my plans shift back three years. I won't be happy about that.'

'What do we do? Do we change him or carry him to the election?'

'Scandal is the traditional way of changing leaders – either that or polling.' Windsor brushed lint from his knee. 'I expect this IR bill going through could be his downfall.'

'How so?'

'As Rafflesy said, let's pivot against it. If Chopra is for it, you table a negative report. If he is against the legislation, then you bring in a positive committee response.'

'I think there might be a better way?' Morgan said.

'What might that be?'

'We manipulate Hudson to play patsy.'

'Jack? He's a decent man,' Windsor said, shifting in his chair. 'Why do you want to go after him?'

'I don't trust him,' Morgan leaned forward. 'If he hangs around the parliament, I reckon he may impact both our careers. Let's take him down now. Then get Chopra to throw out a lifeline. Which drags him under the bus.'

'Could work, but we would need something juicy on Hudson.'

'War crime good enough for you?'

Windsor tilted his head, nestling into his shoulder, lifting his eyebrows like a fairground clown. 'You have evidence Jack is a war criminal?'

'No, not yet. But do we need evidence?'

'You are wicked, Stephie. Villainous even.'

'There is scuttlebutt going around implicating him in a war crime,' Morgan stroked her jaw with a talon like red nail. 'We need the government to get onto it and begin an investigation. Chopra then supports Hudson, and when it creates a crisis for the party, we work the numbers for change.'

'Interesting.' Windsor sipped his wine. 'I have an ambitious backbencher on their side who may be keen to rattle a cage to raise his profile. I can talk to him when we are back in Canberra.' Windsor nodded, then paused. 'You honestly want to do this to him?'

'I want to end his career.'

Windsor shifted position in his chair and gazed out at the view. 'This strategy may do more than that...'

CHAPTER
33

B ooker never accepted the police report declaring
Campbell's death as a misadventure. Witness statements
confirmed the minister walking home from Pelican's along the
coastal footpath. One witness could identify him at Time Ball
Tower with no other pedestrians about. Although the police
confirmed Rusnek's movements with an Uber driver, Maddie
couldn't shake her feeling he was involved. It had become
personal for her.

Her editor pushed her for other stories, but she couldn't
leave Campbell's death alone. No matter the political stories
she had floating about her notebook, and she had plenty, her
focus kept returning to Rusnek. As she flicked through her
notes, an email pinged. She examined the source, concluding it
was from the same anonymous account set up for covert
communication. It was a Gmail account with look4evidence as
its sender. Intrigued, she opened the email.

Booker scanned, then reread it. The email was another allegation against Jack Hudson. It suggested she research a "staff-in-confidence" briefing paper prepared by Hudson's commanding officer. According to the email, Hudson threatened to discipline a fellow soldier soon after a firefight in Malakal. The presence of solid supporting evidence validated the seriousness of the threat.

Booker read the allegation again and wondered if the proposition had merit. Or could it be just a beat-up of the scuttlebutt rumour doing the rounds? She printed a copy and headed to her editor's office, tapping the glass before stepping in. The room stunk of cigarettes.

Andy Giles continued his resistance against the law banning smoking in workplaces, tugging a crumpled tobacco stick from the soft pack.

'Those things will kill you.'

'So, they tell me,' Giles replied with a contorted face as he sucked in the first draw. Then the inevitable cough rasped. 'Always thought this job would kill me. Take a seat.'

'It's not you we're worried about; it's us.' Booker waved in front of her face as he blew smoke in her direction.

He coughed again. 'What have you got for me?'

'Not sure if it is a rumour or fact,' Booker leaned back in her chair, wishing she had stayed at the door. 'I have troubling information about the new chum, Hudson.'

'Who's he?'

'He replaced Campbell knocking off the government candidate.'

'Why are we interested in stories about an inevitable oncer?'

'I share your view, except this story has to do with his military career.' Booker fluttered the smoke as she leaned in with the email.

He scanned the sheet and shrugged. 'It might be something. Try to get Defence to confirm or at least comment.'

'Should I talk to the minister?'

'It's only an allegation from an unreliable source. Wait until you talk to Defence, then push them. It might also be a good idea to talk to Chopra.'

'I should talk to Hudson,' Booker said, moving toward the door.

'Of course, but not yet. We want the heat on once you know more.'

Booker left the office, taking a relieving deep breath, then sniffing her sleeve, checking for any acrid aroma. She made a move outside to rid herself of the pong, taking with her technology for research over a coffee at Aussies.

On to her second latte, she reviewed the military action in Malakal where Islamic State fighters reattempted to gain a strategic foothold in Sudan by overrunning and then settling in the city. Allied troops battled for eight months, curtailing the insurgency and drawing significant casualties. The battle honours included seven bravery awards, including a Victoria Cross and four Gallantry Medals. They did not list Hudson among the recipients.

As she began packing up and relocating to her office, she

received a call from a Defence spokesperson. 'I can confirm there have been two internal inquiries undertaken on issues I am not cleared to speak about. I can confirm one inquiry involved Captain Jackson Hudson.'

Booker pushed her way through the heavy glass security door on her way to the second floor. 'Is there any way we can make this public?' Booker said.

'Ma'am, this is an internal matter, and Defence takes national security seriously.'

'Yes, but this is not national security, is it?' Booker smiled. 'This is two blokes having a go in barracks, isn't it?'

'Ma'am, if you would like further information, can I suggest you contact the minister's office?'

'Will she provide it?'

'The minister has access to everything.'

'I'll do that, thanks.'

Booker hung up, scrolling through numbers until she found the one she wanted as she waited for the elevator. 'Chrissie, it's Maddie,' she almost whispered. 'Can we talk? I need to tell you something.'

'What have you got?'

'Is there any cloud over Jack you know about?'

'He has disclosed none. Why?'

'There is a suggestion he has been under investigation and subject to a military inquiry a few years back about his time in Sudan.'

'He's clean. I'll bet a dinner on it.'

'Oh, why did you say that?' Booker struggled to manage the

button in the elevator. 'That means I need to work harder to prove it.'

'Or you could just let it go, and buy me dinner,' Woodward said.

'You temptress. Damn you,' Booker said. 'Okay, here's the deal. If I have nothing within a week, then I'll buy you dinner. But if I find something, then you buy it before you get mad at me.'

'Why would I get mad at you?'

'I may have to go hard on your man.'

'Bring it on, sister.' Woodward ended the call.

CHAPTER
34

The laneway coffee lounges in Melbourne are renowned for their ambience, the wafting odour of fresh grinds, and the hissing of milk warmed to the exact temperature by a barista. Oleg Rusnek knew of no other place that brought all these elements together, offering a coffee culture worthy of snobbery. He didn't go every day, but when he left his building site, he took his time to savour the flavour and relax, to enjoy people bustling about him.

Manaaki Henari learned his lesson well delivered by Rusnek. He called the union boss to further discuss his idea of taking over national politics. He was eager to increase his political influence and was aware of the importance of voting numbers. All he needed was for Rusnek to approve the scheme to expand his operation.

Rusnek negotiated everything, like a poker player. His face didn't move, keeping a steely gaze, unsettling those wanting to complete a deal. Henari sipped his latte as he waited for Rusnek to say yes or no to his offer.

'How many of your people have you enrolled?'

'Our strategy is to bring them in gradually so as not to create suspicion. This will take two to three years.'

'Don't you listen?' Rusnek hadn't moved. 'How many?'

'We have two thousand already signed. We just need to assign them a branch. This gives us the numbers in six state seats and two federal.'

'Are they winnable?'

'All safe seats for the Social Democrat Party.'

'Really? So can you move in the next round of prese-lections?'

'We have that option, but it'll be a challenge,' Henari sipped his coffee. 'Our choice is to work with the current member as it gives us continuity. We threaten them by saying we can't guarantee their preselection, which is our leverage point. If they don't do what we say, we take them out.'

Rusnek laughed. 'Continuity, good word.'

'Most politicians want to keep their job. Most will do what-ever they can to protect themselves.'

'Even compromising themselves.'

'They will do anything.' Henari checked out a young woman walking past 'Those who don't do what we say, will end their career.'

'Nice one.' Rusnek picked up his glass and paused. 'Why do you want a deal with me?'

'Once we prove our credibility with you, we will then

outline the process to grow the membership of the union, allowing you to control the state council. Ultimately influencing senate preselections.'

'I've had thoughts about that.'

'What is your view?'

'Are we able to flip parties?'

'Join the Nationals?'

'Yes.' Rusnek smiled. 'I'm not aware of any electoral laws restricting membership. Can we influence the other party with your numbers? In particular, senate preselections?'

Henari glanced about the cafe, shrugged, displaying a face of zero expression. 'I suppose we could do whatever we want, so long as we keep our enthusiasm for changing politicians under wraps,' Henari said. 'Why would you want to do that?'

'We don't want to run the country. What we really want is legislation that favours us. Why not work on both sides of the fence?'

'I've never thought about it. It's possible I suppose.'

'Could we influence the next round of preselection in the National Party?'

'It's a big ask, given we are so close to the election. We need stealth, not a gun blazing macho-man.'

'Are you talking about me?' Rusnek snapped.

Henari shifted in his seat, creaking it under his weight. 'Not at all, but it will take time to get in without suspicion.'

'I need the threat, that's all.' Rusnek drained his coffee. 'Are you able to provide me copies of signed membership applications with the branch and the member details redacted?'

'Easy enough, sure.'

'Then get them to me as quick as you can.'

'How many?'

'A thousand should get what I want.'

'Done.'

Rusnek moved to leave, finishing his coffee.

'I can do that for you, but you have to do something for me.'

'Why should I do anything for you?'

'A favour delivered gets a favour returned.'

Rusnek gazed at him, his mouth turning into a scowl. 'What do you want?'

'We want the Gellibrand preselection.'

Rusnek didn't react.

'You had a shot last time and now we want to have one of ours stand for the seat.'

Rusnek's eyes narrowed as he tilted his head back to gaze along his nose. 'What makes you think we are allies?'

'We will do a lot for you. Now we ask for you to do this little thing for us.'

Rusnek nodded. Henari didn't respond, waiting for Rusnek to answer.

'What I can agree to is your candidate to stand for preselection. We can have the local members decide.'

'The members are your people.'

'Not all of them. I guarantee not to influence them.'

'Will you run the same candidate?'

'Hell no.' Rusnek scoffed. 'I haven't seen him.'

'Our plan has always been to win Gellibrand.'

Rusnek raised an eyebrow. 'Why is that?'

'It suits us locally,' Henari said, his face not moving. 'You had the deal done after Campbell. We were too slow getting a candidate.'

'Too bad.'

'It will be ours soon enough.'

'Good luck.'

'Just be fair and let the politics decide.' Henari raised his hands.

'Fair enough.' Rusnek stood. 'Deliver me those applications within a week.'

'Sure.'

'Pay for the coffee,' Rusnek said, striding off.

Henari watched him go. 'Your day will come, Russian.'

CHAPTER

35

Madeleine Booker parked her car near the National Gallery before strolling down landscaped parkland toward the lake, where she was to meet her contact. She sat at the designated park bench at the arranged time, scanning the area for her mysterious visitor. A little girl giggled while chasing a fluffy dog under the watchful eye of a woman nearby. A cyclist zipped past, and enthusiasts jogged or hurried along the path. Despite her vigilance, no one seemed to fit the description of her informant.

As she gazed across the lake toward defence headquarters at Russell, Booker pondered the peculiar placement of the American War Memorial. The towering column, crowned with a distinctive eagle, loomed over the landscape, the centre around which the nation's military complex had grown since its initial construction.

'Miss Booker?' The sudden voice startled her, making her twitch in surprise.

'Oh, sorry, you scared me.'

'Nothing to be frightened of.' The woman approached the bench, checked behind her, and smiled. 'I'm told you have been asking questions and getting few answers.'

'Yes,' Booker admitted. 'I've been trying to get answers from the minister, but it's proving futile.'

'We decided to meet, to provide you with the information you may want.'

Booker nodded, and shrugged. 'I'm not sure what I am trying to find.'

'It seems there is a political game afoot, and it might implicate one of ours.'

'You'll have to explain.' Booker scratched her head. 'One of yours?'

'Miss Booker, we are aware there has been misinformation circulating. We suspect you might be involved in this political game.'

Booker furrowed her brow. 'I'm confused. What do you mean?'

'There's a conspiracy to make it appear Defence is covering up war crimes.'

'Are you affiliated with Defence?'

'I'm not at liberty to say. What I can say is that the allegations are baseless. We have found no evidence to support them.'

'What is your name?'

'I'm not at liberty to say.'

'You can't tell me your name, or who you work for, but you tell me a story I am following is fake, and I'm being used in some sort of political game.'

'Yes.'

'Who's driving the game?'

The woman checked about her. 'The government, but mostly the opposition.'

Booker frowned, scratching her head as she looked away. 'For what purpose?'

'Power,' the woman said, rubbing her fingers across her chin. 'We just want to make sure we balance all perspectives in reporting.'

'What can you tell me?'

'I am authorised to tell you there was significant military action over a four-day period in Malakal. The fighting was unrelenting and lethal, sometimes hand to hand. We awarded various decorations for the battle, and most troops operated with distinction. There have been claims of inappropriate conduct in breach of standards. We investigated these claims and determined that no further disciplinary action was necessary. We assume the parliament is showing interest because one of the decorated combatants is a member of the House of Representatives.'

'Jack Hudson?'

'Yes.'

'Was he under investigation?'

'I am not at liberty to provide specifics, but I assure you we cleared every soldier investigated and their files confirm no investigations took place.'

'What was the investigation about?'

'I am not at liberty to say.'

Booker blew a raspberry and sighed. 'You are not at liberty to say.' She rubbed her jaw with the back of her fingers. 'Is there anything you can tell me?'

'I can say there was an operation, fierce fighting, a death of a family, including children during the mission. I can also tell you there was no action which concerned us.'

'You investigated the deaths?'

'Yes.'

'Australian troops killed them?'

'Conflict collateral damage, unfortunately.'

'Was Hudson involved?'

'He was in the battle, yes.'

Booker leaned forward, gripping the edge of the bench, feeling its cold metal against her palms. 'If there is nothing to see, then why is this narrative gaining traction?'

'You'll need to figure that out.'

'You're telling me it is a false narrative?'

'It's my experience that politics is the manipulation of perceptions,' the woman mused. 'Work out who gains from this narrative. Then you may find the reason this allegation is getting legs.'

'Why are you telling me this?'

'Two reasons,' the woman said, holding up fingers. 'First, as a serious journalist, investigate and present the truth. Second, there is an alternate political narrative that deserves exploration. We'd prefer Defence to stay out of it.'

A faint smile crept across Booker's face at being recognised as a serious journalist 'If I need information, will you provide it?'

'If I am at liberty to do so, yes.'

'Will you point me in the right direction?'

'Just focus on who is raising the issue,' the woman said. 'Rather than go back and try to open something that doesn't exist. Why not go forward and uncover what is going on?'

'And what might that be?'

'Ambition.'

'Can you give me anything for me to investigate?'

The woman smiled. 'A name already out there for you to have a chat is William Tyrrell. I wouldn't expect you will get much from him. Anything he says you can verify with me.'

'You didn't give me your details.'

'If I told you, I would have to kill you?'

Booker glared at the woman. 'Are you kidding?'

'Yes,' she said, laughing. 'My name is Debra Dallas and here is my number. Don't call, just text. I'll then contact you.'

Booker took the number, glanced at it, then turned to the woman. 'That can't be your real name.'

Dallas laughed. 'See, I told you you are good.'

CHAPTER
36

'It's all set. I have a question today. The other side will then follow up.' Windsor chatted on his phone with Morgan as he strolled to the chamber. 'I submitted it to the strategies committee. They have given it to me to ask. Isn't that delightful?'

'Are you sure the government will respond?'

'I don't know how they will respond, but respond they will, I can assure you.' Windsor checked over his shoulder for anyone listening. 'We just need to link it to Chopra.'

'Leave that to me,' Morgan said.

Windsor ended the call as he entered the chamber and took his allotted seat. He swiped through social media until the bestial behaviour of question time opened. The noise was rowdy during the first seven questions. He rehearsed his question, waiting for his scheduled turn. When the prime minister resumed her seat, he stood waiting for the speaker.

'I call the Member for Adelaide.'

'Thank you, Speaker. I would like to direct my question to the defence minister. I refer her to the recent Auditor General's report on defence spending and equipment procurement and ask if the government has plans to recover the allocated budget and cut expenses. Will she be seeking to increase spending in the budget, or will you leave it for the next government to clean up your mess?'

'Hear! Hear!' the opposition members supported him.

'I call the Defence Minister.'

'Thank you, Speaker, and I thank the honourable member for his question. Yes, the Auditor General made comments regarding expenditure in defence, but we should take those comments in context. Defence over the last decade has maintained security forces offshore during extended campaigns against terrorism. We assign these support units to battle zones, and we support them with as much equipment and resources as they require. We do not believe in cutting back our support for our fighting personnel. The contingent we provide to a coalition of allied countries does not come cheaply. As we weigh the contribution, we make in bringing freedom and peace to our friends, we must always take into account the cost of such support. Across this side of the chamber, we firmly believe that fighting for freedom against tyranny is a worthy value and remain committed to supplying our allies with the essential resources. We will allocate budget resources as needed; the opposition's policy on these matters is something we have yet to learn.

The minister resumed her seat.

'The Member for Cowan.'

Ramsey MacDonald nodded his thanks to the speaker. 'Following on from the answer to the last question, I direct my question to the prime minister. I ask, why are there extraordinary expenses allocated for internal reviews within Defence, and should we be aware of how we can reduce these costs by ensuring our frontline troops are well resourced?'

'The Prime Minister.'

Irene Mosely tugged a sheet of notes from her file, moving to the Despatch Box. 'I thank the member for his question. Our defence personnel, especially those on the frontline, receive extensive training and prioritise a spirit of comradeship. Australian military units have a fine reputation with our allies for being the best fighting units in the world. They are at their most lethal when faced with extraordinary resistance. My government supports our defence personnel and will not tolerate any suggestion they do not work as a team and provide the support for each other.'

Windsor cast an eye to Hudson at the back row of seat, appearing to listen to the prime minister.

'Defence chiefs are well aware of my direction to rid themselves of unnecessary expense and search for a better way to manage discipline and any wrongdoing,' Mosely glanced at her notes. 'I advise the House that Defence has completed several investigations into conduct within theatres of conflict administering costly investigations leading to military inquiries, including classified assessments.'

Maddie Booker sitting in the media gallery above the chamber glanced over to Hudson, leaning back in his seat with crossed arms.

'I have directed chiefs to apply a more open system of inquiry otherwise risk the support of the government and the Australian people, we will not tolerate criminal acts in the name of a military operation. We will always hold all military personnel to account for any breaches of codes of conduct, no matter their rank or station.'

Windsor wiped his face, covering his smile.

'I further inform the House that I have asked the minister to report to me on all open cases and matters requiring my attention.'

Booker texted Chrissie Woodward for a response.

'Finally, I wish to reassure the Australian people that my government will always ensure our military represents all of us. We will never condone criminal behaviour on the battlefield.'

As the prime minister resumed her seat, Ramon Chopra stood erect at the Despatch Box.

'Speaker, on indulgence.'

'Leader of the Opposition?'

'I want to support this unexpected statement of principle by the prime minister. I wish to assert the opposition's position that we will never approve of Defence expenditure being misused to cover up criminal activity of military personnel. It is our belief that open and honest communication within defence is necessary. We also hope we will expose criminals.'

Windsor nodded, his hand still covering his mouth. 'Perfect.'

Hudson left the chamber.

CHAPTER
37

E ddie Collins watched question time from his office at the Chronicle. He rubbed his hands together as he moved from the couch to his desk to write an editorial about the need to support veterans. As he tapped away, he wove in the need to separate criminals from veterans who served the nation with distinction. He omitted mentioning Hudson but crafted a story that could apply to him if evidence emerged.

Once he had his five hundred words he sent a transcript to Senator Morgan. Seven minutes later Collins accepted the senator's call.

'I would print it in your next edition if I were you.'

'Why?'

'The government will disclose a war crime case against a soldier from special forces and they may name him,' Morgan said.

'Hudson?'

'Not confirmed. It might help your cause if you get it out as soon as you can.'

'Should we take him out at the election or at pre-selection?'

'What are you thinking?'

'Expose him, then replace him at preselection,' Collins said.

'What? And have some dowdy small business owner stand?'

Collins paused for a moment. 'When can we talk about my preselection to the senate?'

'Again, you're querying me?' Morgan huffed. 'I have already told you. Soon enough.'

'You have said nothing like that,' Collins said. 'You have used my numbers at state council for years and given me nothing in return.'

'Your numbers are my numbers. Never forget that, Edward,' Morgan snapped.

'That's a curious response,' Collins said. 'Are you sure you have the numbers for your own preselection next month?'

'Are you threatening me?'

'Not at all,' Collins said. 'I just think I need certainty for my future.'

'Believe me, Edward, your future is assured,' Morgan said, before ending the call. 'Must go, bye-bye.' He didn't hear her next comment. 'Dirty little perv.'

Collins examined his phone, a touch bemused by the sharp end of the call. 'Maybe I should bring the entire house of cards down.'

COLLINS LEFT work that evening after putting the next edition of the Chronicle to bed. They would deliver it to mailboxes the following day with the front-page editorial no doubt creating concern for his local federal member. 'Here's hoping,' he said to his lead printer as the press rolled.

It was a little after eleven when he snuck through the garage door, only to find Alice working on a computer at the dinner table, an almost empty glass of red nearby.

'Hi honey,' Collins said, kissing her forehead. 'What are you working on?'

'I'm crunching numbers that can reflect where I can improve the cafe business,' Alice said, scratching the back of her head then combing relief with her fingers. 'To be frank, we need an injection of funds, otherwise we're done for.'

'So, this is not the time to raise your preselection application for Gellibrand,' Collins joked.

'You are kidding, aren't you?' Alice's jaw dropped as she glared at Collins. 'This whole political bent of yours is driving me crazy and costing us a fortune.'

'It has done us okay.'

'It doesn't pay the bills, Ed. That's what's killing me.'

Collins moved to the kitchen, pulled a beer from the refrigerator, and joined his wife. 'How much do you need?'

'Right now, eight thousand,' Alice said. 'If we can get past this trade period, then I reckon it'll come back. Otherwise, we should sell.'

'Then what?'

'I come work for you.'

Collins took a slug of beer, then gnawed at his bottom lip, considering the prospect of Alice knowing what he does every day. 'If you become mayor that creates a nice little earner.'

'I won't be able to do both. That's for sure.'

He nodded. 'Maybe I should go harder with my preselection?'

Alice sniffed disdain. 'I don't understand why you keep helping Morgan so much. She gives you little in return. Can't you go around her?'

Collins leaned back, nodded, then raised the bottle to his lips. 'You may be right,' he took a slug. 'She's not giving me credit for anything.'

'Look Ed, you have given that party everything. In return, they give you nothing. You wanted me to run for Gellibrand. Maybe I could have won, but they took it away from you. You provide the numbers for Morgan, and what does she give you in return? Christmas drinks. If it wasn't for you, this whole electoral division would be a wasteland.' Alice paused for a moment. 'You owe them nothing, so why not use your influence to get what you deserve?'

'If I get rid of Hudson, would you want to run?'

'I'll do what you want me to do, but I reckon I should go for the mayor's job and leave others to fight the good fight with Hudson.'

'We then sell the cafe?' Collins asked.

'You run for the senate, and we then appoint a manager to drive the newspaper.'

'Interesting idea.' Collins finished his beer. 'Shall we?' He offered his hand to his wife.

She glanced up and grinned, taking his hand. 'Are you going to get rid of my headache?'

'Your wish is my command my darling.'

———

THIRTY MINUTES later Collins slipped from bed, padding to his office, switching on the computer. He brought up his banking accounts and transferred ten thousand dollars to the cafe's trading account. He then opened the party's trading accounts and completed a payment appropriation for print advertising with the Williamstown Chronicle, listing an invoice and purchase order number for ten thousand dollars.

As his finger hovered over the enter key, Senator Morgan's last comment, "Your future is assured," echoed in his mind. 'Yes, it is senator,' he tapped the key. 'Yes, it is.'

CHAPTER
38

Ramsey MacDonald's political journey began as a bright-eyed member of the Social Democrat Party, curious about the world of politics and the allure of power. University life led him to join the Social Democrats Club, where he ascended to president, gaining valuable insights into the inner workings of politics. From state and national conventions to meetings with federal politicians, he honed his skills and dreamt of federal politics.

Ten years ago, when a retirement in the safe seat of Cowan was made public, MacDonald evaluated the numbers. Despite seven worthy candidates, advisors informed him that vying for preselection would be futile. Undeterred, he entered the process, recruiting numbers, emerging victorious with a clear and absolute majority in the first round against union-backed candidates. Now his political acumen and organising skills became highly respected.

He knew that a West Australian would never become prime minister. Nevertheless, this insight did not dampen his enthusiasm for seeking a position on the front bench. With patience and strategic finesse, he waited for a vacancy, garnering support from new members joining the backbench because of retirements or winning a seat. While some suggested he ingratiated himself, he knew the value of forging a social connection with members across the aisle, which proved to be more rewarding than usual political alliances.

MacDonald's keen eye spotted a potential collaborator in Alexander Windsor from the National Party when the chatty Adelaide MP entered the parliament. He ensured their paths crossed within the parliamentary halls, leading to convivial coffee meetups at Aussies Cafe. These meetings blossomed into covert dinners, where they exchanged valuable information and juicy gossip, shielded from the prying eyes of the media. While MacDonald would never trust his friend Alex, he welcomed his valuable insights.

'I've got a job for you, Ramsey,' Windsor said, his eyes glinting with amusement.

MacDonald leaned in. 'What's the plan?'

'We need to take Hudson down.' Windsor giggled eagerly. 'He needs a reality check to deflate his inflated ego and spike his career.'

MacDonald chuckled. 'Count me in. What's the plan?'

Their strategy included an initial question to the defence minister then asking the prime minister about ballooning costs in Defence. Based upon the responses they sought copies prepared under parliamentary privilege of incident reports involving the military service of Hudson. The Defence reports they could access provided sketchy information about an incursion team caught in lethal action with the enemy before the four-day battle. This became their focus for research. While lacking detail, it provided enough ammunition to imply misconduct and smear those involved, especially Hudson.

While walking to the parliament chamber for the opening prayer of a new day, MacDonald suggested to Windsor that the report they found wasn't sufficient to implicate Hudson.

'It doesn't have to be,' Windsor replied. 'This is not about him. Although he needs to be cut down. This is ultimately about Chopra.'

'We still don't have a candidate in Gellibrand. I'm betting this will assist my front bench ambitions by helping us win the seat back.'

'This morning, I sent you the scanned copy of Hudson's preselection nomination form. The form has enormous holes regarding his Sudanese service postings and activities.

'I'll have a look at it, thanks,' MacDonald said. 'I should be able to get a question up today or tomorrow.'

'Can I suggest a Grievance speech this morning before question time?'

'What line do you suggest I take?'

'Just raise the report and imply the parliament should take a look at it, without naming names,' Windsor chuckled. 'Just suggest somehow that Hudson is involved. Maybe imply a member of parliament has serious claims to answer. Then let me do the rest with Chopra.'

'You'll owe me.'

'Of course I will, and when I'm a minister, I'll be able to give you more.'

'You're going to be a minister?'

'The way I am reading your side is this. You won't get promoted until you lose government. I know my side will promote me to a ministry when we are in government. It's in our best interests for your side to lose the next election.' Windsor stopped walking to ensure no one could hear. 'I won't be on the leadership team until we do another stint in opposition. So, I will help you win the government benches back. Then you'll be a minister,' Windsor said. 'A win for you and an even bigger win for me.'

'I love the way you think, Alex.'

'Mate, we work together, and we can enjoy the next three decades in this place.'

'Sounds good to me,' MacDonald said, as his eyes narrowed.

'MR SPEAKER, I rise on a matter of grievance today for I have a melancholy duty of exposing a potential war crime and a cover up of such a crime,' MacDonald said, addressing an almost empty parliament.

Madeleine Booker heard the unfolding drama in the chamber drifting to her workstation. Her curiosity piqued by the mention of war crimes, and she tuned in, moving to a nearby television, turning up the volume.

'I have in my possession a Defence Department report numbered ZYR 6983, which was a confidential investigation into an alleged war crime days prior to a four-day battle in Malakal, Sudan as raised in this place with a previous question to the prime minister. That battle is historic for the heroism of our fighting unit to withstand enormous opposition. The numbers against them created a significant imbalance on the battlefield, but Australian troops were victorious and gave cause to all of us to celebrate their success in the fight against terrorism.'

Chrissie Woodward picked up her phone when a message pinged, then rushed to the television in Jack's office to tune in.

'We all know the spirit and willingness of our Australian fighting forces to engage. They have a reputation for lethal resistance, and we are grateful for their service. But, Mr Speaker, we should never accept the compromise of our moral compass when we breach ethical boundaries.'

Woodward texted Hudson, suggesting he should return to the office.

'Two days before the Malakal battle, the military deployed a squadron of special forces with orders to find and kill an insurgent who was known to be recruiting terrorist fighters in a village located fifty kilometres away from Malakal. They travelled by helicopter to the village searching for the alleged insurgent.'

'Order.'

MacDonald stopped speaking and waited for the speaker.

'I am paying close attention to the Member for Cowan and enquire if he is about to reveal sensitive matters that could be considered inappropriate within this place.'

'Speaker, I have a report, which I can table, if you think appropriate, which was obtained through numerous freedom of information applications.'

'Are you seeking leave to table the report?'

MacDonald paused and cast an eye toward Windsor sitting at the back of the chamber, who placed a finger to his lips and shook his head ever so slightly. 'I will reflect on that Speaker.'

'Proceed, but I caution the member.'

'Thank you, Speaker,' MacDonald nodded. 'Testimony from a medic during the deployment stated he cared for a wounded farmer shot in the abdomen and other wounds until he was in a stable condition. He stated that as he attended the wounded farmer, a ranking officer advised, the farmer was to go with him. Two troopers assisted the farmer to another location. Some ten minutes later the officer returned advising the medic he was no longer needed and to return to the communication position.'

'What's going on?' Hudson asked as he entered his office.

Woodward pointed to the television. 'The government is reporting an alleged war crime.'

Hudson stepped forward, eyes fixed on the television.

'Speaker, the medic reported the matter to his commanding officer and provided a formal statement. He was unaware of the officer's subsequent actions, but he felt he needed to report the

incident. He heard nothing further until this clandestine investigation conducted by the department. I'm not suggesting there
has been anything untoward other than reporting to the House
an investigation into the allegation was completed. I also advise
the investigation remains with the Defence Department and is
yet to make any charges or recommendations for further action.
Defence informed me the medic has since left the military. I'm
advised the officer in question is now working in a community
leadership role.'

'Boom.' Windsor smiled behind his hand.

'Speaker, I have raised these matters today because it is
unacceptable that we have operatives within our military who
have stepped over the moral compass line, allegedly taking part
in a monstrous crime. But Mr Speaker, as these allegations are
very serious, the incident which needs investigation is not the
crime. What really needs answers, and at the very least, further
investigation by the parliament is the cover up of these allegations. I call upon the government and indeed this parliament to
investigate these matters further. For the sake of all the heroes
within our military who fight to protect us, I ask that we
unmask the truth regarding these allegations. I thank the
House.'

Windsor tapped his eyebrow with a single finger as a salute,
looking over at MacDonald.

CHAPTER
39

The shrill ring of the Woodward's office phone jolted her and Hudson from their focus on television. She hurried to answer, leaving Hudson transfixed on the screen. 'Jack Hudson's office,' Woodward said, as she checked back through the door at Hudson.

'It's Maddie. What does Jack say?'

'On the record, we do not know what the Member for Cowan is talking about,' Woodward replied. 'Off the record, sounds like a potential beatup to me. I do not know where they are focussing.'

'You think it's Jack?'

'No idea, frankly.'

'Come on, Chrissie, something must be going on.'

'I don't know what I can tell you. Jack is relaxed about it.' She glanced into the office to see Hudson taking a seat on the couch. 'If I hear anything, I'll let you know.'

As Woodward returned to the office, she found Hudson texting. 'Do you know anything about that speech?'

'Nope.'

'Were you involved?'

'Maybe. I could have been. I just texted Charlie for a view.'

Woodward's phone shrilled again, and she moved to answer. 'Jack, it's Dale on line two.'

Hudson moved to his desk. 'Put him through.' He prodded the speaker function and motioned Woodward to join him.

'Jack, I just took a call from Eddie Collins.'

'Oh, yes. What does he want?'

'He referred to the speech by MacDonald and asked me flat out if he was referring to you?'

'What was your response?'

'I said I had no information and couldn't provide him an answer.' Bower hesitated for a moment. 'He then said he would be running another lede story tomorrow about it.'

'No kidding. What a surprise.'

'Jack, this could be significant trouble for us, especially amongst women.'

Hudson peeked up at Woodward. She raised her eyebrows, pursing her lips. He then shrugged. 'Not sure where this is going, Dale. I guess we will know soon enough. I suspect it could be bigger than the women of Gellibrand.'

'I'll do some testing overnight.'

'Why would you do that? I'm not mentioned.'

'Alright, fair enough. I'll wait a few days and see what Collins does in the Chronicle,' Bower said.

'I think we should all relax a little.'

'Jack, I don't know what Chrissie thinks, but this is a potential problem for you. You are the only one who has served in the military in the parliament. It is obvious the government is moving against you.'

'Relax Dale, it'll be okay, mate.'

'Once I know more, I'll get back to you,' Bower said. 'This sounds like a setup – expect something in question time.'

Woodward nodded.

'Jack, just be careful. There are sharks circling – blood is in the water,' Bower said.

'It'll be okay, Dale. Just relax and let's see what happens.' Hudson ended the call, slumping back in his chair.

'He's right, this could be a problem,' Woodward said.

'Why?'

'Maddie Booker rang me, asking about you?'

Hudson nodded as he rubbed his hairless face. 'I wonder what she knows?'

'Not sure, but I'll stay close.'

Hudson nodded, examining her. 'Where's your glasses?'

'They're an accessory, Jack, not a prescription.'

Hudson snorted. 'Accessory?'

'Camouflage.'

Hudson smiled. 'Ah, I get it. Nice one.'

'So, what do you want to do?' Woodward asked, trying to make sense of his question.

'Let me talk to Charlie O'Brien and flesh out if there is anything we can do.'

CHAPTER
40

Senator Morgan finished her daily workout in the gymnasium, displaying a level of physical ferocity putting the few parliamentary colleagues in the gym to shame. She had undergone a personal transformation years ago, confronting her own body image and working hard to reshape and maintain a physique she deemed worthy.

As she left the facility, she answered her phone. 'Edward, hello, how can I help?'

'You may or may not be aware that a government member delivered a speech to parliament this morning alleging a war crime ten years ago.'

'Oh yes, what did they disclose?'

'There was an investigation. It seems there may have been a coverup.'

'Names?'

'None, other than a perpetrator may be involved in community service at the moment.'

'Excellent,' Morgan said as she passed Aussies Cafe waving to a colleague.

'I contacted Hudson's office for a comment,' Collins said.

'Your speculation is unwarranted, since no one has been named.'

'I'm running the story on page one.'

Morgan paused, wiping her face with a towel draped across her shoulders. 'Just be careful not to mention or even imply Hudson is involved. We don't want this blowing back on us.'

'I won't. But I will mention his service in Sudan and that his office made a *no comment*, when I sought a comment from Hudson. His refusal to speak about it may be self damning.'

Morgan resumed her stroll with a hand resting on her hip. 'Just be careful, this is important.'

'I will, don't worry,' Collins said. 'Speaking of things to worry about. I received interesting information from the head office the other day.'

Morgan's impatience displayed itself. 'What is it?'

'We had almost a thousand members join in the last week.'

'A thousand? Where?'

'All over the state but mostly in safe state seat branches.'

'Any talk of who is harvesting votes?'

'None,' Collins smiled. 'They won't be eligible for this year's preselection, but they will be next year. They may impact all state seat preselections and the next senate selections.'

Morgan breathed in, filling her lungs. 'Are you sure there is no talk?'

'I assume the AGM season will see changes to preselection delegates; therefore, I expect preselections will face challenges.

'What are you saying?' Morgan reached her office.

'I'm saying that it might be time to add me to the ticket.'

'Again? Don't you ever give up?' Morgan snapped. 'Your time will come.'

'It seems so will yours,' Collins quipped.

'Edward, we have spoken about this type of toxic language,' Morgan tugged the towel from her shoulders as she arrived at her desk. 'If we are to work together, then I need you to stop tossing these micro-aggressions at me.'

'No aggression, just a statement for you to chew on,' Collins said a smile in his tone. 'I'll send you a copy of the front-page.'

'Thank you, Edward.' Morgan dropped the phone to her desk, peeling off the wet lycra. She kicked off her shoes and tossed her steaming clothes into a pile before entering the bathroom suite. She checked her image in the mirror and nodded.

THIRTY MINUTES before scheduled question time in both chambers Windsor paid a visit to Senator Morgan. 'I come to you with news,' he announced as he walked into her office.

'Oh yes, Alexander, what news do you bring?' Morgan stood by the window, using the natural light to complete the slight touches of makeup.

'Crumbs, are you going to a function? You look sensational.'

'Just pour a little water on your burning testosterone,' Morgan scoffed.

'I bet you say that to everyone – girls included.'

'Give it a break will you, Alexander?' Morgan frowned as she snapped shut her touch-up purse. 'I would argue you are being too provocative with your sexual references. You well know we have a code of conduct.'

'Oh Stephanie, we're mates.' Windsor collapsed in a chair at her desk. 'If a mate can't say something, then life would be very boring.'

'That may be so but keep them between you and me.' Morgan grinned as she took her chair.

'I really do have news for you.'

'Then you better tell me what's what.'

'The government is raising a question about Malakal today following an earlier speech by our man. It seems there may be a cover up of war crimes.'

'Who covered up what?'

'Defence covered up an inquiry ten years ago, just before we lost the government benches to Mosely.'

'Why is that good news?'

'How soon we forget.'

Morgan narrowed her eyes at Windsor as she thought through why he would be excited. Then she realised. 'Oh, I see what you mean.'

'Chopra could be up to his neck in it.'

'He wasn't the defence minister for that long.'

'Doesn't matter, does it?'

'If we tarnish him, then we can move him out.'

'When is Peter thinking about challenging?'

'Within a month, so we need to start counting votes.'

Morgan scoffed. 'Don't you just love politics?'

CHAPTER
41

T he noise in the chamber subsided when the speaker asked for question time to begin. The first to seize the floor was Chopra, directing his enquiry toward the prime minister concerning the ongoing investigation into business activities of registered organisations. In response, Mosely suggested in a blunt reply they would enact the legislation soon, depending on the outcome of the current inquiry.

'The Member for Cowan,' the speaker announced.

'I direct my question to the prime minister, and I ask, have you been advised by the Department of Defence regarding a confidential war crimes report? Will you respond in the parliament to the allegations which have been exposed?'

'Prime Minister,' the speaker called.

'I thank the Member for his question.' Mosely tugged the briefing notes before her. 'I'm aware of a discovered internal report concerning alleged war crimes committed by Australian special services during an operational deployment in Sudan a little over ten years ago.' She allowed a moment for the gravity of the issue to settle before continuing. 'You may recall my government was then yet to secure the government benches.'

'You won't have them for much longer,' interjected Windsor with a derisive cackle.

'My honourable friend makes a joke during a very serious report to the House regarding war crimes.' Windsor's broad smile disappeared. 'I have a report from the department which provides an interesting communication trail. It reports that the department sought advice about the matter from the Chief of Defence and the minister. The Chief advised that the department should conduct an inquiry at the lowest possible level and complete a comprehensive report, which should involve securing evidence and recording witness statements. The Chief also directed that those involved conduct the inquiry confidentially, with the highest levels of security.'

A hush settled over the House as politicians paid closer attention. Jack Hudson, engrossed in files, directed his focus toward the prime minister.

'The House may think this command may be important, but it appears this is standard practice for Defence when they investigate themselves. What is clear from this inquiry is that a thorough investigation was needed, and this did not happen. The report concludes there was no evidence of a war crime, and it recommends against further action. Defence Chiefs reviewed the report and agreed.'

A pause punctuated the prime minister's words, allowing

her gaze to rest on Chopra, who met her scrutiny with a sense of uncertainty as he twiddled his pen.

'Considering these revelations,' Mosely's voice gained a measured intensity. 'This afternoon I will appoint a Justice of the Supreme Court of Victoria, a former Brigadier, and counsel for the Army to reopen the investigation and review the evidence. The government will investigate and review the evidence to determine whether horrendous war crimes were committed and whether further legal action against those involved is necessary.

'I have instructed the Justice to investigate whether the government hindered in any way the inquiry. Attention shall focus on the conduct of the then Minister who now leads the opposition, and the behaviour of the minister in directing the Chief of Defence.'

'Boom,' Windsor whispered into his hand.

Chopra's demeanour remained unchanged, absorbing the implications of the Prime Minister's words.

'I will release further detail, including terms of reference at a media conference later today.' Mosely glanced up from her notes. 'We on this side of the House hold honesty and integrity in high regard. These values shall continue to underpin all facets of governance, including the Defence.'

'Hear, hear,' the government members responded.

As the prime minister resumed her seat, Chopra moved to the Despatch Box. 'On indulgence, Speaker.'

'Proceed,' the Speaker said.

'The Prime Minister has just implied I suppressed information about a Defence inquiry some ten years ago. Nothing could be further from the truth. I vehemently reject this insinuation and welcome a judicial inquiry to restore my tarnished reputation. I thank the House.'

High above the chamber in the media gallery, Madeleine Booker took notes. She shifted her attention to Jack Hudson, observing he seemed relaxed with the prime minister's response to the question and Chopra's intervention.

CHAPTER
42

Alexander Windsor's daily routine sidestepped the parliamentary chamber and its routine committee work. Such matters were far too trivial to capture his attention. Windsor was a politician with unwavering focus, his sights set on leadership within the party. His guiding principle was clear: to rise in the ranks, the existing leader must go.

Day after day, he prowled the corridors like a predator stalking prey. Conversations with colleagues were a means to an end. He'd scribble notes on a small pad in the corridors, jotting down impressions from meetings before moving to the next office. He would charm representatives and senators with his banter, luring them with the latest whispers of gossip. Unbeknownst to them, Windsor compiled a weighty dossier, gathering information that only he would bother sifting through. He anticipated ministers' allegiances could shift as the leadership battle approached; however, he focused on discerning the loyalties of ambitious backbenchers.

Returning to his office, Windsor would ponder over his notes, transferring key points into the template files he maintained for every contact. Legislative matters took a backseat to his network cultivation. He knew their preferences, their pets' names, their favourite drinks, and the ambitions they harboured for their constituencies and their personal career goals.

While the rest of the world disregarded such minutiae, Windsor delved into the details, never missing a birthday, not just his colleagues but their spouses and children as well. The same care extended to party members outside parliament, earning him gratitude for his attention to detail. A former member learned the hard way that Windsor's support was no guarantee of preselection security. A promising political career came to an abrupt end because of Windsor's numbers.

'Howdy, Jack. How are they hanging?' Windsor shrieked, barging into Hudson's office.

Hudson glanced up and smirked. Windsor always brought a ray of sunshine to his gloomy days. 'Alex, nice to see you. Have a seat. Would you like a cup of tea?'

'Yes, please.' His posh accent seemed even more posh. 'But none of that peppermint crap you forced on me last time. Do you have anything with a pleasant aroma?'

'We have French Earl Grey, which might just be your cup of tea,' said a smiling Chrissie Woodward, standing at the threshold of the adjoining office.

'Then that sounds fabulous, gorgeous, thank you.'

Woodward disappeared to brew the tea, closing the door, adding a touch of privacy to his visit. She was conscious of Windsor's political tactics and didn't want any other party staffer stumbling in on their meeting. She warned Hudson when he first came calling, but Jack kept a soft spot for him.

'What's going on, Huddo?'

'Don't you read the papers?' Hudson said.

'This army thing has nothing to do with you, does it?' Hudson didn't respond. 'I mean, it's a very long bow to link you to the incident they are talking about.'

Hudson pouted his bottom lip, shrugged, and nodded.

Windsor frowned. 'It's not connected to you, is it, Jack?'

Hudson shrugged. 'I don't have all the details. My unit cleared a village, and I was injured.'

Windsor hid his great fortune. He wouldn't have to do any research on the army records. 'These things blow over,' Windsor opined. 'My only advice is to keep your head down.'

'Not the first time I've heard that.'

Windsor shook a confused look, then realised. 'Oh yes, I see what you mean.' He chortled. 'Nice one. Keep your head down.'

Woodward reappeared with two mugs of tea, leaving them on Hudson's desk before withdrawing. Windsor wasted no time in taking a sip.

'Nice one, Chrissie,' he yelled, assuming she couldn't hear. 'This tea is fantastic. Where did you find it?'

'Sassafras, a charming spot up in the mountains. Perfect for a leisurely Sunday drive.'

Windsor eyed his colleague over the top of the steaming black tea. 'Seriously, Jack, the only person who should be worried is the leader.'

'He wasn't there.'

'He was the minister. And when a department messes up, the minister takes the fall,' Windsor said. 'Or they're supposed to according to Westminster precedent. Recent years, to be honest, have rather tarnished that protocol.'

'It was ten years ago.'

'Irrelevant in this political bubble. You stuff up, no matter how long ago, and the sharks come hunting for a kill.'

'We're not in government.'

Windsor sighed. 'Jack, my dear you have much to learn about politics. It doesn't matter if we are in government or not. If someone wants you smeared and you stuffed up in your life, then they will use it against you.' He sipped his tea. 'Trust me.'

Hudson rocked his chair as he leaned back. 'So, no matter how much good you've done,' Hudson tilted his head. 'They use a mistake, a weakness, or an accusation from way back against you?'

'That's the way it works in this game. Remember that attorney general who was forced out because of a weird story about him when he was a teenager?'

Hudson nodded as Windsor sipped his tea.

'If we force the leader to stand down,' Windsor drained his cup. 'Who would you support?'

'He will not stand down.'

'He may have to do it as a result of the cover up.'

Hudson nodded. Windsor's words lingered. 'I will support him if he needs it. No one should be accountable if they were never there.'

'It's the cover up.'

'It could be classified.'

'No one knows. There is no public information about what happened.'

'And if there was?'

'Then Ramon wouldn't be under threat.'

'Interesting.'

'Yes, it is,' Windsor changed tone. 'Now tell me, what do you think of Peter Raffles?'

'A gentleman.'

'A potential leader?'

Hudson didn't respond, examining Windsor. His staffer's advice playing in the back of his mind. Be careful. 'Are you promoting him?'

'Noohoohoohoo,' Windsor squirmed. 'I just think we first termers need to be prepared.'

'Prepared for what?'

'A leadership challenge.'

'Why would there be a leadership challenge?'

'If we want to win the next election, we need a new leader,' Windsor said, watching for a Hudson's reaction, but getting none.

CHAPTER

43

'We might face an issue with Hudson,' Windsor said, easing into the comfortable lounge in Peter Raffles' office. 'Seems like he's leaning towards Chopra.'

Raffles reclined in his chair. 'Why? He will never get promoted, whilst Chopra is leader.'

'I'm not sure the lure of ambition has the young man prepared to barter his vote,' Windsor mused, his fingers finding the armrest's intricate patterns.

'Did you ask him directly?' Raffles asked.

'Not in so many words, but he said he was loyal to the leader, no matter the leader.'

'Interesting position to take.' Raffles nodded. 'Support your leader even if you don't agree and never challenge the leadership.'

'I suspect it's a soldier's mindset,' Windsor scoffed. 'You know, all that jazz about loyalty and other sanctimonious stuff.'

Raffles swung back and forth in his chair as he considered what to do. 'I don't think we need him,' he finally said. 'In fact, it might be prudent for us to get him out of the parliament. I'm not sure he will be a team player in the future. I reckon he may be on a trajectory to a leadership position if we are not careful.'

'You think?' Windsor seemed sceptical.

'Good looking military man,' Raffles nodded. 'Yeah, I reckon he could be a future contender.'

'Morgan wants him gone for the same reason,' Windsor said. 'He apparently sends a chill through her.'

Raffles sighed, pinching the bridge of his nose. 'If she's wary of him, there might be substance to it. She might know something about him.'

Windsor made a mental note to probe the senator's concerns.

'When is she planning it?' Raffles asked.

'She wants him gone at preselection, which will black mark him forever.'

'Why not let him run and lose the election?'

'That's precisely the point,' Windsor said. 'If he loses at a general election, he might earn another shot in a more favourable constituency. Morgan wants him nutted as soon as possible.'

'Risky, but it makes sense, I suppose.' Raffles acknowledged, fingers drumming a soft rhythm on his desk. 'How?'

'We can associate him with the current Chopra scandal – then claim both scalps.' Windsor said his lips curling into a sly grin.

'Just be cautious about leveraging the military angle,' Raffles said. 'It may come back to bite us if we're not careful.'

'Point taken,' Windsor nodded. 'MacDonald is up again today with a question and is providing more revelations. Apparently, he has a letter from an investigative psychologist reporting back to Defence.'

'Exposing what?'

'A coverup,' Windsor said. 'MacDonald is convinced this will destroy Chopra.'

'History shows the cover-up is always more damaging than the initial action.'

'For leaders and ministers, that's for sure,' Windsor said. 'Not sure why they just don't come clean and admit their mistake, apologise, and then move on.'

'Politicians can't help themselves. It's all about ego.'

Windsor cackled. 'You're right there.' After the laughter ebbed, he mused. 'When shall we move on Chopra? We almost have the numbers. This coverup may swing others across to you and be the end of him.'

'Let's spill some blood on the floor in the chamber.'

Windsor prepared to leave, rising to his feet. 'I'll prompt the government to crank up the intensity. Maybe I can convince them to raise it during the Matter of Public Importance today.'

'Good work, Al.'

'It's Alexander,' Windsor corrected him as he left the office.

WINDSOR MOVED through the corridors to Ramsey MacDonald's office at the other end of the building on the first floor. He spotted him at his desk as he entered the lobby, so moved through to the office, craving privacy as he closed the door.

'Alexander, what can I do for you?'

'Ramsey, I think we need more than just questions about Chopra.'

'I have one today.' MacDonald waved to a chair. 'What are you suggesting?'

'I have an idea for you.' Windsor said, taking the chair offered. 'If I talk to the selection chair, would you be happy to lead a Matter of Public Importance debate after question time?'

MacDonald considered the idea, nibbling on the end of his pen. 'Maybe.'

'If I can persuade Chopra to let me speak as second for our side after the shadow minister,' Windsor said. 'I'll start with a conciliatory tone. Then, pivot and critique the coverup and its lack of transparency.'

MacDonald considered the idea, the pen now between his fingers. 'Maybe we could invoke the Yamashita Convention.'

'The Yamaha what?'

'Not Yamaha, Yamashita. I stumbled upon the Convention recently.' MacDonald dropped his pen onto a pad. 'Australia apparently executed a Japanese general for war crimes that took place when he wasn't in command.'

'Why would that be relevant to what happened in Sudan?'

'It establishes the concept that a commander can hold

responsibility for their troops' crimes, even if they weren't directly responsible, aware, or capable of stopping crime.'

'Seriously?' Windsor said.

'That means we can bring everyone associated with an incident to account.'

'Even a minister?'

'Especially the minister.'

CHAPTER
44

Once the business of the House resumed after a fiery question time, the Speaker stood and announced. 'I have received a letter from the Member for Cowan seeking that a matter of public importance be debated; namely, the covering up of alleged criminal actions of our defence personnel in Malakal, Sudan. I ask those who support the motion to rise in their places.'

Government members stood with a rousing 'Hear, hear.'

Hudson remained seated, rubbing his forehead.

'The Member for Cowan.'

'Thank you, Speaker,' MacDonald began, his voice measured as he read from his paper. 'It gives me no pleasure to be raising this issue of war crimes...'

'Alleged.' Hudson interjected.

MacDonald glanced up and nodded, acknowledging the point. 'The member is quite right. We must exercise caution in discussing such matters in this hallowed space, given they remain allegations.'

As MacDonald warmed to his presentation, Hudson left his seat and walked to the table, sitting next to the shadow defence minister. 'Who is our second speaker?'

'Windsor.'

'Interesting,' Hudson said. 'When did this get added to the notice paper? I thought there was another topic listed.'

'There was indeed, but the government orchestrated a late change via the Chair of the Selection Committee.'

'Do you have everything you need?'

'I think so,' said the shadow minister. 'It's an attack on the leader as he was the defence minister.'

'Why doesn't he speak?'

'Good question,' the shadow minister said. 'He may need to face the media in the coming days if this gains traction. It will depend on the national broadcasters' reaction to these allegations.'

'This is nonsense to raise now,' Hudson said. 'Defence has investigated and there is no cover up.'

'So close to the next election the government's strategy is to pin this on the leader,' the shadow minister said. 'Our job is to prevent this from escalating into a full-blown crisis for him.'

'Need any help?'

'I have my notes, so should be okay.'

With a nod, Hudson retreated to his seat as MacDonald began explaining behaviours he considered inappropriate within the military.

'Speaker, I regret to inform you that this hidden report has uncovered alleged atrocities that need to be mentioned. The report is clear in identifying loss of discipline within special services leading to a warrior culture where units would enter war zones as part of their deployment and not meet the standards of war as prescribed by the Geneva Convention, for which Australia is a signatory.'

'Referring allegations of civilians being murdered during the Malakal deployment to Defence inquiries and taking no further action is unacceptable. There is an anguished question that needs to be asked. If these allegations are correct, then why does the Australian public remain uninformed? Why does the Defence leadership not know? Why did the Minister for Defence at the time not know? Because he should have.'

'As I stated, we are signatories of the Geneva Convention, which provide guidance for war and the rules we must abide. From the reports of these alleged incidents of murder and mistreatment of Sudanese civilians, we have not. So, who is culpable?'

MacDonald paused for a moment, looked around the chamber, determined who was listening, and settled his eyes on Hudson. 'Every soldier who was involved should be brought to account to reveal what they know. Speaker, this is not good enough. Australia subscribes to the Yamashita Convention which holds the entire chain of command liable irrespective whether the commanding officers were aware.'

'This must then mean the Minister who issued the orders for Australia to be in Sudan and therefore Malakal. This means the defence minister at the time should and must bear responsibility. That minister, Speaker, remains in the parliament. That minister is Ramon Chopra, the leader of the opposition.'

Hudson took a note.

'I acknowledge the prime minister has initiated a review with a judicial officer. However, I am seeking a reopening of the inquiry so that the Australian public can have a full and frank discussion about the behaviours of our military service men and women. We must courageously expose what is hidden, or we will never rid the military of those who dishonour our nation.

'I also call upon all of those service personnel who were present during the Malakal deployment to speak up and tell us what happened.' MacDonald glanced over to Hudson and then turned to the speaker. 'Speaker, I note the Member for Gellibrand is in the chamber. I also note the member served during the Malakal deployment and when asked about these issues during his recent election campaign, he mentioned he could not answer questions because of national security. Well, I ask the member, what did he know and when did he know it?'

Hudson doodled on his pad. He did not look up.

'If the honourable member has something to contribute to these matters, he should go on the public record. Speaker, if the Member for Gellibrand abstains from doing so, it casts a shadow on transparency, raising suspicions about whether his silence shields the opposition leader.'

A slight wince etched its way across Hudson's expression.

CHAPTER

45

When Hudson reached his office, a heavy shroud of exhaustion enveloped him. Fatigue gnawed at his bones, and his mind drifted from the present moment to the future and its uncertainty. A looming challenge for the leadership approached with its significance amplified by his silence about his service.

The shadow minister defended Chopra, presenting a compelling argument against holding him accountable for decisions made over a decade ago. Yet, this defence unwittingly cast Hudson into the limelight, insinuating that it was the voices of those who were there that should unearth the truth. Whether the allegations were fact or fiction, the burden of addressing the issue seemed to poke him.

As he nestled into the lounge for a brief rest, a steaming mug of tea materialised, courtesy of Woodward. He managed a grateful nod as he sat up to accept the warm comfort. 'Thank you, Chrissie,' he said. 'I appreciate it.'

'What do you want to do?'

Sipping his tea, Hudson mulled over the question. 'Why should I do anything?'

Her response was sharp. 'You can't leave the doubt out there.'

'What doubt?'

'That you were involved in killing civilians?'

Hudson's chest heaved. He puffed out his cheeks, exhaling heavily.

'You can't afford to ignore this indefinitely.'

'The debate is about Chopra.'

'No, Jack, listen,' Woodward sat on the edge of the lounge, 'it's not about Ramon anymore, it's about you. You were there and you will need to address it. Otherwise, they will tarnish you with the same allegations.'

'I can't say anything.'

'Can't or won't?'

Hudson's gaze shifted to her, eyes weary but resolute. He took a sip of tea. 'It's classified.'

'Why is it classified?'

'I can't divulge that.'

Woodward rose, gnawing at her lower lip. 'Jack, if you don't address this, it could cost you the election.'

'It'll blow over.'

'Yeah, nah,' Woodward said, moving to her office. 'I've

fielded ten media requests in the last half hour. This is just the beginning.'

'What does Dale think?'

'He believes Collins is desperate to smear you with any hint of criminality. He thinks the government handed him ammunition today.'

'Tomorrow's fish and chip wrapper.'

'Jack, you are joking,' Woodward snapped. 'This could be the end.'

A moment of tense silence hung in the air, broken only by the sound of Hudson draining his mug. 'It's a government back-bencher suggesting I might know something, that's all.'

'The way I see it,' Woodward began, 'MacDonald's comments demand a full explanation from you.'

'The question is if I should provide information, not if I should explain myself.'

'Jack, get real, will you?' Woodward placed a fist her hip. 'Perceptions matter more than reality in politics. Right now, the perception is that you're guilty of a war crime.' Hudson sighed. 'If you don't change that perception, then I suspect your career might be over.'

'How should I do that?'

Woodward shook her head, thinking through options. 'I'll give Maddie Booker a call; maybe she can help.'

'The media?'

'They can be allies when the situation calls for it,' Woodward moved off. 'I'll call Dale as well.'

THIRTY MINUTES later Madeleine Booker sat poised at Hudson's desk, pad open ready to take shorthand notes.

'Why do you think the government is running with this story?'

Hudson winced. 'I suspect it's less about the events in Malakal and more about undermining Chopra.'

'Were you in Malakal during the period they are talking about?'

'They deployed me to Sudan three times, including the Malakal conflict.'

'Is it uncomfortable to ask you about this?'

Hudson offered a wry smile. 'I served with honour and distinction. Sometimes soldiers become calloused and tired of their constant edge of being ready to fight.'

'This tiredness of your men you mention. Could this be linked to the war crime accusations? Were our soldiers unaccountable?'

Hudson's gaze flicked toward Woodward, who nodded encouragement. 'They train us to have moral courage and honour the rules of war, even though our enemy does not. War is degrading for everyone involved. Everyone is accountable. We cannot allow the chain of command to dismiss the alleged actions with the blame taken by lower ranks.'

'What guidance did you give to soldiers under your command?'

'When I arrived, I observed two types of warrior culture.

One based on worshiping war through ego and self-adoration. The other humbler in their duties prepared to fight but knowing the rules they were fighting under.'

Maddie's notetaking ceased, her eyes fixed on Hudson as she processed his words. Clearing her throat, she spoke. 'Are you saddened by these allegations?'

Hudson brushed his knuckle across his lips. 'War generates scabs of burden. The toxic personalities in a company can have a negative impact on soldiers deployed under orders to kill or capture. Especially those who have been deployed for too long. They risk their lives fighting in a war that others think is important. I don't judge. I defend those men under my command who fought with honour.'

Booker cleared her throat with a short cough. 'I'm sorry for you having to feel that you're ensnared in this political frenzy.'

Hudson steepled his fingers. 'I served with honour. I'm untroubled by the accusations for myself or my men.'

'Do you stay in touch with your men?'

'I see them at commemorations or regimental events.'

'What is the message you want to give to them, and others interested in this story?'

'War is hell. The troops sent to fight do so with honour and moral courage.'

Booker nodded. 'Fair enough.' She closed her pad and stood, offering her hand. 'Thanks for your time. This has been helpful.'

'Why helpful?' Hudson said, standing as they shook hands.

'I hate war, and all things involved with it. But talking to you challenges my view of those entangled in it.'

'History reminds us wars are inevitable, so we must be prepared to fight to protect the values we hold dear, like freedom from tyranny.'

'Jack, thank you.'

They still held hands. 'Madeleine, if you ever need a view about this or other matters, my door is always open.'

Booker dropped her hand, flushed, and turned to Woodward who escorted her out.

Left alone, Hudson's head sank into his hands, the weight of the world pressing down.

Woodward's return offered a glimmer of comfort. 'That went well, Jack. Maddie will handle it with dignity.'

Hudson's voice wavered. 'Why am I doing this job?'

CHAPTER
46

Oleg Rusnek has little interest in the affairs of the nation. He rarely pays attention to headlines and does not listen to the broadcast news. Making money was his paramount concern, ever since he observed how his union bosses revelled in their privileges. He established his own union, employing ruthless tactics to secure access to construction sites by breaking a few arms. Now, he commanded the bustling CBD building sites, granting him cash flow and opportunities to expand. Politics only mattered to him as a means to eliminate unfavourable legislation. Numbers held no sway over him. His approach was straightforward and uncomplicated: comply with his methods or face severe repercussions.

Every weekend, he took his rottweilers to the beach, revelling in solitary moments while Mozart filled his ears through his Bluetooth earbuds. These moments were his sanctuary. Although he remained vigilant, his dogs were ever ready.

Brighton was a bit of a trek from his Toorak mansion. Port Melbourne dog beach, was a closer option, but the drive to Brighton didn't faze him. He kept his beach gear stowed in a metal trunk at the back of his modified Dodge Ram, enabling impromptu beach outings with his canine companions. The rugged Ute served him well for both work and road trips, the rottweilers often lounging in the back. Upon reaching the beach, he released his dogs to terrorise smaller creatures. He staked a spot by the water with his folding chair and returned to his book and music, not caring too much about the trouble his dogs might do in the water and sand.

Soon after settling in, Manaaki Henari and a companion trudged through the soft sand to stand above Rusnek blocking the morning sun. He lifted his sunglasses when a sudden shadow was cast, glancing over his shoulder.

'What are you two dipsticks doing, blocking my sun?'

'We came to discuss our agreement.'

'We have no partnership.' Rusnek flipped his sunglasses back in place.

'I wanted to tell you we shunted new members into Nationals' seats. They are ready for upcoming preselections. Our plan to infiltrate government seats is also bearing fruit. We're gaining substantial numbers in pivotal electorates.'

'This is encouraging news.'

'We are happy for you to use them, but just remember, they remain under our control and will follow our direction.'

'You building an army?'

'More like a stealth force,' Henari scoffed.

'So why are you here casting a shadow over my beach time?'

'It's time we complete a deal.'

'What deal?'

Henari's expression soured at the response. 'Have you seen today's Williamstown Chronicle?'

'I don't follow the news,' he quipped, holding up his book. 'I follow Shakespeare.'

'Good for you,' Henari mumbled, kicking at the sand. 'Our agreement was that we'd show our goodwill by delivering you numbers to influence candidate selection in both parties. In return, you'd permit us to legitimise our businesses under your corporate brand and give us Gellibrand.'

Rusnek let out a sigh. 'Look, the only reason I want Gellibrand is to thwart the legislation suffocating my business. You kill the legislation, then we can do the deal.'

'According to today's newspaper, Hudson is in trouble.'

'We all want him gone, so what's your point?' Rusnek said.

'Why not use him as leverage to get what you want?'

'How would that work?'

'We kill him as a favour to those who wish him gone. They then return the favour.'

Rusnek sneered. 'You don't mean literally kill him?'

'We know Senator Morgan is the one chairing the inquiry. Why not present the proposal to her?'

'Working with politicians is akin to dancing with vipers. They'll slither away once they get what they want.'

'What if we threaten her Senate seat? Would that nudge her towards our way of thinking?'

'It's not Gellibrand that concerns me. My union owns it,' Rusnek said.

'Her committee needs to submit a recommendation to the government,' Henari said. 'If she doesn't like it, her party has the numbers in the senate and can stop it. So, let's go have a chat with her.'

Rusnek flicked back his sunglasses. 'I'm wary of bringing you in on anything.'

'Why are you worried about me?'

'Hmm, let's see.' Rusnek whistled to his dogs as they pestered an elderly woman with a poodle. 'Harassing my workers on the sites. Pushing your drugs. Your continued misconduct is prompting regulators to inspect our sites, causing me problems. And...' Rusnek halted, fixing his gaze on the man eclipsing the sun. 'Maybe your cosy relationship with Campbell and persuading him to introduce this legislation?'

'That's an extensive list.'

'Yeah, it is,' Rusnek said.

'Let's go see the senator,' Henari said. 'Come on Oleg, let's work together on this.'

Henari offered his hand to complete the deal. A bounding, snarling dog leapt at him, stretching for his neck. He reacted instinctively, swatting the dog aside and flinging it over Rusnek. It thudded onto the sand as the second dog now more cautious stayed at Rusnek's feet.

'Call them off.'

'Pyatka!' The dogs crouched ready to respond.

'Call those mongrels off.' Henari said, stepping back and checking his elbow.

'You're safe. There is nothing to fear.'

'You know something, Russian,' he kept a close watch on the dogs. 'I'm doing you an enormous favour and you treat me like dog shit.'

'This is not true. I admire your ambition to steal my business.'

'I'm not here to steal your business. I'm here to talk,' Henari said. 'I'm too old for this crap.'

'You misunderstand.' Rusnek scrambled from his chair, extending a hand. 'I've worked hard to get the territory I own. I'm not interested in your porn or your gambling empire. But I'm prepared to talk if we resolve this legislation dilemma.'

'Well then let's go see the senator.'

Rusnek gripped his hand and squeezed as hard as he could. Henari didn't flinch. 'You have many attributes I admire, but I will not allow you to undermine my union.'

'You see this is the point.' Henari squeezed, hard. 'I'm not wanting to take it over, Oleg. I want to negotiate.'

Rusnek's hand buckled as he returned Henari's stare. 'I'll set up a meeting with the senator.'

Henari released his hand and moved off. 'Let me know, and can we stop this macho bullshit.'

As Rusnek watched him go he worked his thumb into the sore palm. 'Filth.'

CHAPTER

47

Morgan stepped from the limousine, leaving her travel bag, instructing the driver to wait. The driver let out an frustrated sigh and acknowledged the delay to his radio base informing them of the change to his schedule because of the senator's unexpected meeting.

Stepping into her office, Morgan found her staffer, Sandra Addison, waiting with files for signature.

'You have an eleven with two union members?' Addison asked.

Morgan glanced at her watch. 'I pencilled them in the diary yesterday. I would have expected them to be here by now.'

Addison checked her watch. 'Still five minutes.'

'My car's waiting, so ensure they're wrapped up within ten. Call me at ten past,' Morgan directed.

'Will do,' Addison said. 'What's your plan for the rest of the day?'

'I need a run.'

'Okay, I'll defer all calls until Monday.'

'Good girl.'

'Do you want me to offer them refreshments when they arrive?'

'No, I know what they want. It should be a short, sharp meeting.'

As Morgan sat at her desk, Addison placed a handful of files before the Senator. 'These need your signature. If you could take care of them before you leave, it would be very helpful.'

'Thank you, Sandra,' Morgan said, watching her leave.

Before she could open a file, her intercom buzzed to life. The receptionist announced the scheduled appointment. Morgan moved from her desk to greet the union representatives. Her smile faded as she took in the mountain of the man beside Rusnek. She offered her hand. He smiled. 'Senator Morgan, pleased to meet you.'

'Manaaki Henari.'

'Hello, Mr Rusnek, please come through. Nice to finally meet you. Make yourself comfortable in the lounge.'

'I think we might prefer to sit at your desk if that's okay?' Rusnek said.

Morgan masked her disappointment. 'That's fine, whatever you prefer.'

As they settled, Morgan cast an eye over Henari, examining his thick body, lingering on his chest. She smiled when she spotted Rusnek looking her. 'What nationality is your name?'

Henari beamed. 'Australian, why do you ask?'

'It's distinctive. I would have assumed it has islander roots.'

'My family is from New Zealand, but like Oleg here, I call Australia home.'

Her gaze flickered over his tattoos bursting from beneath his snug shirt. A tingle hurried down her lower back, and she squeezed a response. 'How can I help you?' Morgan's tone was now professional.

'We're here for an update,' Rusnek said.

'On the legislation?' Morgan confirmed.

'What else would we want you to update?' Rusnek responded.

'Parliament moves slow. We are still accepting submissions.'

'Will there be a recommendation from you prior to the election?' Rusnek pressed.

'You must remember, I'm not in government. This is your government's bill,' Morgan pointed out.

'Can you speed it up?' Rusnek urged.

'If we win the election, I can assure you we will kill it.'

'We want it resolved before the election.'

'Will you win Gellibrand?' Morgan shifted, then cast an eye to Henari, who cracked a knuckle with a thumb, sending a chill through her.

'We'll field a better candidate and secure the numbers. Gellibrand will return to us,' Henari said.

'We're aiming to oust Hudson at preselection, replacing him with a weaker candidate, but don't underestimate their chances,' Morgan sat forward. 'Remember, it's crucial for you to have the strongest contender.'

'We understand,' Henari concurred, his dark eyes engaging the senator.

Morgan's attention returned to Rusnek. 'Your primary concern is the legislation?'

'Senator, we just need your reassurance the legislation will be dumped, or at the very least deferred until after the election,' Rusnek said.

Morgan flicked her eyes back at him. 'Why is this so important to you?'

Rusnek smirked. 'Let's just say we're expanding our business interests, and we want assurance of protection from the regulators.'

The senator nodded. 'The responsibility for the legislation should rest on your side, not ours.'

Rusnek smirked a scoff. 'We think you will be the one to stop it, Valentina,' he said.

Morgan's tongue moved out to the edge of her lips as she tried to hide a nervous gulp. 'What did you call me?' she asked, her voice quivered.

'Do you think you can live an obsessive life as Valentina in the seedy bars of Melbourne without being recognised?'

'Not sure I know what you are talking about,' Morgan said, shifting in her chair.

'I know more about you and your, shall we say, interesting behaviour late at night than you might realise.'

Morgan sank back into her chair, combing her fingers through her hair.

'If you don't do what we ask, we might expose your alternate life.'

'I am still not sure what you are accusing me of.'

'Please do not play games with me, Valentina,' Rusnek said.

'We are everywhere, senator, and we know everything,' Henari said. 'We even have our people as delegates on your preselection committee next month,' Henari said.

Morgan's telephone buzzed. She didn't answer. It buzzed again. She ignored it, her focus now fixed on Henari. 'You have what?' she inquired.

Henari's smile faded. 'I have sufficient votes to alter your preselection. So you will do what I tell you.'

'Please excuse the coarseness of my friend's language,' Rusnek said. 'He is uncultured in the ways of senators. Proper filth he is, but I must say, he is not one to upset.'

Henari cracked a knuckle; this time a little louder.

'It seems it is time for us to leave,' Rusnek said as he gripped the arms of his chair, lifting himself. 'We shall win Gellibrand, and we will guarantee you are pre-selected. But in return you must assure us this legislation will never see the light of day.'

'Are you threatening me?'

Rusnek scoffed as he moved away. 'Threaten? Not at all. We are merely making certain you know our position and who holds the power, Valentina.'

Henari also stood waiting for Morgan to approach. 'Goodbye, Mr Henari, I'm sorry I could not be of more assistance to you,' she said, her hand extended.

Henari took her hand and tugged her close. 'You will be soon enough. I know you, and I know what you like. I have the numbers in your party, and soon I will control your preselection. You will begin to realise for you to continue doing what you like to do, then you will need learn to do what I ask.'

Morgan winced as his hand squeezed, a finger stroking her stomach. She flinched and resisted as best she could.

'The Russian may want his legislation quashed, and I recommend you listen to him. But I want more from you, especially the succulent fruits you obviously have on offer,' he said, his nose brushing hers. 'Do you understand?'

Morgan scratched at his shoulder, trying to push him away, then resting it on his chest, gripping it. 'Yes.'

'You come to me whenever I call for you, Senator,' Henari said. 'Understand?'

'Yes,' she whimpered, her hand tightening on his chest.

Henari stepped back, releasing her hand, and eyed her. She gasped; her hand cradled against her chest. 'It was a joy meeting you, Valentina. I reckon we will have a very satisfying time together. I hope we talk soon.'

Morgan watched him go, massaging her hand. She moved back to her desk, taking a chair. 'What the hell was that?'

CHAPTER
48

The shrieks of children resonated through Commonwealth Park every weekend, a familiar commotion as families gathered at Williamstown's foreshore for picnics beneath the canopy of trees. The park's breathtaking waterfront view of the city skyline attracted tourists and locals alike. On this particular day, three mates settled onto a hard park bench at the water's edge. Though they preferred their coffee in glass in a cafe, they opted for paper cups in the park to ensure their conversation remained discreet.

'Ever wonder why this Eddie Collins is writing this nonsense about you?' Charlie O'Brien mused, studying the front page of the Chronicle.

'He wants the skipper gone,' Billy Tyrrell said.

'But we're all on the same team,' O'Brien said.

'Nothing to do with teams, mate. Collins wants to evict the skip.'

Hudson took a sip of coffee, gazing across the water at Melbourne's skyline. His legs stretched out, a casual hand resting in his jeans pocket. 'I was just reflecting,' he began, catching the attention of his companions. 'Why the hell am I doing this?'

'Doing what?' Tyrrell asked.

'Politics,' Hudson said, taking another sip. 'It's a mug's game.' Tyrrell exchanged a glance with O'Brien, who lifted his eyebrows, breathing with ballooning cheeks. A squeal from the nearby playground attracted scrutiny. 'Why do you reckon they're targeting us?'

'You mean the regiment?' O'Brien asked.

'Yeah, why now?'

'Like any military operation,' O'Brien responded. 'The brass orders the mission. Then criticise our survival.'

'They don't get it,' Tyrrell added. 'Fight for us they say then ignore us when we get back. Yet the hypocrites say Lest We Forget every ANZAC Day.' Tyrrell stared out on to the water. 'Bastards.'

'Why do you reckon they're coming after you, Jack?' O'Brien asked.

'Beats me,' Hudson sipped his coffee. 'I reckon they're after Chopra.'

'Someone wants you gone,' O'Brien said.

'What do we do?' Tyrrell said.

The three comrades fell silent. Tyrrell jumped up and returned a kid's stray soccer ball.

'Your profile in the Hancock media seems fair,' O'Brien said, flicking the paper.

'I think the journo wants to protect me?' Hudson offered.

'Why?'

'Yeah, dunno,' Hudson said. 'She seems to think the revelations are a beat-up.'

'Well, they are?' Tyrrell said.

Hudson glanced at O'Brien who nonchalantly shrugged. 'War is hell, Billy. You more than anyone would appreciate that cliche,' Hudson replied. 'But did we ever cross a line?'

'My conscience is clear,' Tyrrell stated.

O'Brien leaned forward his eyes fixed on the footpath.

'In Malakal, we made some decisions that might've danced close to the line,' Hudson said.

'As I said, my conscience is clear.'

'Not sure mine is,' O'Brien confessed, head hung low.

Hudson crushed his cup, his gaze sweeping over his colleagues. 'Look at you two,' Hudson said with a lopsided grin. 'You look as if a mate has died.'

'Too many did, Skip,' Tyrrell said, reclaiming his place on the bench.

'That's true,' Hudson said. 'But should we talk about it?'

'I wouldn't recommend it,' O'Brien said. 'Unless you have to.'

'So, I leave Chopra dangling?'

'He was the minister,' Tyrrell said.

'But he didn't give the order,' Hudson said.

'He sent us,' O'Brien said.

They didn't speak for a few moments as they squinted to the city. 'My question was, do I leave him hanging?' Hudson said.

'Are you sure they are after him?' O'Brien asked. 'Who do you reckon is behind it?'

'Our side. I wouldn't put it past Alexander Windsor running the play,' Hudson said.

'How does that link you with the Chronicle story?'

Hudson winced. 'The local party members want me gone. They're exploiting this smear campaign for my preselection.'

'What does the sexy girl have to say?' O'Brien chuckled.

'Who's this sexy girl?' Tyrrell asked.

'Senator Morgan,' O'Brien said with a playful nibble of his lip.

'Morgan?' Tyrrell wrinkled his nose. 'That skinny little thing.'

'Yeah, her.'

'You reckon she might help get Collins off my back?' Hudson said.

'Maybe she is the one who shoved him onto your back,' O'Brien answered.

'She is tight with Raffles,' Hudson said.

'Who's Raffles?' Tyrrell asked.

'Huh,' Hudson scoffed. 'Don't you pay any attention to the national parliament?'

'Why should I? They're all morons.'

'Really?' Hudson grinned.

'Not you of course Skip, but most of them,' O'Brien said.

'Assuming this media assault is designed to topple Chopra and bring about a leadership change, what should my next step be?"

'If we were out on a battlefield, what would you do?' Tyrrell asked.

'Step forward with caution,' Hudson said.

'Yeah, nah,' Tyrrell said. 'You would order in a barrage. During the bombing, you would charge the enemy head on.'

'Maybe,' Hudson said.

'Billy might have a point,' O'Brien said. 'To save you, we might have to risk you.'

'Hang on, that's not the approach we took before.'

'If you want to save your preselection and then win the seat again, you need to get out and advance on the opposition and fight back until they back off,' O'Brien said.

'No more of this ridiculous silence strategy,' Tyrrell said. 'Let's get you out there and show everyone that you are what this community needs.'

'I'm not quite convinced of that,' Hudson confessed.

'Skip, you need to decide,' Tyrrell said as he stood. He then fronted his former captain. 'Either you step up and lead us, or you step away. If you're committed, then get in the fight.'

Hudson glanced up. 'That sounds familiar.'

Tyrrell nodded. 'Yeah, I thought it might.'

'What do we do with Chopra?'

'Never leave a man behind,' O'Brien said.

Hudson bit his bottom lip, watching O'Brien and then Tyrrell. 'Lucky for me you didn't.'

CHAPTER
49

'Boss, are you sure you want to do this?' Bower asked after perusing the speech Hudson requested him to review. 'This is powerful stuff, but it might come back to bite you at the preselection next week.'

'The truth should never be something we fear.'

'I must admit, I'm not convinced,' Bower said. 'The tracking research shows the uncertainty surrounding your involvement in war crimes as a potential vote changer.'

'That's precisely why I think we should tackle it and get on the front foot.' Hudson glanced at Woodward. 'What's your take, Chrissie?'

Woodward blew out her cheeks, shaking her head. 'My advice would be to do it. Collins won't let it go. If there's a leadership challenge, they'll point the finger of blame at you.'

Hudson drew in his lips, gnawing at them, nodding.

'Are you sure you want to provide such graphic detail?' Bower asked.

'It's what happened,' Hudson said.

'I understand, but the content might unsettle some, especially kids,' Bower noted.

Hudson scoffed a smile, a wry glint in his eye. 'You think me talking about a conflict will scare kids who live in the graphic detail of Call of Duty?'

'Maybe,' Bower smiled. 'I'm just saying that what you talk about is quite confronting.'

'Okay, tone it down if you need to.'

'When are you planning on getting to your feet?' Woodward asked.

'I thought I might do it after question time.'

Woodward nodded. 'Solid plan. Do you think you might want to talk to the leader beforehand?'

'Sure, I can do that. Why?'

'Just to help him expect media after you speak and remind him to remain in the chamber.'

'Anyone else we should loop in?'

'Perhaps flick a copy to Madeleine Booker,' Woodward said. 'She can have it ready to run online once you've finished speaking. Give her an exclusive and she will owe you.'

'Owe me? No one should owe me.'

'It's the way politics works, boss,' Bower said.

Hudson shook his head. 'I'm not sure I'm cut out for a career as a politician.'

Woodward raised an eyebrow, exchanging a glance with

Bower who shrugged. 'Why would you think that?' Woodward asked.

Hudson turned away, considering the question, wiping his chin with the back of his hand. 'It's the people I have to deal with,' he said. 'You can't trust anyone. They lie to your face. There are schemes to unseat me, even within my party. I'm not sure I can accomplish anything in an environment like that where I'm watching my back and having to do favours so that people will owe you.' Hudson air quoted.

Bower nodded, while Woodward's expression shifted to one of slight disbelief. 'Are you serious?' she asked. 'Do you think politics should be free from conflict and challenges for achieving things for the nation? Is that what you believe?

Hudson didn't respond, resting his head on his hand.

'You are a soldier for heaven's sake,' Woodward continued. 'You think you're so privileged that politicians should be immune to the struggle of fighting for what's just?'

'I've never said that.'

'You just implied it,' Woodward said. 'Jack, you have a unique privilege, not as a soldier but as a lawmaker. You create laws that ensure Australians can live with a sense of security, knowing that those with integrity and moral courage can defend against those who seek to harm us. That's the battle we fight; against all opposition, against the community, even against our own party to secure a safe and prosperous future.'

Hudson winced, locking eyes with Woodward.

'You have a duty to serve the community until they say otherwise. Serving the community means you fight the horrible people who would undermine our principles and values. If you can't handle the fight and stand up for what's right, then step down. If you do have the moral courage, then don't complain that it's tough. Embrace the struggle and show us why we put our trust in you.'

Hudson avoided Woodward's gaze, shifting in his chair, while Bower tapped his fingers on the armrest, checking out his shoes. 'Chrissie, thank you,' Hudson finally said. 'You're not the first to tell me something like this. I just find the whole Machiavellian game a little unsettling.'

'That's because you are not a prince and you're living your political life as a pauper.'

'Boss, Chrissie is right,' Bower chimed in, clearing his throat. 'Our research shows your leadership favourability is high. Voters like you. They are ready to back you, but you need to be out front leading on issues.'

Hudson steepled his fingers in front of his face. 'Does that mean I should do this speech or not?'

Bower twisted his mouth. 'It's a risk, but then being a leader is risky.'

Hudson shook his head. 'That's where you're wrong. Leadership is about mitigating risk.'

'That's where you're mistaken, Jack,' Woodward said. 'Political leadership is all about risk, those who lead want us to go to the promised land, and like Moses we will follow.'

'They died,' Hudson said.

'But they did so with conviction,' Woodward said, grinning.

'Trust what Dale is doing to identify the issues. Then step up in the parliament and the electorate and tell us what you will do.'

'I reckon the first thing we should do is save the leader. Then let's get our preselection sorted so we can fight the government, who I'm sure wants the seat back.'

'They do,' said Bower. 'Though they're still mulling over who their candidate will be.'

A smile tugged at Hudson's lips. 'Thanks Chrissie.'

'Jack, Dale and I are here to help you,' Woodward said. 'Stop feeling sorry for yourself. You need to understand this is how the game works and how deals are done. Find the middle ground between those in contention and those who shape public perception. Take ownership of your perception and allow us to support you. Get into the game.'

'That just gave me shivers,' Hudson said, brushing his arms. 'Why aren't you sitting here?'

'I will one day,' Woodward replied.

Hudson pouted his bottom lip. 'Okay, folks, let's advance on the enemy and march to victory.'

CHAPTER
50

'S peaker.' MacDonald's voice cut through the hushed expectation, his gaze sweeping across the chamber as he began the last question of the day. 'My question is to the prime minister, and I ask, can the Prime Minister report to the House the outcome of the investigation into the alleged war crimes incident at Malakal during the Sudanese civil war?'

'Prime Minister.'

Mosely collected several papers before moving to the Despatch Box. She turned to MacDonald and bowed. 'I thank the honourable member for his important question. Allegations of war crimes, in any context, are distressing and in this case disturbing. Australians would be saddened by the allegation of war crimes in Malakal, where Australian troops allegedly murdered eleven civilians and a wounded combatant. I asked the Chief of Defence for a report on this incident. His report states, in part, that amid intense combat, our Australian special forces acquitted themselves with distinction. However, there has been a report of deaths of eleven citizens, including six children. They attributed these deaths to indiscriminate use of explosives and firepower.'

'It is vital the recent appointment of the special investigator should adhere to the fundamental principle of presumed innocence.' Pausing, she looked out at the chamber, her gaze shifting. 'I remain eager to ensure all our men and women who pull on a uniform in no way feel reflected upon by the actions alleged by a small cohort within our military. It is vital we provide our serving men and women the support they need. They have earned our respect, and we should provide our thanks for their service.'

'Hear. Hear.'

Leaning forward, Mosely's tone hardened. 'I will also ask the special investigator to review all government communications. We need to ensure that the minister, and indeed the former prime minister, did not sanction this alleged criminal act.' A commotion throbbed from the opposition benches. Mosely held her ground, her gaze intense and focused on Chopra. 'I trust the leader of the opposition will embrace this inquiry, should he have nothing to conceal.' The Speaker intervened, restoring order, yet Mosely's words still hung in the air. 'It appears, from the noise, the opposition may have something to hide.'

With silence restored, Mosely cast a pointed look toward

Hudson. 'Mr Speaker, I have one more directive for the special investigator. I would like them to dispel the cloud of rumours and allegations that surround our esteemed colleague and veteran, the Member for Gellibrand.'

Hudson's attention snapped up from his notes, his eyes locking on Mosely's as he twirled a pen.

'I believe the honourable member will welcome the opportunity to clear his name and reassure the public,' Mosely continued. 'I intend for this investigation to conclude before the next election, granting the honest people of Gellibrand the chance to judge their accidental representative with greater clarity and conviction.'

Mosely turned, addressing the chamber. 'These issues of moral integrity and courage are essential for the nation's well-being. I will not step back in finding the truth and those who are involved should not shield themselves in the dark shadows but step forward into the light and assure us all there is no substance to these allegations.

'In conclusion, the ambassador of South Sudan has contacted me, calling for a comprehensive, impartial, and transparent inquiry into the alleged war crimes. I agree with this request made by the ambassador. I now ask that further questions be added to the notice paper.'

Ramon Chopra darted to the Despatch Box. 'Mr Speaker, on indulgence. I emphatically reject outright the baseless insinuations the prime minister has made upon both the previous government and me as the defence minister. I also dismiss the smear she has made on our colleague, the Member for Gelli-brand. I repudiate her assertion that we are trying to hide or hinder any investigation. Nothing could be further from the truth.'

As Chopra returned to his seat, Mosely prepared to leave the chamber, but not before casting a scornful glance across the aisle, then said, 'One will learn that we, on this side, do not accept accusations of murder and do not take allegations of baby killers among us too kindly.'

Chopra was about to object when he heard a loud voice from the back of the chamber.

'Mr Speaker.'

'The Member for Gellibrand?'

'Speaker, I would like to accept the offer of the prime minister and make a statement to the House concerning her assessment of me in her answer to the last question.'

Mosely paused her exit from the chamber and resumed her seat. Windsor pouted his lips as he glanced at MacDonald. When Raffles turned to glance at him, he winked and nodded.

'The member should seek leave to make a statement,' the speaker said.

'I seek leave to make a statement.'

'Is leave granted?'

For a few moments, several government ministers conferred with the prime minister before the leader of the house moved the Despatch Box. 'Speaker, leave is granted on the condition the member restricts his statement to what the prime minister was addressing.'

'Leave is granted,' the Speaker reaffirmed.

Hudson observed the by-play across the chamber and realised that he needed to put an end to the destructive leadership game he was caught up in. 'Speaker, I want to address the issues raised by the prime minister and refute the implied allegations of war crimes.' He paused. 'How do I know these claims are false? Because I was there.'

As murmurs circulated with some members voicing their objections, Hudson's gaze remained fixed on his speech notes. The House fell into silence.

'Prior to the four-day battle of Malakal I commanded D squadron, which was assigned to secure an airfield along with other coalition troops prior to the major offensive. My orders were to capture combatants securing them for further interrogation. Command ordered me to not engage in direct action that could endanger the lives of civilians. Our orders were to seize and control an area to ensure the safe deployment of personnel. The aim of the whole deployment was to secure the airfield within three hours, as other troops would deploy and begin an offensive, which ultimately lasted four days.

Hudson's gaze lifted, locking onto the prime minister. 'I directed a troop of fifteen special forces to secure the northern perimeter of the airfield. I set up reconnaissance posts and deployed my men to overcome the expected resistance. We were soon engaged, by an entrenched enemy from three bunkers. Our job was to silence those positions. My troopers sustained fierce resistance, and the brutal reality is my battle plan never survived the first shot.'

Madeleine Booker was watching from her media gallery office following Hudson's speech from the papers he provided her before question time. Several colleagues joined her.

'Under heavy fire, we secured the first bunker, silencing nine combatants and capturing three, which we tethered for interrogation. One of these captured combatants explained through an interpreter that his family was being held as a shield by the enemy. He sustained wounds in his abdomen and hand. He was coherent enough to express major concern for his family and pleaded for us to save them.

'I discussed the challenge with my NCOs and decided we should reconnoitre the area. I advised our medic to release the combatant to my care, and directed him back to the communications position. We escorted the combatant to show us where his family was held. I took him to a knoll overlooking a small village cluster of maybe seven solid buildings. He told me his family was being held in the rooftop room of the largest building. I made a command decision to determine the safety of the family by moving to it. I came under heavy enemy fire from various sites before reaching the building. From the high point of the building, I radioed enemy positions to our machine-gunners. We then overcame enemy resistance and secured the building. The Sudanese interpreter joined me with the still tethered prisoner. They pointed out a doorway on the roof, so I cut his ties and indicated to him to take me to his family.'

'He led me through a massive, draped opening then along a darkened passage to a large candle lit room where I found a dozen women and children cowering in a corner. It surprised me they did not react with joy to see their husband and father coming to save them. As I turned to check the prisoner, I recognised he now held an explosives vest with his hand ready to detonate the bomb. In a split second, I made a choice. I responded with lethal force, eliminating the threat.'

Hudson's eyes found Mosely's again. 'The incident identified in parliament as the alleged murder of a wounded prisoner was this event. But the story doesn't end there.'

Mosely wiped her mouth.

'As I checked the prisoner's vital signs, a young boy came at me, snatched the vest and scampered to the others still cowering in the corner. As he reached them, he tossed it to a woman, possibly his mother, who cried Allahu Akbar as she detonated the explosives.'

Hudson paused for a sip of water, composing his voice. 'The group suppressed the impact of the explosion. As the shockwave washed over me, it tossed me against a wall. The explosion injured my back and also ruptured my eardrum. Once the room cleared of smoke, several enemy combatants entered and dragged me to another room. It seemed my ordeal was far from over. They beat me then stripped away my equipment, ripping open my clothes. They burnt my chest and sliced and nicked my shoulders to weaken my arms.'

Mosely now gripped her face, her hand covering her mouth and nose.

'On seeing the explosion, my sergeant, Charles O'Brien, led a small recovery team to extricate what they then believed to be my corpse. The creed of the special services is to never leave a man behind. I'm thrilled the sergeant took this action. Otherwise, I would not be speaking to you today.'

'Hear, hear,' Chopra said.

'Let me read O'Brien's citation for a gallantry medal, and I quote. "Sergeant O'Brien led his team in silencing the enemy's position while under heavy small-arms fire. Then, he took it upon himself to rescue his seriously wounded commander. With disregard for his own safety, he drew the fire from an enemy machine-gun position with bullets hitting the surrounding ground as he carried his commander to safety."'

Hudson continued after scanning the chamber. 'While this rescue action was happening, Corporal William Tyrrell moved from cover and charged the enemy. He used his automatic weapon to eliminate two machine-gun positions. In one instance, he engaged in a hand-to-hand exchange with the enemy, using his pistol at close range. With his bravery, he drew the enemy's fire away from the rescue extraction point. In addition, he rescued the interpreter who was now wounded. They described his actions as being of the highest selfless act and in keeping with the finest traditions of the special services.'

Hudson took another drink and winked at Chopra, all eyes upon him.

'We awarded Corporal Tyrrell the Victoria Cross for his bravery. I owe my life to both him and Sergeant O'Brien. Mr Speaker, a nation needs people who run to the sound of guns who are prepared to fight and destroy our enemies. These brave souls are prepared to die by doing so. Those soldiers exist and serve or have served our nation with distinction. They have done nothing wrong and we in this place should uphold their valour and their vital mission to protect us.'

Hudson's voice held both sorrow and resolve. 'To all those who cast shadows on our soldiers' actions, I say this: war is brutal and unforgiving. Yet, we must not allow our leaders to exploit the media and present only fragments of the truth for their own gain. History says there will be more wars, and we must be ready. We do not need our nation's leaders questioning the moral courage of our soldiers for cheap political gain. War is violent, escalatory and degrading, and some of our lethal force can lose their way and become hard of heart, especially after multiple deployments.'

Hudson's gaze locked onto the speaker. 'Mr Speaker, during that offensive, I did not seek permission to save a family that day. I did not ask for approval to take decisive action that required immediate leadership and sacrifice. And I have no expectation that any special investigator will find me culpable of wrongdoing. What I find, however, is an attempt to undermine the leader of the opposition and his exemplary leadership.'

'Hear, hear.'

Hudson's voice grew resolute as he addressed the chamber. 'We must not allow rumour and unfounded claims to taint this House. We cannot allow baseless accusations to erode the faith we have in our own colleagues.' He looked toward Mosely, with the tension between them obvious. 'To suggest war crimes during a day when bravery was recognised with our highest medals for valour, is a sombre moment in our parliamentary history.'

Drawing in a steadying breath, Hudson concluded. 'Mr Speaker, I apologise for the requirement of diminishing the Office of the Prime Minister, but enough is enough. Those who peddled rumours as truth, regardless of their status or affiliation, should bear the shame brought upon this parliament.'

CHAPTER
51

Dale Bower spent the entire day briefing Hudson, ensuring he was well-prepared for the impending pres-election meeting. Gathering intelligence from his covert sources, he determined Jack's chances were slim, but not insurmountable. The key was to instil confidence in the delegates regarding his campaign strategy. An unexpected request for a meeting at Senator Morgan's city office an hour before the scheduled preselection presentation puzzled them both.

Bower dropped Jack off, promising to wait outside to ensure he would make it to the meeting on time. Hudson adjusted his cuffs and straightened his tie as he entered the senator's meeting room. Before him sat Morgan, Collins, the state president, and the president of the women's division. Seating himself opposite the panel, he offered a polite smile, waiting to hear the purpose of the summons.

'Jack, while we welcome your election victory,' the president began after exchanging pleasantries, 'we have concerns. It seems you're not dedicating enough time to your electorate. There's a perception that you're more focused on Parliament than your local constituents. We'd like to hear your response to these claims.'

As Hudson assessed the panel, a hint of a smile played on his lips. 'I have a preselection meeting in less than an hour. How long do you think we need to outline my activities?'

'We will stay here until convinced you are worthy of representing the electorate,' the president said.

Hudson's eyebrows arched, pouting his lips and nodding. 'If I understand you correctly, I need to justify myself before you allow me to stand before delegates seeking their approval.'

'At the moment, they don't count,' Collins interjected.

'Sixty volunteers don't count,' Hudson mused. 'Now that's very curious.'

'Jackson, perhaps I can clarify,' Morgan said. 'We are seeking reassurance from you that the party will win the seat. We're considering investing money and resources into Gellibrand.'

Hudson shifted his gaze to Morgan, studying her for a moment. 'You get into a little trouble, Senator?' Hudson joked, tapping his cheek.

Morgan shifted in her chair, recalling her amazing previous evening with Henari. 'I bumped into a door this morning while my hands were full of mugs of tea for my staff.'

'Looks nasty.'

'I'm fine, let's move on.'

'Folks, I'm not sure what you want from me. I'm happy to step you through the last campaign and the reluctance of the local party to assist.' Hudson cast an eye toward Collins. 'I can also tell you about party meetings being held when I'm required in Canberra. I can also talk about the disrespectful attitude toward my staff when they wish to report to a local meeting,' Hudson took a deliberate breath, still glaring at Collins. 'I can tell you about headlines in the Chronicle claiming I'm never in the electorate. Yet I have hundreds of photos on my Facebook page with local constituents at my town hall events. Shall I go on?'

The president exchanged a perplexed look with the women's division president. 'We received advice that you've stopped attending community events, especially the local mother's group,' the women's president stated, her face severe. 'Do you have something against women?'

Hudson inhaled, then exhaled through his nose. 'The women's group of which you speak is one of twenty-seven in the electorate and has six members. Of the other twenty-six, I have started community awards in all but two. Since my election, I have engaged a back-to-work intern program in my office for women seeking to improve their office skills and assisted in sixty-seven women finding local employment. The other point to make is that the mother's group you refer organises their meetings when I am in Canberra. Most of the members are party members and have access to me through other forums.'

'These are just smoke and mirror responses,' Collins said.

'The bottom-line is that we want you to work harder and be more visible in the electorate.'

Hudson's eyes locked onto Collins. 'Eddie, you're right. Let me clarify things for you. If you want me to address every point, let's do it. I can discuss first the previous campaign and the local party's reluctance to help.

'Jackson, we don't need to be doing that,' Morgan interrupted, reading the mood. 'We consider it unnecessary for you to have to a competitor against you at preselection. Especially since you are the first National to hold the seat. Our preference is that we ratify you tonight with no trouble and we will withdraw Alice Collins' nomination.'

Hudson leaned back, his eyes scanning the panel. 'That would be a great vote of confidence for the work we have done over the last few months.'

'Yes, it would,' said the president. 'We would like you to agree to a campaign program. This plan would include benchmarks, and if you do not meet them, you agree to step down, allowing us to select a more cooperative candidate.'

Hudson frowned at the president, narrowing his eyes and nodding, beginning to decipher the game. 'I'm in your hands. Set out what you want and place deadlines so we can measure performance and I'll be happy to comply.'

The president glanced at the senator, who nodded. He then sought agreement from the women's division president, who scowled a nod. It was Collins who continued to reject the idea.

'I tell you what, Eddie,' Hudson said smiling. 'You write a list right now and I shall sign it. How's that?'

'Jackson, that is very liberal of you. Isn't it, Edward?'

Collins didn't respond.

Morgan's calm demeanour returned. 'I just happen to have a page here that I would like you to consider and sign where indicated,' Morgan said, sliding a sheet of paper across the table.

Hudson intercepted the sheet, scanning the tasks listed. He checked his watch, then withdrew a pen from his pocket. With a swift signature, he passed it back to the president.

'Thank you, Jack,' the president said. 'I suspect we won't need to refer to this again.'

'It specifies a month,' Hudson said. 'So, I would expect it back at that time.'

'Of course,' the president confirmed.

'As I understand it now,' Hudson glanced about the panel. 'They will confirm my endorsement at the meeting this evening. Do I give the brief speech or the long one?'

Collins frowned. 'Do the short one and don't waste their time.'

'Understood.' He looked at Collins. 'And Eddie ... you'll be there, won't you?'

'I'll be there. Just don't prolong the event; we are already running late.'

As Hudson stepped from Bower's car in front of party

headquarters in Exhibition Street, a cluster of journalists rushed to him.

'Are you confident, Jack?'

'The party will decide tonight.'

'What are your chances, Jack?'

'The good people of Gellibrand will make the right decision for them.'

'Is Senator Morgan behind this showdown?'

'There is no showdown.'

'Do you support Ramon Chopra?'

'I support the leader.'

Hudson pushed his way through the pack, past the cameras, and up the steps into the building. Woodward was waiting as he entered the lobby.

'What's happened? Where have you been?'

'I just did a deal with the party.'

'What deal?'

'Alice Collins has stepped down. I am standing unopposed.'

'Why?'

'No clue. But hopefully, this will be over within the next thirty minutes. Let's celebrate with dinner, shall we?'

'Stay focused, Jack. Let's not think about dinner until you secure your endorsement.'

Hudson nodded, stepping into the elevator and waved goodbye as the doors slid closed. They reopened on the fourth floor, and he moved from the elevator into the meeting room with anxious members waiting. Without hesitation, he headed to the lectern. He switched on the microphone and addressed the members. 'My apologies for the delay. I have been directed to provide a condensed overview of the past few months and a brief outline of what we plan for the campaign.'

Hudson scoped out the plan and spoke until some members began shifting in their seats twenty minutes later. He closed the address and asked for questions.

Eddie Collins was first on his feet. 'Jack, based upon that brief presentation, I believe I'm speaking on behalf of the delegates when I say that was inadequate. You've given us little insight into voting trends, strategies to increase your visibility, and how you plan to engage with constituents. If there was another candidate, I couldn't endorse you. How can you improve?'

Hudson scanned the room, his mind racing for a response as Collins resumed his seat. He noticed a few nods with others shaking their heads lowering their eyes from his gaze. 'I'm sorry Eddie, given the absence of other contenders I assumed we all wanted a swift resolution.' He stared at Collins who was sitting to the side, legs crossed, the palm of a hand cupping his face, his eyes twinkling with a leering smile.

'I can see some delegates share your sentiment, so let me step through the entire campaign plan.' He moved to the desk where he left his leather satchel, pulling out a thick spiral bound document with Gellibrand Campaign imprinted on the cover. 'This is the campaign plan and allows me to connect the PowerPoint presentation for those who prefer visuals.'

Hudson moved to the projector, fitting his small USB, working the tabs to bring up the presentation. Then, like addressing troop leaders before deploying them into a hot landing zone, he led them through the minutiae of the campaign. He covered all aspects, including the resources required. He distributed paperwork for each delegate to complete, now obliged to join the campaign.

By the time Hudson finished collecting the personal details of each delegate, almost two hours later, Collins had had enough and called for the vote.

'Delegates, I would like to thank Jack for his thorough presentation, and perhaps, ask him to consider condensing it next time.'

'I thought I did so earlier, which you said wasn't enough.'

'I now call upon the motion to endorse Jackson Hudson as the National Party's candidate for the electorate of Gellibrand at the coming federal election. All those of that opinion say aye, to the contrary no. I think the ayes have it. I declare Jackson Hudson the candidate for Gellibrand.'

As delegates began moving to leave, Hudson was quick to the microphone.

'Delegates, thank you for your support. Please feel assured I will not let you down.'

———

TWENTY MINUTES later Hudson was hosting a late dinner with Woodward and Bower. A bottle of French champagne popped for toasting. 'Thank you both, and if we win, I will be in your debt forever,' Hudson declared as they clinked glasses.

'Forever sounds like a long commitment,' Bower said.

'You get me the votes and we will be together forever, Dale.'

Bower blushed while Woodward let out a husky chuckle. 'I expect a senate position in New South Wales.'

'All possible if we win, Gellibrand. I think the new prime minister will help you attain your goal.'

'Here's cheers to you, Jack,' Woodward said, holding up her glass.

'And to you gorgeous.' Hudson said, with a warm smile as he clinked her glass..

Woodward blushed.

'Can we eat?' asked Bower. 'I'm so hungry.'

CHAPTER
52

Alexander Windsor leaned back in his office chair, his gaze focused on the sun casting long shadows across the parliamentary precinct, canvassing a picturesque scene contrasting with the storm brewing within the walls of his mind. He swivelled around to face his colleague, Peter Raffles, his expression a mixture of determination and unease.

'Hudson ruined everything with his speech.' Windsor sipped his coffee. 'Then what happened with Morgan's assurance of sacking him at preselection? Nothing. She talks a big game, that one, and we see very little action in return. Just like a penny-banger, she promises an enormous explosion, but we only get a small fizzer.'

'More like a Catherine wheel,' Raffles smiled, scratching his chin. 'All smoke and colour; just spins out of control and goes nowhere.'

'The election is creeping closer, and timing becomes critical,' Windsor asserted. 'We need to reshape the troops and bring in talent that can provide us the leverage to take over.'

'Like you, do you mean?'

'Young and enthusiastic, that's what we need.' Windsor laughed. 'All we have is a fat bloke who loves Tim Tam biscuits.'

'He has the numbers.'

'Does he though?' Windsor said. 'Why don't we test them?'

'How do you suggest we do that?' Raffles drained his coffee.

'Simple. We test Hudson,' Windsor said, a spark of mischief in his eyes. 'Let's see how firm his support is.'

Raffles sighed. 'Your ideas have a way of getting us into unexpected, no-win circumstances. Remember the last one?'

Windsor snickered, his eyes dancing. 'Ah, but that was a small price to pay for the lessons learned.'

'Hudson is becoming a potential problem, isn't he?' Raffles admitted, nodding. 'He's been here five minutes and he already has the national media attention. Just as Stephanie warned he would.'

Windsor's gaze turned thoughtful. 'Can he win the election, though? Gellibrand is supposed to be a stronghold for the government.'

Raffles spoke after a moment of silence. 'You know, I might pay a visit to the leader. Get a feel for the waters, so to speak.'

'Just make sure you don't get swept away,' Windsor quipped, a smirk tugging at his lips.

Raffles chuckled, rising from his seat. 'Let's hope I can stay afloat in this turbulent political sea.'

As Raffles headed for the door, Windsor offered a parting shot. 'Remember, Peter, there's no lifeguard is on duty.'

————

RAMON CHOPRA RECLINED in his office chair, enjoying a cup of tea paired with a chocolate Tim Tam, a small indulgence amidst the pressures of leadership. He looked up as Peter Raffles tapped on the door, then waved him in.

'I was just thinking about you, Peter,' Chopra said, sipping his tea.

'Good thoughts, I hope.'

'Hmm, good thoughts?' Chopra smiled. 'Some good and others are not so good. Leadership inspires a variety of reflections.'

'About leadership?'

'Leadership, of course,' Chopra said, chuckling as he bit the chocolate biscuit. 'Plus, your goals and current plans.'

Raffles raised an eyebrow. 'Should I be concerned?'

'Concerned? Perhaps. Intrigued? Absolutely. I've been thinking about the challenges that lie ahead.'

Raffles shifted in his chair, his posture alert. 'Challenges in what sense?'

Chopra leaned back, savouring the biscuit's chocolate. 'Leadership, of course. Your ambitions and the plans you're orchestrating.'

Raffles hesitated, then asked, 'what's on your mind, Ramon?'

Chopra's eyes narrowed. 'I've been considering our leadership strategy. What we're made of. What we're willing to do.'

Raffles chuckled. 'Sounds like deep thoughts for a cup of tea and a biscuit.'

Chopra's smile held a touch of humour. 'There's more to it than meets the eye.'

'Concerns about my goals?' Raffles inquired.

Chopra's chuckle radiated warmth and comfort. 'You know, Peter, I've learned that timing is the key to success in leadership. Timing determines winners and losers.'

Raffles nodded. 'That's a truth we can't ignore.'

Chopra took another sip of tea, then met Raffles' gaze. 'So, my friend, what do we do about it?'

'We all have ambition, Choppy,' Raffles said. 'It's about timing and recognising opportunities.'

'That's what I'm thinking. You want my job, but we are too close to the federal election for you to challenge, because we have a slight chance of winning.'

'You think it's time for a change?' Raffles asked.

Chopra's smile seemed cryptic. 'You want the job, and I want to keep it. This is a gamble with small odds but with dire consequences.'

'Not confident in our chances of winning the election?' Raffles prodded.

'Yes, I am,' Chopra said. 'It'll be a battle, a seat-by-seat struggle. We need just six to secure victory.'

'Do you believe your leadership will get us over the line?'

'Do you think yours will?' Chopra sneered.

Raffles hesitated, then answered, 'I have a chance, just like anyone else who thinks your leadership is wavering.'

Chopra examined his rival while finishing his tea and biscuit. 'Here's the reality, Peter. If we win the election, I know you and your allies will come for me, sooner or later.'

Raffles speculated on how much Windsor had revealed to Chopra.

'Here's my proposition,' Chopra continued, leaning back. 'Let's settle it now. A leadership spill. You and me.' He pointed, touching his chest. 'If you do me now, I may as well leave the parliament at the election.'

Raffles blinked, then shook his head. 'Are you suggesting what I think you are suggesting?'

Chopra scoffed. 'And what's that?'

'You want a leadership spill?'

Chopra cocked his head and shrugged. 'Why not? You have been doing the numbers for months and waiting for the right time, so why don't we get it done?'

Raffles moved his jaw as if chewing gum, sizing up the leader and questioning if he was being set up. 'When?'

'I'm thinking before question time.'

Raffles grimaced. 'I may have to talk to a few people.'

Chopra released a hearty chortle. 'That's got to be a joke,' he said. 'You and Windsor have been talking to everyone with a vote. In some cases, a touch of political bullying exists. Don't tell me you're getting cold feet.'

'It's not that.'

'Then why are you hesitating?'

Raffles shrugged. 'Maybe because this is unexpected. Perhaps something else is going on.'

'I can assure you, if we are to change leadership, then it has to be done today so we can stop your team from leaking to the media.'

'My team isn't doing that.'

Chopra pinched and squeezed his nose. 'There's only one condition.'

'What's that?'

'The loser leaves the parliament,' Chopra said, studying Raffles, enjoying the sudden expression of fear in his rival's eyes as they flicked about.

Raffles cleared his throat. 'I will keep my counsel on that decision.'

'Pete, it will not work like that,' Chopra said, smiling. 'I either have that agreement in writing or I won't be calling a spill.'

Raffles breathed in deep. 'When do you want it?'

'I just happen to have a copy for your approval right here.'

Chopra flicked open his folder and drew out a sheet, passing it to Raffles, who scanned it.

'Can I make a call?' Raffles asked.

'Of course you can.'

Raffles left the room to talk to his advisers and perhaps squeeze in a call to Windsor.

———

An hour earlier Jack Hudson requested a meeting with the leader. He wanted to express his gratitude for Chopra's endorsement and unwavering support during his preselection and explain the document he signed.

'It means nothing, Ramon,' Hudson countered when Chopra challenged his judgement in signing the agreement. 'It's too late to alter the endorsement. They are now incapacitated and pose no substantial threat.'

Chopra nodded; his lips pouted duck-like. 'This means they can use this against you at any time.'

Hudson's response was sharp. 'What can they do? Give it to the media and expose themselves?'

'They could give it to the other side,' Chopra said, tapping his fingers together. 'Who do you think has been orchestrating the campaign against the military that ensnared you?'

'I thought it was the government wanting to do a job on you.'

'Not likely. Why would they create a potential issue for themselves mere months before the election?' Chopra said, leaning back in his chair. 'No, this campaign is designed to undermine my leadership, so a challenge is imminent, I'd wager.'

Hudson nodded, then cocked his head as if he beginning to understand messages he had been receiving. 'That being the case, then I should tell you I've heard whispers. There will be a challenge.'

'When?'

'Soon,' Hudson said

'Who?'

'Alex Windsor seems active working the numbers. I have a feeling Steph Morgan might be keen for a change of leader.'

Chopra raised his eyebrows. 'I thought you were a Morgan soldier.'

'She may have spoken for me last time. I now realise she wants me out of the place.'

Chopra gawked at Hudson before stroking his jaw with the back of his fingers. 'That surprises me. I thought you were one of hers.'

Hudson smiled. 'I support the leader.'

'What should your leader do to end this campaign to get rid of me?'

'Frontal attack.'

'How would that work?'

'Bullies always back off when you stand your ground,' Hudson said. 'If I were you, I'd call them out.'

'Risky.'

'It seems to me they are trying to weaken you by incrementally slicing off your flanks, piece by piece, so your supporters begin questioning your leadership. They then listen to other voices and before you know it, chaos is within the ranks, and we're all decimated.'

'I'm not sure I should expose myself.'

'Ramon,' Hudson leaned forward, resting his elbows on his knees, 'if you don't get control then you die. You are just deferring the inevitable. Take control of your leadership under your terms. Attack.'

'Easy for you to say.'

Hudson nodded. 'Yes, it is, but if you don't, you lose control. Control the controllables is the mantra in any organisation. Politics is no different. Seize control.'

'If I do, will you support me?'

'I support the leader.'

'But what if someone else assumes the role?'

Hudson grinned. 'For that to happen, they would need to secure leadership. I support the leader.'

'Regardless of who that leader might be?'

'Embrace risk and call a leadership spill,' Hudson said. 'Win or lose you walk out with respect and leave a solid legacy.'

'It's an unprecedented move.'

'That's precisely why a leader leads.'

————

RETURNING TO CHOPRA'S OFFICE, Raffles smirked as he settled back into his chair, sliding the now signed agreement across the desk. 'Ready to shed the gloves and enter the ring with me?'

Chopra's response was a scoff, a mix of amusement and determination. 'We shall see.'

Raffles pushed. 'Should we proceed before or after question time?'

Chopra's response was unequivocal. 'Right now.'

CHAPTER

53

'Does this mean you have to resign from parliament?' Windsor asked.

Raffles scoffed at the question. 'Hitler said of Chamberlain's peace in our time declaration that it was only a piece of paper, nothing more.'

'Phew. That's good,' Windsor said, hiding his disappointment.

'One vote,' Raffles said. 'Just one damn vote.'

Windsor speculated. 'I would wager that vote was Hudson's.'

'An ironic twist, isn't it?' Raffles sniffed. 'We celebrated his victory in the by-election and now we can't wait to get rid of him. If it weren't for him, I reckon I would be leader.'

'Pete, you know you're the best bet for the party.' Windsor scratched his grimacing face. 'What happens if we win the election?'

'It's unlikely we'll secure a victory under Choppy's.'

'But, what if we win?'

'Then we'll have to buckle down and give it our best, and if he falters like Rudd, we'll have to bring him down.'

Windsor brought his clasped hands to his face to hide his smirk. 'What do we do about Hudson?' he asked.

'I'm not aligned with the senator's perspective,' Raffles said. 'We may need his seat to win government.'

'I can manage him,' Windsor said. 'If he wins, we'll keep him busy and out of our hair.'

'Perhaps I could have him as my parliamentary secretary?'

'You're supposed to be resigning, remember?'

Raffles chuckled. 'Choppy knows I won't. He was testing how serious I was.'

'Sneaky sod.'

'An excellent move, because it did put the wind up me.'

'What's our next move?'

'Simple. We win the election.'

'I'M TOLD your vote may have been the difference,' Booker said.

Hudson smiled as he stirred his coffee at Aussie's Cafe. 'I have always said, I support the leader.'

'So, what now for you?'

'Winning the preselection marked a significant step for team Hudson. We can now focus on winning Gellibrand and, with a bit of luck, forming government.'

'Are you expecting more challenges from within the party?'

Hudson didn't respond.

'We're off the record here, Jack,' Booker said, reassuring him.

Hudson managed a smile. 'I'm sure we are. It's just that I don't know.'

'Who's applying the pressure?'

'I'm still not sure who is driving the local folks, but my suspicion leads to Senator Morgan.'

'I don't get it. She seems supportive.'

Hudson sipped his latte, enjoyed the flavour then sipped again. 'Maybe I pose a threat to her?' Hudson said, without enthusiasm.

Booker scoffed. 'I would have thought no one threatens her.'

'Yeah, maybe.'

Booker drained her cappuccino. 'One of the many reasons I wanted to talk to you was to determine your position on the union bashing bill.'

'Who refers to it as the 'union bashing' bill?' Hudson asked.

'It's centred on unions and employer groups exploiting their business model taking advantage of the zero income tax arrangements,' Booker said. 'It means unions will have to change their business model.'

Hudson nodded. 'What I don't get,' he said, 'is why would the government want to hurt a major source of revenue for their party?'

'Do you think there are links between Campbell's death and the legislation?'

'The police say it was a misadventure death.'

'They have no proof otherwise. They say he drowned, but I reckon the manner he hit his head would have caused it,' said Booker.

'The manner? What do you mean?'

'His injuries suggest he may have been driven into the rocks.'

Hudson raised his eyebrows and cocked his head. 'He was a big man,' he said. 'Hard to lift and toss I would have thought.'

'Ever play rugby?'

'No.'

'It's called a spear tackle. They rub them out for weeks if they do it to an opponent.'

'You think he was gang tackled and speared headfirst onto the rocks?' Hudson said.

'The possibility of that happening is just as plausible as the police's claim he fell nearly two metres headfirst,' said Booker. 'I would have thought there would be damage to his arms or hands from protecting himself.'

'Yeah maybe,' Hudson lifted his coffee. 'Do you think someone associated with the unions murdered him?'

'Union. The BWU?'

'What would be their motive?'

'They ran a candidate against you.'

'They won preselection, so what?' Hudson finished his coffee. 'Why would they do Campbell in just to get the seat?'

'To exert influence over the bill.'

'But they don't need a parliament member for that.'

'This is what I don't understand,' Booker said. 'Killing Campbell who was a union man ends their influence. Senator Morgan's committee will report soon, so why get rid of your influence?'

'Maybe they didn't?'

'Then who did? Who would want Campbell out of the picture?'

'You're the investigative journalist – maybe you need to investigate.'

'Very cute, Jack,' Booker smiled. 'That's why I'm talking to you.'

'I'm just a humble backbencher trying hard not to be a oncer. What would I know?'

'You're on the committee and must know what's happening.'

'What do you want to know?'

'Why has the Chair taken leave?'

'Sick leave I believe. Some sort of mental health issue.'

'Which conveniently allows the opposition to chair the inquiry,' Booker said, resting her chin in her palm.

'Why is that convenient?'

'It'll be an opposition recommendation to disallow the bill.'

'Meaning?'

'The government can run a campaign against the opposition during the election, pushing the perception it approves of union fraud.'

'But the bill is about business enterprises, not fraud,' said Hudson.

'You think that will be the message from the government?'

Hudson nodded, learning more each day. 'You think this is a set up?'

'Win-win for the government if I read it right,' Booker said. 'Leverage the opposition into rejecting the bill helping them during the campaign. Or sending the BWU to the wall by forcing them to divest their assets, ensuring they lose their power within the party.'

'So why kill Campbell?'

'He was in the way,' Booker said.

'Of the government or the union?'

'Both, maybe,' she said.

'Why are you talking to me?'

'Two reasons,' Booker said. 'I want to know if you have had any pressure from anyone concerned with the inquiry?'

'Nothing.'

'And the second,' Booker paused for a moment, studying Hudson as she locked eyes. 'On second thoughts,' she dropped back in her chair, 'the second point is not important at the moment.'

'Fair enough.' Hudson moved to leave. 'If I get any information about the committee, I'll let you know. We meet in a few days. Morgan wants to advise us of her recommendation.'

Booker nodded, acknowledging Hudson's willingness to cooperate. Hudson walked away. She sighed as she watched him.

CHAPTER
54

People in the street can hear the throaty rumble of a Harley Davidson exhaust before they see it. When there are two, the commotion is irritating. When there is a mob, there is trouble. A gang of bikies set off earlier in the day and now thundered into Williamstown's tourist precinct, roaring exhausts shattering the peace and rattling windows of local shops. There must have been about fifteen riders. No shop owner wanted them to stop. They figured the bikies would parade past the police station, displaying their contempt, and head for a bar for a few beers. Britannia Hotel, their usual haunt, disappointed them when it upgraded to hipster decor. Still, it was just a stone's throw from their western compound on Aitken Street. Some parked their machines outside the bar while others lined their machines near their compound.

Henari arranged for Rusnek and his crew to meet at the compound to discuss all political and business matters. After waiting more than an hour, he suggested his crew have a beer. They settled into their favourite bar with its view on the street, allowing ever-watchful eyes to scan for trouble. The pub's owner remained apprehensive when his big spending clients were around. He knew they never tolerated aggravation from anyone brave enough to cross them. Construction workers never back down, so he hoped the gazetted Rostered Day Off would not have them arriving for a beer.

The bikies were onto their third round of drinks when several vans pulled up across the street. No one paid much concern until men began stepping out of the three vans. The pub owner winced when he saw someone twirling an axe handle like a baton.

'Boys, take it outside,' he shouted.

Henari barked several commands, his crew filed out to confront the threat. The bikies gathered as a tight group, sizing up the twenty workers who seemed intent on seeking trouble perhaps as retribution for an incident at a construction site the previous day.

Calling for attention, the crew's sergeant-at-arms raised his voice, and they stepped into a V-shaped formation. In a haka-like fashion, the bikers started slapping themselves in rhythm, reminiscent of a traditional Māori war dance. While slapping thighs and chests, stomping their right foot to the rhythm of the powerful chant, the men countered with a response as the sergeant continued bellowing.

The crew began shouting, 'Ka mate, ka mate! Ka ora! Ka ora!', moving up in formation on the workers, blowing forcefully, wide eyes, extended tongues, some workers stepped back, while others tightened their grip on weapons.

The haka's cry intimidated even innocent spectators, scurrying elsewhere in search of safety, prompting someone to call the police. The pub owner began sealing doors, hoping the combatants wouldn't smash his windows.

Amidst the looming cloud of battle, tension thickened as both groups were ready to crack heads at any moment. But just before it erupted, an SUV screeched into the street, coming to a sudden halt between the two factions.

Rusnek stepped from the cabin.

'All right, enough!'

The crew continued their intensity, blowing cheeks, thrusting tongues, wide eyed, bracing for battle.

'Back off! Both of ya,' Rusnek ordered.

For a moment, they hovered on the brink of violence, both sides poised for a fight. But then, when the tension seemed unbearable, Henari shouted a command from the rear. The crew members retreated, straightening as they did so. They remained cautious but acted as if nothing transpired, leaving Henari standing alone in the middle of the street.

'What's this about?' he called out at Rusnek.

'You don't know?'

'We are ready, but we would like to know why.'

'You attacked one of our building sites yesterday,' Rusnek said.

'We had business.'

'You wrecked our site office and bashed one of my men.'

'He had business.'

'We run the sites, and we do not tolerate outsiders barging in.'

Henari stepped closer. 'As I suggested, he had business with us.'

'Union business?'

'No.'

'Why do it on our site?'

'You need to ask him.'

'I would, but he is in a coma.'

'Then consider it a lesson learned.'

'Why didn't you speak with me?'

'Nothing to do with you.'

Rusnek moved toward Henari.

'Look, I know you think you can force yourselves into our union, but there are preferred ways to do that.'

'We don't need your blokes befriending us then doing the dirty.'

'What did he do?'

'He grabbed one of our girls without approval and we punished him.'

Rusnek didn't respond.

'He took what wasn't his, and we either wanted cash or restoration,' Henari said. 'He informed us in no uncertain terms to go fuck ourselves, so we paid him a visit.'

Rusnek tightened his face. 'You need to talk to me.'

'No, we don't.'

'I take care of my blokes,' Rusnek said. 'You have a dispute with them, then come to me.'

Henari glared at him.

'We are working together. Or we are not?' Rusnek said, 'You choose.'

'Seems to me you need to make the choice,' Henari said. 'I have the political influence, not you.'

Rusnek turned to walk away but paused, peering over his shoulder. 'If you have the political power as you say you do, then stop the legislation. If you do, then let's talk about unification,' he said. 'Until then, stay off my sites.'

The workers loaded back into the waiting vans and Rusnek clambered into the cabin of his SUV and drew away; the vans following. Henari watched the leaving cortege. He then gestured and beamed at his crew. 'Not a bad effort, boys, but I think we need more drill practice.'

CHAPTER
55

The gymnasium at Parliament House is for the privilege of politicians when the parliament is in session. At other times, parliamentary workers use the facilities. Madeleine Booker enjoyed a routine of swimming laps every other day when parliament was not sitting. On this day, it surprised her to find Senator Morgan slumped over the handlebars of the exercise bike, legs pumping at a rate that could have placed her in the sprint at the velodrome at the Olympics. Booker straddled the unit next to her, whirling the pedals at a more leisurely pace.

Morgan pumped her legs, raising her cadence to a furious pace. Sweat tumbled from her chin, her gaze fixed ahead, her head rigid. Booker didn't interrupt, watching the demands Morgan placed on her body. Then, as if she crossed the finishing line, the pace slackened, and the senator straightened, taking a gulp of water from her bottle.

'Oh hi, Madeleine, been there long?' she asked, gasping to control her breath.

'Long enough to be impressed.'

Morgan chuckled as she slowed further, her hands resting on her hips. 'It's good,' she said. 'My body needs a rigorous workout every day. I think I'm addicted to it.'

'How often do you do the bike?'

'I mix it up,' Morgan said. 'I do a bike session about two times a week.'

'Everything at that intensity?'

'I swim, box, lift weights and even enjoy dance classes. Whatever I can do to bring the heart rate up.'

'No wonder you're in such great shape.'

'We all have the capacity to do it,' Morgan grinned. 'Some people just don't bother. As I said, I think I am obsessed.'

'Well, good on you.'

'Just do yourself a favour and raise your rotations. You'll feel better,' Morgan advised as she stepped from her bike, plucked up her towel, mopping the wet saddle and handlebars.

'I try to swim but my shoulder is plaguing me so I thought I would ride today.'

'Keep at it.'

Morgan, sopping wet, moved to the weights station. Booker eyed her as she stood before the mirror working dumbbells. Forty minutes later she staggered off the bike, thinking a shower would do her good to refresh her burning muscles.

The change rooms were no different to any other. White tiles, wooden benches, and lockers, plenty of fluffy white towels and the smell of disinfectant. Booker sat heavily on a bench, battling to loosen her shoes. She yanked off one and was untying the other when bare feet appeared before her. She glanced up at Senator Morgan completely naked before her.

'Madeleine, I was just wondering, do you want to grab a bite?'

Booker didn't know where to look and felt self-conscious as her eyes darted over Morgan's toned body. She noticed a tattoo of a fern leaf wrapped around a hip, its stem extending from a tiny tuft of hair. Her eyes flashed past and shifted elsewhere.

'Sure, now?' Booker tried to regain her composure.

'I was thinking of dinner.' Morgan placed a hand on her hip. 'I'm in town for the last report writing of the Registered Organisations legislation tomorrow and I thought you may like a briefing.'

'Why me?' Booker gulped, avoiding the temptation to stare, now struggling to pull off her wet top.

'You have an interest in the BWU, so I thought you may like to get a briefing,' Morgan said. 'Do you want a hand with your top?'

Booker stopped struggling. 'If you wouldn't mind.'

Morgan leaned forward, grasping the bottom hem of Booker's top and whooshed it from her like a matador, revealing her sports bra.

'What time?' Booker asked.

'Early, let's book for seven if that's okay.'

'Sure, where?' Booker gnawed at her bottom lip.

'The Ottoman is always good.'

'It's expensive.'

'My treat.'

Booker smiled. 'Then it's a date. See you then.'

Morgan nodded once, turned, and headed for the showers. Booker chuckled as she ogled her.

THEY WERE PECKING on the dips and tearing bread at the restaurant. The Ottoman was famous as the location of planned leadership coups, political scandals, and policy promises at various tables over the years. Now the place was almost empty.

'What are your plans for the campaign?' Morgan asked.

'I have had a chat with my editor, and he suggested I concentrate on seats expected to change hands, which I will do,' Booker said. 'I thought I would also sniff around Gellibrand.'

'I'm afraid that's likely to go back to the government.'

'That might be the case. I like the way Hudson has gone about it.'

Morgan lifted her glass, sipping her white wine. 'In what way?'

'Oh, I don't know,' Booker said. 'The way he handled the war crimes allegation. His preselection survival. There's just something about him.'

'Is that your professional view or a perspective of a horny woman?' Morgan said, leaning forward, dunking a piece of bread.

Booker laughed. 'Professional.'

'You're right, he has something about him,' Morgan said. 'But he will be lost to the parliament if the government selects a stronger candidate.'

'I hear the other side is having a battle to select one.'

Morgan lifted her eyebrows. 'What have you heard?'

'The BWU wants a candidate. I'm told the numbers are fluid and there is talk another candidate may win.'

'Do you know who?' Morgan asked.

'No, I don't. I hear within the party there is a troubled discussion over it.'

'Troubled discussion. What a curious turn of phrase,' Morgan said. 'Who has the numbers?'

'I'm uncertain. There have been claims of branch stacking.'

Morgan smiled. 'Yes, well, those things happen.'

Booker nodded, taking a sip of wine then looking at the menu. 'What are you recommending?'

Morgan gazed at Booker.

Booker looked up and smiled. 'The Committee, what are you recommending?'

'The government should pass the legislation.'

'Seriously?'

Morgan smirked. 'Why are you shocked?'

Booker shook her head. 'Your party is against over regulation and interference in organisations. The government has proposed the bill, and you would receive praise for blocking it. It has no impact on workers.' Booker scratched an eyebrow with her thumb nail. 'I could go on.'

'That's enough,' Morgan responded. 'If we deny the government, they'll accuse us of enabling unions to rip off members. That's the issue here.'

'But the legislation is about paying a fair share of tax.'

'I know, but the perception is fraudulent activities. The government wants to regulate so they can collect more tax. If we say no, then we stand accused of abetting those shonky activities.'

'Are you facing any other pressure?'

Morgan sipped her wine. 'What have you heard?'

'Your preselection is at threat.'

'Where did you hear that?'

'A party member reached out.'

'Cockroaches live everywhere, don't they?' Morgan said, smirking.

'Journalists thrive on them,' Booker grinned.

'Let's just say I always work on my numbers. I will do whatever is necessary to maintain them.'

'Interesting,' Booker said. 'What did you have to do?'

'Nothing I didn't want to do. Let's put it that way,' Morgan said, sliding her tongue along her bottom lip. 'Quite enjoyable.'

Booker leaned back in her chair and finished the remaining wine. 'You seem to take pleasure when you can.'

Morgan eyed her for a moment and smiled. 'Would you like more wine here or on the balcony at my apartment?'

CHAPTER
56

Hudson didn't like the temporary electorate office allocated after his election. It was not as lavish as Minister Campbell's, and it was barely serviceable. Tucked away from foot and vehicle traffic along a seldom-used side street of the Williamstown's main shopping precinct. He figured if he was successful at the election he would apply to the department for a new office. He saw no point in squandering taxpayer funds if the tenancy was short term.

His primary concern was the safety of his staff and campaign volunteers parking cars in dark community carparks, making them a potential easy target for the various creatures of the night. He insisted on a protocol of staff being accompanied when leaving late at night. One late night Chrissie Woodward had a disturbing encounter with a homeless woman, prompting Hudson to double down on taking greater care with personal safety.

He didn't like the cramped offices, which did not allow for community meetings. They crammed in the campaign resources into various nooks. His military training insisted on adapting to the surroundings, so he never complained to the department, but made it clear to them his team would move if he won the election.

His key advisers ate dinner most evenings collected by Dale Bower from local restaurants. When together, they discussed campaign strategies and what they needed to do before the prime minister announced the election.

'When do you reckon Mosely will call it?' Woodward asked.

Hudson shrugged. 'What would I know?' He popped a hot chip into his mouth.

'I reckon she'll announce it after the next sitting week,' Bower said. 'The government needs to clear a few bills, and they want to respond to Morgan's recommendation. I'm not sure they want to call a parliamentary vote on the Registered Organisations bill before the election.'

Hudson stretched back in his chair, hitting the wall and readjusting. 'What's our position on it?'

Woodward glanced at him. 'What's your position?'

Before answering, Hudson gnawed at his lip. 'I reckon we should reject it.'

'Did you vote against it when the committee considered it?'

'Morgan never consulted us or took a vote.'

'Interesting.' Woodward glanced over at Bower, who was taking a massive bite of hamburger. 'What do you think?'

Bower wiped mayonnaise from his mouth as he gulped his food. 'The electorate doesn't care,' he swallowed. 'They believe unions work to enrich themselves, so if this legislation stops that, then they support it.'

'What's their view on freedom?' Hudson asked.

'So long as it doesn't break the law, they support it.'

'What if the law is wrong?'

'Voters want peace. They will give up their rights if we leave them alone.'

Hudson smirked. 'Why then do we send our troops overseas to fight for freedom?'

'They don't care,' Bower said, ready for another mouthful. 'They don't want to be bothered by it.'

'I hear a rumour from the leader's office that the party will support the legislation,' Woodward said, twirling chopsticks into a box of noodles.

'That's strange,' Hudson said, linking his hands behind his head. 'I would have thought the party would support free enterprise.'

'We do, but only some enterprises, like small business,' Bower said in between bites.

'Are you saying it's a mistake for me to speak out against the legislation?'

'We need to be cautious, Jack,' Woodward said, scooping up another mouthful of noodles.

'Caution?' Hudson glared at Woodward. 'We have been very cautious and look where that got us.'

'That was a smear campaign against you,' Bower said,

preparing his hamburger for one last assault. 'Speaking out against the leadership can mark you within the party and it is risky.'

'Huh,' Hudson sat forward, 'the same party that worked against me during the last election? Or the party that tried to strip me of my preselection?'

'No, the party you want to be a success in,' Bower said, stuffing his mouth.

'Jack,' Woodward interrupted. 'If we vote against the bill, they will see us as supporting fraudulent behaviour and allowing tax evasion to prosper.'

'So you're suggesting I fall into line?'

'What's the point speaking out on an issue Dale tells us is a low-ranking with voters,' Woodward said.

'Just comply, is that it?'

'It's not complying, per se,' Bower mumbled. 'It's keeping your powder dry for a more important issue.'

'What's more important than entrepreneurial freedom?'

'I would think winning your seat would be a worthy contender,' Bower said. 'Once you secure that, you can focus on the significant issues affecting your constituents.'

Hudson filled his lungs through his nose. 'This is what I'm trying to understand. What's the point of being here if I remain silent on issues that are important to our culture and economic system?'

'Jack, you need to get over yourself,' Woodward said, stabbing her chopsticks into the noodle box and leaning back in her chair. 'Yes, step up and be assertive, but choose your battles wisely. You can't fight them all. You need to compromise.'

'I agree,' Bower said. 'There is no traction with industrial relations in the seat, so let's just concentrate on policy that affects the young mums, like affordable childcare.'

'Am I not allowed to make a speech in the parliament next week on this issue?'

'If you do, the wrath of many will fall upon you,' Woodward said.

'Which side of the aisle?'

'Both sides, I reckon, boss,' Bower said.

'I can't not say anything?'

'I'll draft you a speech about the aged care facility threatened with closure,' Woodward said.

'So I should just get out and knock doors and kiss babies, is that it?' Hudson asked.

Bower nodded. 'Now you're getting it.'

CHAPTER
57

Hudson wore out another pair of shoes over the week while door-knocking his electorate before heading back to Canberra. Unlike his campaigning gear, he appreciated wearing fine Italian leather shoes and a collection of suits he left in his suite at Parliament House. This arrangement spared him from hauling outfits back and forth each week, allowing him to travel light, carrying only his paperwork, without the hassle of luggage.

After changing out of his casual travel clothes, he strolled the corridors to the leader's office, enjoying the comfort of well-made shoes. Upon reaching the Whips' office, he checked the speakers' board and saw that they had scheduled the debate of the Registered Organisations legislation in the House. He noted Alexander Windsor already listed to speak, as did another colleague from Queensland. He glanced over his shoulder to the Whips' administrator, who was busy matching backbenchers' names to travel lists for overseas delegations.

'No chance those delegations would go ahead, is there, Sue?' Hudson queried.

'Mr Hudson, I take nothing for granted,' she replied, without glancing up. 'These delegations will go ahead even if they are after the election, so your colleagues will want to know if they are successful. The leader has allocated them. I just need to make sure the file is complete.'

'Did I secure a trip?'

She paused, glancing up at a smiling Hudson. 'Too soon for you, but if you return after the election, I'll make sure you are on top of the reserve list.'

Hudson laughed. 'I notice we expect the Registered Organisations bill in the house. Will it get up before the government prorogues Parliament?'

'Not sure. There is discussion about it, and it seems they might defer it,' she said. 'The committee report is due to be tabled this week. It might be better to wait for the report if you want to speak on the legislation.'

'Do I need to list my name?'

'No, but I'll make a note for the Whip to add you to the speakers' list, if you would like? You may only have a couple of minutes because it is time limited to fifteen minutes.'

'Sue, you're a tremendous help,' Hudson said. She blushed when he stepped closer. 'If you could manage that for me, that would be great. Anything I can do for you?'

She looked away. 'Not right now but just make sure you get re-elected.'

'I'm working on it, Sue, I honestly am,' Hudson grinned as he left. 'I went through another pair of shoes last week.'

She watched him go and sighed.

Hudson continued his stroll, passing the Chamber on the way to the leader's office. He was keen to speak with Chopra and discuss the recent leadership challenge.

'Jack, good to see you,' Chopra walked around his desk to welcome him. 'Nice to see you.'

'Leader, I've come for advice and to tell you what I plan to do.'

'Sounds ominous. Should I have someone take notes?'

'Relax, it's not serious,' Hudson said, sitting on the couch as Chopra chose a chair.

'I want to thank you for your role in the leadership challenge.'

'What role?'

'You inspired me to shirtfront the enemy,' Chopra laughed, 'so I did.'

'I wasn't expecting a full-scale leadership spill,' Hudson said. 'I thought a more subtle approach might have been an option.'

Chopra steepled his fingers. 'I must also praise you for voting for me.'

'It was a secret ballot.'

'You support the leader though, right?'

Hudson nodded and grinned, 'Yes, I do.'

'So, you voted for me,' Chopra said. 'If you weren't in the Parliament, I would have lost. Thank you.'

'You may not thank me after we talk.'

Chopra frowned. 'What do you want to discuss?'

'This legislation regulating unions.'

'We treat fraud seriously,' Chopra said. 'This is why we are supporting the government.'

'Why don't we support entrepreneurialism?'

Chopra grimaced. 'I understand where you are coming from, but if we don't support the government, they will cane us in the media.'

'This is what everyone talks to me about, political pragmatism,' Hudson said, crossing his legs. 'Give up what you stand for and keep a low profile.'

'Yes.'

Hudson was surprised by his reply.

Chopra added. 'I would rather be in government.'

'Can't we do that without compromising our principles?'

'Political purity keeps us in opposition.' Hudson shook his head and Chopra studied him. 'You are learning a lot about politics?'

'It's very different from my lessons in the military,' Hudson said. 'I was intending to speak in the chamber on the legislation.'

'It's not going to a vote before we head into an election,' Chopra said.

'Why is that?'

'The government doesn't want to enact it.'

'It's their legislation and they don't want to enact it?'

'They wanted to use it as leverage against me. Now that the leadership threat is over, they're calling for it to be deferred, so we're accommodating them.'

'I understood politics was a battle of ideas?'

'It is, but only if you are in government.'

Hudson nodded. 'I want to express my opposition to the legislation before the election.'

'No can do. I'm afraid.'

'Ramon, listen to me,' Hudson said. 'Just because I support the leader does not mean I do what the leader wants me to do. I feel obliged to express my view and I'll do so if an opportunity arises this week.'

'Concentrate on your constituency, Jack. Leave the politics to us.'

'My electorate wants me to speak in the parliament.'

'Then speak about schools and health.'

'Ramon, I think you're mistaken about this,' Hudson stood. 'You are mobilising the union movement against us.'

'It's the government they will fight, Jack,' Chopra said. 'Not us.'

'You're wrong,' Hudson said as he reached the door. 'They are the government. They will organise against their enemy. You have given them that opportunity.'

'Keep doorknocking, and leave the strategy to us.'

'My strategy is to win. I don't want hordes of union members doorknocking in my seat.'

Two DAYS LATER, Hudson stood in the chamber seeking leave to speak on the tabled committee report. The deputy speaker granted his request, and Hudson thanked her.

'Australia needs flexible, sophisticated representative bodies advocating for workers and employers. These organisations need to be nimble and adaptable in the modern workplace and not restrained by outdated industrial age-old thinking and restrictive laws. These organisations must fund their member services ethically, and adhere to their legal requirements.'

'Deputy Speaker, we have too many government regulatory bodies overseeing the manner organisations conduct business. We safeguard consumers with stringent laws carrying heavy penalties. However, as more services move online, these organisations are losing membership. The high fees they charged in the past for their services are no longer sustainable as members move on.'

'To remain relevant, these organisations need revenue. Allowing them to seek legitimate revenue streams would assist them in serving their members and providing a strong advocacy voice for them.'

'It is unacceptable to allow this government to stifle the opportunity for these organisations to prosper. It is imperative that we do not let them wither and die by denying them the freedom to seek revenue and develop better business models.'

'Order, the member's time has expired.'

'I will conclude by saying that if I remain in this parliament,

I will continue to fight for the right to express our views and opinions, and to build enterprises that increase employment opportunities for all Australians. Laws should never impede our fundamental freedoms.'

'Hear, hear,' Ramsey MacDonald said.

Hudson sat glancing across the Chamber to notice MacDonald nodding.

IN SENATOR MORGAN'S OFFICE, they could hear a smashing glass. 'He's such a bastard.'

Ramon Chopra was following the speech from his office. 'Brave lad.'

Oleg Rusnek was watching on his phone at a construction site. 'What the hell is going on?'

Prime Minister Mosely asked as she refilled Henari's glass. 'Perhaps you should pay Mr Hudson a visit.'

CHAPTER
58

E very morning at the corner of the highway and the main road through Williamstown, Hudson stood shaking a corflute message just like some employee from a fast-food joint. He wasn't sure passing drivers even recognised him or if it would sway votes. But he was certain the female government candidate was nowhere to be seen campaigning in the electorate.

Each evening Bower researched the electorate, and his morning brief to Hudson had been disheartening. The polls projected that the government would reclaim Gellibrand, and they would record Hudson's position in political history as insignificant. He asked Dale if there was any progress. Bower reported an unusual reluctance among voters toward survey questions and engaging with pollsters. Typically, those who already made up their minds were eager to express their views, aligning themselves with the winning party, but not this time.

'What are they afraid of, do you reckon?' Hudson asked.

'If I was a betting man, which I'm not,' Bower said. 'I would say they want to avoid disappointing their party by keeping up the pretence, they support the government.'

'That's ridiculous,' Hudson scoffed. 'Why would they do that?'

'I'm no Freud, but I reckon they are grappling with political identity,' Bower said. 'They have voted Social Democrats for so long they have forgotten why they do it. They want to support you but don't want anyone to know.'

'Yeah, righto,' Hudson said, picking up his ice chest of water bottles. 'You keep telling me that and maybe I'll start believing you.'

'You don't think you'll win?'

'Dale, I will fight until the end, just like Custer.'

'Didn't his men get annihilated?'

'Exactly,' Hudson laughed as he left the room. 'Keep getting the mail out,' he called over his shoulder.

A car honked as it drove past. Hudson responded with a thumbs up. He checked his watch. He had to be at the crèche in thirty minutes.

The van went unnoticed amongst the traffic until it mounted the kerb and parked on the footpath, making it impossible to ignore. A burly bloke emerged from the driver's seat. He sported a wild mane of hair, his eyes hidden by sunglasses, and a bushy beard concealed his face.

'Mr Hudson?'

'Could be. Who are you?'

'My name is Pascale. I am here to invite you to meet Mr Henari in Williamstown. He would like to buy you a coffee.'

'I have a meeting in thirty minutes, so thank you, but no.'

'You will only see five mothers at the crèche. Mr Henari would like to discuss bigger numbers for your campaign.'

'And who is Mr Henari?'

'He is a local business identity. He'd like a word with you.'

Hudson weighed the offer, waved as a car tooted, then said. 'I'll follow you.'

'Sweet, I'll phone ahead.'

Hudson watched him as he left for the van. He waved to another car, he walked towards the side street where he parked his vehicle. By the time he unlocked the trunk to stow his gear, the van was waiting nearby. He then followed it back to Williamstown where they arrived at a small coffee hole-in-the-wall kiosk nestled within the Prince of Wales Hotel. Henari was waiting with a latte for Hudson.

As Hudson approached, Henari stood and ushered him to sit and make himself comfortable. 'I believe latte is your preferred drink. Please enjoy.'

'Thank you, but I would rather skip the pleasantries and get to the point. What do you want?'

Henari smirked. 'A man who wants to get down to business, and not muck about. I like it.'

'Who are you?' Hudson said, returning Henari's stare.

'I have a vested interest in the seat of Gellibrand,' Henari said, lifting his glass, encouraging Hudson to do the same. 'Let's just say I would prefer you to win the seat and not the BWU candidate.'

'I don't do deals.'

Henari frowned. 'I find that offensive. I'm not here to broker any deals.'

'Then why are you here?'

'As I mentioned, I have an interest in Gellibrand, and I would like to have the member supporting me rather than working against me.'

'What's your line of work?'

'I'm in the consumer goods industry,' Henari said, sipping his coffee. 'A wholesaler. I want to ensure legislators help my business and not impede it.'

'I don't do deals.'

Henari laughed.

'This is what I told prime minister Mosely, when she suggested I speak to you,' Henari said. 'I told her, Mr Hudson will not entertain any deals, and we will need to win the seat back.'

'Look. Mr Henari,' Hudson said, moving to leave. 'It's been a pleasure meeting you. It seems we cannot get any common ground. You support the government and I'm not likely to engage in any discussion with you.'

'Let me just say, before you go,' Henari leaned forward, 'we want to win the seat. But not with the union candidate. So, we want to help you.'

Hudson frowned. 'You want to win the seat from me, but not yet?'

'Exactly.'

'You want to support me to defeat the government candidate intending to win the seat back for the Social Democrats at the next election?'

'Someone said you were sharp,' Henari quipped, clicking his fingers.

Hudson scoffed, relaxing back into his chair with a smile. 'And how do you propose to do this?'

'You won with a tiny margin last time.' Henari offered his thumb and finger in a pinch. 'Current polling has you losing the seat by maybe two thousand votes.'

Hudson shook his head, not realising the polls were that bad.

'We can provide you with enough votes to win.'

Hudson stroked his chin. 'How would you propose to do that?'

'You pick the booth, and we will have two maybe three thousand people vote for you at that booth,' Henari said. 'You can then have obvious proof we voted for you by the result in that booth.'

Hudson studied him, nodding. 'And if I agreed, what do you want in return?'

'Nothing.'

'Nothing?'

'Oh well. Stop talking about industrial relations, especially the legislation before the parliament. The prime minister would prefer you didn't.'

Hudson nodded, gnawing at his bottom lip.

'Nothing,' Henari said with a cheeky smile. 'Though, if you come across any information about local planning issues, that might be valuable to us, we would appreciate a heads up.'

'Ah, and there it is,' Hudson said. 'The deal-breaker.'

'You don't do deals, remember?'

Hudson stood, extending his hand. 'Thanks for the coffee. I'll think about it and let you know.'

Henari shook his hand. 'That's all I ask. Take your time.'

CHAPTER
59

'Did he actually guarantee two thousand votes?' Dale Bower asked, a look of scepticism on his face.

'Maybe three,' Hudson said, his feet on the desk in the cramped office.

'At any polling booth we choose?'

'Any booth, preferably not a busy one.'

'We have two,' Bower said, pointing a ruler to the map behind him. 'The one I would recommend is in Bayview Street, plenty of parking with less than five hundred votes. The perfect place for this to happen.'

'You are not considering doing this?' Chrissie Woodward asked.

'We are falling behind,' said Bower. 'If it costs nothing, then maybe it's worth considering.'

'How do you reckon it would look in The Chronicle?' Woodward responded.

'He hates us,' Bower said, scowling. 'What is his problem, anyway?'

Hudson shrugged.

'He wanted his wife to run to increase her profile for a challenge at the local council,' Woodward said.

'Why does he run negative stories about us?' Bower asked.

'He's bitter and twisted,' Hudson said. 'The piece he ran the other day was downright shameful.'

'He has a political motive I would wager,' Woodward said.

'What political motive?' Bower said. 'What does undermining our campaign do for his political reputation within the party?'

Woodward tapped her nose. 'Have you ever thought he may be under riding instructions from another authority?'

'Who would be so dumb as to use Collins as a political operative?' Bower said, chuckling. 'The man is a moron.'

'He holds the numbers in Gellibrand,' Hudson said.

'You win the election, and you'll replace him as the authority in Gellibrand,' Woodward said.

Hudson nodded. 'And that, my friends, is his motivation.'

'Listen, Jack,' Woodward said. 'If you win Gellibrand, you threaten the senator and all the others who are ambitious for promotion.'

'How can I influence the party structure?'

'Charismatic authority,' a beaming Woodward suggested.

Hudson shook his head. 'Is that it?' he said. 'No depth of character. No policy ideas. No support for the leader. No campaign skills. Just a smile and a good suit.'

'Jack, we've had worse as prime minister,' Woodward scoffed. 'You are the complete package. Winning the election assures your future, even though no one expects you to win.'

'Until Henari runs a candidate at the next election, and I lose.'

'You win this time, and we then run a community campaign that will not only secure your margin but also ensure your victory in every election,' Bower said. 'Demographics are rapidly changing, so boundaries will shift voting margins to you. We just need to win the election.'

'If Henari can offer me three thousand votes, what's stopping him from bringing them in and using them against me?'

'Your smile,' Woodward said.

Hudson shrugged, shook his head, stood, and left the room.

Bower cast an eye at Woodward, raising an eyebrow. 'We don't stand a chance on current polling.'

'When it comes to elections, there's always a chance.'

'Easy for you to say when you have a job waiting in the leader's office,' Bower moaned. 'If he becomes prime minister, even better for you.'

Woodward grimaced. 'My loyalties lie with Jack.'

'At the moment,' Bower said.

'We'll give it a solid crack.'

'He won't win unless he increases the numbers, and that seems unlikely,' Bower said.

'Increase his numbers,' Woodward said.

'I can if I have access to three thousand votes.'

'What happens if we use them, and he wins?' Woodward asked.

'We say thank you very much and go on our way.'

'I suspect these types of business folks,' Woodward fingered air quotes, 'will want their pound of flesh.'

'A bit hard when they're dealing with a federal member.'

'You recall what happened to the last member for Gellibrand?'

'No charges, no evidence, so what do you mean?'

'Could they have made the same deal with Campbell? Perhaps he never did what they asked him to do.'

Bower shook his head, chewing on the end of his pen. 'Do you think someone killed a federal member because he didn't do what he was told?'

Woodward shrugged. 'He was having trouble with the IR legislation. Unions weren't happy.'

'But he was the minister. What was he supposed to do?'

'Maybe nothing. They capped him because he didn't do anything,' Woodward said.

Bower pouted his bottom lip. 'That's a long bow to suggest they killed him because he wasn't following orders.'

'Maybe it is,' Woodward said. 'It could happen, though. If Jack does a deal for votes, who's to say he won't end up the same way?'

Bower rubbed his mouth and pinched his nose, then scratched his ear. 'He won't win without them.'

CHAPTER

60

Hudson busied himself packing corflute signs and brochures into his car in the parking lot across from his office when a taxi pulled up, and Madeleine Booker emerged. 'Hi Jack, I wasn't expecting you to be here,' she said, strolling over.

'Maddie, I should be doorknocking, but I ran out of brochures,' Hudson said, closing the boot lid. 'I have a street meeting in an hour, so I came back to stock up.'

'Sick of it yet?'

'Sick of what?'

'Campaigning. It seems that's all you've been doing the last few months.'

'I've been knocking doors every day when I'm in Melbourne,' Hudson said. 'When I won the by-election, I kept campaigning, knowing the national election would be in a few months, so we are well ahead of the other candidates.'

'What have you learned?'

'Folks couldn't care less about politics. They don't know me from a bar of soap.'

Booker laughed, 'Hey listen, have you got time for a coffee?' she asked.

'Sure, let's head around the corner. Jo serves great coffee.'

Hudson locked his car and picked up Booker's overnight bag. She slung her handbag and satchel over her shoulders. They exchanged small talk until settling at a table on the foot-path outside Parade Deli, waiting for their coffees.

'Jack, I wondered if we could talk about your experience in parliament since you were sworn in,' Booker said. 'I'm doing profiles on first term politicians preparing for the election. I would be interested in getting an idea of how it has been for you.'

'There must be others more worthy of the publicity,' Hudson said. 'I think I've had more than enough.'

'Why do you think you've had enough?' Booker flicked her hand around her handbag, dragging out a well-worn spiral pad, flicking over pages until she had room for notes. She titled it Gellibrand and dated it. Hudson waited, checking about to see if there was anyone in earshot who may be interested in what he had to say.

'I came into politics wanting to serve the community and the nation,' Hudson said. 'But what I have found is an entirely different world full of horrible people.'

'Can I quote you?'

'Hmm, maybe not,' he said. 'And that is a good example of

what I mean. I must be cautious about what I say and who I say it to. It's such a difficult thing to do.'

'What is?'

Hudson frowned. 'Not trusting anyone. I have to check over my shoulder all the time to see if anyone is listening, and I must be careful when I speak to the media and even then, they take you out of context.'

'Do you trust anyone?'

'My staff.'

Booker scoffed. 'Not even me?'

'Yeah, nah,' Hudson grinned, 'you'd do me in if you had the chance.'

'Probably,' Booker laughed.

Hudson studied her for a moment, then grinned a grimace. 'I'm not sure why I'm doing it now,' he said.

'What's getting you down?'

'Doorknocking, voters always wanting something from me, and no recognition,' Hudson scoffed. 'I fixed a woman's reticulation the other day and then two days later she rang the party complaining she had seen no one from the party.'

'You're kidding?'

'Indeed, I kid you not,' Hudson said, welcoming his coffee. 'I had a cuppa with her, and we chatted about all things politics and then she forgot me.' He laughed. 'This is why I think I should do something else – I'm doubting my ability to break through.'

'Your parliamentary work must provide some satisfaction?'

'Of course it does, but I don't have a voice with developing policy.'

'You've only been there a short time.'

'Yes, but I can contribute more. They lock themselves into their ideas and refuse to listen to a new kid.'

'Give it time.'

'According to polling my time is running out.'

'I'm sorry to hear that.' Booker said, lifting her coffee. 'You have no chance?'

'I have the party working against me.'

Booker raised an eyebrow. 'The party is active against you?'

'The local president, who is on the party's executive and owns the local newspaper. He attacks me almost every day.'

'What's his problem?'

'They took the preselection off his wife and installed me.'

'But you won the election.'

'Yeah, I know, right?' Hudson laughed. 'I've since learned they didn't expect me to win.'

'But you did,' Booker said, shaking her head and taking a sip.

'I can't prove it, but I think Senator Morgan is setting me up.'

Booker peered at him, taking a note. 'In what way?'

'She keeps spreading rumours about me that just aren't true.'

'Like what?'

'She said I voted against the leader. She claims it was her vote that tipped the scales in his favour.'

'That could be true.'

'She voted for Raffles.'

'What makes you say that?'

'Windsor told me when he tried to secure my vote.'

Booker fell back in her chair, pen in hand poised on the pad. 'I find her forthright and honest when I deal with her.' She shook her head. 'This surprises me.'

'Surprises you?' Hudson said. 'It kills me I have to fight against my own.'

'What do you plan to do if you lose?'

'I said polling is bad, not that I am preparing to lose.'

'You just told me your own party is working against you, and the polling doesn't look favourable. Of course, you're going to lose.'

'I'm working hard.'

'Sadly, I'm not sure knocking doors and waving poster signs are enough.'

Hudson glanced across the street, gnawing his bottom lip. 'I had an opportunity of securing votes the other day.' Booker left her pen on the pad, crossing her arms. 'A community leader approached me offering me two thousand votes.'

'A community leader?'

'Some bloke. A business manager who claims he can have his people go to a particular booth and vote as one.'

'Who was he?'

'A local businessperson. He told me he was eager to keep the union out of the seat and is prepared to lose the seat this time and win with his candidate at the next election.'

Booker shook her head and frowned. 'Why would he do that?'

'He asked me to go soft on the IR bill, he said the prime minister would prefer it.'

'Do you have a name?'

'Henari.'

Booker's jaw dropped. She slowly outlined her upper lip with her tongue. 'You know who he is, don't you?'

'A local business owner tight with the government.'

'Involved in the business of drugs.'

Hudson didn't respond as he stared at her.

'He's somehow involved with Rusnek from the BWU,' Booker said. 'I'm trying to figure out their connection because they only seem to be at each other's throats whenever they see each other.'

'But why would he want to help me win the seat?'

'If he is tight with the prime minister, I suspect it has something to do with the IR legislation.'

'Why would he want to have a link with the union whose candidate is running? Then come offering help?'

'I don't know,' Booker said. 'My theory is that Rusnek had something to do with Campbell's death. Maybe it's connected?'

'Well, I guess that ends that idea.'

'You weren't going to do a deal were you?'

'Desperate people do desperate things, Madeleine, especially in politics.'

'You got that right.'

CHAPTER
61

The Williamstown Chronicle distribution strategy shoved free issues into over fifty thousand letterboxes with a further ten thousand cleverly placed at cafes, newsagents, and other high consumer traffic areas. Each edition overflowed with community news and advertising, catering to the active local community eager to support their own. The editorial focused on local identities. Each edition, during the election campaign aimed to expose Jack Hudson as an inadequate political representative. It highlighted his no-show attendance at events and silence on important issues.

When Hudson unfolded his latest copy of the Chronicle, he almost dropped his tea. 'Dale? Are you in?' he bellowed.

No reply came.

He fanned out the newspaper to read the story. A photograph of Hudson and Henari having coffee under the banner headline BIKIE BUSINESS splashed across the front page.

With heavy innuendo, the article insinuated Hudson was colluding with criminals during his recent meeting. Hillary Duff, a clearly fake name, wrote the report implies the Gellibrand member's involvement in organised crime. The photograph was all the evidence the community needed to reject Hudson at the election.

He flicked to the nominated page for further information. He felt dumbfounded when he saw a double-page spread dedicated to his short political career. It featured a photograph of his empty chair at the opening of a community park when he was in Canberra. Another photograph depicted him standing at the edge of the road, appearing worn-out and abandoned, amplifying the negative emotions surrounding his early morning traffic campaign. ALL ALONE. NO PLACE TO HIDE. The seven articles included quotes from residents all of which were negative. Even the woman who wanted him to fix her reticulation had a photograph and comment attributed to her, *"Wherever he is, he is never in Gellibrand"*.

'Yeah, thank you Mrs Carmichael.'

Hudson closed the paper when he heard the cheery voice of Dale entering the building. He was with several volunteers gossiping about the campaign and the overnight polling. 'Dale, can you come in, please?'

Bower took a moment but finally arrived in the doorway. 'Morning boss, when did you get in?'

'I'm just on my way out to the train stations, but I needed more brochures,' Hudson said. 'Have you seen the Chronicle?'

'I never read it. It's a rag.'

'They did a job on me.' Hudson slid the newspaper across the table.

Bower stopped the spin, reading the headline. 'Geezus.'

'What is wrong with that guy?'

Bower shook his head and shrugged. 'I reckon we need to take it up to him,' Bower said. 'He should not be allowed to get away with this.'

'You don't believe in the freedom of the press?'

Bower raised his eyebrows. 'I do, but this is beyond fair reporting. This is editorialising a campaign against you.'

Hudson took a deep breath, then harrumphed it out. 'We need to campaign against this at a grass roots level.'

'Getting you out more?'

'Let's do rallies so I can speak to voters.'

'Yeah, not a good idea,' Bower said, shaking his head and staring at the floor. 'Our opponents will be there tossing tomatoes and eggs.'

Hudson sighed.

'Just keep doorknocking, Jack.'

'Clearly, that's not working if a voter forgets I repaired her reticulation.'

'The work we are doing on the telephones is affecting the polling. This is what I wanted to talk to you about.'

'Is it good news or bad news?'

'Both,' Bower said. 'Good news is the margin is narrowing. Bad news is we need more money to keep doing it.'

'How much do you need?'

'Twenty should see us through.'

Hudson dropped his hands to the table, shaking his head.

'Told you it's bad news.'

'So, without it we can't win?'

'I didn't say that,' Bower said, wiping his face. 'I just think if we are going to get over the line, we need cash.'

'Cash and people,' Hudson said, rubbing his forehead with his thumb and fingers. 'We have neither.'

'Normally, that means a losing campaign.'

Hudson glanced up and shook his head. 'You carry little tact in your bag. Don't you, young man?'

'My job is to tell the truth.'

'Yeah, that's true, but sometimes, you need to read the room.'

Bower wiped his hands on his shirt and fidgeted. 'I reckon you can win, Jack. You just need to believe it.'

Hudson squinted, offering a smile.

'Hi,' A call came from the front door. Chrissie Woodward arrived four hours after leaving for home. She appeared at the door and looked at the men. 'What's going on?'

Bower shuffled his feet.

'Reality has made an entrance,' Hudson said.

'What does that mean?' Woodward snapped, flicking a glance between the two of them.

'Dale has been giving me a run down,' Hudson said. 'Take a look at the local paper.'

Bower shoved the paper across. Woodward scanned the headline then flicked to the spread. She shook her head when she closed it.

'He's supposed to be supporting us,' Hudson said.

'Welcome to politics, Jack,' Woodward said. 'We've talked about this.'

Hudson didn't respond. Bower swayed, focusing on the floor.

'You need to be out on the hustings, Jack,' Woodward said, her face tightening. 'Can I encourage you to get moving?'

Hudson didn't move and avoided her stare. He brought his fist to his mouth and worked the knuckles into his teeth.

'What's up?' Woodward demanded.

'Why bother?' Hudson continued to avoid her gaze. 'It seems pointless now. We should just focus on polling day and help the senate vote.'

Woodward said nothing. Hudson glanced up at her.

'I'm tired and it's too much for too little result,' Hudson said. 'Sometimes you have to cut your losses, retreat ground and protect your base.'

Woodward shook her head, glanced at Bower and then back at Hudson.

'You are kidding me,' Woodward said. 'What a load of crap you are loading up there, Jack. I'm not working my guts out to have you give up.'

'Why would you bother?'

Woodward fisted her hips, her mouth and eyes wide. Then changed her face to a frown. 'You selfish bastard. You are a damn selfish bastard.'

'Chrissie, wait up,' Bower said.

Woodward shoved her palm his way as she stepped toward

Hudson. 'When are you going to get it into your thick skull that you have an opportunity, Jack?' she said. 'When are you going to respect the work volunteers and staff are doing for you, because they believe in you?'

'I've heard this story before.'

'Then damn well hear it again because it seems you are too privileged to realise how much you are needed,' Woodward said, straightening and tilting her head back. 'You think you can swan around with your chest full of medals and expect an easy road? You think you have served your country once and that you can take the easy road to community service? It's clear you have little regard for the hours we put in here.'

Hudson avoided her eyes, glancing at Bower who cocked his head.

'Of course, it is hard. Of course, there are horrible people trying to end your career,' Woodward said. 'Just stop whining about it and get on with it. You have the capabilities you just need to get out there and stop your moaning.'

'It's not working, that's the point.'

'How would you know unless you're out there?' she said. 'Do you get negativity? Are people abusive to you?'

'No, they smile and chat.'

'If it was as bad as you think, do you reckon that would be the response?'

'I don't know.'

'That's the point, you don't know,' Woodward said. 'We do and we reckon we are still in this.'

'We need money,' Bower said.

Woodward turned. 'What?'

'We need money. The party isn't giving us any.'

'Why not?'

'Collins doesn't want to give us any,' Bower said. 'He wants to invest in the seats we can win.' Hudson watched the by-play. 'That's rubbish, he can't do that,' Woodward said.

'He is doing it. We have no money for poll tracking.'

'What can we do?' Hudson asked.

Woodward looked askew at him. 'You still here?'

Hudson exhaled sharply and shook his head, crossing his arms, and leaning back into his chair.

'There's a party executive meeting this afternoon, right?' Woodward said.

'If you say so,' Bower said, shrugging his shoulders.

'Let's send Jack to plead our case.'

'He won't be able to get in.'

'If I use my connection with Chopra, we might have him address them with a campaign update.'

'That might work.'

'He then asks for more funding in line with other seats.'

'He could provide...' Bower said.

'Excuse me,' Hudson interrupted. 'I am here. Perhaps we could include me in the discussion.'

Woodward turned and smiled. 'Jack, you need to be at the train station ten minutes ago. When you come in for your break, we will provide more information for you.'

'Do I have a say in anything?'

'No.'

CHAPTER

62

Hudson discovered himself that afternoon seated at the board table within the National Party's headquarters in the CBD with instructions from Woodward to get the money. He occupied the chair opposite the party president, with Senator Morgan seated at one end. Among the other office holders seated opposite in a panel configuration was Treasurer, Eddie Collins.

'The leader directed us to receive a briefing on your campaign progress. We look forward to learning more about what is happening in Gellibrand,' the president encouraged Hudson to begin his presentation.

'We are putting in a lot of effort to keep the seat. However, we have encountered several issues we hope to resolve today.'

Senator Morgan leaned forward. 'What issues might they be, Jackson?'

Hudson turned his gaze toward her, grinning. 'It's the view

of my campaign team that certain elements within the party seem inclined to see us lose the seat.'

The president frowned. 'That's not a claim we want to hear. What evidence do you have?'

Hudson glanced at Collins, who shifted in his chair, biting his thumb's nail. 'The local newspaper has been running negative stories in every edition for the past three weeks.'

'The party supports freedom of the press, Jackson,' Morgan said.

'As do I,' Hudson said. 'But it is worth noting the newspaper's editor is sitting at this table.'

'I only print what the community wants to know,' Collins said.

Hudson smirked and shook his head. 'I have no issue with the truth being told. It's when fake news is published that my team takes exception.'

'What news do you consider fake?' Morgan asked.

'The story about me doing deals with criminals,' Hudson said, tossing the edition on the table. 'To suggest I'm colluding with criminals for personal gain is wrong and damaging. Your reporter, whoever she may be, didn't even seek a response.'

'She claims she called your office, but no one answered. Everyone had gone home,' Collins said.

'Not true,' Hudson said, shaking his head and glancing at the president. 'My staff are at the office until 2 AM every day.'

'Regardless, it's already out there. Nothing much we can do now,' Morgan said.

Hudson gawked at her and then turned back to the president, waiting for a response.

'What do you want to happen?' the president asked.

'I want the newspaper to provide fair coverage of the campaign. Acknowledge the work we are doing.'

'We don't publish puff pieces,' Collins said.

'Like the article concerning the government's candidate the other day?' Hudson said. 'You even included a photo of her having coffee with you.'

'Is that true?' the president asked.

'I'm a community leader. She is working in the retail district,' Collins said, stroking his chin. 'I seldom see Jack on the shopping strip.'

Hudson smiled. 'I don't need puff pieces. Just report the news, that's all,' Hudson said. 'I'd appreciate no more hatchet jobs on me until after the election.'

Collins cupped his face in his hand and peeked at Morgan, who nodded. 'I can do that.'

'That's good, thanks Eddie. Anything else, Jack?' the president asked.

'Yes, we could do with some party people to help the campaign.'

'You have plenty of party members in Gellibrand. Why do you need more?' Morgan asked.

Hudson gazed at Collins. 'The local members aren't willing to assist at the moment.'

'Why is that?' the president asked.

'You should ask the president of Gellibrand. Perhaps he can provide an explanation.'

All eyes turned to Collins, who once again shifted in his chair.

'I have provided all the contact details for all the members in Gellibrand for the campaign.

'Is that right, Jack?' the president asked.

'We have spoken to all of them, and together they all seem to have excuses for not coming out and helping. Many of them are volunteering in Lalor and Maribyrnong.'

'And none are available for your campaign?' the president clarified.

'Not a single one.'

'Edward, can you perhaps let the executive know why this might be the case?' Morgan asked.

Collins clasped his hands, twiddling his thumbs. 'I do not know why they don't want to work for Jack. Maybe they don't like him.'

'All of them?' the president pressed.

'I can't be responsible for their personal preferences.'

'You are their Branch President,' Hudson said. 'It would be helpful for an email of support encouraging them to help on election day to support the senate vote. I'm sure Senator Morgan would be appreciative.'

'You're right, Jackson, the senate team would be grateful for their help,' Morgan said. 'I'm sure you can write to members, can't you, Edward?'

'If you believe it might help, then I'm happy to email members.'

'I'll draft the email. If you could distribute it tomorrow, that would be appreciated,' Hudson said.

Collins nodded, his lips pouting.

'Anything else, Jack?' the president asked. 'We have an agenda to get through.'

'We could also use financial help.'

'Everyone could use more funds, Jackson,' Morgan said.

'According to the information I have, other federal campaigns are receiving financial support, but Gellibrand is not.'

'That's not what our accounts say,' a director said.

'Yes, Gellibrand has received a fair allocation of campaign funds,' the president said.

Hudson frowned and shook his head. 'I must be missing something.'

'According to the financial reports presented earlier, we have allocated fifty thousand dollars to Gellibrand for the campaign,' the president said, scrutinising the ledger sheet. 'Just a few weeks ago, the party received an invoice for printing and posters from a supplier named WCC Press, amounting to thirty thousand dollars.'

Hudson leaned back and scratched his ear. He stared across the table at Collins, who glanced away and then back, fidgeting in his seat. 'That seems a little high. What was it spent on? Was it cash transfers? Is it all from the same supplier?'

'Let me check,' the president said, scanning the ledger

sheet. 'Yes, it is. I must admit, that seems like an excessive amount of printing.'

Hudson nodded. His mouth curled down. He glared at Collins again. 'Yes, well, we've put a lot of brochures into letter-boxes over recent weeks.'

'How much more do you need, Jackson?'

Hudson switched his gaze to the senator, then back to Collins. 'We need twenty thousand to work the phones and our social media campaign.'

'That's quite a substantial sum of money; it would push your campaign expenditure well beyond seventy thousand, higher than other electorates of similar size,' Morgan said.

'I could query those figures and request an audit. Couldn't I, Eddie?'

Collins cleared his throat. 'Yes, you could.'

'Or maybe I could get a donor to contribute to that portion of the campaign.'

Collins avoided Hudson's gaze, wringing his hands together.

'You think you could raise the money?' the president asked.

'Well, it's either that, or we have an audit to verify the recorded funds.'

'What are you suggesting?' Morgan asked Hudson, glancing at Collins.

'Nothing at the moment. I just need the money for the campaign. I'm exploring all available options.'

Collins straightened in his chair and cleared his throat.

'President, I think I may have a solution to Jack's current challenges.'

Hudson frowned at him.

'The WCC is the commercial arm of my newspaper, and we have been managing the campaign's account,' Collins said, avoiding Hudson's gaze. 'As a gesture of goodwill, I would like to offer the campaign the twenty thousand they need for the telephone canvassing campaign.'

The other executives responded with applause and good cheer.

Hudson smiled. 'That's very generous, Eddie. We accept your very gracious and substantial contribution.'

'I'm pleased to help,' Collins said, nodding at Hudson.

'I'm sure you are,' Hudson replied with a hint of irony.

CHAPTER
63

Hudson raised an eyebrow as he checked the bank statement on his computer screen and Bower couldn't help but ask, 'How did you manage that?'

'If I read him correctly,' Hudson said. 'He might be doing a fiddle.'

'Embezzling money from the party, do you mean?'

Hudson nodded. 'That's exactly what I mean.'

'Why didn't you toss him in?'

Hudson leaned back in his chair, contemplating a response. 'I've learned a few things about politics over the last few months, and I reckon we might leverage that information.'

'Hence the twenty grand?'

'Exactly.'

'Boss, now you're getting it,' Bower chuckled, closing his computer and preparing to leave for the evening. 'Are you heading home?'

Hudson shook his head. 'I have a couple of emails to write. I won't be far behind you.'

Bower collected his sweater, tossing it over his shoulders, and left. Hudson watched him go, then turned to his screen and began an email to Madeleine Booker. He wanted to reinforce his new financial support, and his campaign was back on track.

Everything is running smoothly, and we will give it a proper go.

As he pondered how to sign off, he contemplated whether to keep it business-like or add a touch of friendliness, given her interest.

We should make a small wager. Dinner if I win?

His finger hovered over the mouse as he reread the email, searching for any mistakes, and then breathed deep and sent it. He checked his watch. It was late. He straightened his papers and looked forward to getting much-needed sleep.

His computer popped a muted noise.

Hi Jack, you are working late. Great to hear you sorted out your party problems.

Let's hope it makes a difference. Let's do dinner no matter who wins.

Maddie x

Hudson read the message again, a furrow forming on his brow. He couldn't help but feel a sense of unease, especially about the kiss emoji. What did it signify? Should he respond? After some thought, he decided to let it go for now, opting to send a note tomorrow after his morning church visits.

He logged off, scooping up his keys. He walked through

the office and locked the front door, checking it before striding off across the street to the car park. As he stepped through bushes, he noticed a solitary figure leaning against his vehicle.

'Mr Hudson, I presume?'

'Who's asking?'

'My boss is waiting for an answer.'

Hudson detected a New Zealand accent. He was big and hairy. Built like he worked out every day and the dumbbells were grateful when he stopped.

'Who's your boss?'

'Mr Henari expects an answer from you today. Do you have one?'

'Mr Henari?' Hudson said. 'I understood him to be a business manager.'

'He is,' the big guy moved closer. 'I'm his personal assistant.'

'Messenger boy?'

'That's not a nice thing to say,' he said. 'I'm just doing my job. I would like an answer to the proposal Mr Henari provided the other day.'

'Or what?'

'We deliver you a message.'

'We?' Hudson checked around. 'I only see you and me.'

The big guy let out a shrill whistle, and two dark figures emerged from the shadows wandering over. Not as big, but just as menacing. Hudson took a deep breath, watching for sudden movements, hair lifting on his neck.

'I'm guessing your boss only wants one answer.'

'He is eager for you to understand how disappointed he will be if you choose to reject his proposition.'

Hudson nodded and grinned as he checked the other two, thinking through his options, weighing the benefits of attack versus defence. He was thankful he left his jacket in the office. 'Could you please relay to Mr Henari that I appreciate his kind offer, but on this occasion, I'm going to decline.' Hudson's grin widened as he observed the assistant's anxiety, and the hesitant glances exchanged between the other two men.

'I think you should, maybe, reconsider given the new information before you.'

'I suspect that is why you remain a lowly assistant,' Hudson said, as he paused, watching the big guy. 'You don't think.'

'There is no reason to insult us with cheap disrespectful humour, and not expect the shit to be kicked from you.'

'Okay,' Hudson said. 'I want it on the record that I do not want this. It is you who will take time to recover.'

The big guy scoffed, and his two mates stepped in behind ready to protect his back and step forward when required. Without warning, he ran at Hudson, aiming to tackle him to the ground so the other thugs would sink their boots in. Hudson already presumed the big guy was a wrestler and prepared for the attack. He stepped aside like a matador handling a charging bull. He punched him as he brushed by. The big guy dropped to a knee glancing back. He straightened with clenched fists, moving toward Hudson.

Hudson kicked the assistant's right knee, crippling him and eliciting a painful cry. He then stepped forward and landed a knee to the man's chin, shattering teeth and likely breaking his jaw. The big guy collapsed to the pavement, clearly incapacitated. Hudson delivered a final blow by stomping on his groin.

This prompted the next attacker to step forward, who spun, sending Hudson a well-executed karate-kick soaring through the air like a ninja. Hudson crouched as the kick sailed over him. Grabbing the outstretched leg, he gripped it under his arm, causing the ninja to struggle maintaining balance.

Hudson glanced to the other thug who hesitated. 'Really? Are you still thinking about it?' He then fisted the over balanced ninja to the ear, grabbing his testicles squeezing as if crushing a chocolate Easter egg. The ninja wailed until Hudson released his grip and the thug crumpled to the bitumen. He then swung his left foot into the thug's face, breaking his nose and splitting his eyebrow.

Hudson held up the palm of his hand to the advancing thug. 'Someone needs to drive these blokes to casualty, so choose wisely.'

The thug appeared anxious, glancing around for backup that was nowhere to be seen. He hesitated, and Hudson took a step forward.

'No, wait,' the thug stammered. 'I'm done.'

'Wise choice,' Hudson said. 'Go bring your vehicle over. I'll leave you to it.' Before he walked to his car to drive off, Hudson punched the thug in the nose, causing a split. 'Just in case your boss asks why you aren't injured.'

CHAPTER
64

The early dawn filled with the calls of waking birds on a secluded street. A vehicle remained hidden from the view of the CCTV cameras coming to a stop among the trees. As the driver opened the door, the car emitted a repetitive loud ping, prompting a hurried closure to silence the warning.

Moving to the trunk, the driver popped it open, retrieving a can of solvent and two bottles of kerosene, both stuffed with a soaked rag as a stopper, placing these items on the bitumen. The driver scanned around the street. The hour was too early for pedestrians, although a late-night reveller may still lurk about. He saw nor heard anything suspicious.

Tugging a balaclava over his face and donning surgical gloves, while pulling up his hood, he collected his bottles and can. He continued to scan the parking lot, attempting to avoid the watchful gaze of the security cameras until he could no longer do so. As he reached the building, he uncapped the can, splashing its contents against the front door, window alcoves, and along the front walls of Jack Hudson MP's office.

Stepping back to the other side of the lane, the driver ignited a kerosene rag wick, waiting for it to burst into flames. When it did, he hurled it at the door. Suddenly, a burst of flames erupted as the makeshift firebomb struck the frame. The flames, fanned by the solvent, engulfed the front of the building. The wooden door offered little resistance as it was consumed by the fire.

Igniting the second bottle, the man threw it harder at a window, smashing it, and watching the liquid splattering across desks and papers. He surveyed his handiwork for a moment, satisfied his mission was a success, before sprinting back to his car and departing.

The fire fanned throughout the old building. The inadequate sprinkler system was no match for the fierce blaze. A smoke detector began pulsating, and a fire alarm from a neighbouring building blared. The distant wail of a first responder siren echoed through the area.

The fire had been raging for ten minutes before the fireys trained their hoses onto the seat of the flames. It didn't take long, maybe five minutes, to have the fire under control and a further twenty minutes to have it extinguished. The firefighters were almost on their way when Hudson arrived, moving through the early morning walkers and spectators who ventured from nearby homes wondering what the commotion was all about.

Chrissie Woodward, in her gym gear, chatting to a police officer as Hudson joined them.

'Was Dale the last to leave last night?' Woodward asked as the police officer took a note.

'No, I was,' Hudson said, scratching his head as he gazed at the damage. 'Have you contacted him?'

'I can't get a hold of him.'

'You're not suggesting he's in there?' Hudson said, shaking his head, still looking at what had once been his office.

'We've found no evidence of anyone, sir,' the police officer said. 'The first indication is that this was arson. Any ideas?'

Hudson turned to the police officer. 'I have a few, but none of them would be stupid enough to do this.'

'We'll know more once our arson investigators examine the scene.'

'Will you check those cameras?' Hudson asked, pointing to security cameras in the carpark.

'We will. If we discover anything of interest, we will come see you,' the police officer said.

'Anything salvageable?' Hudson said, turning to Woodward.

'Most of our critical data is in the cloud, so that should be fine,' Woodward said. 'It's just the printed material that we can't use and all our hard-copy files, of course.'

'Some of them could still be recoverable if they are in fire-resistant cabinets,' the police officer offered.

'What about our volunteer information?'

'Only Dale would know,' Woodward said.

'Where is the boy? Give him another call. He should be here by now.'

As Woodward stepped away to make the call, Hudson's phone buzzed. 'Dale? Where are you?'

'I'm at my computer going through the camera footage.'

'How is that possible?' Hudson asked, shaking his head.

'You must get across this thing called technology, Jack,' Bower said. 'I have access to our digital recordings from the cloud.'

'So, you can see who did this?'

'And the exact time.'

Hudson grinned. 'Good lad, can you get a copy prepared for the police?'

Bower made a noise. 'Not sure you want to give this to the police, given your visitors last night.'

'I have nothing to worry about.'

'Not a good look for a federal MP to be kicking the crap out of someone.'

'They attacked me.'

'The media won't see it that way, and neither will Collins.'

CHAPTER
65

P olitics consumed Alexander Windsor. His fervour for the political arena had begun during his primary school years when he campaigned for various positions, from house captain to school captain. Windsor pursued votes while his peers engaged in childish antics in parliament. His dream of becoming the prime minister took root early and remained unshaken. Every day he laboured over the numbers, engaging in conversations with those who could aid his ascent. Windsor's cheerful disposition endeared him to others, providing a pleasant reprieve from the stresses of their daily lives. However, beneath that cheerful facade lay a Machiavellian mind, adept at extracting and filing away information and gossip. His jokes and anecdotes had a purpose. They encouraged loose lips, filling his files with valuable material for future use.

Windsor's systematic information gathering remained a critical element of his long-term strategy to secure the role of prime minister. He forged close friendships with colleagues, exploiting those connections until they could no longer serve his advancement. His close alliance with Peter Raffles crumbled after Raffles lost the leadership ballot.

Now he supports Ramon Chopra.

His ambition led him to Melbourne three days prior to the election, where he attended the Oleg Rusnek's site office. As he waited in the busy lobby area, the chill in the air made his jacket ineffective. He noticed a worker in a fluorescent vest and a hard hat adorned with stickers delivering coffee and food in paper bags to the office. Laughter and loud voices emanated from behind the flimsy walls. Despite the snub, Windsor's objective was to speak with Rusnek, so he endured the discomfort.

Workers entered and exited the office, paying little heed to the young man in a suit. Ninety minutes passed the agreed meeting time, before a worker indicated to Windsor to enter and meet with Rusnek. The office offered a warm, stark contrast to the cold outer room. Behind a cluttered desk, Rusnek sported a polo shirt with a BWU logo.

'Why are you still here?' he asked.

'Can I sit?' Windsor asked.

'If you must,' Rusnek said, gesturing to a chair. 'You have five minutes.'

Windsor sat in a rickety chair, which wobbled beneath his weight.

'I offer you a solution to the problem you have.'

'Are you stupid?' Rusnek said.

'Not at all, Mr Rusnek,' Windsor said, checking over his shoulder to the man standing by the door. 'You have a problem, and I can provide you with a solution.'

'What problem do I have, dipstick?'

'Interesting.' Windsor paused, smiling. 'You want legislation postponed indefinitely. You have little support in the government and not much in the opposition.'

'What can you offer me that I don't already have?'

'A solution.'

Rusnek regarded Windsor, then glanced at his man by the door. 'A solution?' he mused. 'A mincing poodle wants to provide me with a solution?' The man laughed. 'What does a politician of such little significance have to offer me?'

'Well, for starters I'm offended by the epithet,' Windsor said, glaring at Rusnek. 'I've come here in good faith. I don't appreciate being kept waiting and then subjected to insults by someone I'm offering a favour.'

Rusnek grinned. 'You've got balls, kid.'

'Look, I've spent enough time here in this grimy place. Do you want my help or not?'

Rusnek still grinning, glanced at his man who, raising his eyebrows, smiled. 'Okay, what have you got?'

'My interpretation of the election is that it's close, but Chopra will win.'

Rusnek pouted and shook his head.

Windsor continued. 'We need six seats. We'll get five in Queensland and pick up one or more elsewhere. Our only probable loss is Gellibrand.'

'You seem quite confident?'

'Confident enough to predict who the next industrial relations minister will be.'

'Not the current shadow?'

'Absolutely useless.'

'Who?'

'Senator Morgan.'

Rusnek nodded. 'And you know this how?'

'I peddle in information and arithmetic,' Windsor said. 'I collect information. I listen to stories. I overhear gossip and I keep a dossier on every politician in the parliament. Some files are inches thick; others have little information.'

'And what does this have to do with anything?'

'I know, for instance, your prime minister is exceptionally close,' Windsor air quoted his fingers, 'to one of your associates. If you know what I mean.' Windsor tapped his nose.

Rusnek glanced up and his man shrugged. 'How could you possibly know that?'

'I have comrades on the other side, and we share information,' Windsor said. 'For instance, I know the prime minister threatened Campbell with expulsion from the party if he did not comply with his request.'

'Why?'

'The prime minister is doing a favour for someone close to you.'

Rusnek thumbnailed his teeth as he studied Windsor. 'Why are you telling me this?'

'I don't want Senator Morgan promoted.'

'And you want me to do what?'

'Allow me to explain,' Windsor said, leaning forward. 'I can guarantee you I will bury the IR legislation you want deferred forever. But there is a condition.'

Rusnek raised an eyebrow. 'A condition?'

'Morgan was influential in having the legislation deferred until after the election,' Windsor said, grinning. 'She is taking her riding instructions from the same person the prime minister is helping.'

'What you are telling me makes no sense.'

'Mr Rusnek, this is not about the legislation, this is about you and your union.'

Rusnek shook his head.

'Someone is coming to get you and your union,' Windsor said. 'The legislation is being used to ruin your plans and push you into retirement.'

'They have no chance of doing that.'

'They will if they enact legislation targeting your activities and enabling criminal sanctions against you and the others.'

'It doesn't do that,' Rusnek held up his hand, 'it only stops non-member commercial enterprises.'

'That's what the legislation proposes, but once the election concludes, regardless of who wins, lawmakers will amend the legislation to include criminal sanctions for past practices.'

'You know this how?'

'Senator Morgan and my contacts within the government suggest your associate is in control and pulling the strings to his advantage. It seems he has a fondness for powerful women. He rewards them with product and a good session every now and then. In return, they assist him by doing nothing other than working against you. The deferral is only a ploy to keep you quiet until after the election. They don't want you interfering with numbers in the party.'

Rusnek shook his head. 'What are you suggesting?'

'Stop the legislation by stopping Morgan.'

'How do I do that?'

Windsor raised his eyebrows, took a deep breath, and said, 'You know about her different lifestyle.'

'She likes a bit of fun, so what?'

'That sort of lifestyle is not what the public is prepared to accept. They do not want their tax dollars wasted on the salacious activities of their politicians.'

Rusnek pouted his bottom lip, nodding. 'What's the deal?'

'I get any thought of the legislation stopped by the parliament and you release evidence you have on Senator Morgan to me.'

Rusnek clasped his hands in front of his face as he examined Windsor. More interested in punishing the rival working against him than exposing Morgan. 'What assurances do I have?'

'If you expose Morgan, I will make sure she doesn't get promoted. The legislation dies with her career.'

'Why do you think I know anything about her?'

'The same way I know about your rival,' Windsor said. 'When you need to know who that is we can strike another deal.'

Rusnek worked his tongue into the side of his mouth.

'When we win the election and end Morgan's career, we will end your rival's influence,' Windsor said, preparing to leave. 'Once we do that, you will be free to keep doing whatever it is you are doing.'

Rusnek watched Windsor leave. 'I've always thought there was something bigger going on,' Rusnek said, his feet on the desk, leaning back in his chair, clicking a pen. Campbell should have told me he was under pressure.

'Who do you think it is?'

'Who hates us and would want to see harm come our way?'

'The BLF.'

'Are they smart enough to be orchestrating a coup?'

'They play the numbers better than us.'

'What do you think of the mincing poodle?'

'He wouldn't come to see you unless he knew something.'

'What have we got on the senator?'

'Photos and a recording.'

'Enough?'

'More than enough to pique the media's interest.'

'Should we act before or after the election?' Rusnek asked.

'I would recommend after,' his man said. 'It won't matter unless they form government.'

'If they don't win, what then?'

'Our girl in Gellibrand will be our voice.'

Rusnek nodded. 'Only if she beats Hudson.'

CHAPTER
66

Senator Morgan accepted the invitation to the election night campaign headquarters shindig at the Melbourne Sofitel hotel, but uncertainty shrouded her as she waited for the results. If they won, she expected to be promoted to the front bench as industrial relations minister. Her obligation remained clear. She received instructions from Henari to ensure the passage of the Registered Organisation bill through the parliament. If she didn't, she would face dire political consequences and perhaps physical harm.

Inside the bustling ballroom, big screens broadcast television pundits from the national tally room in Canberra. Animated politicians, familiar to voters, provided commentary on the closely contested election, fuelling further uncertainty about the outcome. Interviews were underway with both victorious candidates and vanquished politicians exiting the national stage. The government lost eight seats in Queensland, losing a senior minister.

As Morgan mingled with familiar party members, the atmosphere grew more charged, with each government seat lost. The likelihood of a change in government loomed. Amidst the revelry, she noticed a rowdy young campaign worker who caught her attention. She thought she would quite like to punish him, making a mental note to seek him out later.

Spotting Peter Raffles and Alexander Windsor arrive after completing duties at the head office, she navigated her way through the jubilant supporters. 'Colleagues, how do you feel?' Morgan asked. 'We've made it.'

'We have a meeting with Ramon tomorrow, so ask us then,' Raffles said.

'What meeting?'

'Some of us are convening in Sydney,' Windsor said. 'Have you not received a call from him?'

Morgan didn't respond.

Raffles turned his attention to her, shifting from the big screen. 'Steph, he only called me thirty minutes ago. Don't worry, he'll be in touch with you.'

'When did he call you, Alex?' Morgan asked.

'About an hour ago.' Windsor casually turned to the screen, hiding his smile.

Morgan gnawed her upper lip, crossing her arms and fixating on the screen.

'Look, the government hasn't conceded. Read nothing into

it,' Raffles said. 'It's just a meeting of advisers. There won't be any official announcements.'

The three stood and watched the telecast in silence for a few moments.

'How did we fare in Gellibrand?' Raffles asked.

'The bastard kept the seat,' Morgan said.

'Based on the current figures he did so easily,' Windsor said.

'That means he may be a thorn in our side,' Raffles said.

Morgan wanted to go home but first cast an eye around the room for the campaign worker. 'It seems that way.'

———

BEFORE POLLS CLOSED in the afternoon, a courier arrived at the Sydney headquarters of the opposition leader. As Chopra sifted through papers and polling data, the courier delivered an A4 envelope, placing it on the table next to him. The polling data showed he was likely to form the next government, and he was crafting his potential ministry.

Chopra reached for the yellow envelope, tugging open the seal. Once able, he extracted several photos, the first of which had a post-it note affixed.

This woman does not deserve a ministry and if you think otherwise, she will be your first scandal.

He studied the grainy black and white shots of a woman enjoying herself with a big man in a public convenience. The images were fuzzy, but he recognised a familiar hair style.

Chopra crossed out Senator Morgan's name, adding Alexander Windsor.

––––––

THE CELEBRATION at the Gellibrand campaign party began after the polls closed. Initial results were promising, but as each booth reported the numbers the celebrations became rowdier. It became clear Jack Hudson transitioned the once-safe seat for the government into a safe seat for the Nationals.

'I don't want to say I told you so,' Bower said, his face beaming, 'but I told you so.'

'Yes, you did young man, and I am grateful.'

Bower and Hudson sat a table in a quiet room, watching the live telecast, fielding calls from booth captains reporting the election counting.

'Even in the high progressive suburbs the count swung in your favour,' Bower said. 'A swing of seven percent in one case.'

'Which booth was that?' Hudson asked, surprised by the result.

'The high school junior school campus,' Bower said, checking his notes. 'There's just seven hundred votes taken there, but this time we recorded two thousand.'

Hudson sat forward, gesturing for the spreadsheet. Bower slid it over and pointed out the result compared to the last three elections.

'It's consistent at seven hundred, but this time there is a significant increase.'

'What was the vote?'

'It's normally a fifty-fifty split. This time you have a winning margin of sixteen hundred,' Bower said. 'We also have this booth to the west, which you won by a few hundred last election, but this time it is over a thousand.'

'Any idea why?'

Bower scratched his head. 'Not a one. The result in these two booths has put you across the line.'

'I won by twenty-four hundred?'

'Heck no,' Bower said. 'More like forty-eight hundred, which is a significant margin compared to just a few months ago. It means you convinced twenty-four hundred to change their vote.'

Hudson shook his head. 'I'm not that good.'

'It doesn't matter,' Bower smiled. 'You won and won well. Given the crap you faced, this is a tremendous campaigning result.'

Hudson seemed unconvinced, gazing at a beaming Bower.

The noise in the room increased as Chrissie Woodward slipped in, a glass of champagne swaying in her hand.

'Jack, come on. People want to see you and toast your magnificent victory.'

Hudson smiled and stood. 'Keep this analysis on the down-low please, Dale.'

'Sure boss.'

CHAPTER
67

A change of government reshapes a nation, but the morning after an election no one cares, as life carries on. Hudson enjoyed the sun as he sat outside a cafe opposite a park with spectacular views back to the city. He perused the newspapers, reading about the Nationals' resounding victory, his own triumph receiving just a few lines. Several residents paused, offering congratulations during their morning strolls. He was already on his second latte when Eddie Collins limped by, prompting him to call him over.

'Congratulations, splendid effort,' Collins said as he wandered over.

'Grab a seat, Eddie, and let's have a chat,' Hudson said, gesturing to a chair opposite. 'Did you hurt yourself?'

Collins tried to downplay his difficulty. 'I stubbed my toe this morning. It's still a little tender to walk.'

'Would you like a coffee?'

'No thanks. What do you want to talk about?'

'I received a notice on Friday from head office asking me for a campaign audit,' Hudson said as he took a sip. 'Maybe they thought I would not win.'

'That surprises me.'

'I thought you were the treasurer?'

'I am. I didn't request an audit of any campaign.'

'This request may have come from the national office,' Hudson said. 'Perhaps they are double-checking the state's finances.'

Collins wiped his mouth, his eyes darting about.

Hudson noticed, probing him further. 'Where did all that printing material go?'

Collins dropped his head for a moment then gazed out to the bay. 'Several reasons, none of which matter now, especially since the fire.'

'All the printing went up in smoke, apparently,' Hudson said with a grin and a wink. 'However, I must say, we stored our election day materials elsewhere, so none were destroyed.'

'I don't understand. What are you getting at?'

Hudson studied him for a moment. 'Eddie, I reckon you've been ripping off the party.'

'Get stuffed!' Collins shifted in his chair, checking around him.

Hudson scoffed. 'Never kid a kidder, mate,' he said. 'Without guessing too hard, I would suggest you have been milking the party and banking a handsome amount for yourself.

You got off easy handing back twenty grand. I reckon that is just the tip of the iceberg.'

'You can't prove nothin'.'

'You're right, the fire fixed that,' Hudson smiled.

'So what?'

'I assume the party would appreciate my giving an audit of our printing costs and what we received.'

'Nothing to do with me.'

Hudson scoffed. 'Are you just going to deny everything? Is that it?' Collins shifted in his chair. 'Look, Eddie,' Hudson leaned forward, 'I think we should stop this feud we seem to have.'

'I'm not fighting you.'

'I was not responsible for Alice being replaced,' Hudson said.

'You stole the nomination from her.'

'If you want to blame anyone, blame Morgan.'

Collins leaned back in his chair, a scowl wiping over his face. 'What does the senator have to do with Alice being overlooked?'

'Morgan recommended it.'

Collins gulped but tried to hide it, squeezing his thumb and finger into his eyes, before pinching the end of his nose. He took a deep breath, gazing into the umbrella over the table.

'Not what you wanted to hear?' Hudson said.

He straightened, gazing at Hudson. 'I suspected it. It's a surprise to have it confirmed.'

'I'm never surprised by what the senator does or says,' Hudson said.

Collins snapped forward. 'You know she wanted you gone – don't you?'

'I suspected it,' Hudson said. 'Do you know why?'

'She doesn't trust you,' Collins said. 'Nobody does.'

Hudson pouted his bottom lip and nodded. 'Here's what I reckon,' he said. 'She's been playing you. She doubtless promised you a safe seat.'

'Senate,' Collins corrected.

'A senate seat,' Hudson agreed. 'She is yet to deliver and, in the meantime, you've been working hard to gather her numbers.'

Collins nodded.

'She has asked you to work against the party.'

'Not the party, just you.'

'Fair enough,' Hudson said. 'You feel slighted, so you've skimmed the books with false invoices for the Gellibrand campaign – am I right?'

He didn't answer.

'She no doubt suspects this is what's happening. Now she has a grip on you and is squeezing hard.'

Collins shifted in his seat, looking uncomfortable.

'What can I do to help?'

His eyes widened as he cupped his face, crossing his legs.

'You are going to be found out, especially if the senator knows,' Hudson said. 'I reckon you should pay back the money and get her off your back, otherwise you'll never get selected.'

'What do you want?' Collins asked.

'Nothing,' Hudson said. 'Other than you back off and end this incendiary war you have going against me. I want to help Alice in her campaign for mayor. I want to help you get your seat in the parliament. The work you do in the community needs rewarding.'

Collins shook his head, grimacing.

'We should fight the other side, not each other.'

He straightened out of the chair. 'I'll think about it.' As he moved away, he said. 'Congratulations on your win.'

Hudson watched him hobble away, suspecting more than a stubbed toe.

STEPHANIE MORGAN WAITED for a call from the leader. It never came. When the telephone did buzz, she rushed to it, expecting her promotion.

'Senator, it's Eddie Collins.'

'Yes, Edward, what do you want? I'm waiting for a call.'

'I just bumped into Hudson.'

'He must be pleased?'

'He told me you have been active in stifling my progress to the senate.'

'How would he know?' Morgan said, tapping her lips with a finger.

'He is a two-time winner. He has influence now, it seems.'

'Not yet he doesn't.'

'He put a proposition to me,' Collins said.

'What could he offer you that I can't?'

'A seat,' Collins said, attuned to any change in the senator's tone.

'Interesting,' Morgan said. 'Edward, you need to make a choice. If you align yourself with Hudson, we will expose you for fraudulent embezzlement of party funds. It is as simple or complicated as that.'

Collins expected the ultimatum, but the tone surprised him. He now knew who to support.

CHAPTER
68

Darren Sweeney, the local real estate agent, organised temporary office accommodation for the federal member in the tourist district of Williamstown, with the hope the government would negotiate a deal with him for Hudson's new office. The burnt-out shell of the previous office suffered structural damage, necessitating a new office for the Member for Gellibrand. Hudson didn't object.

The temporary office above Customs House hotel offered stunning views back to the city. The former hotel accommodation was now a rabbit warren of walls and offices not suitable for a business, let alone a federal member of parliament. Hudson's team were thankful to have a base and set about resetting the digital files they maintained in the cloud.

Sash windows provided a view of the park, and the cafe strip below attracted locals and tourists. On weekends the area buzzed with activity. When the weather was sunny, the foot-paths heaved with visitors.

Hudson was at his desk checking through congratulatory cards. A throaty rumble of Harley Davidsons' exhaust could only mean the Maru Hunters were heading to their clubhouse. Hudson moved to the window to watch the procession. Around thirty riders in black, with matte helmets and wraparound sunglasses passed. The roar of engines unsettled anyone with sensitive hearing. The rumble shook the woodwork around the windows, causing the glass to rattle.

Once the procession passed, order returned, dogs quieted, and parents comforted anxious children. Hudson moved back to his desk, continuing to flick through the cards. Fifteen minutes later Dale Bower tapped on his door before stepping fretfully forward.

'Jack, we have visitors.'

'Who?'

'Err,' Bower said, wiping his hands. 'They look as if they just roared past.'

Hudson stood, looked outside but couldn't see any bikies. 'What do they want?'

'They said they want to talk to you.'

Hudson rubbed his bottom lip. 'Show them in.'

Bower ducked out. Henari stepped into the doorway and took a chair by the desk. The other visitor stood by the door, blocking Bower trying to enter.

'Mr Hudson, congratulations,' Henari smiled.

Hudson nodded a few times, eyeing Henari. 'Thank you.'

'I assume you'll be getting a new office soon,' Henari said, looking about the shabby fixtures.

'What do you want?'

'I'm here to congratulate you and wish you well.'

Hudson steepled his fingers, resting his chin on his thumbs. He had a sense there was a reason for Henari being there. He just needed to wait for it to be exposed.

'Anyway, I wanted to come and confirm a few things with you.'

'Such as?'

'Firstly, I want to apologise for the poor behaviour of my blokes the other week. They were acting without authority. I want to reassure you I hold no grudge for them being injured.' Hudson nodded. 'I also wanted to tell you we did not firebomb your office.'

'I reckon the police agree with you.'

'Phew. I hope so. I wouldn't want the police paying a visit,' Henari said, his dripping sarcasm obvious.

'Is that it?'

'No,' Henari smiled. 'I also wanted to let you know the votes we corralled for you were a gesture of goodwill.'

Hudson narrowed his eyes. 'What votes?'

'The ones we organised for you to ensure you would win against the union backed flake.'

'I'm a little unsure what you mean.'

Henari tossed his head back and grinned. 'You know, and I know you would not have won the seat without our votes.

Hudson's throat tightened, clearing it with a cough. 'I don't know that at all.'

'Fair enough, you can play that game if you must.' Henari leaned forward, and the chair creaked. 'Just be aware those votes won't be available at the next election, so enjoy your time while you can.'

'You think I will lose the next election with a four percent margin?'

'I know you will. We will shift votes away from you.'

Hudson tightened his lips. 'Can I ask why?'

'My organisation now controls preselections for the major parties. As you have seen, we can be the difference between winning and losing.' Henari rested his elbows on his knees. 'We have been trying to secure one of us into the parliament. We would prefer this safe seat of Gellibrand as our first.'

'Why?'

'It suits us and our strategy.'

Hudson leaned back in his chair, glimpsed to the doorway to see if Bower was listening. 'And what strategy would that be?'

'A dedicated local member, focused on the community, champions various area developments.'

'Such as?'

'Because the ever-changing climate policy emphasises renewable energy, we want to be a part of the rezoning of Crown land designated for industrial development out west.'

'Are you for real?' Hudson scoffed. 'Do you know how legislation and policy work?'

'Of course,' Henari said. 'I'm more interested in having ears in meetings, introductions to decision makers and the opportunity to invest money in fresh developments in Gellibrand.'

Hudson shook his head. 'Well, good luck with that.'

'This is the reason we wanted you to win,' Henari said. 'If the union won with their stooge, we would never have an opportunity to win the seat. They would hold it for ever.'

Hudson frowned. 'Why are you telling me this?'

'So, you can decide about working with us or losing your seat at the next election.'

'I already gave that message to your boys.'

Henari laughed. 'You surprise me, Mr Hudson. This is why I seek agreement with you now.'

'I told your boys I'm not interested.'

'Fair enough,' Henari said as he stood and leaned over the desk. 'Just so that we are clear. I'm going to take your job away at the next election.'

Hudson smiled. 'Did you end Campbell's career?'

'Campbell was a pawn in a much bigger game, which the government lost. Others may have been interested in his career. We weren't.'

'Did you set me up for that photo in the Chronicle?'

'I play it straight, Jack, as you will learn.'

Hudson scrunched up his face and smiled. 'I don't want to learn more about you. I don't expect to hear from you again.'

'Fair enough,' Henari left the office. 'When you need the numbers, come see me.'

'That will never happen,' Hudson said as the two men brushed past Bower.

'That was intense,' Bower said, entering the office.

'Did they give us the election?'

'Maybe,' Bower said, pushing his glasses up his nose. 'I'll do some modelling and predict what it might look like in three years.'

'I don't want to be a oncer, Dale,' Hudson said, dropping back into his desk. I have no desire to have those blokes as friends. Did they firebomb us?'

'I'll get a better copy of the CCTV off the coppers.'

'Good lad.'

'I'll also crunch the numbers to see what we can do to cover for this loss of votes at the next election.'

'When's the next redistribution of boundaries?'

'Two years.'

'Maybe we should prepare a compelling submission to secure this seat into a more stable position for us.'

'Let's work toward that,' Hudson said.

CHAPTER
69

'Alexander Windsor has just arrived and wants to see you,' Sandra interrupted Senator Morgan.

'Come to gloat, has he?' Morgan's lips curled into a sardonic smile.

'Not sure, Senator, but he seems chirpy.'

'Who wouldn't be?' Morgan stood, stepping around her desk, leaning against it. 'Send him in, and we don't need any refreshments. Hopefully, he isn't here for long.'

'Stephanie,' Windsor declared as he strode through the door. 'You look gorgeous. Come here and give me a hug.'

Morgan hesitated for a moment as Windsor forced himself on her, giving her a squeeze and a gentle tap on the rear as he stepped toward the couch.

'Why are you here?'

'I have come to discuss the future with you,' he said, flopping onto the couch. 'Take a seat,' he waved to a chair, 'and give me a look at those fabulous legs.'

Morgan chuckled as she bounced off the desk. 'You are incorrigible.'

'If we can't be friends and admire the things we do, then life isn't worth living,' Windsor said, grinning as Morgan sat, crossing her legs.

'Congratulations on your appointment,' Morgan said.

'Unexpected, but I'll take it.'

'Why was it unexpected?'

'I didn't vote for Chopra, and he knows it.'

'Maybe he thinks you would be better in the tent.'

'That's a huge mistake on his part if he thinks that.'

'You are not going to be faithful?'

'Of course I will,' Windsor scoffed. 'Until it suits me to do something else.'

Morgan nodded, pursing her lips, eyeing the junior minister. 'I would have thought I would have been appointed to your portfolio.'

'You deserve to be Steph, but I think a graphic photograph doing the rounds changed the prime minister's mind.'

Morgan raised her eyebrows. 'What photograph?'

Windsor cleared his throat, turning away. 'You and a rather large, tattooed man in a somewhat compromising position in what looks like a dunny.'

'What type of tattoos?'

'I haven't seen it, but I'm told they may have been Islander designs.' Windsor grinned. 'From what I have been told, you seem to be enjoying yourself.'

Morgan tightened her lips and pinched her nose before breathing, filling her lungs.

'Chopra had it presented to him the day before the election. He changed his mind about you.'

Morgan dropped her mouth, shaking her head while looking at the ceiling. She tried to recall the moments. She felt a flush in her stomach as she remembered what happened. 'And you know it to be me?'

'The profile and the bangles you wear occasionally give it away,' Windsor said. 'Can't see the dude's face, but he is a solid unit.'

Morgan shrugged and shook her head.

'It's not the end of the world, Steph. You can come back from this.'

'Who has it?'

'Chopra has it. Raffles has seen it,' Windsor said. 'That's it, as far as I know.'

'And Chopra didn't appoint me because someone photographed me in a... let's call it a compromising situation?"

'That's what I'm told.'

Morgan gazed out the office window at the bay. 'Well, stuff me.'

Windsor guffawed. 'I think someone already has done that, girlfriend.'

Morgan snapped a fierce look, then melted, joining the laughter. 'Teach me to keep my mouth closed.'

Windsor squealed, then abruptly stopped laughing. 'Who do you think sent it?'

Morgan shook her head, scratching behind her ear. 'I suspect I know who sent it. I just don't know why.'

'To kill your career would be my guess.'

'They have succeeded then, haven't they?'

'This is why I'm here.'

Morgan sat forward, then stood, moving back to her desk, and prodding a number on her telephone. Sandra answered, and the senator ordered two coffees. As she resumed her seat, she said, 'I assume it is too early in the day for a wine.'

Windsor flicked his arm to read his watch. 'Yeah, maybe.'

'What do you want to discuss?'

'The prime minister is working out positions in government and the parliament as we speak.'

'What's that got to do with me if he has evidence of a compromised position?'

Windsor scoffed a half laugh. 'You previously mentioned that if the front bench was unavailable, the president of the senate position would be welcome.'

Morgan studied her colleague, waiting for him to speak. 'Go on,' she said.

'He has said he will offer it to the most senior Victorian. It seems there are not enough Victorians in the ministry.'

'I would agree, given you took my spot.'

'That may be so. Anyway, he thinks the president should be Saunders.'

'That old chump does nothing and will not survive the next

preselection,' Morgan said, waving to Sandra to deliver the coffees to the table. 'Thirty-five years he has been in the senate and has done very little.'

'I think you should get the gig.'

Morgan nodded. 'Thanks for that, but if Saunders is the longest serving Victorian, then that will not change Chopra's mind.'

'Unless he leaves the parliament.' Morgan didn't respond as she picked up her coffee. 'If he goes now, you are then the longest serving. The PM then has to promote you.'

'Yeah, nice one,' Morgan sipped her latte. 'But I don't think Saunders will go anywhere, as his numbers are rock solid. I will need to work hard to get rid of him at his preselection in a couple of years.'

'Unless, of course, he is not suitable and goes now.'

'The guy is lazy. He has done very little, and he is always promising numbers to the leader whoever it is.' Morgan said, as she sipped again. 'He never delivers, and that's why nobody has ever promoted him. I get he does the deals, but he gets nothing in return.'

'That's because he studies colleagues, and collects information.'

Morgan scoffed. 'Just like you.'

'Maybe, except for one problem.'

Morgan raised a cynical eyebrow. 'And what's that?'

'I have his file.' Windsor leaned to reach for his coffee and sipped.

'What does it say?'

'He is more salacious than you.'

'Really?' Morgan leaned back in her chair. Her coffee held on her knee. 'He is such an unattractive man. That surprises me.'

'Darkness doesn't care if you are ugly.'

'What are you saying?'

'I have a file on him that has him claiming allowances to enjoy the comforts of others whilst in Canberra and Sydney.'

'Not Melbourne.'

'Never shit in your own nest, Stephanie. Perhaps, you should learn that lesson.'

'I thought I had,' Morgan laughed.

'Anyway, he enjoys the favours of, shall we say, forbidden fruits?'

Morgan raised her eyebrows. 'And you know this how?'

'I have financial statements about his use of commonwealth cars and claiming for services against his travel allowances.'

'He can do whatever he wants. He is travelling.'

'Not visit a bathhouse and have cars waiting. Then claim expenses against entertainment.'

'He's gay?'

'I wouldn't know.' Windsor smiled. 'He likes to visit places where clients might be assumed to be,' he said.

'He's married with four children and ten grandchildren?'

'And your point is?'

Morgan shook her head.

'I'm thinking if someone were to have a private chat with him. You know, confront him about a journalist raising these allowance issues and seeking comment. Maybe suggesting they are fraudulent expense claims. Then perhaps this colleague he trusts could provide counselling on what to do. Mainly that he will need to defend himself once the news breaks. As it no doubt will.'

'Yes, I see what you mean.' Morgan nodded. 'You're a devious little bastard, aren't you?'

'Senator, if you aspire to be Senate President, then you need to counsel your friend.'

'Or what?'

'Or you sit on the backbench without a job, and you may as well call it a day.'

'You wouldn't leak the information you have?'

'Why would I? I don't care who is president.'

'I've underestimated you, Alexander.'

'Stick with me Senator, and I'll have you farting through silk.'

'Oh please, don't be so crude,' Morgan scoffed. 'What do you want from me?'

'I want two things. I want your numbers when I need them, no questions asked.'

'Okay.'

'That's no questions asked.'

'I said alright, and what's the second?'

'Next time you travel to Chile for your meet and greet.' Windsor poked out his tongue and bit it with a smile. 'I want to go with you, Valentina.'

'GET this done and his seat will be yours.'

'Can I have that in writing?'

'Don't you trust me, Edward?'

'No, I don't, quite frankly.'

Morgan smiled as she didn't respond. Collins looked around, waiting for her answer. He could hear her but decided to play along a little longer. 'Do you want me to text you?'

'I want it on paper.'

'It'll be available at the front desk at three o'clock.'

Collins punched the air. 'How do you want me to do it?'

'Use the pretext of administration of expenses. Suggest the party has asked you to clarify his interstate expenses.'

'That won't get him over the line.'

'Then suggest rumours are circulating within the political media of his dalliances,' Morgan said. 'Suggest photographs are circulating of him coming and going from a house of disrepute. Suggest it might be easier for his legacy and his family that he retire. Otherwise, the party won't be able to control what happens.'

'I'll need more than hearsay.'

'Okay, let me think.' Morgan considered the issue for a moment. 'Text me when you enter his office, and Madeline Booker will call.'

'You can get her to call?'

'Edward, Booker won't actually call, but he'll get a message that she did.'

'A little mischievous, wouldn't you say?'

'You either want his seat or you don't,' Morgan said.

'Don't worry, I'll give him an offer he can't refuse.'

'Yes, okay, Edward,' Morgan sighed. 'Keep me advised.'

CHAPTER
70

O leg Rusnek often relished the early morning sun opposite the Victorian Parliament at the European restaurant. The bohemian charm of the décor and the allure of outside tables evoked a sense of Europe for those who sought the elegance. Rusnek was savouring his espresso when Windsor joined him.

'Congratulations on your promotion,' Rusnek said, once his guest placed a coffee order.

'It's a healthy start for the new government, I feel humbled to be entrusted with the responsibility of serving the workers of Australia.'

Rusnek suppressed the urge to laugh. 'You're for the workers?'

'Oh, absolutely,' Windsor said, nodding to the waiter who served his latte. 'You know the workers united will never be defeated.'

'Then why does your mob always want to screw us?'

'That is a political myth. I will ensure we debunk it while I'm the minister.'

'Interesting,' Rusnek said, with a smirk. 'A pro-worker conservative. Nothing surprises me in politics.'

'You have a different approach to making money. I know that,' Windsor said, sipping his coffee. 'But I suspect we share some common goals.'

'Which are?'

'The freedom to do whatever we please without interference from nosy regulators.'

Rusnek knocked back the last of his coffee with a quick tilt of his head. 'What's going to happen to the legislation controlling unions?'

'And employer groups, it's not just about unions.'

'Them too.'

'I'm withdrawing it within the first week of the new parliament, as per our agreement.'

'You used the photograph?'

'Oh yes, it worked a treat,' Windsor said, with a grin. 'Not only with the prime minister but also the good senator, who now owes me big time.'

Rusnek smiled and waved to an attentive waiter, ordering a red wine and another coffee. 'I expect we will work together to get the things we need.'

'I'm a government minister. I will work with anyone who is keen to provide a better system for employers and workers.'

'My plan is to develop access to the infrastructure policy

the government announced as part of its election campaign.'
Rusnek engaged Windsor with a steely stare. 'I'm expecting a
good hearing from your advocacy.'

'That's a little presumptuous, wouldn't you say?'

Rusnek glanced around the footpath and across the street to
the parliament. He didn't identify any interested parties, so
leaned forward, grasping an A4 envelope at his feet and placing
it in front of Windsor.

'What's this?' Windsor asked as he checked about.

'It's an agreement for you to consider,' Rusnek said. 'It
states we will share information that may or may not assist
either party.'

Windsor nodded and spun the envelope so that he could
flip it open. He looked inside, expecting paperwork, and saw
four stacked bundles of $100 notes. Once he recognised it, he
snapped the envelope closed. 'What the hell is this?'

'A donation to your cause.'

'You can't do that.'

'I can,' Rusnek smiled. 'Now make a decision. Will I, or
won't I?'

'I don't understand.'

'I'll deliver an envelope every month whilst you remain
minister. Strictly cash, of course, no trails.' Rusnek smiled.
'What you do with it is up to you.'

'What do you want?'

'Nothing other than information when I need to know it.'

'How much is it?'

'Ten big ones.'

'A month?' Windsor said, doing the mental sums.

'Should cover your mortgage.'

Windsor pouted his bottom lip and nodded. 'We can discuss the rate every year.'

Rusnek scoffed. 'Cheeky bastard.'

'My soul comes at a much higher price than ten a month.'

'Okay, we can talk each year.' Rusnek sipped his wine.

'Fair enough,' Windsor said, shoving the envelope behind his back into the chair. 'If we are going to have an open and honest relationship, then you have to tell me what is going on with the branch stacking in Victoria.'

'One of my contacts is keen on controlling both parties.'

'That will not work for us.' Windsor frowned. 'Frankly, it will not be good for you. Who is it?'

'The Māori one percenter.'

'Henari?'

'That's him.'

'Isn't he close to the previous PM?'

'I'm not sure,' Rusnek said, shifting in his seat. 'I know he was doing a number with the senator.'

'Is he at the meal she is eating in the photo?'

'You could say he provided her with a generous the sausage.'

'This is making sense now.'

Rusnek shook his head, confused.

Windsor smiled. 'You are no good at politics, are you?'

'I know muscle works on building sites and in boardrooms.'

Rusnek shrugged. 'I'm still learning about politics. Campbell let me down.'

'Why would Henari be bonking a senator from the opposition at the same time doing the same with the former prime minister?'

'He enjoys playing with powerful women?'

'Yes, but what else is he after?' Windsor said, shifting in his chair, crossing his legs.

Rusnek shrugged, shaking his head.

'Once Campbell was gone what should have happened?'

'The legislation should have stalled. That's what I expected.'

'Right, but it didn't,' Windsor said, finishing his coffee. 'Why did the PM bring it on, only for the senator to obstruct it?'

'This is why I'm talking to you. I don't know.'

'Could Henari have anything to do with it? And if so, why? Why would he be growing numbers in both parties? What's his endgame?' Windsor said. 'I'm guessing that it has a lot to do with access to building sites and your business model. I wouldn't put it past him that he wants your organisation for his own criminal activities.'

'You're delving into conspiracy theory crap.'

'Am I? What's Henari after?'

'He wanted Gellibrand for one of his men.'

'Why?'

Rusnek shrugged.

'Find that out, and you may uncover why he is meddling in

legislation that directly impacts your operation,' Windsor said. 'He wants to end your influence.'

'You're a conniving little snake, aren't you?'

'Not every battle is won by force, Ollie,' Windsor said, as he stood, tucking the envelope under his arm. 'It seems to me you may have a few issues to sort out in your own backyard. You need to end the Māori's influence.' He smiled. 'And that my friend is my first consultation.'

Rusnek gazed up at the minister above him. 'I would suggest you never call me Ollie again,' he said, his eyes narrowing. 'Are we clear?'

Windsor extended his hand. Rusnek flicked the back of his fingers across Windsor's groin, the sudden discomfort bending him over.

'Are we clear?'

'Christ, righto,' Windsor grimaced.

'Just remember the hierarchy structure in our agreement. You report to me.'

'You didn't need to do that.'

Rusnek smiled as he drained his glass and stood. 'Sometimes we need muscle to re-establish lines of demarcation with any agreement. Settle the bill and we'll talk in a week.' He disappeared into the pedestrian flow as Windsor blew out his cheeks, trying to suppress the sting.

CHAPTER
71

Madeleine Booker scanned the buildings, searching for a number to identify Hudson's temporary office. The various businesses along the street bewildered her as she searched for an entrance. Despite being told he occupied the first floor, there appeared to be no obvious entry point to an upstairs office. She wandered back and forth along Nelson Place, shielding her eyes with her hand, but with no luck seeing where she could enter. Her text messages and email had gone unanswered, adding to her frustration. Hoping for an answer rather than being redirected to voicemail, she again called his office.

'Hey, Maddie?'

Booker turned, trying to locate the source of the voice, but couldn't see anyone grabbing her attention.

'Maddie? Up here!'

Hudson leaned out, peering down from a window above. She gazed up and smiled at the absurdity of it all.

'Do you want to come up?'

'How do I do that?'

'Go through the bar and into the dining room. You'll find a set of stairs in the corner. We're toward the front.'

'Yeah, nah,' she said, squinting at Hudson, her hand shielding her eyes, 'not going to happen.'

'Okay,' Hudson said. 'You want to see me, so I guess you have to decide.'

'Maybe you come down and I'll buy you a coffee just here.' She thumbed toward the cafe.

Hudson glanced over at the empty tables outside Schwabs Cafe. 'Grab a table in the shade and I'll be right down,' Hudson said. 'Order a latte.'

Booker ordered coffees and found a table as Hudson joined her.

'Have you had a busy day?' Hudson asked. 'You're a tad late.'

'Don't start with this nonsense,' Booker snapped. 'No street numbers, no phones answered, no emails responded to. When was the last time you checked your phone for messages?'

'It seems I need to apologise for stuffing you around.'

'This is a perfect addition to my expose file.'

'Maddie,' Hudson sighed. 'There is no need to get me further into trouble by that gossip column.'

'Further into trouble?' Maddie softened her tone. 'How so?'

Hudson watched her as the coffees were served, a cheeky

smile across his face. 'Back to business,' Hudson said. 'And here I thought it was a social call.'

Maddie sipped her coffee, hiding her smile as Hudson spooned a dash of sugar into his latte.

'My editor has directed me to write a piece on you,' she said, placing her glass back on the saucer. 'It seems there are a lot of unanswered questions regarding your political journey.'

'I stand on the shoulders of giants.'

'Yeah, nice one,' Booker winced. 'I'm not interested in writing a puff piece.'

Hudson's eyes narrowed. 'Then what are you after?'

'In a nutshell, this is what I know,' she stretched for her coffee, 'someone murdered a minister, forcing a by-election. The preselection committee discards an unknown candidate lacking political experience. Then a higher authority overturns that decision. He then wins a by-election by a small amount...'

'Four votes.'

'Four votes.' She took a sip of coffee. 'He was set up and exposed in Parliament over a sensitive military action. Then, they challenged his preselection, forcing a deal to save him once again. He then had a conservative independent run against him and a strong union candidate. During the campaign, someone firebombed his office, and attackers assaulted him in a carpark late at night.

'How do you know that?'

Booker tapped her nose. 'I'm an investigative journalist, remember?' she smiled. 'Anyway, your party reallocates resources away from you. Members don't want to help, and they then accuse you of doing criminal deals. There's also tension between factions of the government. Overlay this with contentious legislation that has various local identities fuming. It's a recipe for disaster.'

'The way you lay it out, it certainly seems that way,' Hudson nodded, taking a sip.

'Everyone expects the novice to lose,' Booker said, wiping under her nose. 'The polls are against you. The commentators mark you down as a loss, and your leader, now prime minister, says you will be a significant loss to the party. Even you were showing signs of wanting to get out of this life.'

'I wasn't too far from giving it away, I can tell you.'

'Then lo-and-behold you win,' Booker said, shaking her head. 'Not just scraping over the line, but you win again with a huge margin, almost securing Gellibrand into the safe seat category.'

'Amazing, isn't it?' Hudson smiled.

'You are a political genius or there are other dark forces operating in the shadows.'

'Well, I'm not a genius, I can tell you.'

'Which implies that the seat, and by extension, you, have been manipulated for the betterment of others,' Booker said, as she sent a steely gaze to Hudson. 'The question I have for you is this: who are these people, and what do they want from you?'

Hudson smirked and turned away to scan along the foot-path. He noticed a familiar face walking toward him from his cafe on his way to his newspaper office.

'Here comes one of them now.' Booker turned around to see who Hudson was referring to. 'Do you know Eddie Collins?'

'I sort of know him, but he hasn't been on my radar.'

'His wife ran as the independent,' Hudson said, watching Collins approach. 'Apparently, she has mayoral aspirations, and she thought running would boost her profile. I suspect it didn't help. They have a cafe down the road they are refurbishing. You probably know him from his columns in the Chronicle.'

'Of that's Collins,' Booker checked him again. 'I wondered who the columnist was. He hates you.'

'He's no fan,' Hudson confirmed. 'He serves as the party treasurer in Victoria.'

Booker noticed the moonboot. 'Did he hurt himself?'

'He was limping a while ago, so maybe that has something to do with it,' Hudson said. 'Hurt yourself, Eddie?'

Collins seemed embarrassed but didn't stop. 'Hi, Jack, nice to see you.' He kept walking not wanting to engage.

Hudson watched him go.

Booker shook her head. 'Nice fellow.'

'He is an enemy, but he also owes me and hates it.'

As they chatted about politics, they worked their way through the coffee. Hudson shared what he could without revealing too much, especially not discussing the bikies and their threats.

'Will Chrissie stay with you?'

'No. She's in Canberra working with the PM,' Hudson said. 'That was always her plan. I hope she gets the gig she wants. She has an interest in foreign affairs. I suspect they will appoint her the minister's chief of staff. So, it's just me and Dale at the moment.'

'Will you set up a different office structure now that you are a safe seat member?'

'It means nothing unless I win the next election, so we'll continue campaigning.'

'Not interested in any spoils of government, then?'

'On the record, I'm more interested in serving my constituents. Off the record, I will consider any position the PM offers.'

Booker nodded as she scribbled notes. 'What do you think happened to Campbell?'

'The coroner ruled it as misadventure.'

'Murder, suicide, or accident?'

'On the record, I offer my continued condolences to the Campbell family who remain living in the electorate. I will ensure we recognise him with a memorial during this term,' Hudson said. 'Off the record, people think he was just as bad as the thugs he was involved with. It's possible the BWU played a role in his misadventure.'

'He was a creep, that is for sure.'

'What do you think happened?'

'Rusnek topped him.'

Hudson scoffed. 'You going to print that?'

'Not likely. I'll keep looking for information that might lead to evidence he was involved.

'That is a dangerous game you play, Maddie.'

Booker felt uncomfortable with Hudson's gaze and shifted

in her seat. 'It's been enlightening dealing with you, Jack. I appreciate the candid nature of your comments.' Hudson smiled, and she wished he hadn't.

'I'll look forward to working with you more in Canberra,' Hudson said as he stood. 'You have treated me fairly, unlike many of your colleagues. I appreciate that.'

Booker scooped up her things and stuffed them into her oversized bag. 'I can't promise this article will be favourable, as there are still many unanswered questions. Senator Morgan has a different perspective to you.'

He nodded. 'That's to be expected, I suppose. Her dealings with me have been rather strange.'

'I'll bear that in mind as I investigate further,' she extended her hand. He took it and tenderly shook. They didn't release as they stood eyes locked. 'It's been a pleasure, Jack. I'll make sure I send you the copy before it goes to press.'

She leaned in and planted a warm kiss on Hudson's lips. The kiss lingered, and they enjoyed the surprising, unexpected moment.

'Take care,' Booker said as she left a speechless Hudson touching his lips as he watched her stride towards the hobbling Collins.

CHAPTER
72

'Hey boss, where have you been?'
'Downstairs with Booker from Hancock Media,' Hudson said as he squeezed around Bower's desk, grabbing a chair to sit and chat. 'She is doing a profile piece.'

'Nice one. Look, I have a couple of things to discuss with you and need direction.'

Hudson smiled. 'You seem across all the issues. Do you want to be my chief of staff?'

'That's what I wanted to talk to you about.'

'You know the ropes,' Hudson said. 'You've been through a campaign, and you know what's going on.'

'Jack.' Bower leaned back in his chair. 'That's very kind of you to say so.'

'But?'

'I'm a nerd. A computer geek,' Bower said. 'Technology is my jam, not politics. I know nothing about government policy.

459

I'm not interested in following the news. I go home, eat pizza and drink beer, then play games until the wee hours of the morning. I'm a fat, ugly bloke that just prefers to be left alone. You gave me an opportunity, and I have loved it. Thank you. I'll get you re-elected. Well, maybe,' he scoffed. 'Then I'll do whatever you want me to do. But don't ask me to do anything else.'

'You undersell yourself, young man.'

'A man's gotta know his limitations,' Bower said, attempting a weak impersonation of Clint Eastwood. 'I know mine. I know how to work best for you. If you want me.'

'Of course, I want you,' Hudson smiled. 'With Chrissie gone, you are the only one who knows me, and what I want to achieve.'

'That's what I want to talk to you about,' Bower shifted a thick file toward him. 'These are the applications for the roles we have. I have given them a grade and checked their backgrounds. There are some excellent candidates amongst that lot, including some I know through the party.'

Hudson flicked through the file, scanning the applications. 'I remain unsure as to the mix of capability we need. I wonder if we need organisers like the unions.'

'That could be a good idea,' Bower said. 'I think we need a seasoned political policy operator for the chief of staff position. We also then need an office manager to manage constituent inquiries. We also need a media guru to drive local and national media. I'll handle your data research and number crunching and perhaps we need support staff for constituents and campaigning.'

'That's already four. What's the allocation?'

'Five,' Bower said. 'But here's the thing, we can tap into employment programs for interns, indigenous employment, and even bring in full-time volunteers in addition to your back to work program.'

'Who would want to volunteer to work for me?'

'You would be surprised,' Bower said. 'My dad volunteers at the local community centre and practically runs the joint. He loves it. It gives him something to do.'

'I suppose there are folks who would want to help the community and enjoy the prestige of a politician as their employer.'

'Now you're getting it.'

'So, when we get to our new office, we should consider more workstations and introduce hot desks.'

'I agree,' Bower said. 'All that office space is going to waste when most of us are in Canberra.'

'You see?' Hudson smiled. 'This is why I reckon you're underselling yourself.'

Bower blushed and turned away. 'Any chance Chrissie might come back?'

'I'm having lunch with her in Canberra after the swearing in ceremony. The gossip is that the PM promoting her to the foreign minister's office.'

'She always had a passion for policy in that portfolio.'

'Good for her and it will help on her CV for when she puts her hand up for the senate.'

'Not in Victoria, surely?'

'No, she wants New South Wales,' Hudson said. 'You sounded a little surprised. Have you heard something?'

'Just some chatter online about the next preselection and it seems a senator might retire soon.'

'In Victoria?'

'It appears so.'

'Is it Morgan? I heard she was disappointed that she didn't get a portfolio.'

'I haven't heard, but apparently, there are storm clouds coming.'

'Hmm, interesting.' Hudson began to move.

'Boss, before you go, I received the CCTV footage from the coppers this morning.'

'The fight with the thugs or the fire?'

'Both, and I must say, I'll stay close to you whenever trouble comes.'

'I'm a little out of practice.'

'It's the firebombing footage that caught my eye.'

'Can you identify them?' Hudson leaned over the desk to check the screen as Bower swivelled it. 'Was it the bikies?'

'I can't tell for certain, but I reckon no.'

Hudson gazed at the screen to see an image of the criminal moving through the shadows.

Bower pointed. 'This is where it becomes interesting.'

He slowed the footage and then enhanced it, not enough for facial recognition, but when the culprit tossed the bomb, it exploded, forcing them to cower, stepping back. Their foot landed in a pothole near the gutter, twisting and hyperextending the ankle. The figure then limped away, staying hidden in the shadows.

Hudson nodded. 'Interesting.'

'Didn't I see Eddie Collins limping the other day?' Bower asked.

'He was wearing a moonboot this morning.'

'Do you think it could be him?'

Hudson stood to leave. 'We can't prove it, but that doesn't mean we can't use it.'

'I'll get a copy for you.'

'Are you sure you don't want the top job?' Hudson asked as he left.

'I told you,' Bower called after him, 'I'm the geek.'

CHAPTER
73

Rusnek sat at a small outdoor table sharing a sandwich with a union comrade, reviewing an Excel spreadsheet detailing the booth results for Gellibrand. He couldn't help wondering why the voting was so out of whack with the numbers from just eight months earlier. 'It just doesn't seem right at these two. What do you think?' Rusnek asked, his brow furrowing.

'It looks as if there was a reason for the increase,' his associate said.

'There was no significant increase in total registered voters from the by-election.' Rusnek scratched his face. 'But there was a significant increase in these booths, and one flipped to Hudson.'

'Do you think someone is sending a message to him?'

'What are you saying?' Rusnek leaned forward.

The associate leaned back in his chair after biting his sandwich and grabbing a few hot chips. 'If I promised a certain number of people would vote for you, how could I prove I fulfilled my promise?'

Rusnek leaned back, stretched his hand high, then dropped it back before nestling his head into the crook of his elbow, while scratching the back of his neck. His associate, still munching on chips, watched as Rusnek nodded and then straightened. 'Someone brought the vote out in those booths and gave them to Hudson.'

'Sounds like it.'

Rusnek pouted and nodded. 'I reckon I know who.'

The associate stopped chewing as his throat tightened. 'Are you thinking what I'm thinking?'

'The Meat Axe?'

'Yeah.'

'I wouldn't put it past him. He wanted Gellibrand for one of his mob, and when his candidate lost preselection, he thought he would undermine me.'

'We don't have any evidence.'

Rusnek tightened his lips, squinting. 'He has been causing trouble for me for months now. Campbell was sweet with him. I know he was influencing Mosely.'

'Why would he bother?'

'He claims he wants the opportunity to influence planning and rezoning of industrial sites in the electorate. He reckons it's worth millions to him,' Rusnek said.

But I'm beginning to realise that his ambitions may be bigger.'

'But a backbencher can't influence rezoning decisions.'

'Exactly,' Rusnek said, nodding. 'But they would have a seat at the table.'

'Our candidate could have done that for him. Now he has nothing.'

'He's thinking long term,' Rusnek said, steepling his fingers. 'I reckon he thinks he will get it next time.'

'Destroys our candidate's chances and then, at the next election executes Hudson?'

'Exactly,' Rusnek said. 'He wants us out. If we won the seat, it would have been ours until she retired, and they miss out.'

'Politics is baffling,' the colleague said, shoving another chip into his mouth. 'This is why we shouldn't get involved.'

'We're involved because of Campbell's damn legislation,' Rusnek said. 'For some unknown reason they want us out of business.'

'Well, that has now been dropped in the bin.'

'Hopefully,' Rusnek said, pulling at his lower lip. 'We just need Windsor to do as he promised.'

'What do we do about Henari?'

'I'm not sure. He seems unpredictable. I'm rethinking our merger talks, as I suspect he wants the lot.'

His colleague finished his sandwich, screwing up the wrapping. 'I reckon that sounds like a wise idea.'

Rusnek wrapped his scraps, then said, 'I'm meeting him tonight, so we shall see.'

HENARI AND RUSNEK left the historic Steam Packet hotel in Williamstown after sharing a meal and a few beers. They discussed the potential merger and the benefits it could bring to the union, especially commissions from Henari's criminal enterprises.

Rusnek remained reluctant to commit, and the business negotiations still seemed in the early stages. Henari's enthusiasm for merging to leverage the union's corporate identity and bypass the stringent regulations surrounding his money laundering operation remained steadfast. Suspicion still clouded them as they prepared to bid farewell.

'Can I drop you anywhere?' Henari said as a black Porsche SUV came to a halt at the corner.

'No, I'm good.'

'Yes, you are,' Henari said, with a smirk, thrusting his hands into his pockets. 'I suspect we are no further in agreeing.'

Rusnek looked about him to see if ears were listening. 'Tell me something. If you wanted a deal with me, why would you send your votes to Hudson? What kind of deal was done with him?'

Henari scoffed. 'I've made no deal with him.' He raised his eyebrows. 'He took out a few of my boys before the election and he now refuses to talk with me.'

'So, I heard. Yet, you still went ahead to get him elected.'

'You didn't want to give it up. I thought I could get it next time.'

'Then what?'

'Then, I will have increased numbers within the party.'

Rusnek shifted his weight and leaned away from him. 'Why is that important?'

'Oleg, I want my organisation to have no trouble from the legislators, the regulators or my clients. I don't ask for much, just a legitimate path to walk so I can have peace of mind.'

'And you think I can provide that?'

'You or the party can, yes,' Henari said. 'Don't get me wrong. I don't want to get involved in politics or politicians. They are all scum, as far as I am concerned. But I know I can get what I want if I control their numbers.'

Rusnek turned away as if to leave but then stopped and turned back. 'Were you involved in getting Campbell to introduce the legislation?'

'Mosely, pushed him into it.'

'What did you do to influence Mosely?'

'She enjoys the white powder, and exercising with a vigorous man.'

'It was you behind the scenes pushing that policy?'

'I admit I had a hand, but others were more vocal. I only ever wanted you to come to the negotiating table.' Henari shrugged. 'Then the other side of politics got involved. For them, it became a leadership struggle. I had to manage their numbers as well. The senator became just as compliant as Mosely.'

'How did that work out for everyone?'

'Yeah, not well,' Henari scoffed. 'That's the reason, I don't like those dirtbags.'

'See you,' Rusnek turned and moved off. 'Not sure when, or if at all.'

'Oleg,' Henari tightened his tone. 'I must insist you get in the van.'

Rusnek stopped, glancing back over his shoulder. 'Yeah sure.' He didn't see the man slip into his blind spot before cracking his jaw.

The sound of vehicle doors opening and men pulling Rusnek from the vehicle brought him back to awareness. They were now at the time ball tower. The dim lighting made the place eerie when no one was about.

'Let's get this over with,' one man said.

'What the hell are you doing?' Rusnek gasped, struggling against the tight hold of the two men.

By the edge of the wall where Campbell was tossed months earlier, Henari warned, 'This is where your luck runs out.'

'Wait, what's this about?' Rusnek protested, resisting their attempts to move him toward the edge.

'There are folks who don't like you, Oleg,' Henari said, peering down at the water. 'Get him to hit that one.' He pointed to a ragged bluestone boulder. 'I want to see more damage to his head than Campbell's.'

'Who doesn't like me?'

'It doesn't matter,' Henari scoffed, stepping away. 'We don't like you rewarding ministers of the government with paper bags of money. We don't like you, trying to take over other unions.'

'Who's we?'

'It doesn't matter,' Henari dismissed him. 'When you are

gone, the union will be looking for leadership and that's when I step in.'

Rusnek almost broke free from their hold as he tried to get to Henari. 'I'm going to kill you.'

'You see, Oleg, for me it was only ever about the union and gaining access to your business model. You had the regulators on board, and I need them,' Henari said as he moved to the edge and checked below. 'Okay, let's do it.'

'Yes, let's,' Rusnek said, stepping to Henari. 'You think I'm so stupid that I don't know what ticks through your stupid, thick brain of filth?'

Henari spun around to see his men stepping aside and allowing Rusnek to withdraw a Glock.

'What the...' Henari didn't have time to finish.

Rusnek stepped to the edge of the wall and fired off two more rounds as Henari lay across the bluestone boulder.

CHAPTER
74

The opening of a new parliamentary session brims with protocol, process, and remnants of pageantry. Speeches resonate through the hallowed halls, and the Governor-General officiates the parliament's commencement. Members of the House of Representatives take an oath, and then a welcoming parade introduces each member to the Speaker of the House, the President of the Senate, and the Governor-General. The Chief Justice of the High Court usually accompanies the Governor-General as their deputy. Jack Hudson cradled his King James Bible as he entered the chamber for the swearing-in ceremony and later patiently queued to greet the welcoming dignitaries.

Contrary to public perception, members of parliament are often congenial and work collaboratively. Ramsey MacDonald joined Hudson in the opulent marble Members Hall, an expansive area beneath the iconic towering flagpole that dominated the atrium. 'Hi Jack, welcome back.'

Hudson glanced over his shoulder and broke into a warm smile as he accepted the extended hand. 'Ramsey, nice to see you. Congratulations on returning.'

'Not quite an achievement when compared to your solid win,' MacDonald smiled. 'Winning a safe seat off the other party is unprecedented. You have etched your name into the history pages.'

'Thank you.'

'I've been meaning to talk to you,' MacDonald said.

Hudson drew closer, wondering what he wanted to say.

'I just wanted to ask, how are you holding up? You must be exhausted after enduring all the vitriol of the past few months.'

'I'm fine. I didn't expect performing as well as I did.'

'I want to acknowledge that I said some pretty nasty things about you in the last few months. I just want you to know that I didn't mean them. I quite respect and admire you.'

'Thanks for that. I appreciate your honesty.'

'This place is the colosseum for ideas and sometimes it becomes gladiatorial. In the heat of debate, people often exchange harsh words without considering their impact.'

'Hey Ramsey, don't sweat it.'

Hudson's turn to meet the Governor-General arrived, and he enjoyed a brief conversation with the decorated former military officer. He then greeted the newly elected Speaker and President of the Senate. 'Madam President, congratulations on your promotion.'

Morgan took his hand and squeezed. 'Thank you, Jackson. Congratulations to you for your remarkable success in Gellibrand.'

Hudson nodded, still holding her hand. 'We did well. The support from you and the party was unprecedented.'

She dropped the pretence. 'We should have a conversation.'

'Only if we are shooting in the same direction, Senator.'

'We should talk,' Morgan said, releasing his hand.

'Then I look forward to it,' Hudson said. 'Is Collins going to get the nod for the senate vacancy and then join you?'

'Edward is in the mix.'

'I look forward to working with you both,' Hudson said as he stepped away.

Those who had finished their welcome stood like sheep waiting for a jam and cream scone with a cup of tea. Hudson wanted a coffee and cut away toward the cafe some fifty metres along the parquet flooring.

He joined the queue for a takeaway coffee and, once served, exited the cafe, intending to return to his office.

'Jack?'

Hudson stopped and scanned the area to identify the familiar voice. He spotted Madeline Booker making her way toward him with an air of awkwardness.

'Hi Maddie, how are you?'

'Jack, I know you're busy. I just wanted to apologise for the other day.'

Hudson frowned. 'What for?'

'It was unprofessional and inappropriate. I hope we can move on from it.'

Hudson smiled as Booker wished he hadn't. 'What are you talking about?' Hudson checked over his shoulder to see who was about. 'I thought the article was fair. I note the comments you got from Collins.'

'Yeah, he was good. Gold actually.' Booker glanced at the floor. 'No, not that. It was when we said goodbye. I just wanted to apologise.'

Hudson peered at her, waiting for her to lift her face. When she did, he said, 'Nothing to apologise for. I've stuck it into my fondest memory file.'

Booker felt a flutter and glanced back at her friends who weren't watching.

'It's just that...'

'Hey Maddie, I understand,' he nodded, 'don't sweat it.'

Booker glanced at him and nodded as he moved away.

'Oh, and by the way,' Hudson stopped and turned back to her. 'I know this is inappropriate, but a nice frock,' he said, pointing. 'It suits you.'

Booker smiled and dropped a small curtsey. 'Thank you. I think I might wear them more often.'

Hudson watched her return to her friends before resuming his path back to his office.

Bower was waiting in the lobby when Hudson reached his office. 'You have a visitor,' he said, eyes wide and head bobbing.

'Calm down,' Hudson said. 'Who is it?'

'You'll see,' Bower motioned for him to enter the office. 'I'll make sure you're not disturbed.'

As Hudson entered, he spotted the visitor lounging on his couch, scrolling through her phone.

'Hi Chrissie, what are you doing here?' Hudson said, placing his coffee on his desk, then facing her. 'How's foreign affairs, are they treating you well?'

Woodward put aside her phone and looked up at Hudson, then smiled. 'I have been thinking about my future and how I make a run for the senate. I had a chat with the prime minister, and he agrees with me,' she said. 'I've decided if I want to achieve my ambition for the senate, it is in my best interests I work with you and help you grow your career. So, if you want me, I would like to work with you.'

Hudson's eyes welled up as he rushed to embrace her. 'Oh, Chrissie, thank you.'

DID YOU ENJOY HORRIBLE PEOPLE?

I sincerely hope you enjoyed the first episode of the Jack Hudson MP series and follow him as he develops his political career in the Australian parliament. Episode 2, *COVERT AFFAIRS*, will be out shortly.

Authors thrive and rely heavily on the opinion of readers. I wonder if you could help? If you enjoyed the read, I would be extremely grateful if you let other readers know what you thought of *HORRIBLE PEOPLE* by considering leaving an honest review on Amazon or Goodreads or even posting a review on your social media such as Instagram, including the tag, **@852press**. I'd really appreciate it if you did. Thank you!

If you would like to communicate with me, then please do. I always respond to emails and enjoy chatting about future projects and seeking opinions about some of the issues raised with my writing.

If you would like to be added to my Advanced Readers list, then please let me know: **readers@richardevans.com.au**

Unlike other folks in the publishing industry, I don't send tiresome newsletters or offers every other day, but I do write an autumn and spring update every now and then.

Best wishes and enjoy your next read.

RICHARD EVANS

COVERT AFFAIRS

JACK HUDSON MP – EPISODE 2

Jack Hudson MP thought winning the election was the hardest part—he was wrong.

In *COVERT AFFAIRS*, the next thrilling instalment of the Jack Hudson MP series, former special services officer turned politician Jack Hudson, is finally settling into his new role in government. But goodwill remains elusive. With a target still firmly on his back, Jack finds himself relentlessly blackballed by the vengeful Senator Stephanie Morgan, who seizes every opportunity to undermine him.

When Jack attends a high-stakes security conference of Asian nations in Singapore, his future political career is the least of his worries. As the conference unfolds, a vicious terrorist attack plunges Jack into a harrowing situation. Amidst the chaos, Jack faces an unimaginable dilemma: saving the life of his political nemesis, Senator Morgan.

Can Jack navigate the treacherous waters of political sabotage and international terrorism or will his efforts to save Senator Morgan cost him everything?

As a political insider, Richard Evans served as a federal member of parliament for the seat of Cowan in Western Australia during the turbulent 1990s. After a successful career as an Australian industry leader, he now specialises in writing crime thrillers, writing about the exotic characters in the mysterious world of the Australian Parliament. He lives in the coastal village of Airlie Beach, the gateway to the Whitsunday islands, with a view from his writing desk overlooking the Coral Sea.

For more information about his other books, or to contact Richard visit: **richardevans.com.au:**

Visit Instagram for updates on Plots, Publishing, Politics and Personal news.
instagram.com/**richardevans_author**

A MESSAGE FROM RICHARD

Thank you for reading Jack Hudson's initial foray into politics. My plan is to follow his career over ten episodes, and I have no idea where it will lead, although I reckon, he will have a challenging political career ... or will he?

What I can guarantee is that they will be stand-alone stories and will draw upon the pompousness of politicians and their desire for power and spending your money.

Building a relationship with my readers is the very best thing about writing and I enjoy hearing from them, no matter where they are.

Join my VIP Reader Club for information on new books and deals, plus, receive a free eBook of my Democracy Trilogy.

Just visit www.richardevans.com.au and click on the free book.

We are an independent publisher, helping Australians tell their story.

We are keen to share our experiences and processes with Australian writers so they can self-publish their own works. If you have a story to tell, visit our website for a range of resources, services, and events.

Also, if you are interested in receiving Advanced Reader Copies for review, please contact us at write@852Press.com.au

Visit our website for more information.

852Press.com.au